sexxxressions:

Confessions of an Anonymous Stripper

sexxxfessions:

Confessions of an Anonymous Stripper

A novel by
ANDREA
BLACKSTONE

Q-Boro Books
WWW.QBOROBOOKS.COM

An Urban Entertainment Company

Published by Q-Boro Books

Copyright © 2008 by Andrea Blackstone

ISBN-13: 978-1-933967-31-8
ISBN-10: 1-933967-31-5
LCCN: 2007923118

First Printing February 2008
Printed in the United States of America

10   9   8   7   6   5   4   3   2   1

This is a work of fiction. It is not meant to depict, portray or represent any particular real persons. All the characters, incidents and dialogues are the products of the author's imagination and are not to be construed as real. Any references or similarities to actual events, entities, real people, living or dead, or to real locales are intended to give the novel a sense of reality. Any similarity in other names, characters, entities, places and incidents is entirely coincidental.

Cover Copyright © 2007 by Q-BORO BOOKS, all rights reserved.
Cover layout/design by Candace K. Cottrell; Cover photo by Eric Glenn
Editors: Candace K. Cottrell, Latoya Smith

Q-BORO BOOKS
Jamaica, Queens NY 11434
WWW.QBOROBOOKS.COM

ACKNOWLEDGMENTS

To God: Thank you for watching over us when those who believe in you need your protection and favor the most.

To Ayanna: Wherever you are, I pray your life is improving. I miss you.

To the many people who looked out for me, especially, V.N. and S.I., it was much appreciated.

To Andrea: Thank you for giving my story time and effort.

To Mark, Candace, and the people behind the scenes at Q-Boro Books: Thanks for giving authors a vehicle to use their creative voices.

—Mystique

DEDICATION

This novel is dedicated to every wife and mother out there who is secretly struggling to feel loved, beautiful, and appreciated.

This novel is also dedicated to every single woman or mother trying to hold it down alone, now caught up in some kind of hustle gone wrong.

I acknowledge your existence. Don't give up on loving yourself, no matter how tough it all gets.

—Andrea

PROLOGUE

Like it or not, we've all done our share of private dirt that we'd prefer to forget. But despite shame or regret, let the record reflect that there's always a risk that lies will fall apart. No matter how hard we wish for otherwise, the truth can't hold and keep it together, and understands what real love is. Secret lives rarely remain secret, forever. Sure, most of us have been taught not to put our private business out in the street. But the thing is, circumstances don't always unfold pretty and neat. Eventually, the truth will probably rear its ugly head, whether it be exposed in full or revealed in pieces, in life or in death, or in front of one million, or just one. And I get the feeling that our society thrives on prying into other people's private lives, although most would cringe at the thought of having people dig up skeletons from their own past. It is easy to say someone ought to know better to have done this or that, but that judgment usually is made when we forget that we haven't walked a mile in someone else's shoes—to hell and back. If it were us sitting on the cusp of rage and fury, would we want someone to empathize with our blues down deep . . . really?

Putting all this aside, what if someone you love was living a naughty, secret life? If you found out something that cut you deep, would you make that person quietly pay a high price, solely out of anger and spite? And if your dirty linen was aired for all of the world to see, would you push your pride to the side and confess and claim your dirt, or swear it wasn't you? Just as Paul Lawrence Dunbar said, "We wear the mask that hides our cheeks and shades our eyes!"

What should be judged, and what should be excused, as we walk through this journey called life? After the messy dust has settled, what about the sliver of forgiveness that hangs on the edge of pain and disappointment—does it even have a place? If what was done in the dark comes to light, just what do you do when your world has been turned upside down, then broken in two? Many of us have been there in some way, shape, or form. Be honest . . . have you? As three characters living secret lives wear masks to hide their eyes, morning noon and night, think about everything said thus far, down to the origin of why what was done ever came to be. And lastly, God is the only judge, but telling the truth will set any of His children free.

Dear Readers,

This is a crazy story about the pain of being played and how I tried to flip a man's cheating game because of that unbearable pain. Consequently, something toxic took up residence in my heart. That something toxic is otherwise known to many as revenge.

I never thought I'd open up to anyone about the events that occurred in my life, and in lives of those close to me, but I'm ready to let go of the guilt. Thus, I hope this confession can lead to more spiritual and emotional healing. Although marital counseling has proven to be quite beneficial to me and my husband, whom I did eventually get even with, it still feels like a substitute of some sort. He has no idea that I put this story out in the universe, by giving insight to an author who could get this into print. Who I am is irrelevant; it's the message that counts. Names have been changed and some locations have not been mentioned. Ya dig? If he ever finds it, he'll just have to live with it. After all, "this" all started because of something wrong he did, and I get to do things my way now. Yep. I run shit—nice twist considering the shoe was on the other foot a while back.

I started to abandon this project after my sister never came back home. She is an author you may or may not know, but discussing Ayanna's disappearance is a true sore spot. I guess telling this story without her was just how it was supposed to be. Why, I don't know. I made it a point to attend Andrea's book signings after I first heard about her on the radio. I told her I had a story to tell—what I felt was an unusual kind of story about why I became a suburban mother who got caught up in some mess while strip-

ping in secret, for the thrill of the attention, *not* for the
money.

I know she probably hears that "I've got a helluva story
to tell you" line all of the time, but she listened anyway. We
grabbed a cup of coffee, and I told her a little about what
I'd done and why. After that, she interviewed me over dinners and private email exchanges. I wanted her to write
this because it may help some woman out there in pain—
single or married. I sat in that dark place, and I know how
it feels to suffer from the breakdown of love and self-
esteem, and then try and build all of that back up. Ayanna
was in pain, and I think I have an idea how she felt too.
With that said, these few pages are the only ones that will
come directly from me, aside from some thoughts at the
very end. I'm no writer. I'm just a suburban mother who
works in some dry-ass law firm, with a few naughty secrets
stashed in my panty drawer. Still, Andrea insisted that I
should be the one to introduce my story, so if I fumble
through it, please excuse me. I hope my introduction
makes sense and you can follow where I'm trying to go
with this thing. Really, I do.

How does a woman feel when she finds out that she's
not the only one? When she's been committed to a
man, mind, body, and soul, for fifteen long years. When a
woman wears a ring that a man slid on her on her finger
after exchanging vows, and she has the displeasure of
finding out that she's been played. It feels like the world
has stopped turning. It feels like warm sunshine has instantly turned to icy rain. When reality of indiscretion sets
in, that's when you feel like crying. When you're tired of
feeling sorry for yourself through the tears, then you feel
like sighing as your stomach twists in hundreds of knots,
double looping while cutting off your ability to digest the
sour taste.

After reality sets in, you ask yourself, "now what?" What should I say? If he appears to be sorry, should we start over again? What should I do? Should I let him take a walk that won't stop until he sits his ass in front of a judge in a black robe? What about the kids who would be dragged through issues of being raised in a broken home? What about visitation? What about *myself*? Then you start blaming yourself, flipping the script. That's the mind game we women play on ourselves—asking ourselves a whole string of questions, making a whole lot of statements. Maybe I should've acted more of this way or done more of that. Maybe he thinks *she's* sexier, prettier, or more interesting. Maybe I overlooked the red flags that he was not on the same page with me . . . maybe. There are so many thoughts. Too many thoughts that overwhelm a woman at a time like that.

You feel crushed, scarred, scared to love again, betrayed, duped, and super stupid, all in the same breath—or life. This is how it feels when a woman finds out that a man that she loves has stepped out of the relationship, breaking a bond that was supposed to be strong as iron. I've been there. I am there. I sit in this ugly place I'd rather not be. I felt like I needed to take a few puffs from a cigarette, and a sister doesn't even smoke!

When it happened to me, I sat there stunned and plain hurt that my husband Donavan would abuse my trust and shatter the word love until it dripped down my chin, fell in my lap, and stung me hard. I'm either in your corner all the way, or I'm just not digging you whatsoever. I'm no backstabbing bitch, and he knew I was a one hundred percent real woman, no smoke and mirrors, no games under my thumb. I wondered if he thought twice about me, about us, about the life we said we'd build with our children. I never cheated on him, and I just couldn't understand why he did what he did that night. He said I was a good woman he loved enough to settle down with—so why did he do that foul shit? He didn't even go in a back room or private place to get down. He did his sexual dirt out in the open, *and* he managed to get his ass captured in the act, on tape. Dumb move. That made two of us. I'm not sure who was dumber—me for believing in him at the time, or him for crossing me so boldly.

I struggled hard to hold myself together in one piece, replaying what I saw in my head, after I viewed a tape that exposed the truth. How could a man who said he loved me go to a forbidden place, all in the name of fun with *a stripper* the night of his bachelor party? The day before our marriage even got started, it was doomed, but I was the last to even know. The vows, a lie. My wedding, a farce. The honeymoon, a waste. Sacrifices made on Donavan's behalf, all undeserved. Bitterness, I owned it.

I pushed my children Brittany and Brian out of my womb—children that came from his seeds. I endured morning sickness, swollen feet, and labor, not him . . . not her. I rubbed his back even when mine ached. I plucked the forest of black hair from around his ears with tweezers. I sewed the buttons back on his shirts whenever they wobbled and fell off. I woke up at four AM to drive him to the airport whenever he had to fly out for business. I loved him unconditionally, even when I didn't feel like it. I did all of this and more. I was his super woman, yet still, it wasn't enough. He threw away a collection of many moments in time, built up over years, getting down with some paid-for slut with a loose, stank pussy. Vicious fucked God knows how many men the same way she did him, but none of that mattered to Donavan. He still wanted her like that. Men!

Sharing this is very embarrassing, but some of everyone from trophy wives, stay-at-home-mothers, chicks who make six figures, to any women out there who have held it down for the good of her family and her man, has had this shit jump off. The only difference in my case is that I caught my man with his Calvin Klein drawers down as he starred in his own movie—*The Unfaithful*! Not all men get busted. To this day, some women are completely unaware that this has happened to them. Since I did become privy to the situation, I took matters into my own hands, although the origin of further discovery of Donavan's neglectful hiatus came with a price. I don't know why he even wanted to get married at the time. Obviously, he just wasn't ready. Now if you agree that a woman scorned is capable of anything, my story will go to prove that theory is right. I'll stop here and let Andrea lead you through the rest of my journey. Adios.

Signed,

A former anonymous stripper

1

CHEATING 101: LEAVE NO EVIDENCE

My life-changing personal odyssey began the morning after my kids headed to summer camp, on June 15, 2007. Since I was used to letting Brittany and Brian run me ragged with their many activities, and getting about fours hours of sleep because of it, I tossed and turned in my sleep until I just couldn't take it anymore. As a result, I yearned to feel Donavan's strong arms wrapped around my curvaceous frame. I missed my babies. I felt lost. Everything was too quiet and far too calm in our household. Hell yeah, I wanted some action and attention.

At the very least, I yearned to cuddle with my soul mate. In fact, I craved having the comfort of my husband's presence, as opposed to downing Nyquil just to force myself to drift off properly after the kids took off. Little did I know, what was meant to be a simple request would snowball into something far greater.

"Honey, don't you want to come to bed?" I said, gently stroking my husband's back as I stood over him as he lay on the couch. Smiling at someone I thought was a man with whom I shared an indestructible bond, I slowly bent down and softly kissed him on his neck.

"No. It's time for me to get up soon. I'm comfortable here," he answered, half-mumbling.

"But, I just don't understand why you want to sleep on this raggedy old couch in the basement. You've been doing this for the past month. Enough is enough. I have a hard time sleeping without you. It's rare we have the house to ourselves. Come on. Get up, baby. I might even give Daddy something nice this morning to get your day started right," I flirted, pulling on his elbow.

Donavan sounded more lucid, obviously waking up a bit more, although his eyes were still closed.

"Aren't you the one who used to complain about my snoring?" he answered when I stopped.

"Yeah, but I never said sleep on the couch because of it. You don't snore all of the time."

"Like I told you before, I don't want to disturb you when I get in late. I'm working on a big project with a tough client. Do you think I enjoy seventy-hour work weeks?" he said, scratching his chin.

I let my fingertip gently massage the top of his head, still trying to coax him to get up. His knees were pressed against the back of the tattered leather couch. It was obvious that he wasn't comfortable.

"I know you work hard and you're under a lot of stress. You always have big projects and difficult clients though. That will never change. You're an investment banker. Why are you making excuses, Donavan? I'm just trying to—"

"Mystique, stop nagging me. Leave me the hell alone! I take care of my responsibilities. I've been a rock for my family. What more do you want? Is a little space and peace too much to ask for? I have a long day ahead of me at the office. Back off!" he said, nearly swatting my hand away in annoyance. "You're tripping! Just stop all of this madness and go back to bed," he snapped.

I withdrew my arm as he quickly rolled over. That's when his cranky ass fell clear off the couch. He hit the ceramic tiled floor with a gigantic thump.

"Damn it. Look what you made me do!" he commented, blaming me. I watched my husband crawl back up on the couch.

"Yes Donavan, you do take care of home. But right now, you're not taking care of me! What is it? You don't love me anymore? Do you find your wife boring after fifteen years of marriage? Is it that I'm so repulsive that you don't want to even sleep with me now? You never used to treat me this way. I don't know what's going on with you lately! Fuck it. This doesn't make any damn sense. We've got a king-sized bed upstairs. You used to be so affectionate toward me, and now you suddenly want to stay on some couch our old dog used to sleep on! Go ahead, get a crook in your neck. I'm not going to beg you anymore. I hope fleas come out of hiding from the cracks in the cushion and start biting your stubborn ass," I rambled, my heart pounding in anger.

Feeling rejected I stormed out of the room. I was so frustrated that at four-thirty in the morning on a Friday before going to work, I started working on washing a pile of clothes. Since Donavan suddenly appeared to no longer respect my needs, I wasn't gung ho about giving him the same courtesy. The laundry area was on the other side of the wall of where he was sleeping in the basement, but I told myself I should bring on the noise, so I did. I sorted clothes and also noticed a small pile he'd left on top of the washing machine after his Thursday night outing. I dropped in several pieces of dark clothes that were in the hamper, then I began working on the clothes I assumed

Donavan wore last, as the water in the washer rose upward. I dropped his socks in the water first. Then I grabbed his pants. I took the red and white Starlight mints out of my personal devil's pocket, and also a number written on a piece of small, jagged paper. I grabbed his shirt. I sniffed it and it smelled just like smoke, combined with some pungent, cheap body spray that I wouldn't be caught dead wearing. When I examined it again, I even detected faint traces of make-up on his shirt. Seventy-hour work weeks my ass!

I swallowed hard, wondering who'd written the number down. Peeved and confused, I let the lid on the washing machine drop, not bothering to fill the machine with other clothes or even add soap powder. I suddenly ran out of the laundry room and bolted up the stairs while tightly gripping that piece of paper. I sat on the edge of our king-sized bed, staring at it as I bit my lip and sighed. I grabbed the phone, dialed the first three numbers, then put the receiver back down. I decided to think about it first, as opposed to letting my emotions take over.

I tossed and turned until day break. There was only one other woman, aside from my unmarried sister, I could trust to give me an objective opinion. I felt that I needed some advice from another wife who I knew wouldn't tear me down, gossip about me behind my back afterward, or straight up insult me if I chose to open up my heart and share my personal business. That wife's name was Janet. I met her at my wedding fifteen years back. Her husband and mine were friends. They grew up in the same neighborhood. She was a pharmaceutical sales rep, turned stay-at-home mom, who took a few years off to spend time with her first child. Aside from my sister, Janet and I had become best friends.

Around six AM, my husband left the house quietly, with no additional words sent my way. I had a nagging feeling finding the mystery number was a timely sign that I needed to search for answers right then and there, so I did. Within thirty minutes, I found myself dialing Janet's number. After she agreed I could swing by, I dressed, showered, and paid her a visit not long after rush hour began.

"So what is it you wanted to talk to me about so early in the morning?" Janet asked. "Did you come by to volunteer for my husband's House of Delegates seat campaign? We could always use one more supporter. I think he really has a shot of winning, you know," she told me, smiling a bit.

"I'm truly glad to hear that, but I came to see you on my way to work because of this," I said, showing her the piece of paper. "I'm sorry about the time," I said, noting that she was still wearing her robe and cold cream on her face.

"What is that?" she asked, frowning at it, then looking at me.

"I found it in Donavan's pocket after he got in early this morning," I told Janet.

"Oh," she commented somberly, realizing it had some number scribbled on it.

"So what would you do, if you found it? I mean, would you call this number or what?"

"Mystique, let's just say that your husband could never run for politics."

"What is that supposed to mean?" I questioned defensively.

"I should not have said that," Janet said, covering her mouth with her right hand, realizing she let something slip.

"What is it?" I asked. Janet just gave me this funny look like she didn't know what kind of face she should make.

She dropped the hand from her mouth. It began to tremble.

"He's one of my husband's buddies, Mystique. I shouldn't

have said anything. I mean, I'm not supposed to know that. Some things are better left unsaid. I mean, you're not supposed to ever hear about . . ."

"Janet, if you know something, tell me! You're my best friend in this town, aside from Yana."

"I know, but it's none of my business," she told me, shaking her head. "The only reason I know is because I was snooping through Scott's porn collection one day. I was just trying to watch a flick, which is unlike me, but I was curious."

"Look, please tell me whatever you know. I swear this won't come back to you. From one woman to another, please let me in on the information you have. I won't say a word. If you were in my position, I'd tell you. I swear I would, Janet."

After Janet made her unusual comment, I begged her to explain her Freudian slip, so she finally broke down in the name of married sisters helping married sisters.

"There's a tape. A very bad tape that could destroy many lives. That's all I can really tell you about what I know," she said, playing with the loop on her robe, dropping her head.

"Please, Janet. Show me the tape. I've got to see it," I said, grabbing her face, forcing her to look me in the eyes.

"Are you sure you really want to?" she asked.

"Yes, Janet. I'm sure. Things have really gotten out of hand at my house. Donavan has been acting very strange lately. Everything was fine. But out of the blue, he started acting cranky. I feel like Donavan and I are roommates these days, not husband and wife. I need to know the truth, or anything that can help me figure any of this out. If you know something, please help me," I insisted, wiping the cold cream into my hands like lotion.

Janet sighed while grabbing a tissue from her pocket to smooth the goo on her face, then told me she'd be right back. When she returned she summoned me to the basement. On my way out of the living room, she locked all the doors in her house, and even slid the bronze-looking chain across the top of the door.

"Is all of this really necessary?" I asked, cutting my eyes at her like she'd lost her mind. My heart raced as I wondered what the hell was on that damn tape. I could tell it had something to do with my husband. Seeing it seemed like it was taking forever, considering Janet's "rituals" and so forth.

"I'd say it's necessary, just in case my husband forgets something and turns around to come home. He does that on occasion," Janet explained.

I felt like we were sneaking down to the basement, and into the entertainment room, like two mischievous teenagers. Janet popped the tape in the VCR, but stalled as long as she could. I could tell that she hated to show me whatever I was going to see on that flat screen, high definition television of hers. Even so, I insisted that I wanted to watch it. She handed me the remote.

"Just press play, but before you do, remember that you can watch this, but I have to put it back in my husband's secret porn stash."

"Okay, Janet. Stop being so afraid. I'm not going to try and take it. You know me better than that," I explained, trying to convince her to open the bullpen.

When the tape began to play, an exotic dancer appeared holding a sex toy. She flirted with my husband a bit, then grabbed a can of whipped cream. I was glued to the television as my mind flashed back to the night of my husband's bachelor party. The dancer shook it down to the floor, then came back up and sprayed whipped cream all over my husband's chest and nipples as he smiled. She seductively licked the white, frothy cream off of him, flicking her tongue in long strokes, then handed the can to what appeared to be a random man in the crowd, instructing him to coat her nipples with it. After he sprayed the cream in circular motions, he tasted her nipples with his mouth and tipped her. She handed a different man her dildo and motioned for him to stick it in and out of her mouth as she she sat down on my husband's lap and started to work him over. The dancer rubbed her apple-shaped ass in his groin while bending and moving in various positions.

Next, she stood, laid down on the floor, then motioned for the man to return her toy. She looked into Donavan's eyes as she slowly slid the plastic pole in and out of her pussy. The men's eyes were glued to her as she continued pumping it in and out of her slit, until her body convulsed and her back arched like a poetic pose painted on canvas by an artist. Money rained down on her as a wild orgasm welled up inside of her and burst into one big explosion. For her grand finale, she did a split, swung her legs around, and slowly parted them, exposing her creamy goodies in front of my husband, one last time. The dancer kissed him on the cheek, scooped up her many tips, and left the room full of noisy men who hooted with approval.

"I don't have a problem with her performance. This is nothing. So he was having a little fun at his bachelor party," I said, half-laughing, waving my hand in the air. "To think I was worried over nothing. I feel so much better now. I've been paranoid, I suppose."

"Keep watching," Janet urged in that same somber pitch.

As I continued to watch the tape, it was obvious that Donavan was sloppy drunk by the time the second and third dancers appeared. Although the lights had been dimmed, I could still make out his facial expressions. I frowned as I noticed that the leggy one was dressed in a bright red devil costume. Her head was topped with horns.

A red garter belt was positioned on her right thigh. Her bra was red and I even recall seeing a tail sticking out, when she turned to the side. Although I didn't know a thing about strip clubs, I knew that no dancer would dress that way on stage. That was a private party moment, surely. I suddenly recalled that Donavan told me that he and a few of his friends were meeting at a strip club setting to have drinks and watch a few dancers in public. We both agreed we wouldn't have formal parties. In fact, I went out to dinner with the girls. I didn't even want to drool over male dancers.

"Wait a minute! That's not a room in a club. That's a hotel room. No it's not, it's a house party!" I exclaimed, moving close to the screen, squinting my eyes. "He wasn't supposed to do that. What in the fuck was going on that night?" I muttered as I moved backward, shaking my head in confusion.

Rick James's "Super Freak" blared as one dancer took off her sparkling sequin-filled costume, and the other shed her tacky looking devil get up. They both laid down in the middle of the floor. The short one dropped a large ice cube on the taller one, then stuck it in her mouth, slowly gliding it over top of her dance partner's nipples, belly button, and between her thick thighs. By the time it melted, they both were busy sticking large dildos inside of each other. One dancer twisted one around, pumping the toy in and out of the other. By the time she moved it faster and faster, she was licking on her partner's clit at the same time. When the recipient of that insane mess came, the other took it out of her pussy, but the show didn't stop there. The pair took turns sucking her juices off of the dildo. Next, they played around with each other a while, grinding and licking skin and kitty kats even more, giving the men a girl-on-girl show. Those freaks didn't waste a single drop. The partygoers showed them lots of love, quickly tossing bills. Apparently, the men loved that pornographic looking shit.

Next, the shorter dancer got up and dripped hot candle wax on Donavan, as the second one who entered the room moved toward Donavan to the familiar beat, twirling and switching around his chair that had been placed in the middle of the room. In fact, it reminded me of some king's throne. The dancers behaved as if they were a part of his harem of women, and Donavan was a king. Both dancers moved their hips in unison from side to side as they stood in front of him, making their shoulders rock, as they bent there knees.

"Dayumm! Can those things clap on their own?" Donavan asked, nearly salivating over the women's backsides. I heard other men laughing at his comment.

When Sir-Mix-A-Lot's hit "Baby Got Back" pumped strong, both dancers turned around and quickly jiggled their asses with a vengeance. As if they'd planned it, they began making their ass cheeks clap and pop as they bent over with their hands on their knees, one on the left side, and one on the right. Some men high-fived each other, while some pointed as the women showed off their "talents."

"I guess you got your answer. Smack those phat asses hard, player. Leave hand prints on those hoes. Pow! Pow! One big booty for each hand," an attendee said as the girls continued to flex their glutes rapidly to the beat of the music. By the time the hook played, Donavan smacked their asses, still smiling, as he melted with lust.

Toward the end of the song, the taller dancer turned around swaying her hips, as the other dancer drifted off into the crowd, then I couldn't see what happened to the shorter one at all. The remaining dancer tugged at one of Donavan's fingers, instructing him to stick it inside of her mouth. Her head bobbed as she gave him a sample of her tongue tricks. When Prince's cut, "Cream" played, she ducked down, took off both of his shoes, pulled one of his socks off, then sucked and licked on his big toe. After that, the dancer licked on his calves, giving them a tongue bath. Next, she unfastened his belt, unzipped his zipper, and peeled off his shirt.

"Awww shit! Here we go. Now I see why she was wearing that devil costume. Let's get the real party started!" one of the men yelled, wearing a button down shirt and slacks.

"Don't cheat my boy. Get 'em, girl," another commented when the dancer helped Donavan to stand as she helped him to remove his pants.

When Donavan sat back down in the chair with his legs gapped open, he let his arms dangle over the sides as he laughed and grinned. A big smile was plastered on his face. I wanted to choke him until I reminded myself that this was a tape, not something that was unfolding live and in living color. I could feel my jaws tighten as I watched the dancer bend backward, making her back touch the carpet. When she returned to the normal position, she slithered around Donavan like a panther. Then she got low again, like she was going to hit some really slick move. That's when she slapped a condom on my husband's erect pole and went to work with her mouth.

"That's what I'm talking about!" Donavan said, grabbing the woman by the back of the head as it moved up and down the middle of his crotch.

My eyes widened like they were dilated during some eye exam. Donavan was having a ball. My mouth fell open as I watched my former six foot four hero getting a covered blow job from a scantily clad young woman in front of a room full of wild men who were egging him on to enjoy himself beyond reason.

"Oh shit!" I exclaimed. "What in the fuck?" I mumbled, losing my cool.

"You okay?" Janet asked. I suddenly felt frozen, barely able to breathe.

"That son of a bitch! That sneaky, trifling, black son of a bitch!" I screamed, rising to my feet, rage boiling up within me. My heart pounded as I struggled to understand.

The second stripper got up and pulled the condom off of Donavan's dick. When Prince sang about getting on top, the dancer directed my husband to lay flat on his back in the middle of the floor. After that she began shaking her ass over top of his face, barely a few inches away from it. Money was flying from every direction, like confetti in Times Square on New Year's. It began to coat the floor with a thick layer. In response, the stripper continued the hardcore freak show. I'm sure the bitch got what she came there for—a big pile of cash.

When some of the men in the room chanted loudly over the music, "Get on top! Sit on his face! Get on top! Sit on his face!" she lowered her kitty kat on top of my husband's face, as suggested. Without hesitation, Donavan curled his tongue and stuck it up the wild acting woman's kitty kat, exploring her labia and pink creases.

"This is your last time to play in any other piece of pussy, playboy," someone I couldn't see yelled. "Everybody knows D's been with Mystique since he had his first wet dream. He never even sniffed no other pussy. Try something new. Suck this bitch's pussy 'til her face caves in!"

Not only did Donavan lick it when the dancer got on top of him, without reservation, he licked, sucked, fingered, and had her shit gushing like a busted water main, as she panted during the wild escapade. His boys began to hoot and holler like adolescents. I couldn't believe my ears or my eyes. The person I loved the most was acting like he was that uninhibited porn star, Mr. Marcus or something. The man I thought I knew was nothing like the one I watched. Who I saw on tape was some evil body double with a whole lot of freak tendencies. As my heart bathed in hurt, that's when I regarded the woman as a prostitute *posing* as a stripper, based on everything that she'd done.

"Mmm," the stripper moaned as my husband licked and sucked her juices down.

"Oh yeah, baby," she said loud as her nipples began to point outward as she bit her bottom lip.

After that, the other men looked as if they wished they were the groom to be. Their johnsons were bulging out of their pants, and some were unconsciously rubbing themselves over their slacks and jeans as they watched the freaky sex show. The stripper lifted herself from the squatted position, as several men crowded around with beer bottles, lit cigars, and shot glasses in hand, in close perimeter to she and Donavan. A few of them smacked the stripper's ass, then she whispered something in Donavan's ear. When the giggling stripper pulled my husband by the hand, helping him up, the tape cut off abruptly. When it ended, I thought of many things, wondering what jumped off after that point. Was giving and receiving head the beginning or the end of the *fun*? Unable to come to grips with what happened, all I could do was appear dazed, until I shook my head a few times. My feet just started moving with no warning, then I blew my top.

"Mystique, are you okay?" Janet asked as my fingers curled around my keys, and I slung my Tumi Vista Drawstring bag on my shoulder.

"He kissed me the next day!" I shouted, feeling sick to my stomach. "That's what I get for marrying a pretty boy! You were never really down for me—you were just out for ace number one. Fuck the big house we live in, your six-figure job, the closet full of shiny wingtips and designer threads you rock, and that candy apple Porsche you have sitting in our garage—you ain't shit! See, this is why women don't want men to have those fucking bachelor parties. Dirty-ass hoes! I should kill him. I should get my hands on a gun, drive up to his job, and blow Donavan's fucking balls off. That bastard! Who does he think he is?" I said, ranting and raving like an insane mad woman, stomping up three steps.

"No, honey. Don't. You can't. I mean. Shit! I knew I shouldn't have shown you that tape," Janet told me, probably thinking of herself.

"How long have you known about this?" I asked Janet, making my mouth form a mean point like I was some half-possessed monster. She didn't answer, so I backed my friend up against the wall. Looking terrified, Janet leaned back against it as far as she could, nearly shaking from my intimidation.

"Answer me! Answer me right now," I yelled, hollering in my friend's face at the top of my lungs.

"Three years," she said, beginning to cry, turning her head sideways.

"I guess you had no reason to open your mouth about it since *your* husband's face wasn't on that tape. Damn, Janet. You and God knows who else knew about this and let me make a fool of myself. I thought you were supposed to be one of my best friends!" I ranted a bit quieter, blaming the messenger.

"I was thinking of you. I was thinking of the kids. What was I supposed to do? It was not my place to—"

"You were content keeping your fat mouth shut while I let twelve years of my life waste away with that jerk, so save it," I said, cutting her off while moving backward. Throwing my left hand outward, my palm showed. I needed someone to blame, so I lashed out at Janet for not pulling my coattail about the situation after she found out. I tried to force myself to appear cool outside, but I couldn't simmer down. My blood was still boiling, and on the inside I counted the ways that I could try to demean that playboy who I married. I shot out of Janet's house in a blur and unlocked the door of my Lexus using my wireless remote.

"Come back in the house. You're in no shape to drive," Janet said, catching up with me, then pulling on my arm.

"I'm okay. Let me go. I've got to get to work," I told her, pulling away.

"You're *not* okay. I don't want you to have an accident. Please come back inside."

"I said I'm okay. I know when I'm okay! I'm really really okay and . . ." I said, finally breaking down, falling to the ground in my navy blue Jones New York business suit. I curled up next to my car, hunched over in a *U* shape. Before I even considered how I looked, I found myself cupping my hands over my eyes, beginning to catch teardrops.

"Shhhhh. Oh, sweetie. I'm so sorry this happened to you. Go ahead and let it out. It's going to be all right," Janet said, stroking my hair tenderly, as cars whizzed by. I could hear her sniffing as I sniffed. Our sniffs and cries were staggered. My pain became Janet's pain—at least at that moment.

"I thought he really loved me. We promised each other that no one would ever come between us. I gave my virginity to him. He was the only man I've ever slept with. I can't believe he betrayed me like that," I told her. "I trusted him!" I screamed, getting heated all over again. I felt a stream of snot tickle my lip as my body began to tremble. "What if he's still taking money out of my household budget and throwing it away on greedy whores with no morals? I bet this is why he hasn't been sleeping with me for the past month. I bet he's hanging out in strip clubs. I bet he was going to those seedy places the whole time we were dating. Why do strippers wreck homes like this, and what do these women have that I don't? Okay, maybe my body isn't perfect after the two babies. I have gained a little weight."

"Slow down, Mystique. You're upset. I'm sure all sorts of scenarios are suddenly coming to mind, but stop getting ahead of yourself. This mess happened fifteen years ago at his bachelor party. It really doesn't mean that a stripper has anything to do with what's going on in your marriage now," Janet suggested.

"You're absolutely right! If he's really working seventy-hours a week, he could be banging his secretary on his desk right now," I ranted.

"That's not what I meant either. Donavan not sleeping with you could mean something, or it could mean absolutely nothing at all. And for the record, you look great. There's nothing wrong with you. You filled out in all the right places after having Brian and Brittany. I know it hurts, honey. I know," Janet told me, trying her best to coax me to calm down. "As far as what he did at that crazy party, other men would line up to have a good woman like you in their lives. I'm not trying to talk badly about Donavan, but he's such a fool. All I can tell you is that men will be men. Women mature so much faster."

"Bullshit! I wish they'd close every one of these whorehouses down and outlaw bachelor parties! I swear I suddenly feel like giving up on my marriage. It if weren't for our two kids and our financial obligations together, we might not be having this conversation, Janet. If a man gives a woman a ring, or he commits to date her exclusively, he better man up!"

Janet was still busy trying to coax me to go back into the house, and collect my faculties, but I wouldn't hear of it. After I cried a while and promised her I wouldn't hurt Donavan or myself, I rose to my feet, wiped my burning eyes, and got into the car. Janet talked to me a solid twenty minutes more as she ran out of words and apologies for something she wasn't even responsible for.

"You could've said something long ago!" I told her while starting up the car. "There's no excuse for that behavior, and I needed to know about it."

"I know exactly how you must feel," Janet responded.

Hearing those words made me angry all over again. She didn't know how I felt, and I was insulted. Usually, I was a lady who walked away from situations with style and a level head. But when it came to the man I loved, I completely lost my head.

"Oh no you don't. You can't even begin to fathom the pain. As far as you know, you've got the clean-cut altar boy who can run for politics, and I'm stuck with the cheating man-whore, remember?" I replied in a hostile tone. "I'm not about to take this sitting down. Only weak women will allow that shit, and I'm not weak. Don't ever call me again, Janet. I don't need a so-called phony-ass friend like you. If you even think about ever calling me again, I'll tell Scott about his darling wife's little snooping habit. I don't think he'd appreciate that when he's trying to win a political race," I told her. I wiped my last tear that fell, and Janet ran into her house, tears flying all over the place. I knew I hurt her, but I didn't even care at the time. As if seeing the tape wasn't enough, I still had the piece of paper that got my wheels turning in my pocket.

Now that I had that sucker's number, I fantasized about how I could make my husband's hurt equal mine. Filled with rage, I wanted him to understand that he thought he was going to get way with everything, but in the end, he wasn't going to get away with anything.

I began plotting and planning to make him pay when the time was right—emotionally, financially, maybe even physically. I was driven to helping karma along to make sure my pain became his pain. After I made it out of the development, I sped down the street, squealing tires when I leaned into the first curve. By the time I made it to the expressway, I hadn't realized that I was on my way to make trouble at my husband's job in McLean, Virgina, at the rate of eighty mother-freaking miles per hour. I dialed his work phone number and was in the mood to demand answers, starting with what else happened two days before we got married at the bachelor party that went too far. And so much for not blaming the messenger . . . I lied.

2

WHEN IT RAINS IT POURS

"Mystique, it's me," Janet said

"I already told you. I don't want to talk you. I need my space," I reminded.

"Instead of getting mad at me, try bitching at the man who stabbed you in the back. I'm tired of being nice to you while trying to help you through this fucked up drama. I don't have to take this abuse. You don't have to worry about me dialing your number one more time! Your wish has officially been granted!"

"Fuck you, you stuck up genie bitch! Wait 'til your plastic world melts too. You may be next if some competitor digs up dirt on your old man," I yelled.

Hating on Janet was only the beginning of my screwed up morning. With new suspicions about Donavan's fidelity, I couldn't help but to question if there was something more to Donavan's behavior. They say that cheaters usually repeat their behavior, so seeing that damn tape only added fuel to a raging, blazing fire. After the harsh reality set in, I found myself putting the pedal to the metal, wanting to ask my husband a long string of questions. Did you go to strip clubs? What are you really doing with your time? Is there another woman you're cheating with now? So many unanswered questions swarmed around in my head. I felt lied to, misled, and deceived. If Donavan hid all of that dirt from me for fifteen years, I wondered if I even knew my husband at all. I wanted answers, and I was determined to get them.

Five miles from my husband's work exit, I saw the multi-colored lights of a state trooper police car swirling around. As I looked in my rearview mirror, I knew I was in deep trouble.

"Shit, that damn speed trap!" I said, inhaling deeply. I pulled over on the shoulder of the road. I got my license and registration ready, then prepared to collect my ticket on one hell of a morning.

"Do you know why I pulled you over?" the state trooper asked with a serious look.

"Yes. I was speeding," I answered as the trooper took my license and registration.

"Next time, leave the house on time," he suggested.

"It's not that, Sir. I just found out my husband cheated on me once, and I suspect he's at it again. I must admit that I'm a bit upset. I was on my way to confront him about it and I wasn't paying attention. I am sorry, officer."

"Yeah, right," he said. Then the asshole chuckled like my story was that far-fetched. "Your eyes are very red," he said, staring at me. "I think you've been drinking," he added before walking away.

"Great!" I said, throwing up my hands.

When he returned to my car, the officer gave me a breathalyzer test. I swore I wasn't drunk but he wouldn't take my word for it until I proved to be one-hundred percent sober.

"I told you I'm not drunk," I said.

"If that speed trap hadn't caught you, some innocent

victim could've ended up dead, or you could've killed yourself. It's not our fault your husband can't keep it in his pants."

"It's just like a man to say something like that. May I just have my ticket please?" I said with far less respect.

"Ma'am, step out of the car," the man said with his hands on his hips.

"For what? Because I'm a black woman having a screwed up morning? You're just out to give me a hard time," I commented.

"Step out of the car!" he shouted in a stern tone.

As cars whizzed by, the state trooper handcuffed me. When I heard the click of the shiny silver handcuffs lock, I began shaking so badly my knees were nearly knocking together. I was completely humiliated. I was ordered to sit in the back seat of the patrol car for what seemed like forever. I wasn't sure what would become of me. I'd never had any type of run-in with the law. The experience made me feel helpless and at the mercy of a sadistic stranger.

"That damn Donavan," I said to myself. "This is some really fucked up shit." Shortly thereafter, another patrol car pulled up. I watched a female state trooper get out of the vehicle. The short woman with a wide-brimmed hat spoke to the one who stopped me, then she began walking toward my direction. When the door of the patrol car I was sitting in opened, a humongous lump rendered me speechless. If I had to talk, I couldn't have managed to utter a single syllable.

"Step out of the car, ma'am," she said. I noted her authoritarian stance.

This time, I wasn't bold enough to ask any questions. My stomach was doing super-sized summersaults as I questioned my fate. My heart pounded when she turned me around and began inspecting every crack and crevice on my body. I was still dressed but I felt naked. People were slowing down to rubberneck, probably thinking I was some fugitive that had been caught on the run. She told me to spread my legs, and ran her fingers over my crotch and between my legs. She even felt between the cracks of my ass cheeks, felt up my legs through my stockings, and groped my breasts. Ten minutes of being fondled by that freak had me wanting to cuss her ass out, but I was too scared to say a word. I'd learned my lesson, trying things that way. After she finished she turned toward me and winked.

"She's good. No need to take her in," she said to her colleague. The first trooper wrote me a ticket for reckless driving and speeding. After I took it I pulled off, scared to even drive the speed limit.

Instead of heading to Donavan's neck of the woods, I took my ass to work. I sat in the full parking lot, staring at myself in the mirror attached to the inside portion of the sun visor. My eyes were watery. I closed them and held my head.

"I've tried so hard to be a good mother and wife. My marriage is falling apart, and I don't even know how or why. Please God, help me to stay strong. I don't deserve any of this. It feels like the world is coming down on me," I commented aloud, sniffing a bit.

By the time I opened my eyes, I inhaled deeply, got out of my car, then prepared to face the wrath of my idiotic boss.

Not even ten minutes after I cleaned up my face—before running into the twenty-story building in Montgomery County, smoothing as many wrinkles out of my suit skirt as possible—part three of my ugly day had begun. After smacking the up button of the elevator five times in a row, I was finally on my way up to the law office where I worked. I didn't have time to grieve or process my pain at that time. I didn't even have time to pull the knife out of my back. My duties at D&R Associates had to come first, not my hurt.

"Forrester, you're late!" my boss yelled, as soon as I turned on my computer and plopped down into my chair. Mr. Jiles was standing by my desk, doing everything but tapping his foot. Still struggling to catch my breath, a light shine from perspiration covered my forehead.

"Good morning. I'm sorry, Mr. Jiles. I'm late because I had a personal emergency this morning, then I got a ticket and—"

"And nothing! Five minutes, two hours, it's all the same. In this case it's two hours late! There is no such thing as a personal emergency. Late is late! Fix these papers. I want you to re-staple them. You know I don't like crooked staples," my boss complained after a pile of papers fell on my desk. "And those letters to clients better be typed and sitting on my desk for my review by the end of your lunch hour, or else. I'll be back from discovery for the Drexel case by then, so make yourself useful around here and earn your damn paycheck," he added.

Mr. Jiles was a stubby, middle-aged man with a comb-over that made me want to break out a pair of scissors and lay his few dirty blonde strands to rest. Every time he walked, it blew back over in the opposite direction. He also had the habit of chewing Tums like candy, and on occasion, he'd throw things.

"I won't have time to actually eat lunch if I type all of the letters to your clients," I reminded. "There's simply not enough time to get that much done, even if I work as fast as I can."

"Maybe that's because you can't do anything right, just like you can't seem to come in to work on time!" he told me in front of everyone in the office.

My head began to pound.

"When you yell at someone, you make it harder to concentrate, Mr. Jiles. I think I do quite well, considering how you communicate with me. I'm sorry you're upset, but I don't make many critical mistakes. I don't think I've ever told you this, but I'm not hard of hearing, so there's no need to yell," I said, trying to speak calmly. Saving money for my children's college tuition stopped my tongue from moving any more than it already had. Although my husband made good money as an investment banker, I wasn't depending on him to think ahead. I'd never even said that much to my boss, so I'm sure he couldn't believe I'd crossed his "don't talk back to me" line.

"I should've known better than to hire *two* women around here. If it's not cramps, it's your kids. If it's not your crumb-snatchers, you expect men to communicate like sissies. I hired you to do a job, and you will do it as expected. If you don't do as I instructed you to, there is a filing cabinet full of people who'd love to take your place here at the firm. I have no patience for lazy, disrespectful employees! There's a simple solution—don't eat lunch so you will have enough time. If I didn't yell at you, you wouldn't get anything done. Now shut up and just get to work," my boss screamed, his cheeks turning crimson, as spit flew in my face.

After he took two paces toward the door, I hit the power button of my small radio, as I continued to bite my tongue. With the volume low, my jazz station, 105.9, was already playing something mellow and new by a talented artist named Stan Ivory. After the song played, I was straining to hear the name of the CD that could help me hold everything together, despite the madness. After I found out the name of it was *Follow Your Dreams*, I decided that I had to remember to look for it, then Kool and The Gang did their thing. But that's when my least favorite grinch struck again.

"Is that music I hear?" Mr. Jiles asked, stopping dead in his tracks.

I didn't reply, so Mr. Jiles walked over to my desk, stomping with his two fists balled up like the grench he was.

"D&R Associates isn't a club, nor is this happy hour time at a bar. Do that shit on your own time," he yelled, ripping the power plug clear out of the socket. Mr. Jiles carried my radio away. "I don't want one more thing out of you today. Not a fucking thing, Mystique!" he continued, kicking my stress ball that fell off my desk.

When he walked off, his comb-over blew in the other direction, just as it always did. I looked out of the corner of my eyes, and just like clockwork, Mr. Jiles pulled a dwindling pack of Tums from his pocket and began pulverizing them with his teeth.

After two and a half hours of typing with no break, my fingers were cramping like a mother. I'd already had one bout with carpal tunnel from typing and data entry. I looked around to make sure Mr. Jiles was out of sight, then stopped, massaging my hands briefly. I popped two Aleve, realizing that my boss didn't care to ask me if I was okay, despite my puffy, red eyes. I washed the pills down with two swallows of Sprite, since I didn't even have time to get up and walk to the water cooler.

When I resumed typing, part of my mind was on deciphering Attorney Jiles's chicken scratch, but the other part of my brain drifted back to my husband, as I questioned how well I really did know that man who left me out in the cold. I was fighting to hold back more tears that wanted to pour from my eyes. I think I would've snapped and done something to land myself in jail for murder if a few things hadn't thrown salt in my game. I suddenly regarded that foul trooper fiasco as a sign from God that I needed to cool my tail down, for the sake of my two little monsters I loved, Brittany and Brian. I think I could've killed my husband if he'd had the audacity to lie about that damn tape when I showed up at his office.

After a minute or so, I snapped back into my world at D&R Associates. I did work through my lunch break, although I knew I wasn't obligated to do so. It's a funny thing that a lawyer would have no problem violating labor laws! Grinch Jiles was giving the boss in the movie, *The Devil Wears Prada* some stiff competition. He nearly lived in the firm, never taking time for a social life, determined to make partner before a heart attack demoted him to a coffin first. Every other day the man was calling me in his office to complain about nothing that he swore was something important. And there was no way I was also going to work eighty-hour weeks right along with him, secretary or not—no Sir. As a matter of fact, when his brother died, he only took off half a day. By the time the coffin was covered over with dirt, he was back at his desk. I believe in working hard and earning what you deserve, but that's just no way to live!

On the way home, the only thing that made me smile was getting a call from my kids at Camp Rising Sun, in the Blue Ridge Mountains. I stayed an extra hour and a half to get some additional work done, but I knew I wouldn't be rewarded with overtime.

"Mommy, I miss you," my youngest said. "So Ma, guess what? I made a really neat dish for you on a real potter's wheel. It's in the kiln right now. After that, my camp teacher says we glaze our work for the second firing. After that, we get to pick whatever paint we want," Brittany continued.

"Oh, that's great! I know it'll be wonderful when you finish," I said, smiling. My son Brian snatched the phone.

"Give me the phone. It's my turn!"

"That thing looks jaaacked up, Ma! It's all crooked and

ugly." He laughed. "She couldn't work the wheel right. I saw it. Clay was flying all around the room."

"Shut up, boy! Mom is going to love it," my daughter defended in the background.

"As I was saying, your son is the one that's got it going on around here. I'm practically running things. I show 'em how I make it do what it do with my trumpet. If the band teacher didn't have me on his team, the old boy would be short," Brian said.

"Yeah, right. It sounds like a retarded man is playing that thing," Brittany commented.

"Who you talking about? If you don't like it, take a nap and go to sleep," Brian said.

"I wish I could when you play, you tone-deaf sucker!" she added.

"Don't be calling me no sucker, *sucker*!" Brian replied, forgetting that I was on the line.

"Hey, hey—now wait a minute here. Brian Christopher and Brittany La Chelle, stop it right this minute! You two better get along because you've got nearly the entire summer of camp to go, and it's not cheap to send you to a program where you stay so long, and get to do so many quality things. You both just may as well behave. If it were up to your father, you'd be right at home sitting in front of the television set watching movies or playing PlayStation. I was the one that thought to send your behinds somewhere nice. In fact, I gave up my vacation money so you two could go to a nice place in the mountains like that," I explained.

"Oh, we having fun, Ma. We are enjoying it here. I have to ask you one little thing," Brian said, sounding too nice.

"What do you want?" I asked.

"Why do I have to want something, Ma?"

"I know my son. What is it?"

"Ok. Did you call the coach about Pop Warner Football? I have to be on that team again. My dawgs need me. You said I could if I got at least a B in math, and as you know, your son pulled his grade up to an A," Brian reminded me.

"It's taken care of. But if any of your grades slip again, you're off the team. You tend to get a little lazy if I don't keep an eye on you," I said.

"Yeeees!" he said, rejoicing. I imagined the way he looked when he did his little stupid victory arm motion.

"Give me the phone back. I want to talk to Mom, too," Brittany complained.

"Hi again, Mom. It's me," she said sounding overly sweet.

"Hi, Me. And what does Me want?"

"Oh . . . nothing," Brittany remarked, trying to lay on her charm.

"I doubt that. Go ahead, Me. What do *you* want?" I questioned.

"Well, I was just wondering if you signed me up for ballet when I get back. Mrs. Bakerfield said I can bend like wet spaghetti, and I'm ready to dance on my toes. You said I could get my new ballet slippers and take more lessons if I did a better job picking up my toys, keeping my room cleaner, and made up my mind on if I wanted to be in Brownies or ballet. Ballet, Mom. I want to get real good and dance like the girl I saw when you took us to see The Dance Theatre of Harlem. I've been thinking it over real good and that was cool. If I miss Brownies, I can be in Girl Scouts. I hate those beanie hats they make us wear in Brownies anyway. They are so corny," Brittany told me.

"That old dance show was boring and dumb. I fell asleep," my son commented.

"Shut up, boy! Well, Ma. What's the dealie, yo?" Brittany said, half-laughing.

"What did you say?" I asked.

"I meant . . . are you going to let me take ballet again when I get home?"

"Yes, Brittany. But you still need to work on that room and you left a trail of watermelon seeds on the kitchen floor after I told you to clean it up before we left."

"I did clean it up," Brittany whined.

"No, *I* cleaned it up. You left most of them on the floor. Someone could've slipped and hurt themselves. I am sick and tired of picking up your crap. I'm not your maid."

"Sorry, Mom," my daughter said.

"If you forget these things again, I'm going to change my decision about registering you. And stop trying to sound like your brother. One teenager is enough. You're only seven."

"I'm seven and a half, Mom. I get to take ballet. Yippie! Thank you, thank you, thank you!" Brittany exclaimed.

"You're welcome, Me," I answered, smiling from my daughter's obvious happiness.

"What color do you want me to glaze your bowl—anything you want," Brittany offered.

"Do something crazy and surprise me," I said cheerfully.

"Ok, I will," Brittany answered, then giggled. "Mom, we have to go. It's dinnertime now. I love you. Bye, Mom."

"Bye, sweetie," I said to my daughter.

"Give me the phone!" Brian said. "Hold it down for me 'til I get back. Ya feel me?"

"You mean 'til *I* get back. You always trying to act like you the man. You make me sick. I should tell how you almost wet your pants 'cause someone was in the latrine and you couldn't get in yesterday."

"You better not roll your eyes at me again, and you better get your hand off your hip. Who do you think you are? Just get out of my face before I bust you in your eye, Brittany, with your big ole head looking like a runaway slave.

Did you tell Mom that you plucked out your cornrows that took eight hours for you to get done? By the time she picks us up, you better work a miracle and get that stuff back in braids, fool," Brian commented.

The phone call ended with the line going dead. No matter how hard I tried, my children never seemed to stop fighting, and that's part of the reason I needed a long break from them. Nevertheless, at least I knew *they* loved me, although it still didn't ease the pain of my suddenly troubled marriage, or my hideous work environment. Everywhere I turned, stress was pulling me down. Feeling burned out, I wasn't sure which way to turn. I had no idea more surprises would be in store for me on that memorable Friday. As if the day hadn't been hectic enough, it turned out that my husband wasn't the only one who was close to me, hiding a big secret. My sister was next in line, delivering shocking news.

3

SOMETHING DIRTY SHE DID FOR MONEY

By the time I'd reached my house, my emotions were all over the place. I pulled out all of my wedding albums and tapes from my big day. After I studied nearly every picture of Donavan, I finally sat Indian style on the floor with a glass of cranberry juice in hand, watching the tape of my wedding. Tears fell as I watched Donavan slow dance with me. We swayed to tender melodies, feeling joyous and excited. As I watched my husband stuff wedding cake in my mouth, I tried to reconcile how I felt then with how I felt after all of the most recent hell began to break loose, but I couldn't.

After the tape of our reception ended, and I drank the last drop of Ocean Spray, I worked up the courage to call that number. I cleared my throat, dialed it, and let 'er rip.

"Here goes nothing," I said to myself.

"The number you dialed is temporarily not in service. If you feel you've reached this recording in error, please try your call again."

"Damn! Maybe they're on to me and had the phone cut off," I said, putting the receiver down.

I knew I was jumping to conclusions again, but nothing seemed to make sense. Although my effort to speak to the holder of the number turned out to be a dead end, I felt like venting about Donavan's betrayal. If not to that mystery person, I had to go there with someone else. I decided that after I finished washing the load of clothes I'd abandoned early that morning, I'd wear out my baby sister's ear a little. I'd been holding it in until I punched the clock to leave D&R. That took a lot out of me, to say the least. Just imagine holding some heavy shit like that in all day long. After the reality of Donavan's actions set in, I had more questions for my tight-lipped pal Janet, realizing that I screwed up royally by swearing her off. Finally acknowledging that she was the messenger that wasn't responsible for the message, I decided that I didn't want to drag Janet back into my marital drama, even if I could beg my way back into her heart. I just didn't feel the same about her either. After all, she probably did regret showing me the tape, but I knew I couldn't trust her the way I once did. Come to think of it, I cut her off and never apologized, although none of that mess was her fault. I just had no interest in facing her.

While I waited for Ayanna to show up, I'd decided to return the piece of paper to my husband's pants pocket after his clothes dried. In essence, I knew all I needed to know. He was a cheater! How many ways did I need to slice that? Ayanna came over to hang out with me for a while, and I fought an internal battle of not letting her know everything. Plus, after I changed out of my work clothes, kicked off my pumps, and pulled off my stockings, I realized that I really didn't feel like spending that Friday alone. Just like before, I turned to chores to keep my mind off of things, so I began cleaning up the kitchen as I chatted with my sister. Since she was a single woman, I

questioned if she could give me a totally different perspective regarding how to handle man problems.

"Awww, isn't that cute! By the looks of your living room,
you were doing some serious traveling back down memory lane," Ayanna said as she walked toward the kitchen.

"What we need in this world is more real love. I'm not
sure there's much of it left. When it comes to love in these
modern times, it seems that everybody does play the fool.
I guess I had to go back down memory lane to remind myself how much of a blind fool in love I really was," I said to
my sister as I washed the dishes. I gazed blankly at my
daughter's swing set that was positioned so that I could see
her play when I looked out of the window, on many days
like this.

"What's all of that supposed to mean, Mystique?" Ayanna
asked, suddenly sounding concerned.

"If you thought a man you were with was cheating on
you, would you stick around?"

"What are you talking about?" Ayanna asked.

"I know it's not good to discuss personal relationship issues with relatives, but I have to talk to someone about
what's really been going on between me and Donavan. I
know you're busy with law school, but I called you over
here to talk because I'm not sure I'm willing to ignore his
dirt, just because he's a man and I'm a woman."

"What dirt would that be?"

"Donavan makes lame excuses to justify why he stopped
sleeping with me. For one, he claims that he doesn't want
to wake me up when he gets in after pulling late-nighters
at the office."

"Maybe he is grinding that hard, Mystique. Big incomes
come with long hours. You know how that goes. Having a
big corporate job is a Catch-22. Plus, I can't imagine the
pressure of being a black investment banker."

"It's not just that. We haven't had sex in a month. When

we did go there last time, it was terrible. He fell asleep inside of me when he was supposed to be working me out. I stared into space, just laying there like a wet mop because he wasn't into it at all. The emotional component of the act was non-existent. I can't even have an orgasm with that man anymore. Sex with my husband used to be the bomb."

"Damn. So it's like that?"

"Yeah, unfortunately it is just like that. To add insult to injury, he sleeps on that couch in the basement so much that the shape of his body imprint remains embedded in it at all times. Since there have been no recent walks, talks, and kisses with the man I married fifteen years ago, I now walk around in night gowns to my ankles and sport generic sweat pants, running shoes, and a ponytail. My husband doesn't seem to give a damn if I step up to the romance plate or not."

"So take a trip to White Flint Mall, and find something to spice things up. What's so hard about taking control of the situation?"

"It's hard to want to feel sexy under the circumstances. I guess my only option left is to focus on my motherly duties. Last time I tried to inspire his ass, he turned me down."

"Look, it's probably nothing to worry about. Most couples go through these kinds of moments in a marriage, so I hear. It's probably some harmless phase."

I wanted to tell Ayanna the rest of the story about the bachelor party gone wrong, but I had to bite my tongue regarding that part of my dilemma. The scarred part of me wanted to tell Donavan that I knew all about his little kitty licking experience, but I knew I couldn't because he would've realized that one of his buddies ran his mouth to his wife, then Janet would catch holy hell for telling me the truth. Instead, I chose what I wanted to say. Plus, my sister had so many ducks in a row, it was ridiculous. I didn't want to feel embarrassed by sharing my screwed up life with someone who was making so many positive moves, so young. I was supposed to be setting the example for her, not vice versa.

"There are those fleeting moments when I still feel close to him, but most of the time he doesn't keep his promises, Ayanna, and he treats me like a stranger. He tells me one thing, then comes creeping home at four AM," I commented as I held a plate in my hand and looked out the window.

"Where does he go? What do you think he's doing with his free time?"

"I don't know. And I don't know what he finds so fascinating about running the streets. I suspect he's hanging out at some bar with his boys. I can't speak beyond that. If I had a dime every time the kids ask 'Where's Daddy?' I'd be rich! All I do is pick up after the kids, help with homework, wash clothes, do dishes, clean toilets, drive to ballet class and football practice, and go to work." My eyes began to tear up and my voice began to crack. "Even at work I get treated like crap. Before I left today, my boss moved me to a smaller office with no windows. I'm stuck in a little box typing legal memos all day, ninety words a minute, while he yells at me to type faster. My husband no longer cares how hard I work in our home and out. Hell, he used to send me flowers at the job from time to time. These days, I don't even get a good morning or good night. It hurts, Yana. I'm not just his wife, I was the one who was his high school sweetheart," I said, feeling my eyes begin to water. I broke my gaze, grabbed a red and white checkered dishtowel, and began drying the dishes.

After Ayanna told me to turn around, she hugged me and dabbed my eyes with a napkin she grabbed from the table.

"Hold that thought. I've got to run to the restroom, sis.

We'll talk about this some more when I come back,"
Ayanna said, grabbing her purse.

"You dropped something," I said, when I heard a small
thump.

"Just pick it up for me. Not to be rude and cut you off,
but it's that time of the month," she told me, shooting
down the hallway.

Feeling as if the weight of the world was sitting on my
shoulders, unhappiness sucked me in to a dark place
within. I turned around, and picked up her little book,
trying to forget how bad I really did feel about my life.
One of the loose pages fell out of it, and I attempted to
stuff it back inside. As I kneeled, I was about to place it on
the table, until I realized what is was—Ayanna's diary. Just
like Janet, snooping was becoming one of my weaknesses.
The bad habit started when I was trying to figure out the
deal with my husband. Apparently, I hadn't learned my
lesson by going through Donavan's pants pockets, though.
I couldn't resist the page that had slipped out of the little
book with a gold palm tree on the front of it. I know I was
wrong for that, but curiosity got the best of me, and speed
reading at the firm came in handy. The downside was that
I learned that Ayanna wasn't so innocent and perfect,
after all. We had more in common than I ever imagined,
and even a connection to *strippers*.

4

BROKE DOWN

Dear Diary,

I can't believe that I just got fired, all because companies buy companies, then I got let go at my new temporary position. I wouldn't screw my boss and suck his dick while we were alone last night at my new place of employment, and all of the sudden I get notified that my last day temping was the very next day. So much for that eight dollar an hour meeting planning shit! My boss was slick about it all because he set up his scheme just right so I couldn't file for unemployment, but he and I both know that I really was plain fired. On top of that, I just got word that an interview for a new job that I was looking forward to was cancelled about three hours before it was supposed to take place. And if that's not enough, my publishing deal got jacked up and my man kicked me to the curb. I'm in law school, trying to make something out of myself. What luck! My life is whack!

I'm only twenty-four years old, and stress has got me by the collar, big time. How can I have three job fiascos in a row? I sent out a big batch of resumés after I got laid off last month. The day after I was let go for the second time, someone left a message saying to call back as soon as possible. I did and was called in for an interview for an entry-level job in journalism. I was ecstatic until my intention of rounding up some quality clips for my portfolio—then tried to step up to a well-known newspaper after milking the opportunity out of a $25,000 a year job—went sailing down the drain not so long ago.

"Your interview has been cancelled. We're not hiring at the newspaper," Debbie said.

"What? But I was told to come in at one-thirty today."

"The publisher of the newspaper changed his mind about hiring anyone else because he didn't get the money he was supposed to. Even my job isn't stable. Goodbye." Click.

When the woman ended the call abruptly, my jaw nearly dropped to the floor. Debbie never apologized on the company's behalf—nothing. She just straight up dissed me. After I recovered from the letdown, I peeled off my dress clothes, then scratched the newspaper off of my job list I was keeping to track my growing list of rejections. The economy already sucked bad enough, and it made me suddenly feel the need to officially panic. You know what they say, three strikes and you're out! Like it or not, I was officially just *broke*! I felt like all of the energy had been drained out of my body, and a sharp pain was shooting through the middle of my chest like a knife is stabbing me in the middle of it. I decided to call my boyfriend since I did need a bit of encouragement and comfort to settle my frazzled nerves.

"David speaking," he said, picking up his work extension.

"It's me."

"Oh, hi, Ayanna," David said, sounding disappointed.

"Look, when are we going to spend some time together? I got more bad news. My boss made inappropriate advances, I got fired in a polite way, and a new job I was supposed to get interviewed for just fell through. It's been another rough week," I explained.

"Can you ever talk about anything else? You always have so much drama with you. Why can't you just get your life together?"

"Did you hear what I said?" I told him, sitting up straight. "All I want is for my man to come over and chill with me tonight—maybe make love to me or something. None of this is my fault. I'm not asking you for money, just support. I haven't seen you in a whole week."

"I need a break from us," he explained, his voice chilly.

"A *break*? What are you talking about?"

"All we do is argue, just like we're doing right now," David claimed.

"No we don't. We're not arguing now either. All I asked for was a little of your time."

"I've got to get back to work. Some of us do have to work for a living, Ayanna. I'll call you at seven," David said. "You're a head case," he mumbled before hanging up. Click.

At that point, I was losing count of how many land mines I'd stepped on in disaster city. David never did call me at seven. After playing phone tag the rest of the evening, I blocked my number and called him. That's when he lost it and hit that girly high pitched voice you don't want to hear coming from a man's mouth, and announced that there had been someone else, the whole time we'd been "exclusively dating." That led me to remove his ass off of speed dial, leave him at least five nasty email messages, and a good sum of long-winded messages on his home and cell phone after I didn't block my number. After seven years of knowing him, and two years of commitment, he cut me off, just like that. I was hurt and felt abandoned. I hadn't cheated on him since we'd become exclusive. I busted my ass as an author to try and show him that I was about something and could bring something to the table in our relationship. That's who I wanted to be with, not who I had to be with. I guess it was all about the chase for him, not the prize.

In a state of confusion and panic, I jumped from odd job to odd job—flier distribution for two days, walking dogs for three, and participating in a painless market research study for one. I registered with a few temporary agencies, but with all of the new kids graduating from college, work for people in my category was more than slow. Every day I pounded the pavement looking for work. Another blow came when I landed an interview at a shelter and was told I was over-qualified for the receptionist job. If I didn't mind making ten dollars per hour, should it have mattered? I just wanted to work, period. After a few weeks of trying to piece gigs together to make ends meet, I began to feel burnt out. One afternoon I lay in bed feeling depleted, listening to Kirk Franklin, trying to find a bit of faith and answers to reassemble my strength. I grabbed the phone next to me after I decided to try to shake off my blues and tell someone other than David what I was going through.

My frazzled state of mind led to me spilling my guts to the first person that would listen. I still can't believe that I had this conversation with X—someone who had been a friend for only about six months. I'm sure he had better things to do than listen to me rant, rave, and whine about my situation. But instead, he stared me in the eye from across the kitchen table, trying to advise his confused and ridiculously broke friend about her limited options. Room temperature water was all I had to offer him, but he sipped it out of that red plastic cup like it was the best shit in the house. I had no idea what X would suggest next.

The solution to solve my problems led to the same something that led to doing something dirty for money.

"Baby girl, worrying never solves problems. It's time to think this thing through, because you need money and you need it fast. If you don't want to sue your old boss for sexual harassment, you've got three ways to make some cash quickly and under the table."

"What? What are you thinking?"

"How many male friends do you know that want to get with you?"

"Nearly all of them, I guess," I answered flatly as my stomach growled.

"Is that right? So there's your clientele right there. The solution is right in front of your face, baby girl. Dance for them privately—problem solved."

"I can't do that!" I exclaimed.

"Then just get one who can afford a mistress. Do you know any wealthy motherfuckers?"

"A few. I dated a millionaire and I know some others."

"Damn, it's like that? Ok, be a mistress then. Hit them up and tell them you require ten thousand a month. You know what you've got to do. Work them over."

"You're crazy! I don't want that bad karma hanging over my head."

"Bad karma, shit. J-Lo did it. Puffy got in trouble and she dropped his ass. Diana Ross had a kid by that white man. That's what smart women do. One minute Destiny's Child was singing about being independent, the next they're singing about can you pay my bills. This is how the game is played, Ayanna. Use your head, here," X said, pointing at his temple.

"If you've missed what I said, I'm not a gold digger."

"Fine—no one said you are. But you better think hard about getting in those pockets while you still can. If I were a good-looking female, I'd do it. When you get a little older, men won't be hollering as much. Do you want to be in the same spot next year? Get a man with some money— a sugar daddy. How many do you know that can afford to donate something toward your finances?"

"You know that's not me, X. I've never wanted any man to do anything for me like that. I graduated magna cum laude, and I'm supposed to set myself back by relying on my sex appeal to make money?" I snapped.

I felt humiliated that paying my dues with my schooling hadn't paid off. I'd worked so hard by keeping my nose in the books so I wouldn't ever be in a position like this. Even so, there I was.

"All I'm saying is make what you have work for you. You don't want to do it with a stranger, then don't. In case *you* missed it, your friend wants to get with you that way. If you were with me you wouldn't have to struggle to stack paper like this 'cause you'd be straight. You could be dipping shrimp in butter sauce at Red Lobster right now if you wanted to. Ya feel me?"

"Like you said, we're friends. I don't sleep with my friends. There's a defined line and there are limits. Besides, I'm not a ho, I'm just broke."

"Now that your trifling-ass old head is out of the picture, you can get with your boy here. If you don't want a relationship just yet, then just let me help you out. It would be a friends with benefits deal, so that wouldn't make you a ho. Take care of just me like that. I'll go to the bank right now and help you out here and there. I'll delete all of those other broads' phone numbers if you say that's what you want to do. I see the potential in you. I know you're a winner. You're smart, good looking, you don't have no kids. And I know that you'd push me in my music career. You're my ideal woman, baby. I always did want to get with you."

SEXXXFESSIONS   43

"No thanks, X. That's not what I want and not how I
want to get it."

"Ok—I'm not going to beg you. When you're ready to
come to Daddy, I'll be right here waiting." He took a sip of
water. "How much are your bills every month?"

I grabbed a pencil and paper and began calculating my
expenses. "The garbage collection is $100 every three
months. The gas runs about $350. My electric, say $100.
My rent is $1,080. My phones and Internet run about
$220. Total, I need at least $2,000 a month. That's not
counting my $35,000 school loan that's due."

"You've got a lot of financial demands on your back.
Sounds like you're gonna need about three jobs to make
it out here. That's what I did back in the day to straighten
myself out. Grind hard like that then. Do ya thing,
momma. Get crackin'."

I threw down the pencil and rested my head in my left
hand. With my right, I nervously began drumming my fingers.

"You know my health isn't that good. I can try to pull
that off, but I can barely get a $10.00 an hour job because
my resumé is screwed up from when I got sick," I said.

"*And* they're going tax you."

"So what am I supposed to do? Medical bills threw me
into debt. That's why I already filed bankruptcy once. To
top it off, I just got a letter that my disability work ticket
expired. My rehabilitation counselor doesn't even want
me to work. I don't want to go back on the system, X. I've
come so far to rebuild my life and the way they treat you is
humiliating. I can't go back to being treated like a second-
class citizen over three hundred dollars a month. I don't
want to be trapped by the past of poor health and a weak
work history, nor do I want to be a burden to my father.
He's on a fixed income, and helping me with a place to

stay is enough as it is. I feel like I'm just existing these days. I want my life back; I just don't know how to make that happen. I'm getting older and I'm scared about not having a stable career, a home of my own, and some sort of financial security."

"Let me explain something to you. It's not about where you start out in life, but where you finish. Take a deep breath. Come on baby, do it. Fill them lungs up with air and blow it out a few times. You look too stressed. I ain't trying to have you croak on my ass! And stop drumming your fingers—that's annoying as hell!" I followed X's instruction, then he continued. "There, that's better. Like I was saying, don't panic. Instead, why not do something to trick the system by taking control of the situation and getting in the mix? I think it's fair to say that you've been struggling way too long. Things can get easier for you, sooner than you think."

"What are you suggesting?"

"You know the shorty on my album cover?" X questioned.

"Yeah," I answered.

"She was a dime shorty!"

"She's cute, but so what?"

"Shorty danced and made that bread. She had her own everything, just from shaking her ass."

"I can't do that!" I exclaimed, my eyes widening.

"Won't and can't is two different things, so choose the right word," he corrected.

"Stripping isn't dancing, it's just stripping. There's a big difference. A dancer is trained in the *art* of dance. Everyone knows that strippers are airheads. What smart girl would want to get paid to give men erections?" I said, then sighed.

"That's not completely true. Maybe some are, but I know a lawyer who did it to get through law school, and now the sister has her own practice and charges four hundred dollars an hour. Many a woman in our community has done it because more of us have financial shit going on and no one to help us out. Ain't too many of us born with silver spoons in our mouths. You ain't no better or no worse than any one of them smart sistas who used dancing to their advantage when they found themselves in a similar situation. I'll be honest about it—this is your last option. I don't know what else to tell you. I'm trying to help you find a solution. Treat it like a challenge, and change your mindset. See, it's all about your state of mind. For the record, it *is* an art, and it's legal."

"I don't know anything about stripping. I don't even look like the stripper type!"

"I've seen you dance. You can do it and I can help look out for you. That way you'd have your own money. You would make it for yourself and wouldn't have to ask any of these men in the DC area for it. Trust me; you could get paid like she did with no problem. Dancing would be easy for you, *and* you'd be an independent contractor. Uncle Sam can't track what you make in a strip club. What can giving it a shot hurt? As long as you know you'll have a roof over your head, the only way you can go with this thing is up. Look, I'm on your side. I want to see you make it because I believe in your writing talent. Your shit can't get much worse than the spot you're in right now," X replied.

He totally missed the point. When I said I couldn't do it, I meant I *really* couldn't do it. I am not secure in my looks, no matter what men say. I see no reason why men would want to watch me flirt in a half-naked state. I considered everything he'd said and then got up from the kitchen table. I didn't know where I was going—I just felt the need to get up just for the sake of moving.

"Put a CD in. Let me be the judge of if you can dance or not. I'll tell you, honestly."

"No. I don't want to think about this anymore," I insisted.

X got up and opened my refrigerator. "Come on now. All you've got is some lettuce and a bony, rotting roaster chicken that you need to throw out." X closed the fridge, then opened and closed my pantry cabinet.

"Don't be going through my stuff!" I said, embarrassed that I had no real food. With the exception of one can of tomato paste, that was bare too.

He sat back down, paying my outburst no mind. "Damn, you don't got shit to eat in here. What are you going to eat tomorrow or the next day? What are you going to do—pawn your TV? Then what is next, your furniture? You can keep going until your place is cleaned out, but it still won't fix anything. It'll just buy you food for a very short period of time. You better think about that, plan your next step, and snap out of this pity party of yours. This is a cold, cold world, baby. Don't no one out here give a damn if you live or die just because you stuck to your morals. I been around the block. I ain't stupid. It's about survival out here. You've got to hustle by any means necessary. Toughen up," he added.

"Well I wasn't raised to think that way," I snapped, crossing my arms defensively.

"Look, my parents made me stand on my own two feet like a man. I had to go hard since I was knee high because my dad was locked down and my mother got on that shit. Heroin. Somehow, I still turned out okay."

"I'm sorry. I didn't know."

"It's ok though. All it did was make me want to be somebody—you know, make something out of my life. I'm gonna bring my kids into the world the right way, and give my seeds better. A brother is going to be all right."

A little tear leaked out of the corner of my right eye. I wiped it.

"Now check this out. 'It's Hard Out Here for a Pimp' from the movie *Hustle and Flow* won an Oscar—that should tell you something, baby. Some people took those lyrics too literally. It's hard out here for anyone on the grind trying to make ends meet legally . . . and extra hard for people of color. The American system is set up for only a few cracker pimps to live good at the top. The rest of us will stay hoes, out on the block making someone else rich 'til the day we die, if we don't wake up and find a way to take our own slice of the pie. Too many of us don't know how to work toward a dream while we work for the man. Understanding this is what drives me to do more. I'm gonna eat *and* I'm gonna get mine in the music industry someday—I don't care what nobody say. Fuck that! No one's gonna throw salt in my game."

After X's reality check I found myself becoming curious. *Could I really be a stripper?* I exited the kitchen and walked into my bedroom. X followed me, sat down on my chaise lounge, and watched me insert a Mariah Carey CD into the CD player. The music came on, but I couldn't move. I stood there stiff as a board.

"I can't do this in front of you. We're friends."

"Come on now—have some fun with it. Loosen up and pretend that I'm a customer. It should be easier in front of me, not more difficult."

"Ok. I'll try again." I restarted the song and attempted to get lost in the thumping beat, but I still felt like a quivering mass of jelly. X nodded his head as I tried to let the music pull me into the melodic groove. It was hard though. Everything seemed wrong. It was broad daylight—it's not like I could dim the lights. To cope with my embarrassment, I looked right past him. As awkward as it was, I let him guide me.

"Now slow it down. Move to the beat, but slower. Make it move a little slower," he said, giving me a little constructive criticism.

It was like giving instructions to a new lover, explaining what you like and how. Although I was dancing barefoot in a nightie short set without lipstick or heels, it was an erotic experience that I preferred not to have with a friend. What we were doing was for a lover's eyes only.

I followed his instructions until my confidence grew. I started looking him in the eye seductively like a g-string diva, watching for some type of reaction. He lowered his eyelids, not returning my stare.

"Please watch me while I can let you," I told him half-irritated.

"You've got the moves. That's what the girls do. Now let's go to a spot and try your luck. You ready?" he asked.

I glanced down at his jeans. He'd obviously gotten hard from watching me sloppily grind and wind. X played it off by taking his hand away from his pants, but I'd already caught him running his hand over his fabric-covered manhood. In an odd way I was flattered.

"No, I'm not, X," I told him as the image of a Playboy model type shot through my head.

"Let's go. Stop procrastinating here. You're wasting time, and time is money," X said as he stood and stretched.

"No, I'm staying here."

"You need to put some food on your table, sweetheart. Let's go talk to the manager of some clubs. Now stop being scared. I'm going with you. I'll be right there by your side. I'll look out for you while you're stripping—I promise. I swear on my grandmother's grave," he said, reassuring me.

"I can't. I can't," I insisted.

"You said you don't want to be a burden to your father. The man's not rich, remember?" He paused, letting his words sink in. "Look, it's your decision, but I'm trying to show you a way to get money fast just for shaking your ass and using your looks to get you by until you find a decent job."

"What if someone sees me? If I do become successful one day, I can't afford some scandal down the road."

"No one is putting food on your table and paying your bills. All publicity is good publicity. You know I'd never tell, but if anyone ever found out who you are, so what? It'll push up book sales. Them folks will run out to snatch a copy then, 'cause people will know that you're not perfect either. They love dirt and grit—it's a win-win situation for you. I say you got a plan."

"You seem to have the answers for everything, so I'll go ahead and ask. What plan?" I said as I turned off the music.

"You don't have to do this for long. Just save some money to get your new book out there. Write about what you experienced in the strip world, from the inside. Ain't no black chick I know of done that from a journalist point of view, but a few white ones have. You can get everything you need in one place—money and a damn good story about strip club culture and feminism. I always want you to control your product, from now on. That's the key—to control your product yourself. Only give it up if the big boys come knocking. Until then, keep control. That's what my mentor taught me 'bout the music industry. So anyway, call that joint something scandalous like *Strip Life*. I'll invest in it, but you've got to put something up too. 50 Cent got his own book line now. Urban music and urban books is mixing 'cause people figured out it can be profitable. Now listen, I have to go to work soon so you need to let me know what you want to do."

"Let me sleep on it. I'll call you in the morning after I think this whole thing over."

"Suit yourself, shorty, but just remember that time waits for no one," he said, shaking his head.

After sleeping on it, I called X and told him that I'd decided to take the plunge. Within ten minutes I was sitting on the passenger's side of X's Hummer. I may have been broke, but I had friends on all levels in life. X's first single was doing extremely well in Europe and he was beginning to make some noise in The States. He produced music and rapped, but he was also working full-time until his record got released. In fact, his manager was busy organizing his first real tour. His finances were in order, even after having gone through some of the same things I was dealing with, so I respected what he had to say. He obviously knew how to make and keep money in the bank. I met X at a book signing where I was signing my first title. We became casual friends and made a pact that whomever hit it really big would reach back and help the other one. He hadn't quite made it to the big show yet, but he wasn't about to leave me behind either.

The first stop we made was at a local spot in DC. He opened my door then locked the car. Forget the swanky décor and fancy design schemes they may have in Vegas—this place was anything but glamorous. It looked to be an old fast food restaurant. I could imagine girls piling in cabs to get to what looked to be a blue collar titty bar, or even carpooling to arrive. As we walked toward the old looking structure, I began to feel as if I couldn't swallow properly. X opened the door and confidently walked straight to the bar. A girl who I assumed to be a stripper was sitting on a well broken-in barstool, playing cards on a computer. The club hadn't opened to customers yet.

"Yeah. She wants to talk to someone about dancing," X said to someone behind the bar. I looked in the other direction like he had experience inquiring for himself.

"Hey Cash. Someone out here wants to talk to you about dancing," the person yelled over his shoulder. "The owner's in the back." He made a motion with his head.

"You said you'd stay with me. Can you come with me?" I asked X under my breath.

"I can't go back there. It will look like I'm your pimp and I'm forcing you to make that bread. Go ahead. Just tell the man you want to audition."

I sighed and left. I opened a door and walked into a cramped, cluttered room. I was told that a man was the day manager, but a woman appeared.

"Hello. I'd like to know about auditioning to dance," I told her. I felt my heart begin to race.

Cash's cologne flew up my nose as soon as I stood in front of him. He was a clean shaven, smooth looking, strip club veteran. His flat cap was cocked sideways on top of his big round head, and his shoes had a shine only few could manage. His eyeballs were all over me, so much that I felt like asking him if he needed a third eye! I knew it was his job to size me up though, so I didn't comment about that. He spoke brief and to the point.

"Do you live far?"

"No."

"Got kids?"

"No."

"You not on that shit are you?"

"No."

"Come here," he said. I moved closer. "Turn around," he ordered. I did. Then he inspected me.

"You ready to work?"

"Yes, Sir."

"Go get your clothes and come right back."

"I'll, I'll be back soon, Sir," I stuttered, feeling nervous after being interrogated.

"They don't make them like you anymore. There's

money waiting on you here, so do that," he answered. Cash turned around and walked toward a kitchen area and I went to find X.

"What did he say?" X inquired.

"To come back and bring some clothes."

"They want you to dance today, so be prepared."

"You don't know that!" I snapped.

"You'll be dancing tonight fo' sure. I know what I'm talking about. That's good. It's Friday—you should make some decent bread. Now look, you know you can come back here. Let's go see what's poppin' at a few more spots downtown."

"But I told the man that I'd come right back," I remarked.

"You already know you can dance here. This place isn't going anywhere. You got that one on lock."

Fifteen minutes later, X and I were walking into an upscale gentleman's club in Southeast. The building was huge and impressive—a little closer to the Vegas style. I could imagine women wearing little black dresses accompanying their beau to get turned on, and high profile men wearing tailor-made clothes, puffing on cigars frequenting this location.

"It's nothing to see dudes with Bentleys and limos roll up here. This is one spot where the high rollers come. If you're rich, and you live in this town, you've been through this joint. If you're a high-profile celebrity visiting in this town, this is where you slide through. The bottom line is, this is where da the real money's at."

As I looked at the building while X led, I felt like a tourist in a foreign city.

"Come on, shorty. I keep telling you that time is bread." X strolled in confidently just like before. "Yeah, man. She wants to talk to the manager about dancing," he said to a cleaning man.

"The manager is upstairs. Go on up that way," the brother told us.

X and I walked past a beautiful bar, pink and blue strobe lights, twelve-foot brass stripper poles, and several large stages. The club was complete with plush couches and many VIP areas. If I were going to dance, this was more my speed.

"Yes?" a woman said.

As she spoke I noticed a petite black woman sitting in a dark corner. At first I wondered if my eyes were playing tricks on me. The one who spoke to me looked like she could stand to miss a few month's worth of meals, while the other look liked she could stand to gobble up every rib, fatty burger, and pizza in town. The whole thing was like some sort of optical illusion. Their appearances were that extreme.

"I'd like information about dancing," I told her nervously.

She looked at me suspiciously from behind her desk, then she handed me a white packet of paper.

"Fill this out, copy your driver's license, then bring it back here. If we have any openings, we'll call you," she said without cracking a smile.

"You don't have any openings now?" X asked.

"She can fill out the application," the woman answered.

I began to read it as we left the room. "X, they want far too much personal information. There's no way I'm putting down where I went to high school, if I speak foreign languages, where I went to college, or giving these people a copy of my license. They want to know if they can contact a current employer, if you've ever been in a mental hospital, and even want to swear you'll submit to a polygraph test." I continued reading as we walked. "It's four pages long! There's no way that I'm going to give them all of this information. The point is for me to get this story discreetly, not try and make a career out of this corny shit."

"Just fill it out. You're a writer. Be creative and make some shit up. They ain't going through the trouble of no polygraph test," he said as he looked at the stage below.

"But they're making you swear it's all true. I'm scared to lie. I don't want to break the law," I explained as my palms began to grow sweaty.

"Look, either you do this or you go back to the other spot. You said take you somewhere upscale and I did. What do you want from me? Do you want to dance here or not?" X said in an irritated tone, his patience wearing thin.

"Maybe—I don't know."

"If you want to dance here I'll go back and talk to that broad. You can't be talking all proper and what not, acting like you just want information when you want to dance. You're messing yourself up. You gotta be more alert, and act like you're down for grinding this way, Ma," X said, shaking his head as if I should've known better.

"If you haven't noticed, this is kind of a stressful day for me. I don't know anything about the streets and strip life! I told you that," I snapped back.

"Come on, let's bounce. You can think about it. There's one more spot up the street we can check out."

I stuffed the papers in my junky purse and followed X. He didn't even have to move the car—that's how close the clubs were. I opened the door to the second club. My eyes fell on a pasty, aging white man who was sitting in a chair near the door. X told him I wanted to dance.

"How old are you?" he asked.

"Twenty-four," I said.

"Come back later. The manager's name is Mary Ann."

I thanked him and told X what he said. After that, we

cruised down the highway so that my road dog could get ready for work.

"Were you paying attention to how we got here?" X asked.

"I don't need to know. I was just getting information!" I snapped.

"I've got to go to the crib, switch whips, and go to work. Go up to the first spot and audition. As far as the other two, we'll follow up on them later. You need to grind in at least two clubs, five times a week to get your paper straight. Keep that in mind."

"I'm not going back to the first club by myself."

"I can't go back there with you. I have to make my own bread. Come on now—just go in the joint and audition. What do you think they're gonna do to you in there? Bite you?"

X dropped me off and I was feeling rather unsure about my plan. I looked everywhere for something to wear and I didn't have many clothes. When it came to something sexy to wear for my man, usually thongs and heels sufficed. I was totally confused regarding what to expect— I must've called X four times about me not having real dance clothes. I finally settled on something frilly I was able to squeeze into. The movies *Strip Tease* and *The Player's Club* were my only points of reference, but I knew that stripping in the hood was probably nothing like the Hollywood version of the grind. I didn't think that what I planned to wear looked like something a stripper would sport, but it was all I had. I showered, lotioned, shaved, packed a small bag, and even a sheet of paper to hang over my tag to cover my back license plate.

I was off to see what I was in for by dusk. After all, it was the twenty-fifth of the month and I had no other way to try and pay my bills by the first. And that was the beginning of dancing for dollars in clubs, private parties, and one-on-one shows. Author, law student, and stripper, what contradictions. People talk about how hip-hop culture has impacted women of color, but who is talking about the point that sex sells overall, and the corrupt system in America that leads to all of that booty shaking? That's the story I planned to pen. I've made more money shaking my ass than my book gig and working, put together. How sad is that? Anyway, I'll never tell anyone about something dirty I did for money. In fact, my life at The Foxy Lady is a secret I plan on taking to my grave.

5

BAD GIRLS

"Oh my God! You have no right to read that!" Ayanna said, flying toward me to tear it from my grip. "My diary is personal and private! I said pick up whatever fell, not go through it."

After I lifted my head and shut Ayanna's diary, I was trying to recover from the shock of learning about my little sister's secret life as a stripper.

I stuttered, finally able to speak. "Ayanna . . . you're, you're a *stripper*?" I asked, struggling to digest the fact that my innocent, sensible, little sister took her clothes off in front of strangers for money.

Ayanna refused to confirm nor deny anything. She just snatched her diary from between my fingertips. That's when I realized that entry wasn't part of one of her fictional manuscripts . . . she'd done it for real.

"Are you crazy? Yana, you're straight out of a small town in the suburbs. We were reared in a minister's home that was so conservative that I was grounded just for asking to try out for the high school cheerleading squad. If you recall, we weren't even allowed to ask questions about sex or where babies came from," I told her, watching my sister stuff her confessions deep down into her purse.

"You think I've forgotten all of that? I held it down by twirling around a pole, and I'm not ecstatic about what I did for money, but God is my witness that I saw no other way at the time. I know some people would say I demeaned myself by playing the role of a sex object, but I really don't look at that way. Obviously, I really needed the money for law school, and stripping has been a way to help me get it. With Mom dead and all, I couldn't burden Dad any more than he already has been, and that's real."

"I had no idea you were going through all of that. I thought your little ghetto book was doing well. I saw it for sale all over the place."

"It was—I just didn't get the money for it. I planned to use my royalties to help tide me over. The bad part began when I ran out of books. I didn't have $5,000 for another print run and I was getting many requests for it. As a novice, I needed guidance and an investor. So, a so-called friend of a friend who had a little loot agreed to finance one print run. A ten percent cut doesn't go very far after *three* or so printings. It turned out that many more copies of my book were printed than I was aware of. Let's just say that I ended up buying more books back over and above the person's initial investment, and I was contractually confined to the agreement," Ayanna explained.

"But I thought you said some agent approached you about turning your book into a paperback, and you could sign with one of the majors."

"Well, I never explained why I turned the offer down. After I told the investor I was interested in accepting the offer, I was told that my hands were legally tied since my investor didn't want me to move on with the project. As a result, I was stuck in a bind that would keep me standing in a deep hole. Having no royalty payment for the whole year led me to hit rock bottom and linger down in the dumps. I was unemployed, but ineligible for unemployment, well . . . traditional employment that is. Plus, I owed my lawyer two thousand dollars for the work she'd done to try and get me released from the agreement and to file a copyright infringement charge. How was I going to have money to drive to job interviews, feed myself, and pay my bills until some of the clouds lifted and someone put me on their payroll? Trust me, Mystique, I never stopped loving God but I needed the money."

"I know that's right," I commented, finally feeling Ayanna's pain.

"I decided not to shop my story to a publisher though. They're looking for unusual memoirs, street fiction, and hip-hop lit from new talent. I don't think my circumstance is interesting enough to be worth the trouble. I decided to just keep my typical day-to-day stripper stuff to myself, although between these pages. School keeps me busy enough anyway. I'm over the book fiasco—you win some, you lose some. Just like they say, what don't kill you will make you stronger."

"But wait a second, Ayanna. Why didn't you ask me for help? I may have been able to get you some legal advice at a discount. There was no need for you to struggle that way. And you should never give up on your writing—you have real talent."

"I wasn't going to put you in the position of asking for any favors at work. I know how they are. Most artists get ripped off the first time around. Now that someone tore me a new asshole, I realize that I'd rather be a lawyer than a writer. I can't be a starving artist—I just don't have it in me. Since I never did find a professional job, that's the real reason that I decided to go back to school. If fate is kind, I'll be a lawyer by this time next year. If I have my way I'll go into private practice and we can work together.

Your boss treats you like shit and you do all the hard work at that firm. In fact, you need to get your props officially and at least get your paralegal credentials. You already do a paralegal's work anyway."

"Thanks, Yana. As you know, I just do it for the money. I hate my job, but a good check is good a check. Anytime you need help, just ask. You should've said something. I'm your big sister, remember? I may be married but I'll never stop sharing. You've been such a good little sister. Whatever happens in life, I'll be right there with you through it all."

"Thanks, boo. I couldn't burden you like that though. You know how independent I am."

"Well, at least you started dancing for a good reason and a specific purpose. I know you can accomplish anything. I'll be the first one cheering my sis on when she gets that J.D." I smiled.

"Look, Mystique. You've got your exotic dancers, and you've got your strippers. Some have class, and some are straight up chickenheads. Everyone who dances for dollars isn't bad though," Ayanna said.

"You don't have to explain. I'm sorry for invading your privacy. You've been keeping a diary since you were a kid. You never let anyone read it then, so I had no right it read it now."

"Cut the bullshit, Mystique. I know you've snooped in it in the past anyway. Don't act like you've never read my dirt."

"What dirt? There was nothing juicy in it back then." I chuckled a little bit. "But this time was totally different.

"I'm still mad. Don't think I'm not pissed," Ayanna said.

"This is just between us," I said assuring her. "And as far as that foul-ass David, he wasn't good enough for you anyway. As long as you'd known him, he never even let you meet his family. You can do far better than the likes of him. He underestimated you. Prove that loser wrong."

"Thanks. I'm still not over that shit, but I'm feeling better about it. I have more than enough to keep me busy."

"You're a good woman, Ayanna. One day, someone is going to appreciate you for who you are."

"For right now, I've given up on real love. I sort of feel better that the stripper thing is off my chest, but you on the other hand, you still looked stressed. I wasn't going to say anything, but you always look tired as hell and unhappy. I love the kids, but I'm glad they're at camp. If anyone ever needed a break, it's be you."

"I'm just a married old hag. It's my job to be stressed. Mothers and wives don't get breaks. Our work is never done. It's always something." I sighed.

"I have an idea," Ayanna said, her eyes lighting up brightly.

"What?"

"Don't sit around moping, and don't get mad with the old ball and chain, get *even*! Take that *Leave It To Beaver* mother's apron off, put some lipstick on those lips, and for the love of God, take those beat-up house shoes off! Since you did something foul, you owe me one. I want to go to the movies, and I won't take no for an answer. You're coming with me. And whether you like it or not, we're seeing what I want to see."

"See there, you clean up nice," Ayanna said. "You're just trying to make me feel good," I told my sister.

After I spruced myself up a little, Ayanna drove me to a building that looked like no theater I'd ever been to.

"What kind of theater is this?" I asked, twisting up my face.

"Just follow me," Ayanna said, rolling her eyes.

The place looked like it could be found in some abandoned shopping center. In fact, I believe it was an old fast food restaurant. It was in a bad neighborhood, populated by all the makings of a ghetto: a greasy spoon fast food Chinese place, a liquor store, an over-priced grocery store with a shitty food selection, and a tennis shoe pit stop. There were no cleaners, no watering holes, deli cafés, or banks anywhere in sight.

My sister found a table near the main stage and ordered me to sit down.

"Ayanna. Where in the world have you taken me?" I asked, feeling confused and a little uneasy.

"This is the club where I work. As you can see, there are no head doormen or champagne rooms. Enjoy, Mystique. Welcome to my hood. This is as raw and real as it gets. Sit tight. I'll be back."

Never having been in a strip club before, I looked all around as best I could, considering the lighting was dim as dim could be, except for the stage area that was lined with pink, white, and yellow bulbs near the top. After Ayanna reappeared from somewhere, she finished greeting a few people and returned to the table and sat across from me.

"Yana, tell me something. What in the hell am I doing here?" I asked, looking around with a sweeping glance.

"You haven't figured it out yet?" she asked, smiling. "Order a drink, and enjoy your payback for snooping. What do you want? The waitress doesn't have all day, and everyone has to throw one back. Rules of the house, you know. It's on me."

"Bottled water and lemon please," I politely told the woman.

"They don't have lemon in here, Mystique," Ayanna said, laughing at me.

"I can't drink. I can't even tell you the last time I had any type of alcohol."

"Now's a good time to refresh your memory. Don't listen to little old grandma, T. She'll have Patrón, and I'll have Hpnotiq. No, scratch that. That'll be bottled water for me. Thanks, girl," Ayanna said with a smile. I shot her a nasty look, but my sister just ignored me like it made not one iota's difference to her.

After ordering drinks, I expected to watch the girls dance, but it was still a bit early.

"Hey, wanna have some fun?" Ayanna asked.

"How?" I asked, sounding baffled.

"I dare you to go up there. I double dog dare you," she told me with a big ole grin.

"Up where?" I asked.

"On stage, fool. See how it feels."

"Are you crazy, Ayanna? All that studying has knocked the good sense of out your head. I don't think so," I replied, shaking my head no from side to side.

"No one's here yet. You can even keep your clothes on. I already asked the manager if it would be all right—he said it was fine. Hurry up before the girls come out. They're getting dressed in the back right now. Don't be so self-conscious, come on! This is your payback for snooping on my diary."

"I can't. I already told you that," I snapped.

"I dare you—come on, it's fun!" Ayanna insisted, tugging at my arm.

"How childish," I snorted. "When did you ask anyway?"

"I asked when I disappeared, if you must know. Your problem is that you don't know how to let go. You were going through all of those old wedding albums, all salty because you're convinced it's a man's world. You may be a mother, and even a disgruntled wife, but you're still a woman. You need to take the stick out of your asshole and loosen your conservative ass up. All I ever see you do is crossword puzzles. You need a big girl's time out. Lighten up. Laugh. Do something different."

"Ayanna! Watch your language!" I scolded. "And I am not too conservative."

"You've always been an introvert that acted as if you were carrying the weight of the world on your shoulders. Mystique, that's just no good."

"That's because I've always had a lot of responsibilities—including helping Dad raise you," I defended.

"When's the last time you had some fun?" Ayanna said, ignoring my comment.

"Fun?" I repeated as if it were a foreign word.

"I feel for you. See what I'm saying? You are too uptight. You've been around those anal attorneys at the firm too long. You know, the ones I bet make the most terrible lovers," she told me, waving her hand. "Whatever you do, don't lose your sense of humor in life. That's what I learned and what's gotten me over this hump. I have to laugh to keep from crying. Try it, you may like it."

"You never cease to amaze me, you crazy fool," I told my sister, cracking a slight smile.

I found myself walking toward the stage and no longer caring if anyone was watching our silly behavior. As I stepped up the small steps, I wondered if I was so bad looking that my husband would pick a stripper over me. Ayanna had no idea what I was thinking about though. She giggled and dropped a quarter in a jukebox near the stage. When she did, she walked up on stage with me and persuaded me to try and follow her movements as we listened to T-Pain's hot joint, "U and Dat." There I stood in my jeans, struggling for my eyes to adapt to the glow of the light, getting a crash course in pole dancing from my baby sister. Ayanna had always been a natural actress, and often turned out to be the center of attention, because she naturally stood out in a crowd. She appeared to be completely comfortable with her sexuality, swaying her hips like she was a lead video girl on some *BET Uncut* video. Part of me did envy Ayanna—I found myself wanting to feel the very same way, struggling to figure out how to move it to the beat like she did.

"See, you feel better, right?" Ayanna asked, continuing to move around.

"Don't I look like it?" I commented, gripping the pole with both hands, then slowly rising back up. When I reached the top I alternated kicking my legs out, pointing my toes.

"You go, gurl!" she said.

Half-laughing, I poorly mimicked her crazy moves as T-Pain belted out a mouthful of explicit, but sexy, words. Oddly enough, I suddenly felt pretty and powerful.

After two songs worth of playing around that pole, Ayanna pulled my hand, giggling. We walked off the stage and sat in our seats as the girls began day shift for the lunch crowd. By that time, the waitress had come with our drinks. Since my sister was driving, I finished sipping my drink and shamelessly watched the girls strip as they dug in their toolbox of tricks. I gulped hard and blushed when the first one removed her top, then exposed her breasts and dropped her shimmering thong, while staring directly into my eyes. But when the second one made smoke ooze from the amber glow, as she took drags of a cigarette with her pussy, my eyes were glued to the stage like a child to a circus act. Ayanna laughed at the trick that I'm sure she'd seen before, but I was just plain stunned and amazed. Things were winding down when the theatrics ended. I enjoyed watching the dancers that followed tease and charm customers with their sensuous pole twirling moves. They didn't seem as interested in topping the next girl with odd talents—their beauty and air of confidence was enough to hook men alone. I found myself wishing that I had the guts to tip them myself when a steady stream of men showed them some love, but I didn't. Well, I'm not being completely honest about that one. When a 50 Cent cut about getting money pumped hard and heavy, I began shedding my inhibitions. I was feeling that tune like a groupie at a rap concert, by the time the alcohol hit my bloodstream. Trash talking kept rolling off my lips as I stood in front of the stage.

"Do it girls. Make that money. Tell 'em, 50!" I said as I tipped one girl who made her ass cheeks jiggle to the beat. She popped it like I pro while wearing stripper shoes. The tipsy Mystique was thoroughly impressed.

"I never had problems 'til I got me one of these," I said, pointing to my wedding ring. "Take it from me. That decision was a mistake. Keep your game tight. If you aren't with the drama, don't let this happen to you. Enjoy your freedom as long as you can, girl! Say no, even if that rock was snatched up from Tiffany's."

The first dancer started peeling off her stripper gear. I noticed that activity increased, guessing that if she didn't take it all off before she stepped off that stage, her hip wouldn't lean to the side from all of those dollar bills being stuffed in her garter.

I peeled off five ones. "Work it, Ms. Black and Beautiful. Having nerve enough to do that deserves something a little nice. I see you working hard."

Without realizing it, I admired that she had the guts to show off her birthday suit, while I was battling self-esteem and insecurity issues my husband had invited into my psyche.

The second dancer that stood next to the first crouched down, smiling at me. She bent her knees, bouncing up and down. When she stopped, she put her weight on her right arm and gripped the bottom of her heel. She raised her left foot and placed it behind her head. Home girl set if off. I ignored that don't touch the dancer sign and slipped my hand up her thigh until I reached her garter belt.

After I dropped around ten dollars on the girls, I made it back to my seat as my hips rocked. Men that had been stingy as hell took her move as a green light to give up the dollars. They nearly broke their necks to tip the dancer who showed off her flexibility.

When they filed past me to take their seats again, I studied them in disgust.

"Trifling dogs," I mumbled.

From the back, one observer that I was hating on looked like a man. But after the person finished tipping a dancer, and turned around to take a seat, I could see it was a woman trying to look like a man—equipped with a mustache and all. I was really freaked out, but pretended that I wasn't taken by surprise. That's when I realized that lesbians were lined up in the front row of the other stage. Their eyes were glazed over worse than some of the men. One tipped the dancer so much that she was digging in her pockets for change because she'd spent all of her cash. A fair share of females cracked their wallets wide open and went broke tipping the female dancers. A percentage of the women looked butch, while others appeared to be lipstick lesbians and even straight chicks. I found it ironic that none of these women hit the strip clubs with men. I began laughing aloud about all of this, nearly cracking my side open.

"What's so funny?" Ayanna asked.

"Nothing," I lied.

As each hip-hop, rap, and slow dragging R&B tune played, I found myself snapping my fingers. By that time, the whole club was rocking. Mostly all of the seats were taken.

"T, another drink for me, please. On the rocks," I said. Ayanna just raised her eyebrows, looking at me in amazement.

"What? I dare you to say a word," I warned her. "My representative is on break. The woman who used to know what fun was is in the building."

"I'm not saying nuthin'. Enjoy yourself while your rep is in town. Hell, I don't get to visit her that often."

I playfully smacked my sister's right arm as my once stressed-filled neck loosened. My eyes stayed glued to the stage. Each dancer seemed to offer something different. My sister didn't know it, but just standing up on stage under those colored lights gave me a rush of excitement I couldn't shake, and watching other women work their bodies as men sipped beer around us only heightened my curiosity. More than that, the drink loosened me up, my shoulders relaxed, and my pussy was dripping wet. If I would've been sober I probably wouldn't have realized that I liked the way I felt in that community strip joint. I was turned on by the whole atmosphere. My panties were so wet, my juices were nearly running down my legs. Talk about a straight aphrodisiac!

As I sat there, hour after hour, I realized that my husband was to blame for not paying me enough attention, not the strippers. They were to entertain to make their money, but not one man in the spot gave one dollar up that he didn't want to give.

After a while, a new group of girls hit the stage. I popped up with another fresh drink in my hand, cheering them on to make money.

"Screw my ticket. Screw my husband who won't give me the time of day. Screw my mean boss. Somebody put the needle on the record and pop it!" I commented, swaying from side to side.

"Sit down for a while," Ayanna suggested. I sat down,

only because my legs were beginning to feel like rubber, and the heat was working on me. A mini river was flowing down the middle of my breasts. "Drink that slow. I think you've had enough," Ayanna said as she grabbed my drink."

"Shush. Now listen here. Don't spill my drink."

"It's time to go. Get your purse."

"So early? I came to party didn't I. It's only two-thirty."

As Ayanna peeled me up out of that crusty little joint, I kept belting out that 50 Cent song, all the way out of the door. Giggling as I walked to the car, I spoke to men with a smile on my face.

"Hey, baby. I bet you're broke now, huh?" I said, laughing and pointing.

I was chilling, all the way back home. I felt like I'd been champagne popping with Hollywood stars all night. I was leaning in Ayanna's ride, feeling like I didn't have a care in the world. When we made it to my house Ayanna had such a hard time making me walk, she tried her best to pull me out of the car. Instead of walking up the sidewalk, I walked in the grass until my legs felt like rubber. I fell down and Ayanna helped me up.

"You're a mess," she said.

"No I'm not. That's the most fun I've had in years."

"Get in the house. You're going to have to drink a truck load of water to get this alcohol out of your system."

"I'mma be all right. I feel freeee," I exclaimed. I began peeling off my shirt, right there out in the open. When I made it down to my bra, I threw my arms up toward the sky. Ayanna was completely fed up with me.

"Cool it. What do you think you are, a stripper now?" Ayanna asked angrily, picking up my things. She quickly shoved me forward. I looked at my monster pad, feeling unimpressed by the high price tag of living in one of the most decent neighborhoods off of 495. Back then, we were the only black family living in the development. Donavan's portfolio, as well as our combined salaries, was not making our home a happy place. Although we weren't exactly rich, we were doing far better than the average American family. We had the appearance of becoming an upwardly mobile family whose financial blessings were moving in the right direction, but obviously, our world had lost the shine to the both of us. The pressure of keeping it all was making me sick and tired!

"Stop pushing. Easy. Easy. That's hot," I said, smiling at the thought.

By that time, Ayanna used her key to open the front door.

"Honey, I'm home!" I yelled. "Miss me? I had my first pole dancing class. Surprised, Daddy?" Ayanna forced me to kick off my shoes. "You should've seen your wife do her thing. Woulda, coulda, shoulda. Where were you, Donavan? Who cares. Fuck you, you selfish, cheating bastard! It's about *me* now," I said, singing that 50 Cent tune again as Ayanna pulled me up the stairs.

As we passed under the chandelier, moving up the staircase, I didn't stop mumbling until we turned right and made it to the master suite. When my head hit the comforter topped bed, I fell backward with one sloppy flop. I started snapping my fingers again, and bouncing my shoulders. Ayanna laid my things across the chair, then helped me get dressed for bed.

She put my smokey smelling body under the covers, having no idea how good I felt inside. By the time she turned the lights out, I was out cold faster than I'd drifted off in an entire month. While snoring loudly, I began to have a hell of a dream. In my head, I was getting my A game in place. I planned to take the entire week off as I fantasized about what I'd look like popping my ass with my booty up in the air. All work and no play had made

Mystique a very boring girl, and I finally acknowledged that was nothing but the truth. Call me irresponsible, but I decided to explore my other side, while simultaneously finding out what Donavan saw in strippers that made him want to lick one of there coochies, instead of just having a little light fun in a club. Although I may have temporarily lost my mind, by the time the liquor wore off, I decided I'd become an anonymous stripper, and have a little fun shaking my ass for the same reason Donavan thought I'd never find out that I'd been living with his representative, not the real man I thought I said "I do" to. Since he thought he could get away with keeping a big secret from me, I joined the very same team, but only I cooked up my master plan to also get revenge.

For the first time in years, I somehow managed to find myself craving sexual liberation and adventure. I didn't want more jewelry. I didn't want a new car. I didn't want anything material. I suddenly wanted to do something completely out of character for and by myself, just like Ayanna. Coupled with the unchartered territory of urban life, I was intrigued by the thought of working my hips and bouncing my booty for lusty-eyed men, while my kids were neatly tucked away at some posh summer camp. Right or wrong, instead of being too scared to ever return to a place like The Foxy Lady, that was the beginning of an-other sharp turn in my life.

6

G-STRING DIVA

After I shaved my kitty kat bald, I got my nails, hair, and toes looking right, and packed my Tumi Signature Weekender bag. Yes, you guessed right. I was drunk as a skunk, the previous night. But by the time the sun peaked over the horizon, I still remembered my twisted fantasy. After chiding Ayanna for stripping, I took the same big plunge after her tricky excursion. It stuck in my mind all day. And by that evening, I crept out of my suburban box and drove to the other side of the world where The Foxy Lady was located. When I arrived alone, I parked on the farthest end of the parking lot where my car could not be easily spotted from the highway. I noted the winos preparing to beg patrons for spare change. One was brave enough to hound me as I drew closer. I was afraid to even look at him, so I kept it moving and hoped that one of the bouncers would shoo him back to the corner. As I walked through the club, my ears reprogrammed themselves from listening to Garth Brooks, Stylistics, and Gloria Estefan to 50 and Snoop.

"I want to audition," I explained, struggling to hear myself think straight.

"The owner, Cash, is away. You really should be talking to him first."

"Okay, thanks. I'll try later," I told him. I turned to walk away.

"Imma give you a break. Go ahead and holler at Steve in the back," the man explained. He looked me up and down, then I walked away, content that I made it past the gate keeper.

"I'd like to audition," I repeated to the man in the back, after building up my confidence to say anything to him. He stood crooked like he had a bad disc in his back and needed surgery. I had no idea where they dug him up from.

"You should've come early in the day. But since you're here now, let me see your ID," Steve answered.

I handed it over to him, after explaining I didn't know that. Steve looked at my ID, then peered over the bifocals that were hanging off his nose, trying desperately to put two and two together. Most people don't think I looked my age, and I assumed he was trying to reconcile my birth date and my appearance.

"How old are you?" a dancer asked in between popping gum.

"Twenty-eight," I lied.

"No you're not!" a catty dancer replied. Jealousy rang in her voice as she looked me up and down like she got her information straight from someone's mouth who was there when I was born.

"Turn around—let me see," another said. She sucked her teeth. "Yes she is. Stop hating, Moet!" she replied as she and Moet both looked me up and down, inspecting me with two sets of eyes.

"Yeah, yeah, yeah!" she replied.

Girl after girl kept asking me where I was from. I lied and gave them the name of a county where I lived years ago. Another dancer was being scolded by the night manager for arriving late.

"Mercedes, do you not know how to tell time? Do you not remember there's something called a schedule around here? You're forty minutes late!" the night manager barked at the girl that had just come strolling in.

"D was tripping, Ma. You know how he is," she snapped with an attitude.

"So that's my problem? You better fix your tone of voice and stop bringing your home problems with you through this door—*late!*"

"He walked out and I didn't have a babysitter. The kids are off the hook. They were fighting over a broom and I had to straighten them out. Everyone else I tried to get to watch them steals or gets on my nerves."

"Then move!"

"I *can't* move."

"One more time of this and you're fired from The Foxy Lady. You got that?"

"I put eight hours in at my day job and my check is nothing. My stamps got cut and D's on crack and dope. I need to feed them kids, Ma. I'm trying to do the best for my children. Please don't fine me or let me go."

"Mercedes, every stripper in here has a story. You ain't the only one in here with problems or kids. If it happens again, I'm fining you. I should fine your ass right now since you have such a bad attitude! You got three kids by three different no good men, and you're only twenty-one. No one told you to have kids so young but your damned self! You ever heard of condoms?"

"I hate that motherfucker," Mercedes mumbled under her breath.

The night manager walked away from the girl, looking like a scary old witch with her scrunched up eyebrows. After she knew she was being watched, the girl sulked in silence as she opened her suitcase and sorted through hot pink, lime, black, and turquoise outfits.

"You get dressed, too. Let us know when you're ready," Ma said, turning my way.

I didn't feel safe or comfortable, so I stalled at least thirty minutes before pulling my white cotton shirt over my head to dress for my debut. The dressing room was so filthy that I cringed at the thought of taking off my shoes or dropping my sweats. My stomach felt as if it was tied in sixty knots. Ma finally made me put an end to my stalling tactic. All I had in my possession was a little Victoria's Secret number with a matching thong that used to get Donavan riled up, and a pair of played out stilettos I once bought from Saks.

As music blasted from the jukebox, I walked toward a stage with a shiny silver pole dividing it, wondering what in the hell I was going to do to entertain the crowd. This time, not as many women were in the crowd yet. It looked like a Disneyland for horny men that ranged from fresh looking hustlers, to well fed CEOs with big bellies. The businessmen surely wouldn't dare take their clients to a strip joint like The Foxy Lady. I could pick out a man with Donavan's sort of background wherever I went. I was amazed that even professional and affluent men would risk life and limb to seek entertainment in the hood. Even the area where the girls performed hadn't been maintained.

Mirrors were pasted on the back wall, and fingerprints were all over them. Obviously no one had invested in a bottle of glass cleaner. Since the stage was higher than the area where the customers sat, my crotch would be eye level to every and anyone that wanted to look. Everyone was waiting. I wanted attention and now I was definitely going to get that. With no liquor in my system, I was far more afraid to unleash the freak within. My hands grew cold and clammy and I wondered how in the hell I convinced myself to do something so scandalous.

So what did it feel like to strip for the first time? It was an ambitious undertaking for someone like me. It's hard to describe, but I'll try to explain it. At first, the smell of liquor and smoke was stuck inside of my nostrils, which made it extremely difficult to concentrate of moving my feet. Then I felt like I didn't have any rhythm. I don't know how I did it, but I finally managed to make them move. All I could do was move like I was dancing in a nightclub, not a strip club. I twisted and wriggled to three or four songs. I felt like I was going to suffocate; it was hot as Hades on the stage. I tried to put a little umph in it, but "dancing" wasn't as easy as I thought it would be. Every time I began to worry about feeling too bold or foolish, I tried to pick a friendly face to focus on, and lose control, but I couldn't work up the courage to peel off my lingerie. It just wasn't going to happen the first time around. Thankfully, no one heckled me for being a chicken.

I looked at the sea of black tables, along with countless men that sipped liquor and beer, as the show progressed. I didn't make much eye contact with anyone, as I subjected myself to being analyzed by a room full of male critics. I didn't feel dirty or ashamed, I just felt free, despite what I'd done. It was clear that they liked something about me, so that was a good thing. I exited with what I felt were sympathy dollars that I'd scooped up from the stage. Some were balled up in a tight wad, and others were flat, smelling purely of liquor and smoke. I can't remember much else besides staring vacantly into space as men stared at me up close and far away.

"Where's your garter belt?" a man asked. I later found out that he was a regular.

"I just auditioned. I don't have one yet," I answered as I shot past him to the back room. I hadn't even thought about tools of the trade.

Steve handed me a clipboard. "Fill this out," he told me. "The rules are on the wall."

As I looked around at a yellowing poster board adorned with words written in faded magic marker, I guessed I'd made it through the "audition." Someone was watching me do whatever I did . . . obviously. I was at war with myself. I was scared as hell but tried to pretend as if I wasn't shaken. Although most were thick black girls with phat asses, they came in an assortment of shapes, complexions, and varied as far as the amounts of cellulite or stretch marks they had. Some were big breasted with big asses, while others were just well-endowed on the bottom with A or B cup breasts and a bit on the slimmer side. I really didn't see what was so special about them. Just like women out on the street, they varied in attractiveness.

Although every stripper wasn't a glamour queen, they all had another thing in common: *tattoos.* Those hood celebrities were adorned on their arms, back, legs . . . just everywhere. One dancer had thickly inked Chinese letters trailing down her back. I wondered if she knew what it even meant. Piercings came in a close third. Some had them near an eyebrow, in their tongues, in their nipples . . . and the second pair of lips. I could see that the Playboy model image had been a stereotype conjured in my mind—at least on the neighborhood strip level.

With all of this said, after I made it inside their world, some of my hate index began to decrease. I remembered that. Ayanna seemed just fine. I then dismissed the assumptions society often pinned on free-spirited women, otherwise known as strippers. From what I began to notice, every girl's reason for wanting to make quick bucks were different—physical and mental abuse, drug addiction, missing baby daddy's child support checks, low paying day jobs, school bills hanging over their heads like Ayanna—a host of reasons all tied to real life. And of course, some were there for stereotypical reasons as well, such as plain old lack of ambition, but still wanting to get paid for something.

I was drowning in a sea of ashy, naked butts that were getting lotioned up, tiny g-strings, wigs, and glasses of liquor. Even the girls who looked like what most men would call certified dimes were cussing, fussing and acting like true fools. I could barely hear myself think as I scribbled down my cell phone number and left my home phone blank. I called Ayanna and whispered in the phone as I asked her for advice. I wanted an adventure that would allow me to escape from my boring world, and that's exactly what I got!

"They want my real name, too. What should I do?" I asked.

"What's all of that noise? Where are you? Who wants your real name?" my sister questioned.

"These girls are making noise. It's so loud in here," I complained. I wanted to find a quieter place, but couldn't.

"What did you say?" Ayanna asked, struggling to hear my whispers.

"These girls," I whispered louder. I didn't want any of them to whip my butt for talking about them. "I'm auditioning for a job."

"What job? You have a job."

"Well, you know. The, the, the one you told me you had," I explained, half stuttering.

"What! I hope you're not at The Foxy Lady. Please tell me I heard you wrong."

"That's exactly where I am," I admitted.

"I *demand* that you get your ass out of that place right now!"

"Come on, Yana. Don't flip out. Help me out on this, please. I'm stuck and I don't know what to do. I'm in the back room and everything. I promise, this is the last time I'll come here. I just want to see what it's like to do this for real, for one night only. It's just an innocent fantasy," I explained.

"Damn—you got yourself into some real shit! Why go from zero to one hundred miles per hour in the same day? Why couldn't you have just signed up for a pole dancing class? " Ayanna asked.

Although it wasn't exactly the most ideal time to do so, I wanted to tell Ayanna the *real* reason I despised strippers and preferred to strut my stuff on a stage, as opposed to signing up for some corny pole dancing classes with other suburban wives who heard about the phenomenon on *Oprah.*

"Well, uh, don't put down your first name. Just use your last," she said, sounding flustered. "No scratch that, make up a last name that sounds like it could be yours. The guy who looks at ID cards won't remember what it was," she said, correcting herself. I knew I really caught her off-guard.

"Ok, thanks, Yana," I answered. A rush of comfort enveloped me after she gave me sound advice as someone who had been there.

"Call me back when you're leaving and I'll take a break from studying to meet you out there and follow you home. This is not the end of this conversation, but since you won't leave, we'll have to finish this later."

"Stage name. It's asking me for a stage name. What should I say?" I asked, rushing to squeeze in one more question.

"I don't know. Call yourself Honey tonight," Ayanna suggested.

"Ok, got it. Bye, Ayanna. I'll call you," I replied, excited by my new stage name.

I checked night and day shift availability because I wasn't sure what to check. I also made up a bogus social security number and called it a day. After I returned the form and clipboard to Steve, the woman that had been chewing out Mercedes formally introduced herself to me as Ma. I wasn't sure if she was straight, gay, or bisexual. She told me I had nice legs and complimented me on my hair, which I had decided to let swing freely. After she caressed me with compliments, she delivered one dose of criticism.

"I don't know what you're used to, but if you think you have what it takes to work at The Foxy Lady, you've got to step up your game," she told me, placing her hands on her fat padded hips.

If she's going to step up anyone's game I wanted to suggest hiring dancers without bulging cellulite, stretch marks, or those that look five foot two and weighed one hundred fifty pounds. Yes, I do understand that beauty is all relative, and yes, I understand that perfect is a goal that is not possibly achievable. But, I thought everyone would look tight, right, or at least like they made an effort to keep up their appearances or become pals with a treadmill. Some did, some didn't. Regardless which category they fell into, all of them were comfortable enough with their bodies to entertain men's fantasies for money. Some were very glamorous looking, while others reminded me of the girl next door. Although I was amongst the ranks of them, I had my butt up on my back for a while. I didn't care for any of them until I grew to understand what Ayanna said about the difference between dancers and strippers.

I gave Ma a puzzled look because of the initial thought, then partly because she acted like the place was some crystal palace, and finally because I didn't know what she was talking about until I followed where her eyes had landed. After I noticed that she was looking down at my beat up stilettos—the ones I'd owned for at least five years, I understood.

"Hot Chocolate, what you got in your stash?"

"I'll check, Ma."

The stripper named Hot Chocolate unzipped a large suitcase. Apparently she sold shoes, clothes, and girl toys.

"Find her something, would you?" Ma said.

"Here, try these on. One's a nine. The other pair is a ten."

I didn't speak as I took the shoeboxes from her. I sat down to try them on. I slid my foot into the first pair. They were too small and squeezed my feet tightly, although I normally wore a nine. I slid them off and uncovered the lid of the second box, then slipping on those size tens. I got up and walked over toward a mirror to see how I appeared. To my surprise, I almost turned *myself* on. The shoes were made of clear plastic on the front, and the heels were sparkly like white diamonds. I felt hot as shit. They made my thighs look edible, my calves appear defined, and my legs looked longer and sexier than life. I stood up in the stripper heels wondering how I would pay her. I hadn't made enough during my first set to pay for these shoes that had me jacked up in the air. I knew I had to have them though. I'd never worn anything like them in my entire life. In fact, I didn't even feel like the same plain suburban wife that walked into The Foxy Lady. For once in a long time I didn't feel boring or unattractive. It felt good to transform myself into an anonymous stripper in a place where no one knew me, my name, or my troubles at home.

"How much are they?" I asked with a sparkle in my eye.

"Sixty," she replied casually. Girls began reaching inside

of her suitcase, trying on outfits and shoes. I saw one outfit I liked and asked her to put it to the side for another
time.

"Now look, I'm going to pay her for you. I at least want
half by tonight. If you make enough, you can pay me back
after you do. If you don't, you owe me. Don't make no
fool of me now. I'm sticking my neck out for you," Ma explained.

"Oh no. Thank you. I wouldn't do that. Thanks," I told
Ma.

When we were finished, a man came in the dressing
room, collected the bag, and hauled it off to the girl's car.

"And write down her number in case you need to call
her about clothes. Write down mine too," she instructed
me.

As I did what I was told, I noted that part of me was mad
that I was already out sixty dollars when I made a little
money. Although I wasn't doing it for the money, it was
still fun to imagine that I'd gotten something while par-
taking in my dirty little secret!

Every hour, I was due to dance for fifteen minutes. I was
told that this usually was equal to three to four songs. Believe it or not, it was hard work. I didn't know what to do
that long, so I watched what other dancers were doing. I
noticed they stayed on their knees a lot and jiggled their
asses on cheaply laid plywood and rug remnants. I had no
experience doing this, but I tried my hardest to mimic the
move. Somehow, I managed to let go of my lingerie top
and do my thing in nothing but a g-string. I got on all
fours like a dog and showed the crowd the view of my
backyard, although I never removed my thong that matched
my lingerie set. During this process, I found out that you
couldn't expose your ass cheeks unless you were on stage.
I had to go to the car and get my bag to find something to
cover them when needed. Since I wasn't sure that I would

be staying, I hadn't brought it inside. I found something to cover my cheeks although the dancer who refused to believe I was twenty-eight offered to sell me a pair of new briefs for $10.00.

By eight o'clock, I'd made enough to pay for the shoes, pay a twenty dollar dancer fee, and put a little gas in my Lexus. The night wasn't even over, but already my knees were red and swollen from trying to jiggle my ass on all fours. I made it back in the changing area and stretched out my legs. They felt as if they were on fire.

"What happened to your legs?" asked one of the girls in the dressing room.

I winced in pain. "The rug on the stage," I replied.

She could barely hear me over the chatter of the other loud girls. They were talking about how they were horny and who they had sex with, girl-on-girl, back in the day. It reminded me of a high school lunch hour.

"You're supposed to put a blanket down on the stage when you go up."

"I didn't know that I was supposed to bring one," I answered. I had no idea the girls spent so much time doing what is called floor work.

"Look on top of the lockers. Maybe someone left one."

I looked and found a blanket to drag up to the stage with me for my next set, but by then, my legs were already in bad shape.

"You have those underwear on backwards," a dancer told me as I walked past her.

"The tag is in the back," I answered.

"Why are your underwear on backwards?" a dancer named Seduction asked.

"No they're not. The tag is in the back," I answered again, checking myself.

She rolled her eyes like I was stuck on stupid and continued walking across the room. After she left, I realized that the tag was supposed to be in the front, not the back! I felt humiliated when I realized I'd gone out on stage like that. I turned the panties around and sat back down in the chair. I felt like such an idiot and very much out of place.

Nearly seven hours later, I'd learned quite a bit the hard way. I was plain exhausted from a hell of a work out, compliments of on the job training to keep men interested and inspired to give up the dollars. I could see why pole dancing had become a fad of suburban women like me. It made me work muscles I didn't realize I even had without even thinking about it.

By the end of night, I'd flexed my booty to everything from reggae cuts, southern crunk, and classic R&B. As I attempted to make friends with that stripper pole, I heard every sort of lyric—themes about the system, getting buck wild, rims, gold teeth, sagging pants, cheaters, love, and so on. Along the way, someone shouted that the club was closing and told all girls to leave the stage. Somehow, I made it through a whole night stripping! It was stressful, but in a good way. All of the bright lights came on and bouncers began ushering all of the men out. I had no idea they'd turn on those bright lights and prayed that no one got a good look at my face. By the time I returned to the dressing room for the last time, I was nearly limping the way my son sometimes does after football practice.

"Hey," Ma called out to me. "Be here on Monday at noon."

"I'll see you then," I replied as I carefully dressed. I turned on my phone and dialed Ayanna to make sure she was waiting for me. She was. As I prepared to leave, I chatted with her a little before hanging up.

When I told Ayanna that I was due to report to the club during the day, she clearly had a firm opinion about it.

"Why'd you check day shift? You want to work nights.

That's when most of the money is made. They put the old or ugly girls on day shift. You're a night quality girl."

"I didn't know. I don't know anything about this stuff. I figured it was a good way to practice, so I don't go out there at night looking like a novice. Plus, I am old for stripping. Most of the girls are very young like you."

"It's about how you look, and you can pass for younger. That's a valuable trait. Act confidant about it and the rest will follow," she explained. "I don't know why I'm explaining all of this to you though. You won't be doing this again, so none of this is relevant anyway. Hurry up and come outside. I have a long day in the morning."

I was just about to leave, when a very tall dancer with a crooked nose busted into the room. My guess was that someone had broken it in the past. Ironically, her name was Envy.

"Don't be telling me to get off the stage early just 'cause *she's* new pussy!" she ranted.

Envy pointed at me while arguing at a man in charge of something or another. At some point that night, I was told to go up on the main stage and she was told to get down. I didn't have anything to do with that, but she made a real scene. The man calmly mumbled something as droplets of spit flew from her mouth.

"And I know it was you that told her to go ask my customer for a tip! Keep giving her that kind of advice and it'll get her head cracked open! Everyone in this club knows he's mine, so don't try to get brand new on me and mess up my hustle!"

I discreetly watched her walk away and sit down in a chair. I made note that maybe she was asked to leave the stage early because of her cottage cheese looking ass, not *just* alleged preference that was given to me! The stripper's anger at me made sense. He did tip me ten dollars in one pop, and despite my dancing blunders, he also told me that I was sexy. Apparently Envy had a steady tipper on her hands and didn't want to let go of him—talk about workplace excitement and colleague competition!

Learning to make my hips sway without wobbling in four-inch heels for a long period of time was no fun experience either. Although my shoes looked sexy as hell, those bad boys left my toes numb. Forget feeling sexy. I couldn't wait to soak my feet, wiggle my toes in water, and drift off to sleep, but at least I wouldn't stay awake tossing and turning over *that* man. The kids didn't even ask about their own father when I spoke to them. Obviously, I wasn't the only one that had noticed that he suddenly wasn't bringing much more than paying the bills to the table. Although it was approaching the wee hours of the morning, I may have beat him home myself. If recent history would prove to repeat itself, Pretty Ricky was out on a Friday night, somewhere. Little did he know that his "boring little suburban wife" was contemplating if she wanted to become a part-time g-string diva.

Entertaining men in the club who didn't have a problem making me feel like someone interesting boosted my self-esteem enough to tell me something I needed to know. No matter how cold Donavan had been treating me, I still had it going on. When I realized that most men did find me very attractive, I realized that it was him, not me. I was far from twenty-one, but even with that said I took a poll of how many men stared me down like they wanted to eat me up like biscuits and gravy. Hands down, I still left a fair share of men in need of neck braces! I didn't care what Janet or Ayanna said, I knew I wasn't tripping. Something really was stinking in Gotham City, and my gut instinct told me that time would tell exactly what, or who, it was.

1

GETTING IT REAL TWISTED

"**W**here are you, Forrester? Why in the hell aren't you at your desk? What's your excuse this time?" Mr. Jiles asked, yelling into my cell phone.

"I put in for a little vacation time. You didn't get the memo?" I explained.

"I don't read memos, and I don't give a fuck who approved you to take time off. I'm the boss, and I said get your ass in here right now, go get my lunch on the way, and shut your damn mouth or else, Forrester."

"I told you I was approved to take some time off. I need a vacation, Mr. Jiles."

"Do I have to repeat myself? Get your ass in this firm right this minute!" my boss yelled.

"I haven't had a vacation in three years. I need a mental break from crappy clients, a boss that thinks that a bathroom break is a luxury, and a man who thinks that I'm a peon or an idiot who is beneath him, just because he does what he does, and I do what I do. Either leave me alone on my vacation, or I'll walk," I threatened, finally getting a few things off my chest.

"Then walk! You'll need a reference. Don't expect me to give you one."

"I've been keeping a notebook of your verbal attacks. I'll file a complaint with the EEOC if I have to. I even have you on tape, bullying me."

"You didn't have my consent. I hand picked you for the job, and this is how you thank me, you ungrateful, dumb bitch!"

"See what life at the firm will be like if I'm not there to take your shit. I don't have to take this. I quit, you crazy bastard!" I yelled, hanging up my cell phone.

My head was throbbing and I couldn't believe I quit my job. My mental health was spiraling downward and I was on E. As much as I didn't want to, I called Donavan at the office. I put my pride aside to let him know that we may be one paycheck shorter.

As my heart pounded I dialed the direct number at his desk from my cell phone.

"Yes, may I please speak to Mr. Donavan Forrester," I said, struggling to sound professional.

"Mystique, is that you?" his secretary said.

"Yes, Patty. I need to speak to my husband. He's not in a meeting is he?" I asked. Then I lost it and began sobbing into the telephone.

"I'm sorry, honey, Donavan's not here. That's why his calls are being transferred to me. Is everything all right?"

"No it's not. There's been an emergency at home," I said. "I really need to talk to him when he gets back in the office. It's very important."

"Well that won't be until tomorrow. You didn't know? He took the day off."

"I guess he forgot to tell me," I lied. A pain shot through my stomach. "I'll call him on his cell phone," I told her, struggling to regain my composure.

"Ok. I hope everything works out."

"Thanks," I said, then hung up.

I was livid, questioning where Donavan's ass was, so I did call his cell phone. When I got his voicemail, I left him a message that I needed to talk. I also decided to send him a text too. Since he had a habit of having his phone with him every time he left the house, I figured he'd get the message pretty quickly, one way or another.

"Nd to tlk asap. Smthng important. Am tired of this 2"
"Call after 12. Busy in a meeting."
"U r lying. Fnd out u aren't at wrk. Where r u D?"
"No time 4 yr head games. Tld u in a mtg. At clnt's office."
"Yeah right. Why won't u have sex w me?"
"CAUSE YR PUSSY SMELLS LIKE ROTN FISH"
"So it's like that? Smbdy can kiss my ass!"
"U r being a bitch. U can't be talked 2. Told u aftr 12!"
"Bitch? U r out of line! U nvr called me that b 4!"
"Trth hurts. Why I don't play yr voice m. Just delete now."
"U started this by actn funny!"
"Mkng money. Now I dont feel like tlkng at all."

Insults were still ringing in my head. I could understand Mr. Jiles, but I couldn't believe that Donavan had moved beyond the silent treatment. He'd been so rude when he responded to my text, that I knew that my marriage was officially crumbling before my eyes. A rush of loneliness came over me. I knew Ayanna was probably in class, plus, I didn't want to repeatedly dump my problems in her lap. My life wasn't her life. My marriage wasn't her problem. To block out the pain, I ventured to my great escape. If I stayed at home, it would only make me feel worse. I'd probably tear the place up, looking for clues that he was cheating, torturing myself further. Instead, I decided to vacate home, as soon as possible. I returned to

The Foxy Lady, struggling to deal with it all later, blocking both matters out of my mind.

I assumed my normal parking space and later discovered the main door was locked. I had no idea why the night manager asked me to return so early. The last thing I wanted to do was be spotted by anyone I knew who happened to be driving by. I was rather peeved that I couldn't get in. As I walked away from the main door near a busy street, I spotted a used condom on the ground. When I called and mentioned this to Ayanna, she told me that she saw a girl get into a truck before the police arrived the first night I began working at the club. She said that the girl stayed in the vehicle for at least ten minutes giving anything but a high-priced blowjob. When she parted with the man, she spit something out of her mouth in the parking lot. I don't know why Ayanna didn't tell me about seeing this at first. Perhaps she didn't want me to find out so soon that many girls do extra things for money. Either way, I was about to find out the other seedy aspects of this game.

I walked from the main door to a back door that was meant for deliveries. I rang the bell many times, but no one answered. After a few minutes a dancer named Butter pulled up with a Styrofoam container and a roll-on bag.

"No one's answering," I told her.

She ignored me, walked past me, and rang the doorbell calmly. When no one answered Butter began kicking it and shifting her food to pound on it with her fist. That did the trick—a round-shaped Spanish cook opened the door and let us in. The dancer didn't have much to say to me. In fact, she had nothing to say at all. Butter smacked her pouty lips on greasy Chinese food as we both sat in complete silence. I was learning that most girls view a new girl as potential competition. Unless your swagger somehow earned the right to be in their clique, they had nothing to say.

I sat on top of my blanket, completely clothed. Another dancer named Nasty arrived pulling her suitcase on wheels behind her. She was a bit more chatty and conversed with people who worked in the club.

"How old are you? You look like a baby!" Nasty said. I wanted to laugh since she was way off!

I responded with my standard answer of twenty-eight. Luckily, just as Ayanna said, I look much younger than I really am. As far as this chick went, Nasty looked like life had beat her up and down a New York block ten years ago. Unfortunately, no one had told her that three layers of make-up couldn't hide the old stripper hag look. Although she had a pretty face, her age was telling on her like the neighborhood gossip queen.

By twelve-thirty a song by Chingy began to flow from the jukebox, and someone fired up the air conditioner. That's how I knew The Foxy Lady would be opening for the lunchtime crowd soon. It was time to get dressed. The second dancer began blow-drying her thick wig. I watched her use a paddle brush to make it appear smooth and silky—the girl had skills! Next she squeezed herself into a Lycra outfit. I didn't understand why she selected something that would accentuate lumps and bumps. Nevertheless, she wore it proudly, just like any Coca-Cola-bottle-shaped diva would.

"I need to buy some food for my cat. I hope I make enough money today," Nasty said as she sat down. I was not encouraged by her pessimistic remark. Are the pickings that slim in this club? I know it's no Atlanta, New York, Vegas, or Miami . . . but oh my goodness! Then again, I did watch someone put a bucket in the corner to catch rain. This place was nothing short of a dump. Well, a neighborhood dump. If I were going to make a go at this for real, there was no way I could show the world my goodies for next to nada.

As several girls started to arrive, I decided to take off my shoes and put on my footies. I changed into my bathing suit, feeling overly observant eyes caress every crevice and fold of my body. The night manager was staring me down the same way she'd done the day I first performed. I soon found out that The Foxy Lady was so low budget, the night manager was also the day manager. I guess they were too cheap to pay two people. Sounded just like corporate America to me though.

I couldn't figure Ma out. One minute she was doing me a favor like she was there to help, the next minute she was inspecting the hell out of me! I couldn't read her thoughts. She made me nervous to say the least. I quickly found that most girls weren't going to share any information, and no one who ran the club volunteered anything for free either. On my second day, my inexperience showed. I remained in a constant state of confusion until the evening hours came.

My formal "initiation" began with Ma scolding me terribly.

"You can't bend over like that. No lap dancing!" I felt someone smack my ass. As the stinging sensation increased, I turned around and it was her, the manager. "I want to see you in the back!" she yelled at me, wrinkling her brow.

"I've got to go," I apologetically told the group of men. I felt like a child who had just been called to the principal's office, and just when I was beginning to enjoy their shameless flirtation. I did know that lap dancing was illegal where we were located. In fact, the customers were not allowed to touch the girls except to place cash in their garter belts. I was afraid that I was in trouble, and I was definitely not comfortable in this element.

"I wasn't lap dancing. I was trying to hear what that guy was saying," I explained as Ma stood there looking at me with her hands on her hips.

"He was taking too long to tip you. They all were. I slapped you on the ass for a reason."

I thought deciding how long it took a man to tip me was my judgment call, but I didn't say anything about that. "And move your money to the front of the garter belt," she continued, snatching my money from around my legs.

"I've never done this before," I admitted. I let the cat out of the bag, but I didn't care. This woman was putting too much pressure on me and it was stressing me out.

"They just told me you were new," she said.

"Well I am—to stripping and this club," I said.

"Put this rubber band around your money, then attach it to your garter like this," Ma said, showing me how to fold it over and secure it. "Always keep it on you, and move it to the front so no one can steal your money. All kinds come through here. Some men will distract you while another one snatches your money. And don't talk too long. If they're not tipping, move on!" She ended the conversation and didn't comment further about what I'd said.

"Yeah. Some of them want to look, but they don't want to pay for it," an anonymous dancer chimed in. She reminded me of Blu Cantrell with her striking looks. I suspected that she had butt and breast implants, though. Her body was tight and stiff. I left the dressing room area as I waited for my turn to dance. After prodding a few employees, I picked up a few must-know pointers.

"How do you know when your time to dance is up?" I asked.

"There's a clock over by the stage," Raheem explained.

I soon learned that since his father, Cash, was the owner. He thought he was big shit.

"Oh," I replied, leaning over to look at it. Everyone had a way of making me feel out of the loop—just plain dumb. It's almost as if you need someone to walk you through things, but having that privilege comes with a price. I would soon learn that no one is nice for free.

"And how do I know where I dance?" I continued.

"You alternate. If you were on the big stage last time, you dance on the small stage the next. You keep alternating until your shift is up."

"What about the music? How does that work?" I asked. Since the man was dropping information in my ear, I figured that I might as well take advantage of his openness.

"It's a dollar to feed the jukebox. If there's something you want to hear, go put money in it." I nodded, taking it all in, but then he surprised me. "Look, I want to talk to you about something else," he said, sitting next to me at the bar.

"What is it?"

"Do you want to go shopping? I mean, let me take you out or something. I like you," he told me.

"No, that's not a good idea," I answered.

"We can make some real money together. I've got money. Can I help you with something? What is it? Do you need help paying your bills? Tell me what you need." He said it in a way that was supposed to make me think that he was concerned for my personal welfare—yeah, right!

"It's time for me to dance," I said, ending the conversation abruptly. Luckily, my turn to expose myself to a room full of men was my way out.

My body was on autopilot as I swayed to the music. I was full of mixed feelings and couldn't seem to organize my thoughts into anything coherent. Part of me began to question what was I doing on that stage, and if I'd gotten myself into too much hot water with Raheem. My mind drifted back to the conversation we shared, but another conversation going on around me broke my daydream.

"She doesn't know what she's doing," an older man said. I'd found my first critic.

I looked in the direction that the comment came from and saw two older gentlemen watching and talking about me. Obviously they were strip club connoisseurs, and could tell that I was new and inexperienced. Just as I was starting to feel self-conscious about their remarks, Raheem walked up to the stage real smooth and faced me.

"Slow down. Play with your pussy and get completely nude," he advised as he faced the crowd, half cocking his head every now and then so I could hear him over the music.

"I didn't do that before. I have to take off *everything*?" I asked, trying to question him discretely as I scanned the room. Enough men were watching me that I felt uncomfortable discussing the matter while I was dancing on stage. Although many could figure out that I was a novice, I didn't want to come off like a complete ditz.

"Yes—take it all off. Since touching is not allowed, you have to do that. This is a nude club. Customers come to see it all, not just most of it. Show some pink, too."

Reluctantly, I peeled off my clothes. However, as soon as I was naked, someone else walked up to the stage and told me to arch my back as he held a few dollars in his hand. I turned around and obliged him.

"Yeah, you're gonna be all right. That's what we want to see!" he said as he tucked the money inside of my garter belt. I smiled coyly. Getting completely nude was a bit of a thrill. I felt liberated in a strange way, standing in the only outfit that I came into this big stinking world with—my birthday suit!

When I dressed and left the stage, I was a hot, sweaty mess. That's when I realized that I forgot my water and snacks, and I desperately needed to replenish myself. I asked someone if they sold bottled water at the bar. When I inquired about how much it was, I found out that it was five dollars! I complained about the price—Raheem overheard me.

"Get her some soda," Raheem told the bartender.

"How much is that?" I asked, my eyes drawn to a porn flick playing on a screen at the bar.

"Don't worry about it. I told you I'd take care of you. If you want some Chinese food too I can get you some."

"No thanks. That's not necessary. Thanks for the soda though," I said. The bartender slid it across the bar. He studied me as I took a few sips. Then I put the glass down.

"You need to get with a thug. We can make some real money together. I'm trying to—"

It was becoming clear that by letting him do any small thing for me I was setting myself up for him to dig up in my life aside from things that pertained to grinding for dollars. But what could I do? I needed someone's help.

"You look really good. What's your name?" a man at the bar asked me. He cut Raheem off, severing our conversation. I stalled for a while because I'd forgotten my stage name. I almost slipped and used my real one.

"Honey," I said after taking a long pause to remember what it was.

I took a long sip of fountain soda. Once I told him my name, the man began talking and wouldn't stop jawing. I wanted him to get his ass up off that stool and disappear, but I was trying to be polite. After a few minutes of this, Raheem exploded.

"Didn't you see me having a conversation? I'm talking here and you're just going to cut in. I'm trying to talk to shorty about some business," he ranted.

Before long the two men began to argue. Their voices escalated with each line spoken. I wondered if they'd start swinging. I just didn't know.

"It's not that big of a deal," I said, trying to diffuse things. Although I didn't want trouble to unfold, I felt pampered and spoiled by so much attention being directed toward me. Two younger men were actually arguing over a stressed-out mother on the verge of having a bush full of gray pussy hairs!

Raheem turned to the bartender and began to repeat his complaint to him. The man yanked his drink off the bar, splashing half of what was in the glass on his right hand, and left after Raheem got up in his personal space and whispered something in his ear.

"It's bad when a customer is telling me to tell you to slow down," he said. "I came over to the stage because I was trying to help you. I'm going to teach you all you need to know to make that paper in here. If you keep dancing that way, girls are going to complain they don't want to do sets with you. I've seen it happen. First impressions are everything. You need to work on that before my father gets back in town, so if I were you, I'd meet me in the bathroom. I'm going to help you."

"Why in the bathroom? Show me somewhere in here," I suggested.

"I can't. The girls will get upset if they see me showing you how to dance. You go in first, then I'll come in," Raheem said, laying his trap.

"I'll get in trouble. The manager is already on my case."

"I'm part owner in the place. I'm telling you—you have nothing to worry about. I run things in here. Believe that."

I went into the bathroom. A few seconds later, the black paint-peeled door opened and shut.

"Face the mirror," he instructed.

I did. He moved toward me. I could feel him breathing on my neck.

"Dance slow . . . like you're grinding in a club to reggae," Raheem said, softening his words.

When he reached out and grabbed me by the waist, I began rocking my hips real steady. When I worked up a nice easy rhythm, I could feel his dick get stiff. I began feeling very uncomfortable. It seemed like he was getting too much pleasure from my "lesson," just as any sleazy strip club owner would.

"That's right, that's right. You're thick, just use your hips," he said, pressing up against me. I could feel his body heat clinging to my skin. "Play with the customer. Every now and then wink and flirt. It'll get you more tips," he added.

I let my hand wander around his neck and down his arms, then I winked.

"We're friends now. I like you—I'm going to look out for you. I'll feature you in my spot and make sure you stay in the spotlight. We're about to clear out these girls and get some that look like you and better," he said. "I'm trying to put you on." After that, he quickly hit the light switch.

"Hey, turn on the lights! What are you doing?" I asked, pulling away from him. I could feel his dick touching my ass. My heart began racing. My eyes darted around frantically. I felt trapped.

"It's ok. Keep going. I'm not going to do anything," he lied, breathing heavily.

Before I knew it he was sucking on my nipples, playing with my clit, and begging me to cum. I could hear him unbuckling his pants as he began licking my neck. It never dawned on me that there was no need for him to have contact with me since all the dancers did their thing on stage. Contact with customers wasn't even permitted! What a fool believes.

I squirmed around in the small space until I managed to tear myself from his grip. I shot out of that bathroom like a bolt of lighting. The door slammed. My clothes were all crooked and lopsided, and my heart was still pumping overtime. No sooner than I stepped outside, I heard a voice.

"I want to talk to you about something," a dancer named Sapphire calmly said. She acted as if she didn't observe that I was startled or winded. A stiff dick to keep on the back burner at work never hurts, right? Wrong, especially in an environment like this where you couldn't even have the option of reporting your boss for sexual harassment.

I was so lost in thought I didn't realize the girl had disappeared. I looked around and soon discovered that she was working her voodoo magic on stage. Sapphire had a Bally's Gym tight body, and was a beautiful dark complexion. Her skin was smooth and rich. I calmed myself down by watching her spellbinding moves, taking note of one garter that was bright red, and the other that was lime green. Sapphire was a sexy woman who could truly dance, and definitely had put some sort of thought into her routine—she appeared to be more of an entertainer than a stripper. Gnarls Barkley blasted from the jukebox. When the guitar blared, she grabbed the pole like she owned the thing. I watched one man stand in awe of her. He was completely mesmerized by the way she commanded attention, and others followed suit. Among other things, she made her ass jump to the rhythm of the music as she grazed the stripper pole with her butt cheeks. As a heterosexual woman, even I had a hard time not paying attention to her admirable muscle control of her pert backside with half of a butterfly tattoo on each cheek. When she bounced her ass, the butterfly looked like it was fluttering.

Sapphire spread her fingers apart, raised her arms over her head, and gripped the pole in an extremely suggestive manner. She pressed her flat stomach against the shiny pole, dropping to the floor as she faced the audience while straddling it between her legs. That seductress then slowly stuck out her tongue as she began crawling upward. Sapphire skillfully gripped the steel with her inner thighs, then hung upside down while slowly massaging her clit with a French tipped finger. A herd of fascinated men rewarded her with bills—ones, fives, and tens. I even spotted a crisp twenty. The men nearly knocked each other down to make their way to the stage. Talking about the power of a woman. She had a sexy vibe that some of the most beautiful women could never master. I was impressed over and above the tawdry cigarette puffing pussy that captured my attention the day I visited The Foxy Lady with Ayanna. Obviously, her charisma allowed her to wrap men around her finger. And obviously, she was the most skillful dancer in the club, or at least the top money-making booty-shaker working that shift. I wasn't sure why she was working days, but no one could deny she was like a breath of fresh air in a place like The Foxy Lady.

After she danced her set, Sapphire was chatting with what appeared to be one of her regulars. They both were having a drink together. She obviously knew how to make her money by telling men what they wanted to hear, giving them proper attention.

"Wait in the back for me. I'll be there soon," she told me when she saw me standing there watching her.

A few moments later, she grabbed my arm and pulled me into that infamous dirty bathroom. I began to wonder what the fascination was with the stinky, cramped, germ infested box. When she began pulling down her clothes to urinate, I locked the door. I couldn't believe how free she was. We'd never even spoken, yet she was comfortable enough to pee in front of me.

"Sip some of my drink—it'll relax you. You're too tense," Sapphire said.

I pretended to press my lips on the glass as I turned away like I was giving her some privacy. When she began speaking, I turned back around.

"He tried to fuck you, didn't he?" she asked bluntly.

"He who?" I answered, lying.

"You know who."

"Maybe," I finally admitted.

"Don't fuck him unless you want to, and if you decide to, get something out of it like everyone else."

"I don't want to fuck that dude," I told her. I suddenly realized that I'd survived my "rite of passage." That's when I had a feeling that Raheem had pulled a stunt like that on every dancer in the club.

"Good 'cause it's really not necessary. I'll look out for you and give you some tips," she told me.

I'd been down that same road with Raheem. I had to at least wonder why she wanted to help me understand the game.

"When you come off stage, walk around and shake hands. You can get extra dollars that way and establish relationships while you're here. I don't want none of these assholes aside from what they can give me while they're in the club, but I've got the best business skills of any dancer in this club. I'm good at selling these men a fantasy they can chase. It's not the fanciest spot, but all sorts of men come here because some other clubs were shut down because of that baseball stadium that was put in that area. Not all of them have relocated yet. There's talk that some may never, and the few that are left may be shut down at any moment. So even professional men slide through. Some want or need shrinks, but they won't go to one. They cling to those of us who listen well."

"Yeah, I did notice you were having a drink back there."

"Oh, with that fat one? He puts mad paper in my purse. I was suspended for fighting, but I begged my way back in the door. Ma thought she was cutting me short by telling me I could work day shift for a while. She thinks she's punishing me, but married men like him who sneak out from work in the day are ones that can be the best tippers. I just listen to him—something his wife probably isn't doing."

"That may be his version though."

"Either way I don't give a damn! I even got these people who run this club on lock. You gotta play head games with them. The best part is I got fifteen hundred out of him this month. I'm about to work on his savings next. You see, men fantasize about being with a stripper, but few would marry one. His wife may really care, but all I have to do is act like I do. None of that shit is real. I know how to gas up these men and make them want to come back to see me—that's what it's all about—feeding men's egos. Men play with our heads to get what they want. Here, the game is flipped around. On our turf, they know we don't give shit away for free like those dumb women on the other side of The Foxy Lady's door. Now back to you, you dance too fast. You need to loosen up and just relax. Look chill," she told me.

I soon realized that there were things going on behind the scenes that everyone doesn't see. What Sapphire said made a lot of sense, so I found myself respecting her opinions even more.

"But how? I get so nervous when I'm out there."

"Brush up on your relaxation skills. Whatever works for

you, works for you," Sapphire told me. "I can't teach you all of my tricks. You'll have to figure out some things for yourself. Everyone has their own way of doing this," she added, half smiling. Sapphire winked, then continued telling me things she felt I needed to know.

"Next, don't play with your pussy. Most of these men are married. They can't go home smelling like another woman. You're light. You don't have to do all of that. They will tip you just because of your complexion and nice body. Just go home and practice in front of a mirror. People that don't know how to dance usually end up being the best ones. And don't be afraid to watch the other dancers."

I suddenly felt guilty about something. Even the strip game appeared to have some color hang ups in the mix, although I'm sure some light men preferred to see chocolate honeys.

When Sapphire finished using the bathroom, our conversation ended. She spotted a business card on the floor and picked it up. I caught a glimpse of the words that were printed on the white rectangle. The person on it worked for the federal government and had a high position. I now understood why she picked it up from syrupy pee-lined floor. High position or not, I would've left it where it was. The place was so filthy that I couldn't believe she didn't squat on the toilet. She sat on it like she was at the Ritz Carlton.

"This is for helping me," I told her. I smiled tenderly and pulled a ten out of my garter.

"No," Sapphire said, refusing the money.

"Please take it. I appreciate you helping me. You didn't have to tell me anything. I insist," I said, pushing the money back into her hands.

When the door opened, the other dancers were watching us like they were going to question us from top to bottom. "What were you two doing in the bathroom together?" one of them asked.

"I like red girls—I was eating her pussy!" Sapphire said with a straight face to throw them off. I liked her style, although I was stunned that she said something so vile. Sapphire motioned for me to follow her behind a wall in the dressing room.

"Do you have any wipes?" she asked me.

"Wipes?" I said. I didn't understand why I'd need baby wipes. The last time I touched one, my daughter Brittany was still crawling around in Pampers.

"Yeah—here. Use baby wipes in between sets to freshen up. Also, bring clear roll-on deodorant. And here's the number to the ten-dollar man—he sells clothes."

"When does he come around?" I asked.

"I don't know, sweetie. You can wear one of my outfits for now. Put this on. Hurry up though. I don't want the girls to know I'm helping you out," Sapphire whispered.

I grabbed the electric-orange netted outfit and thong panties. After I struggled to put it on because of all of the holes in the design, she told me to plaster dollar bills on top of my breasts so they wouldn't be exposed. There were so many trade secrets—I fought to remember them all. I returned to the semi-private area where Sapphire was busy organizing her things. She was hunched over snorting coke—I couldn't believe my eyes. Luckily, she didn't see me eavesdropping on her conversation with her "snowman."

My next set went a little better. I remembered all the things Sapphire told me and made sure I did a slower wind and grind. I still didn't escape complaints, of course, but it was the funniest thing that happened to me thus far. A man who had been sitting close to the front, came up to the stage, demanding that I look him in the eye.

"What's wrong—you can't look at an ugly man?" he asked, the smell of cheap beer floating from his breath. I wanted to laugh. If only he knew the truth. It had nothing to do with him being an ugly man! I thought his concern was cute. I had the urge to coddle his ego, just as I'd done for my kids when they needed a boost from their mother. When Sapphire began walking toward the stage, he gave me my tip and returned to his seat.

"How am I doing?" I asked.

"Better, but just remember what I told you," Sapphire said, while stuffing a few dollars in my garter belt to play off why she made it to the stage. Her appearance made me forget about her drug indulgence, and because I saw how confident she was when she danced, I felt a little more relaxed.

After Sapphire left, a businessman type came up to me while still dancing on the small stage. An Angie Stone cut was thumping. It was a number about a woman having done all sorts of things for a man when he was trying to make it somewhere good, but he'd changed after he'd made it. I was feeling those lyrics, and my body was acting like it for once.

"Open your legs. I wish you'd come home with me and sit on my face," he told me as I opened my legs into a wide V-shape. I had propped myself upside down, and flashed my goods. "You have such a pretty pussy. Tell me what that pussy juice tastes like," he said, staring at my kitty kat.

The man hung around near the stage, commenting on the size of my clit, and even asked if I had any children. As I stood and worked my middle nice and slow, I suddenly wondered why I hadn't answered until I realized the inevitable had happened. The thought of having my fantasy discreetly fulfilled was in the front of my mind, but I hadn't thought of the possibility to be attracted to any of the customers. When I finally met a man that turned me on, I couldn't manage to respond, and I hoped that my pussy wasn't beginning to get all juicy. The stranger was tall with a medium build. His suit, his silk tie, his scent, his voice, and his good looks turned me into pure mush. Suddenly, my knees felt rubbery, and I found myself wanting to know every nook and cranny about him. He was the type of man I'd typically date back in my single days, so I felt a bit shy, given what I was doing.

"If you get on your knees and pop it for me, darlin', I'll tip you more," he told me in a flirty tone. I smiled and blushed. "And take off those panties for me; I can see the other stuff on HBO."

Although my knees were still swollen from the previous day, I found myself walking on all fours and sticking my ass up in the air. It was my choice, not a matter of force.

"Mmm, mmm, mmm! You look good in those heels," he said, moving closer. "That's nice right there. Your body is definitely bangin'! You've got some *serious* junk in that trunk, and you smell sooo delicious!" he commented, boosting my damaged ego.

The stranger made dollars rain on me, and I didn't want the green and white shower to stop. As my reward fluttered and fell, I saw a square card drop in the mix. While he stuck a folded one in between my ass cheeks, I began imagining the stranger caressing my breasts, while I gently squeezed his dick. I wondered if he was packing a big or small tool, and how he worked whatever he had hidden under those slacks of his. I was beginning to lust over him and he was returning the same vibe to me.

"Time's up! It's my turn," said Precious, a dancer with high cheek bones and bushy eyebrows.

I snapped out of my fantasy zone, coming back down to reality. I grabbed my money and relinquished my popular spot on stage a few choruses early. It was a bit aggravating, given that I was beginning to enjoy myself. My set wasn't due to end until the song did, but I knew Precious interrupted me because she observed a heavy tipper was in our midst. I let it go, snatched my blanket, and stepped down from the small stage. Before I turned my back good I saw Precious grab the business card that was meant for me to snag, and just like that, my fine tipper was gone.

"Look shortie, I'll pay $500 to fuck you right now. Let's go in the bathroom, but this time that's what I want," Raheem said as I bumped into him in the back of the room.

"No—I can't," I insisted.

That damn perverted Raheem was at it again, only worse. This time he called his cousin Kirk over. "I bet she got that good pussy," he said to Kirk. He shook his head in agreement. "Look, $500 from me, and $500 from him. That's $1000 to hit us both off. Couldn't you use a grand right now? I think it would be well worth your while," he said, as if their combined offer would convince me.

"I said no, Raheem," I repeated firmly, as I stood sandwiched between them. "I have a boyfriend waiting on me at home," I lied.

"You don't want to make no real money," he said, shaking his head in disgust.

He tried to make me feel guilty and stupid, all in one brainwashing. I should've been the one shaking my head. Besides, what made him think I wanted to get with him for any amount of money? For one, he was getting on my nerves, and two, he looked like he'd been playing with his dog before coming to work. His hair looked dry and uncombed, and he just had this grimy looking skin—the kind that never looks clean no matter how long you scrub it.

"If your boyfriend really cared about you and he was handling his business, your ass wouldn't even be here. I've seen goody-goody church girls with so-called boyfriends come in here and change. I give you two months, tops. You'll change by then. We'll see who's right," he scowled, trying to put doubt in my mind.

I walked away from him, past the bar area, and an African man struck up a shallow conversation as he looked me up and down. When I stopped, he put several dollars in my garter belt. Each time he copped a feel of my kitty kat. The last time he offered me a twenty to stick his finger inside of me. I shot him a disgusted smile while noting his wedding ring. I wanted to go home and rub every inch of my skin in alcohol! I wondered if Donavan had done things like that. On behalf of all wives, I temporarily felt overcome with disgust.

"That's a new piece right there," I heard him say when I walked away.

I ignored the chatter of horny men sipping on alcoholic beverages after a long, stressful workday. I felt hands caressing my ass as I walked by, but didn't bother turning around. I went into the dressing room to get away from Raheem and the customers. Just when I thought I was home free, Kirk took a seat across from the chair where I sat to dress. He began pushing his long tongue out of his mouth like a lizard, as I changed my clothes, trying to get me to go in the back with him.

"Stop. You're making her nervous," one of the dancers giggled. She had the hugest tits—they were big and droopy like half-filled elongated balloons, hanging down to her knees. She was unaware of our previous run-in regarding the sexual advance for money. I wasn't going to be the one to tell it.

My unofficial voyeur slouched down in a chair and kept making lewd gestures with his tongue. He got up to leave when a man carrying a large bag came in and displayed his goods on the table that separated the middle of the room. I didn't like his outfits. They looked cheap and irritating to the skin—cheap lace, crotchless panties, and a little more. Nothing my eyes showed me held my interest like those sexy stripper shoes.

"Does anyone need an instant boyfriend?" he asked. When no one answered he held up the toy and added, "Oh, so all of you have it like that? Well this kind of boyfriend doesn't call you on your cell phone every five minutes while you're trying to make them dollars!"

While the girls were huddled around him, I began dressing as rapidly as I could to leave, stuffing my bra and panties and outfits in my bag. Half-dressed, I turned the corner, only to find the tongue-licker following me. Kirk moved close, then began running his fingers through my hair. My effort to avoid him didn't work!

"You would enjoy it, I know you would. I have a big black snake that you can feel all up in them guts. Take it from me, it'll be different from anything you've ever had before. So tomorrow, I'm going to find out how sweet that pussy really is . . . *Honey.*"

"Oh no you won't," I answered.

"If you don't want to be suspended or fined . . . I will."

I bucked and jerked away from Kirk, then bolted out of the door, running scared. One thing I was learning was that no didn't count for anything in the adult entertainment industry. I was accustomed to telling my kids no and demanding that they listen to me, so his pressure tactic really peeved me. I ripped off the flyers of strip events that were propped on my car windows and threw them on the ground. I planned to head home to count my hard-earned money, but Ayanna called.

"I called your home number and didn't get an answer, so I called your cell. I know what that means. You're going too far with this stripper thing. It was meant to be a dare—

a quick thrill to cheer you up, Mystique. You need to quit. You don't belong in the game and you really don't understand everything that's involved. Turn around before it's too late. Sweetie, get out of this. I'm concerned about you going to all of these clubs. You can get raped, then catch an STD—get out now!" Ayanna warned.

"Lighten up. It's only dancing, and I'm really doubting that my husband loves me anymore. Don't you get it? I'm getting paid to live out a fantasy that is awakening my sensuality. I can be who and what I want to be anonymously. There's a power in that. A power that I need rekindled. When I'm done having a good time, I'll quietly go back to my regular life, but right now, I'm not ready to go back to jail! And you're one to talk, you gave me the idea in the first place by inviting me up on stage. Plus, you do it yourself."

"I'm single and you're not. You're mixing apples and oranges here. You're a wife and a mother of two beautiful children. What if your kids or people in your neighborhood found out about this? How would you feel? You're not setting a good example for Brittany at all," Ayanna said.

"Now that you created this monster, you want to take away my chance at liberation and happiness. Leave my kids out of this because it has nothing to do with them. For once, it's all about me," I snapped.

"It's not that I'm trying to take anything away from you—you're just taking this much too seriously. I know you and your husband don't have a perfect relationship, but count your blessings. Use your common sense, and don't let it destroy your family. I hope I don't have to tell your husband because you're lunchin'."

"My husband's the one that started running the streets and treating me badly, remember? You should've seen the shit he texted me today. It's my turn now, so would you just lighten up on me?"

"What are you trying to prove? What is really going through your mind?"

"Don't worry about that, Yana. I hope you take a deep breath and think about what you said about talking to my husband. I'd hate to have to tell Dad what you've been doing to pay for law school at Hovert—he's so proud of his darling baby girl doing it big at an HBCU. If memory serves me correctly, you still live under his roof and I'm not the only one with skeletons in my closet. According to you, you've been popping your coochie for some time, sis," I said, throwing a low blow that would make my sister feel threatened.

"Look, I don't have time to argue with you. I have my own life and my own worries. I said this once and I'll say it again. I will not be a party to this any longer, and there is no way that we can dance at the same club. All I need is for someone to find out you're my sister. Trust me when I tell you that this kind of job and environment ain't for you. You know nothing about the streets. As of this second, you will receive no more help from me as far as stripping is concerned. Got it?"

"That's exotic dancing," I said, trying to get smart.

"If you're so proud of what you're doing these days, it would be a great idea to tell your man you strip. If he's secure in his swagger, he's secure with everything. Do you think the best way to restart a relationship is with secrets? From what you've said, that's what started your problems the first time."

"Are you crazy, Ayanna? I can't tell him."

"Do you still love him?" she asked.

"Unfortunately, I do still love him," I admitted.

"Well sweetie, you can't strengthen a love by keeping something like this from him," Ayanna reasoned.

"I agree, but he's been treating me like shit."

"If you can't be honest about it and tell your husband, quit. It's obvious you shouldn't be doing something you can't talk to your mate about. "

"Saying anything about this is out of the question, and you know it."

"There's a lot at stake that you don't understand about this lifestyle. I wish you'd take my word for it. Do you have a gun?" Ayanna asked.

"Of course I don't have a gun! You know that. Why would I have a gun with kids in the house?" I answered.

"*Get a gun!* You may have to shoot someone. Don't bother, or blame, me when this blows up in your face, okay? Sure, I was the one that suggested that you hop up on stage as a joke to help you loosen up, but I never suggested that you become one of us. I mean . . . everything is not what it seems. I only do it because not doing it may mean I can't finish school, and I want my education that bad. You on the other hand . . . it's just insane to go there. I'd give anything to fall in love with a man and have a beautiful family. I may never have the experience that you have right now. Life with Donavan can't be that terrible. All a woman really wants is someone who cares and someone to love her in small and great ways alike. If you want your man to do better in the relationship, communicate with him. If you have a real thing for romance movies on a rainy night, try buying some flicks to rekindle the romance. What I'm trying to say is that you haven't told me you tried talking to Donavan. You haven't told me you tried being proactive by seducing him or giving him a reason to remember that you still like being made love to. I'm not blaming you, I'm just saying there are other ways to approach your marital unhappiness. Stripping on the down low is not the answer."

"Marriage is not all it's cracked up to be. Don't tell me anything about adding spice to a marriage, or how to deal with marital tension. I have been married for fifteen long years, but all you do is study and go to school. You don't know what it's like to have the pressures of running a family with no room left to take care of yourself. You don't know what it's like for a mate to make you feel like a failure, or that he hates you. I do!"

"Maybe I don't, but that doesn't mean I don't know how it feels to—"

Cutting Ayanna off, I added, "I've got things covered and you don't have to worry about anything up in my face. I'll be happy to give you a break from me because I'm tired of listening to a hypocrite anyway! I want to do it again and that's my personal decision. I won't go back to the club where you work, but that doesn't mean I'm going to give this up just yet. I need to do this for me, Yana, so mind your own business. Stop fighting me. As you know, I can be just as stubborn as you can. Please . . . just let this drop, sis," I suggested, feeling frustrated.

"This isn't like you," Ayanna huffed. "I was just trying to help. Wreck you life—I don't care!"

"Maybe I'm not naturally outgoing like you, but it doesn't mean that I don't have fantasies and desires. I finally work my nerve up to do something for myself that I wanted to do for the first time in a long time, and now you're discouraging me to discover who I am," I snapped. "I'm not happy! I hate my life and I can't stand it anymore. I quit my job today, and I'm on the verge of burning out or having some sort of breakdown. So while you're doing all of this criticizing, do you have any better ideas? If you do, I'm listening," I added, sounding smart-mouthed.

"What are you saying? You did what? Are you having a female midlife crisis or something? You need to get a grip!

Putting a band-aid on your problems isn't going to fix a damn thing. You'll find out the hard way about using the adult entertainment industry as some weird, quick fix. This is the thanks I get for trying to talk some sense back into your head—humph! You don't have to worry about that happening again. Don't call me anymore and I won't call you!" Ayanna snapped. Click.

For the first time since we'd been sisters, Ayanna and I turned our backs on each other. Of course we'd fought like cats and dogs before, but this time was different. The bitterness in our voices was unprecedented and I really don't think either one of us liked how it felt. Even so, that's how things went down. I couldn't believe my normally jovial and loyal little sister laid me out, and hung up on me to boot.

I started up my Lexus and watched a half-drunk patron pee in the corner of the parking lot. As I pulled out of The Foxy Lady parking lot, I questioned if I really was having some sort of female midlife crisis. I quickly dismissed it, pushing that thought out of my mind. I decided that the solution to my sister's disapproval was to visit another club that was a bit more upscale and classy—the few snafus I'd encountered that night didn't have to stop me. I decided I'd figure out the rest on my own, or get someone besides Ayanna to help me to learn the ropes to my new seductive game. Since I decided to continue my new hobby, I decided to hit a specialty store in the morning and invest in an outfit—a *real* stripper outfit. To make money at stripping, and keep men's eyeballs glued on that ass and pussy, you must look the part. Even if I invested in just one outfit, it would be a start.

I knew I was playing with fire. Nevertheless, I must admit that the notion of becoming a confident exhibitionist was turning me on. That evening, I opened my ashtray and picked up my wedding ring to slide it back on my finger.

"Since you're no longer my protector and best friend, right back atcha, Daddy. I need some me time too," I said to myself.

For the first time in my marriage I didn't feel the urge to wear it at all. I closed the ashtray. Then without realizing what I was doing, I reached in my top, gently stroking one breast as I took a deep breath. As I exhaled, I had no regrets about what I'd done, except that I hadn't done it sooner.

8

LOOKING FOR TROUBLE

After I opened my eyes that morning, I realized that Donavan had made an appearance to our home address. I don't know if it was guilt, or he realized that I was legally still his wife, but he tacked a note on the fridge. In fact, the kitchen light was still burning. I guess he wanted to be sure I saw it.

"I'm off for Seattle. Peace," the note read.

I rolled my eyes at the note's cold tone, but part of me was glad he'd left it. Wondering if he was telling a tall tale again, I went into the closet where we kept our suitcases, and two of them were gone. Then I noticed that his toothbrush and cologne were also gone from the bathroom across from where he'd been sleeping in the basement. Instinctively, I felt that he'd taken a legitimate business trip, but I still didn't buy the story about why he hadn't been at work before. That still bothered me and I found myself rubbing my temples. Feeling tense again I decided to do something I hadn't done in a while—get my work out on.

* * *

"Hello, ladies. Are you ready to sweat?" the lady on my aerobics tape said. I stared at the TV as I followed the exercise routine. I hadn't touched that tape in so long that dust collected on the cover. I didn't really want to lose weight, just stay toned and in shape.

After I showered, ate, and did a few things around the house, I revisited the issue of buying exotic dancing outfits. When I was at The Foxy Lady, I thought it was nice of Sapphire to pass along the ten-dollar clothes man's number to me. Still, I preferred to treat myself and enjoy being picky over color and style, given that I rarely bought myself anything. Come to think of it, I lived and worked within a fifteen-mile radius, ran myself into the ground, and outside of loving my hardheaded children, *nothing* in my life brought me happiness. As a result, I felt that spoiling myself was a must-do. At some point in the night Sapphire also gave me her number and told me to give her a call if I ever needed anything—I needed something! I called her to ask her where I could get a really nice outfit. Instead of telling me where to go to make my purchases, she insisted on meeting me in the parking lot of the club.

"I apologize—I know you've got stuff to do," I said. "There's no need to go with me."

"It's easier to show you than to tell you. Besides, I have a few errands to run at the mall myself," she explained.

Sapphire led me to the exact kind of specialty shop I was hoping to find. I never saw anything like that close to my neighborhood on the other side of the beltway. Just looking at the sexy outfits in the window display at a mall in Greenbelt made me want to go inside. They looked so scandalous, they even looked good hanging on plastic mannequins! The inviting store was lit by seductive recessed lighting, and the clothes extended on hooks near the top of the ceiling. The mood the lighting created made me think of sex as I surveyed numerous costumes, thongs, and specialty items. Sapphire told me that she had to make a pit stop in a jeans store, so I had plenty of time to look around at the skimpy, erotic clothes.

"Excuse me. Do you have any large sizes? All of these outfits look like they are for petite women," I asked the clerk, sounding serious.

"Most of our customers are strippers. They're one size fits all, honey." She could've looked at me like I was stupid, but she spared me.

"Oh. Well that's fine. I'm looking for an outfit. I'm new," I said, nearly apologizing for my naivety.

"Good luck!" she said with an odd, harsh tone in her voice. She made me feel as if there was something she knew that I didn't. Two women walked in the store talking so loud, I didn't have to question their dancing credibility. They immediately began grabbing clothes—I could tell they were pros who had been there many times. They were acting like they could snatch and buy whatever they wanted off the racks without looking at the price tags first, so I tried to discretely follow them around as I pretended to browse. I was hoping they'd say something that would benefit a new stripper. I guess I was curious—mostly.

"Girrrrl, I like this. This is cute," one said.

"Hurry up and make up your mind. He's in the car. He gave us $400. Save $100 for your pocket."

"Right," one agreed.

"Condoms—we'll have to go somewhere else for that. You know I have to put out sometimes."

"And lubricant!" the other commented.

As I inspected a host of tiny outfits, wandering around the small store with track lighting, I continued to drink up their conversation. I suddenly began to get scared, wondering if all, or most, dancers were selling their bodies for money. As I stood in line to pay for my outfits, I wondered what had I gotten myself into, and if I had bitten off way more than I could chew. Nevertheless, my curiously and rush of excitement prevailed, so I picked out and paid for several outfits. My bags were stuffed. Sapphire reappeared with shopping bags, too. She immediately walked up to me with a big friendly smile plastered on her face. She always seemed to have a sunny disposition every time I saw her.

"Let me see what you bought," Sapphire said, looking into my bag. "You're going to make all the tips. Don't hurt 'em too bad. Leave something in their pockets for me, please!" she teased. "Mmm, look at you. You even got a chain belt and garter sets in three colors."

"I'm not going back to the club," I explained. That's when Sapphire looked at me.

"You're not? Why not? I know you didn't buy these outfits just to look at them."

Unfortunately, strip life mentality was rubbing off on me. I was setting Sapphire up by giving her half of the story and she didn't even know it. I decided to feel her out to get as much information out of her as I could.

"Paradise said I should quit. Maybe I should. What was I thinking to imagine that I could learn to become an exotic dancer? I should see if I can return this stuff right now," I lied.

"You just bought it, and they only give exchanges," Sapphire said.

"Damn," I mumbled. "If you think they'll fit you, you can take them. At least I'd know they wouldn't go to waste."

"You're just talking crazy! Paradise is just jealous because your body is banging. You can sit a cup on your booty, your stomach is flat, and you have naturally big titties! Do you know how many tips you can get with that ass after you learn how to work it? The bigger the booty, the bigger the tip!"

I chuckled.

"I don't think it's any of that. Paradise is beautiful."

"Yeah, whatever. If you say so. She ain't all that," Sapphire said, rolling her eyes. I didn't know what Sapphire had against my sister, but she obviously didn't like her for some reason.

"Let me ask you this. Do you want to be an exotic dancer?" Sapphire asked.

"Yeah, I do," I replied.

"Then you've got to do this for yourself—it's your life. You should be perfectly fine. It's really not that bad. And usually the girls that are the worst dancers turn out to be the best. Don't be afraid to watch the girls work it, then go home and practice in the mirror. That'll help you develop your own style. You can do this."

"You think so? No joking around?" I asked.

"Really. Don't let Paradise or anyone else stop you from doing this. Girls play mind mind games. Ignore that hateration," Sapphire said, waving her hand in the air.

"I really don't want to run into her again. I would feel uncomfortable after she pulled me aside and got up in my face."

"If she bothers you that much, find another club then."

"I guess I could," I said as if I'd never considered the thought.

Sapphire looked at me, anticipating something else was on my mind.

"What is it now?" she asked.

I told her about the conversation I'd overheard in the clothing shop.

"You think too much, stop worrying! I've been doing this for eight years. I can honestly tell you that you have nothing to worry about so long as you work the system, and don't allow the system to work you."

"I guess you do have a point. I don't know where else I can go though," I explained.

"I don't know how much longer it's going to stay open since they're building some new stadium over that way, and they're trying to push out as many strip clubs in the DC Metropolitan area as possible 'cause Chocolate City is changing, but you could hit up another club that's still open downtown. It's called The Passion Palace. It's geared toward a more distinguished clientele, as opposed to ones with customers. I bet you could make more money there anyway. It's not my cup of tea though. I'm more comfortable in neighborhood settings. They're too stuck up in there for my tastes. I have so many customers who know me. I do just fine at The Foxy Lady."

I couldn't tell Sapphire all of my business, but I didn't want to risk getting caught shaking my hips. It sounded like it could've been a very popular spot. Although I was pissed at Donavan, I had my children to think of. We knew too many people from their school and activities. I managed to convince Sapphire that another spot similar to The Foxy Lady would do, pinning the blame on Paradise. She made a call to another dancer named Mocha. Mocha said she'd set up a little meeting for me with a contact. I guess she really did have everyone wrapped around her finger . . . even other dancers.

"We have some time. Lunch is on me. Let's go. I'll follow you. You pick." I followed Sapphire out of the store and into the main corridor of the mall.

After Sapphire chose a lunch spot, we ate our meals and got a little too personal, too fast. Sapphire paid attention to me like I was the greatest thing since sliced bread. As a result of her superb attention giving, I ended up telling her about my rotten marriage, in detail, blow by blow. I even told her how old I really was and that I had two children that were away at camp. I guess I missed Ayanna more than I thought, because she was the only person I could blab and vent to every day. I should've remembered that there's a big difference between Sapphire and Ayanna, but I got carried away and forgot. All I really learned about Sapphire was that she used to dance in Florida and she snorts coke from time to time, just like a few people I know who work in corporate America. After I got over the initial shock of her drug use in the club, it really didn't alarm me as much as it should've. We hung out all day at the mall, trying on shoes, eyeing designer purses, got manicures and pedicures, and picked out outfits for our girl's night out. It's sad to say that I'd never gotten a professional manicure and pedicure. I enjoyed being pampered—it felt so good! After shopping and hanging out, Sapphire convinced me that we should go back to her apartment to take a nap, shower, and change our clothes. I wasn't sure why she was being friendly to me so fast, but I took her up on her offer anyway.

Before long, the mystery was solved. I soon found out what was really on Sapphire's mind. She opened her trap by asking me if I wanted to see if what they said about dancers was true. I didn't know what in the world she was talking about. When she started caressing my thighs, asking me if I wanted her to spend the night, she soon explained that most dancers were very comfortable with their sexuality. In turn, they are bisexual or gay. The next thing I knew, she had leaned closer, explaining that she'd already fallen for me. I reminded her that I had a husband, turning down her sexual advances. After that, she reminded me that he was treating me badly. I'd put my own foot in my mouth, sharing too much too soon.

"I feel your pain. I've been there with a man I cared about. Men can be such dogs. It is what it is, you know?

They just won't act right sometimes, but I don't expect you to walk away from your husband and kids. You can have your cake and eat it too. I'm not trying to get in the way of what you got at home, if you and him want to struggle to work things out. I'll give you all the space you need when you need to be with him. I promise," Sapphire said. Without warning she firmly pressed her lips against mine and threw a few careless whispers my way as a sticky feeling crept into my panties. I knew it was wrong to tease Sapphire, but I suddenly became very curious about what it was like to kiss a woman passionately, so my lips pressed against hers again, and I briefly let her tongue tango with mine.

"We can have a beautiful relationship," she told me softly when our lips parted.

"I'm straight. No thanks," I told her.

"You liked that kiss. I could tell. There's more where that one came from," she said.

"I think I better go to that appointment alone."

"I'm off today, but suit yourself," Sapphire told me. She grabbed a pen and paper, scribbling down the information. All I wanted to do was get information about how to dance out of a stripper with a drug habit, I wasn't ready to jump into a relationship with a woman who wanted to be my chick on the side. I never would've guessed that in a thousand years. Hell, after all of these years, I still hadn't mastered how to have a relationship with a man. I grabbed my purse and hopped in my car. I wanted excitement in my life, and I was getting exactly what I asked for. As I sank deeper into a world I really didn't fully understand, new things began coming at me left and right.

I called the number Sapphire pushed in my hand before I shut her car door. Apparently, her Rolodex did have some contacts in it, because some guy named Big Tony quickly gave me another number. He told me I should call and ask for Tim since he was already expecting a call from someone Mocha recommended. According to Big Tony, Tim's father owned The Passion Palace, which was the up-scale club Sapphire spoke of, and apparently his three sons ran the spot I hadn't seen yet. I began to wonder if family worked in every strip club venture!

When I called the number, a man picked up. He sounded very calm and easygoing. I could tell that he was black from the tone of his voice. I told him my name, explained that I didn't have much experience dancing, and also dished my true age. Why, I can't even say. Maybe I was feeling self-conscious again, wondering about my worth as an aging woman.

"That's ok. Beauty is in the eye of the beholder," Tim explained.

The truth is I still hated my looks, although men had shown me a little love at The Foxy Lady. I never had felt pretty. Realizing that made me pause after his comment.

"What I mean is if you're a beautiful person inside, you can do this. I'll be here for the next hour, if you'd like to meet. I heard good things about you already."

After speaking with Tim further, I put my contacts back in and headed toward the address. At first I passed it, but it was easy enough to find and appeared to be in a very low rent district. When I walked up to the door I spotted neighborhood under-aged kids milling around smoking cigarettes and running in and out of a fast food chicken joint. When I made it inside of the club, I met Tim and talked with him. I liked his spirit—he seemed fairly easy-going. He interviewed me and explained the club rules and how everything worked at the lap dance club. Fantasies was a no frills environment, even less glamorous than The Foxy Lady. In fact, when he showed me around, an exotic dancer was busy weaving someone's hair. As the other girl sat on the stool, the dancer stitched tiny burgundy Shirley Temple curls in her head like it was nothing to it but to do it!

"You're selling a fantasy. If you can hustle while selling a fantasy, there's good money to be made," Tim explained when we sat down. That's the main thing I got out of the conversation. "Come back tonight. I want you to audition."

Thankfully, I was able to put on a real outfit that I'd bought when I did return to the club. I was still nervous, trying to play the role of a seductive go-getter, but it wasn't as bad as the first time I stripped. When I returned, Tim hadn't arrived yet. Two police cars were posted across the street. I called Tim and mentioned it. He told me that they did that all of the time. My stomach was doing a few extra flips because the club was located deep in the hood, and I was worried that my shiny Lexus may attract the wrong kind of attention. I also had never been to that part of town before, and it was so different from what I was accustomed to. I sat in the car a while and noted everything my eyes could see: stripped junk cars, trash blowing around the parking lot, and occasional stray cats walking by. I looked at the time stamp on my cell phone and waited to see someone walk through the door across the street, hoping this wouldn't take too long.

I mentioned who I was there to see. Someone ushered me to a back dressing room, although I was never asked who I was.

"Get dressed. There are some men out here," someone said.

I wasn't sure if that included me, but I did. I went toward the front of the club to see if Tim had arrived. I was dressed in tight Lycra shorts, a slingshot outfit, and my clear white stripper shoes, perfect for looking at men with fuck-me eyes to help conjure an instant erotic fantasy. My stripper shoes had turned out to be an important investment.

A few men smoking Dutch brand cigars were giving me a *who are you* look, and I threw it right back at them. Hell, I didn't know who they were either. My contact Tim finally stepped forward and introduced me to them—they were partners. Actually, brothers and partners. The other two were named Ray and Reggie. Ray was tall, and Reggie was short and pudgy. Reggie reminded me of a donut. In fact, each of the brothers possessed memorable characteristics that separated one from the other.

"I'm sorry. I would've introduced myself if I knew who you both were," I apologized.

"First things first—you're cool, but *I* approve all of the girls. You came out here half dressed and I didn't know who you were," Reggie continued as he looked up at me. He was so short that I towered over him in my heels. He was power tripping, but I let his chocolate-colored, four-foot-tall ass have his moment. He really stood a bit taller than four feet, but it didn't seem like much more!

I returned to the back room and sprayed perfume on myself. As the burst of coolness hit my skin, I was thinking that the spot was a true underground club—no one even *asked* me to see my ID. It was obvious that they didn't have a liquor license, and it wasn't up for discussion for them to try to purchase one.

There was a narrow piece of carpet running through the small room. Green lawn chairs, a radiator, and a mirror were the main things I noticed. I pushed two sets of curtains back and entered the dimly lit main room. Just after midnight, girls had painted their lips with everything from cheap, clear lip gloss, to a luscious lollipop red shade. Most of the precious hood gems were sitting on one side trying to tempt the men who were lined up across from them to give them a shot. The girls spoke, but as the night wore on, they were less and less friendly when they saw that men were giving me some play for five-dollar lap dances. Yes, I learned the art of crotch rubbing since lap dances were legal at the location where I was. Tim schooled me on what to do a little bit, and just like my experience at The Foxy Lady, he told me to watch how the experienced girls charmed the customers out of the money.

After a while, I saw an around-the-way looking girl named Cinnamon grinding on a guy as J Holiday's "Bed" played. She was wearing one of those pair of panties that had some nasty, sassy saying scribbled on it. Cinnamon perched herself on top of his lap, moving her hips with specific precision. The rhythm of her movement reminded me of straight dry fucking. The only thing that separated them was a small layer of fabric. One guy asked me to go in the VIP room, but I declined his offer. I saw her head turn in my direction and she gave me the most piecing stare, making me feel as if I snatched food straight from her plate. I soon realized that the men at Fantasies walked through that door thinking that the dancers there were more freaky than a no-touching zone like The Foxy Lady. The customer haggled with me about putting a condom on and rubbing up against my ass. His first offer was $100, but his final offer was $150.00. He couldn't understand why I was sticking to my guns. We ended up going in the back, but only for a nude dance. The house got twenty for providing the space. He and I negotiated $20.00 for my time. When I went to pay the VIP fee, I was told it was too low.

"Never charge under $100.00," Reggie told me.

Nevertheless, I didn't feel that any man would pay that

amount just to look at a naked woman. The customer sat in a chair in the dark booth, filling it up. First, I put my ass in his face and made it jiggle as wild as I could. Next, I wiggled my ass in front of him to the beat of the music, sat on Big Daddy's lap, then began grinding. After a few grinds, I removed all of my clothes except my tiny g-string.

"Damn, that feels good," the man mumbled lustfully. His pants legs were hiked up and his clothes were wrinkled. I let him talk dirty to me and found out that he was married . . . just like me. It explained the way he was dressed, including the orthopedic looking shoes on his feet, and I wondered if my husband had done all of this dry fucking in a strip club. Considering the possibility made me play with his mind even more.

"When you go home, I want you to do something for me," I whispered in his ear like a caged virgin, while softly moving one hand up and down his chest.

"What?" he asked, grinning.

"Fuck the shit out of your wife. Think about my touch, my face, you being here looking at all of this," I told him while bending over, then feeling between his legs. "After that, smash that ass so good cum runs down her legs."

To my surprise, I ended up getting hot, sticky, and wet myself. I was everything I wanted to be—sexy, evil, naughty, and powerful.

"I'll pay you to fuck me now," he said breathing rapidly. I noticed a shimmer on his forehead. "I'll give you an extra eighty," he added.

At that point I felt he should. His breath smelled like hot trash, and it was hard staying in the lap of a man with so much belly. We had a battle of the wits. He was playing games, and so was I.

The thing was, my husband had helped my lying game. Stripping was work. A girl's game had to be tight, so I found out.

"Get me hot, and I'll think about it," I lied, trying to say the right words at the right time.

"Move up and down like this," he instructed me. "Is this easier? Now I can feel you—that's better," he told me while sounding as if he were busy stroking my slippery kitty kat. He was only feeling me through fabric, but if he was happier, I was more than okay with it.

I wasn't attracted to him, but I kept everything that Sapphire told me about creating a fantasy for a customer. Additionally, Tim explained that I should count each song as I gave men lap dances to track when they owed me. He also suggested that I keep them aroused so they'd run up a bill, having to hand over money for more than one lap dance. Keeping all of this in mind, I took my right hand and caressed his face, locking eyes with him. As a slow song played that I can't recall, I was trying to bullshit him and only let him feel up my shit. His hands were everywhere; they'd been on my ass, my stomach, my breasts, the small of my back. I was beginning to sweat in the hot booth, but I continued smiling and grinding like I enjoyed it because I did. I got another $32.00 out of him as we played cat and mouse, but I deserved it. When I unbuttoned three buttons on his shirt, I stuck my hand just below his collar. I soon discovered he had back hair thick enough to be mistaken for an overgrown Chia Pet.

Twenty minutes into our private time together, I realized that security was late coming to get me. I later found out that showing up late to retrieve me was a ploy to let me make more money. When I finally heard a coded banging noise on the frame of the dressing room, I told Big Daddy his time was up. He was sweating and nearly stumbled out of that VIP room in a fog. I know he was mad that he'd spent as much as he did and didn't even get his dick wet! But when he started begging me to continue, I knew he was about to bust a big, messy nut in his pants. Mission accomplished, so I thought. Still, he didn't want to let me go.

"Don't stop. Don't stop," he begged.

Ignoring his plea, I snatched the money from his hand and took off feeling rather satisfied. He soon sat in a large room in the corner, wiping his head with a tissue, staring at me through the curtain. I think he wanted to finish our dirty dancing session, but I had no mercy.

"Did you get your money straight," security asked as I gathered my tip.

"I did. I got it up to what it should've been," I said, wiping my face.

"Good." He smiled and shook his head.

As soon as I freshened up and walked back out into the main room another customer asked me for a lap dance. Despite the rules of customers keeping hands to their sides, not touching kittys or breasts, he was a pretty aggressive, middle-aged customer. He didn't want to pay up front, and seemed annoyed when I mentioned money. I placed one hand on the wall, faced him, then pushed my breasts toward him. Under the glow of the light I could see him looking deep into my eyes—the way a man does when he's having sex with a woman. At that point, I turned around and wiggled my ass slow and sensual. I playfully slapped myself while peering back at him. When he reached in between my thongs, I slid his hand away, reminding him of the no touching rule. I got up off of his lap, slid a chair over facing him, then sat down running one of my three-inch heels over his crotch. By the time I got up and grinded on his lap when the third song played, he broke down and openly asked me "the question."

"How much to fuck?" he asked with a sexy, exotic accent.

I couldn't help but notice his piercing gray eyes that

highlighted his deep, rich and dark, skin color. Even in the low lighting, they commanded attention.

"I don't do extras," I explained, although the fantasy of being a naughty slut made tingles shoot through my kitty kat. The man wanted me to grab and fondle his penis, reminding me that no one could see. At first I pulled my hand away . . . then I decided to loosen up because it *did* sound like harmless fun—plus my pussy was now pulsating. I began rubbing my hands over his crotch until he adjusted his pants so that I could grip his tool. When he set his dick free, I grabbed that sucker, and held onto it for dear life. First, I took my fingertips and slowly teased his head. Then I closed my eyes and let my hands do what they wanted to. Before long he was hard as a rock and I was giving him a real good hand job. The thrill of it turned me on. The feel of it brought him to orgasm although I moved my hands just in time. Four songs later, he owed me twenty dollars, and his shirt covered his white explosion. Business was business, I moved on to the next lap after letting him stick the bill inside of my pink garter belt.

When I was about to walk away, he smiled at me and motioned for me to stay put. He stuck an extra twenty-dollar bill in my left garter belt and an extra twenty in my right. I winked in thanks of my bonus tip and walked away. He got up, walking toward the bathroom—to clean himself up, no doubt. I did have fun, playing with that long, pretty meat!

The third customer was the most polite. I got $7.00 or so and a request to see him again. He told me he thought that I could make a lot of money in a certain part of town that was an upscale environment. After we conversed, I washed my hands with the dish washing liquid that was sitting on the sink in the bathroom. Whomever was in charge of buying hand soap was obviously too cheap to make that happen.

By three AM all of the girls headed back to the dressing room. They were staring at me coldly and asking me how much I made that night. I created a barrier around myself by playing dumb. I pretended that I hadn't made anything at all. Reggie pushed the curtain aside while we were getting dressed. When he walked in, I was bent over with my breasts dangling freely. When I looked up he was staring and nearly licking his thick lips like a hungry lion.

"Give me a call tomorrow. How much do you want to make at this?" Reggie asked while handing me his business card.

I threw out a random figure. "$60,000," I answered quickly. That was the same salary I was earning as a legal secretary, given my many years of experience.

"That's nothing," he told me, twisting up his face into a frown. I noticed a very small white girl eavesdropping. White Chocolate was a firecracker who sported ass-length strawberry blonde cornrows and lived up to her name White Chocolate. As soon as he left, she zeroed in on me again, like an annoying wasp. She placed her hand on her waist like she was going to tell me about myself. I wanted to laugh at her strategy to mark her territory, but I let her keep her dignity. I'd already figured out that she and Reggie were bedmates. I didn't want her man—I wasn't there for that.

"That was a long conversation. What were you talking about? What did he say?" she asked, yoking her neck with a black girl attitude.

"He was telling me about the VIP rules," I lied to the sour-acting eye candy.

She stared at me like she wanted to continue her little interrogation, but her time to flip out was up. Ray came around to collect the dancer's fee. He had a clipboard and checked off who paid. Some of the dancers complained they didn't make any money and didn't want to pay the $10.00. They gave us a break and didn't charge much since many men didn't show. I paid and stuffed the remainder of my bills in the side of my bag. I didn't want the other girls to see me counting my money, but that didn't work either. While I was putting on my coat, little stuff came near my bag and nearly stuck her head in the side of it.

"Are you looking for something?" I asked White Chocolate.

"No. I thought you were gonna drop your money," she lied.

I imagined her bony fingers picking up some bills that didn't belong to her, so I made a mental note that some strippers are more than capable of tip robbery. On the way home I called Sapphire. After I'd done it once, it was quickly becoming a habit. Maybe part of me enjoyed her willingness to make a real effort pursuing me.

"What do you think he gave me his card for?" I asked.

"He's going to try to pimp you, watch. That's what they do. Have I been wrong yet?"

"No you haven't," I replied.

"Be extra careful, 'cause that's his next move. In the morning, call to see what is on and popping in his mind but keep holding on and stay out of trouble, baby girl. I'm gonna rap to you until my battery goes out."

I fought to stay awake as I drove home while talking to Sapphire.

"I'm hanging up. My lips are too tired to move anymore," I said, halfway slurring my words.

"Be sure to call me when you get home then," she commented.

"Yeah, yeah. Sure," I remarked, sounding slightly rude. Honey was officially off the clock and Mystique was feeling cranky and tired. All I could think about was pulling back the sheets and my head hitting my pillow. When I finally did, I noticed that a Bath and Body Works card was tucked underneath. A note was tacked to the back of it.

"Get yourself something nice!" it read in sloppy handwriting. I had guessed that Donavan was in a rush by the looks of the letter. Even so, I felt it was the message that counted.

"He did this for me before he left for Seattle. Maybe Donavan is trying to make things right. Maybe my baby is trying to let me know this war is over," I told myself, smiling. As tired as I was, I got up from my bed, found one of his old T-shirts, and put it on. I drifted off to sleep, a little happier that Donavan was trying to open up the lines of communication.

9

DRAMA IN THE CLUB

Minus Sapphire, I returned back to the mall to go to Bath and Body Works. As luck would have it, they were having a sale. With pep in my step, I walked up to the counter to find out how much goodies I could get. One thing was for sure, I wanted to get some bubble bath so Donavan and I could soak in the Jacuzzi together, if he was game when he returned home. I explained to the cashier that I'd been given a gift card, and I wanted to know how much was on it. After accessing some information, she informed me that the number was invalid.

"This is why," she told me.

"What?" I asked, feeling confused.

"It's *merchandise credit*, not a gift card. You must've used this then returned something to get a credit."

I shook my head.

"Oh no. That's not right. My husband just gave this to me. That's impossible," I insisted.

People behind me were getting antsy, wanting me to move the hell out of the way so they could pay for their items, but the woman typed in the number again.

"Like I told you, it went through as a credit," the cashier assured, sounding catty.

"You don't have to be rude, Miss. If you can't help me without being rude, perhaps your manager can help me."

"I'm just saying I told you, *okay*," she answered.

People in line were growing more impatient, cussing, talking trash about me, and doing whatever they could to give me a hint that I needed to move my ass. The person behind me got so frustrated, that she left her basket on the floor and stormed out.

"Other customers are waiting, Ma'am. What is it that you want me to do?"

"Tell me how much is on the card, that's what!" I snapped back.

"Your card balance is thirty-two cents."

"Thirty-two cents!"

"Next in line," she said dismissing me.

By that time I felt like murdering Donavan with my bare hands, wondering what kind of sick game he was playing.

Everything went from sugar to shit, all over again. Our relationship was turning into some sadistic roller coaster ride.

"You think you're so funny these days," I hollered into my cell phone. There was no way I was going to text him again, so I took a chance that he'd answer his cell.

"I don't know what you're talking about," he said.

"Stop playing innocent. You know what you did!"

"Yeah. I left you a note. What more do you want?"

"How about giving me some respect. I am still your wife."

I heard Donavan sigh hard.

"Look, my days of fighting are over. Between the trip and recent arguing, I'm drained."

"That makes two of us."

"When I get home I promise I'll—"

Bam! I slammed the phone down with a vengeance. So much for opening up the lines of communication.

Still heated, I took my stick of cocoa butter and rubbed it on top of my knees that were fighting to heal from my initial audition experience. With all of that negative energy floating around me, I needed another break, even if drama would probably jump off in the club. When you're not at peace in your life, sometimes you just want to be anywhere different from places and spaces you have to be.

I called Tim. He invited me to accompany him to another spot. I was informed that a few other girls were going also. Since I decided that switching up the mix could be harmless, Tim and I agreed to speak toward the late evening to arrange our meeting. In the meantime, I called Reggie, the brother who handed me his business card. He wanted to meet, too.

"Women are always slow," Reggie complained. "Meet me at the club in an hour."

"I'm not your average woman. Twenty minutes is all I need," I answered, sounding sure.

Being in this environment reminded me to always keep people you don't trust guessing. When they think they've figured you out, you're vulnerable. I suddenly felt like I needed Sapphire's expertise so I didn't write her off just then, despite my disinterest in a girl-on-girl affair.

After we met at the club, I noticed no one else was there. I sat in a chair next to him as he smoked a smelly cigar. What the meeting came down to was that he wanted to try to get in my head. If he got in my head on a personal level, I could be "trained." I picked up on that early on in the conversation. He tried his best to understand me, guess my background, and find out why I was stripping in the first place. As he smoked and put his feet up on his desk, he ended up sharing very personal things with me. At the end of his speech, which ended with asking me if I found him attractive, he offered to take me out to dinner and made a few attempts to convince me he was single. I guess he didn't catch on to the fact that I don't care for short men. I know I'm biased to tall men, but that's just the way the cookie crumbles for me.

"I understand that you are single, but I have one question for you," I asked.

"What?"

"There is a certain girl here who was very upset that you came into the dressing room to talk to me. She asked me what we were talking about so long. Were you going to tell me about her?"

He exhaled a nose full of smoke. "White Chocolate's one of the girls I take care of."

"Financially?" I said, assuming I understood.

"No, not financially. Not that."

"Ooooooh, I see. Well, what two adults decide to do is between them. That's none of my business, nor would I judge that."

"I'm glad you understand. Most don't," Reggie said.

My phone rang. I was told to meet the other partner where I already was . . . at the club. "I'm already here talking to Reggie," I explained. Then I hung up.

"Who was that?"

"It was your brother, Tim."

"Why'd you tell him I was here with you? I thought this meeting was between us?" he said, sounding annoyed.

"There is nothing between us. We were just talking. You're not my boss, and I'm not really your employee. I'm an independent contractor. Everything between us is purely professional and will remain that way," I explained. After biting my tongue while dealing with my boss at the firm, it felt refreshing to be able to speak my mind like that

"You're faking—you know you want me! I'm not chasing you anymore!"

"I didn't know you were," I told him, smiling a little.

"What is this really about? You're hiding something. You're always so secretive and mysterious. I can't put my finger on it yet. Why are you so secretive? You work for the FBI or some shit?" he asked.

"How about having a nice tall glass of mind your own business?" I said, showing a little bit of an attitude. "I understand that you want to feel comfortable doing business with me, but my personal life is my own. I'm going through some things and I can't say any more than that."

"Don't get defensive. I'm here for you. You can talk to me," Reggie said, trying to convince me to confess by changing his tone of voice.

I knew I couldn't trust him though. I wondered if he thought I was just some nosey person, but he hadn't figured out why it was the case.

"I'm putting all day Saturday aside for you. What do you like to eat? We're going out on a date," he said, looking me over like he wanted to gobble me whole.

I told him that I didn't like the kind of food he spoke of, then I laughed. I was being difficult on purpose. He wasn't about to break me in as one of his strip club women. I'm not saying he was a bad person, but he wasn't someone I needed to get too friendly with either. He was playing my game and didn't even realize it yet.

"I can't come out tomorrow, even if I wanted to. I'm job hunting, I've got bills to pay," I lied.

"I might pay bills if you start hanging out with me," he told me while running his hands up and down one of my legs. "How big do you like it?" he added.

"That's personal. Keep it professional," I said as I pushed his arm away. His slime ball routine didn't turn me on, but instead allowed me to practice dealing with slime balls that I needed to keep in check.

Midway between our verbal tennis match, Tim called and told me he'd be waiting outside. When I walked toward the door, I didn't see him.

"What are you doing meeting him?"

"Maybe the same thing I was doing meeting you," I joked.

He called his brother on the phone. I know he wanted to ask where we were headed, but he didn't.

"Where are you? I don't want her standing out there in the dark."

I felt the tension building, but I hadn't figured everything out. I was told that Tim was in a parking space in front of the club. He appeared and I left Reggie staring at us through the door.

I followed Tim's vehicle until we stopped several miles away. He backed up into a space and just waited. I pulled into a space and got out when he did. A few other girls got out of the vehicle with him. I didn't understand why they didn't drive themselves.

"Hey Tim, where'd you find her? Damn!" someone said as we walked inside of the club.

"I think she found me," he remarked coolly.

"You can speak," another man said to me.

I just looked straight ahead and pretended I didn't hear any part of the conversation. I was also confused about them asking where he got me from. These puzzle pieces were getting harder to fit by the hour. Tim told me the dancing fee was twenty dollars, but it ended up being thirty. When I heard that I turned around to leave because I didn't bring that much pocket change along, based on what I'd needed in the other clubs. Tim and, who I assumed was the person who sponsored the event, walked away and exchanged whispers. When they returned, my fee was temporarily adjusted.

"No, I want her to dance—I want her business. Just give me twenty and we'll hold your license until the end of the night," the main said.

I dug in my purse until I located my mug shot. A woman inspected it then took it in her possession. Luckily my address had my old address on it from the time before I moved. It was bad enough that my real name, birth date, and social security number was pasted on the plastic square. With all of this, I brushed my worry off and gave my contact the money and he handed it to the third party. I stepped down three steps and he pointed to a door and told me that I could get dressed. The facility was a large open space and very nice inside. A live DJ spun current hits. I noticed a lot of the men wore slacks and button-down shirts, which told me that they were professionals. The place was rather empty though. I would venture to guess that there were only twenty people in attendance.

The dressing room was noisy and the most cramped I'd ever seen. In fact, I think it was a storage space that was being used to serve two purposes. Furniture and miscellaneous items were stacked high to the ceiling. As a result, fifty percent of it was not a functional space. Girls were loud, full of chatter, and the volume was unbearable. There was nowhere for me to sit and I had to balance on one foot to change my clothes. With all of this, I managed to get dressed. When I came out I spoke to a few men. I tried to appear busy, hunted for the bathroom, then walked around the room a few times. A few girls were jiggling their asses on stage, trying to tempt the customers to come up and tip them for showing a glimpse of their love tunnels. Some men walked up to tip them while others lined the walls or sat in chairs, getting lap dances.

Just as I was about to find a seat, a man approached me. He wore a thick coat, sported an earring in his ear, and was a medium brown complexion. He guided me to a dark, isolated corner and asked me for a lap dance. I sat in his lap and began to move my hips to the music. He asked me my name, who I was there with, and seemed like the confident type.

"How good are you?" the man asked.

I smiled coyly, lightly touching his crotch area, then put one leg up on his shoulder while putting my kitty kat close to his face. I took my leg down, then assumed my original position, facing him.

"You be the judge," I said, moving around on his lap.

"How come I never seen you before?" he asked.

"You have. You don't remember seeing me in your fantasies?" I joked, half-flirting like I had a little stripper game.

I smiled at him seductively as he held onto my ass like he was gripping two melons with his hands. I pressed against his hardness like I was mimicking the motions of him stroking me. He pulled out a stack of money and stuffed some of it in my garter. I exposed my breasts, letting him peek at my fleshy mountain peaks. As I felt his hard tool pulsate through his pants, he cupped them then lightly teased both nipples with a few warm fingertips. My nipples began to poke out. Thy got so hard, they almost ached. He began to nibble, lick, and suck on those babies like he was a real breast man. Making them grow larger and thicker, he began flicking them with his tongue, spiraling in circles around the edges of my areolas. I continued to work my hips as he reached down to play with my kitty kat. I hadn't had sex in so long, my clit was swollen and I had thoughts of practically jumping on his dick, right there, since I hadn't pushed his hand away. Just as I felt one of his fingers slither, I bit my lip, anticipating juices running down my leg. When more fingers slipped into my wetness, I began to moan a little and I laid my head on his shoulder as my hips started working hard on their own.

"You want to make any money tonight?" he asked me.

I was beginning to hear variations of this line on a daily basis.

"I do want to make money. It's just that I'm a good girl," I said, still enjoying his fingering.

He shook his head and laughed, still tickling my wet kitty kat. "If you're one of Tim's girls, you fuck. You sound innocent, but I know better," he commented. "The girl in my fantasy did everything I wanted like a bad girl, *not* a good girl."

"I don't do any more than dance. I really don't," I insisted. I said I was with Tim, but I didn't understand why he classified me as one of his girls . . . whatever that meant.

"That's funny 'cause you're doing more right now," he said, pumping his finger in and out of my pussy harder. "I would spoil you," he told me as I fought hard to maintain my composure.

Finally, he pulled his finger out of my wetness and I was glad that he did.

"Here. Hold this," he said handing me a lighter. I tried to fire it up, but it didn't have much juice. After three tries, I saw his fat wad of money. There was at least two grand in his stack. My heart began to pound as I wondered why he was carrying around so much cash on him, as well as how he made the money. I didn't want to assume the worst, just because he was a casually dressed brother. All I knew was that I didn't know what to say or how to act. Despite my efforts not to stereotype yet one more black man, all I could conclude was that he was a hustler. I swiftly changed the subject.

"Why are you giving me such a hard time?" I asked sweetly.

"Never ignore me—never!" he said in a moody tone. That's when I realized he was a real hothead.

"Like I said, why are you giving me such a hard time?" I asked, caressing his arm. I felt the need to keep him calm.

"Because I like you."

When the song ended, he wanted to exchange numbers. I wished I had another phone that I could abandon when all of this was over. I hated using my real cell phone at times like these, but I hadn't thought that far ahead.

"Program my number in your phone," he added. He called my number to make sure I wasn't lying. I was a bit frightened of this one. "Call me tomorrow," he told me before walking way.

"Ok," I lied. I could barely stand, given that I was so aroused. All I can say is he left me wanting to cum hard.

After I walked away I spotted someone staring at me from across the room. I wasn't sure, but for a minute I thought it was Donavan! The person favored him quite a bit, at least from afar. My palms grew sweaty, nearly dripping at the fingertips, but I felt like I needed to know. With every step I took I prayed it wasn't my husband. When I made it close to the man, I played it off by sitting with him to talk, wasting time as my hands dried. I sighed with relief when I discovered we hadn't crossed paths. Before the night ended I was propositioned for sex three times and approached twice about dancing privately on a weekly basis. I didn't make much money that night, as most of the men were looking for something more than a semi-nude bump and grind. In the end, I was more than glad to get dressed.

When I was sliding on my jeans and top, two girls were throwing words like bitch, fight, whipping ass, and outside! I noticed that they were wearing the same outfit, which I think was a catalyst for the big bang. The one that I recalled having a c-section scar was accusing the other who sported a hip-hop honey, video look of stealing two hundred dollars out of her bag. I stayed out of it by getting dressed faster than the other girls who were coming into the dressing room swiftly. Security came in and told a few of them they shouldn't go outside just yet. In the meantime, I slid past him and searched for Tim. When he asked me if I was ready to go, I was more than ready. I located the woman who was holding my license and she wanted to play some sort of cute game with me. She asked me at least five questions as she grinned, including my middle name. I wasn't in the mood to be assumed, it wasn't the time for fun and games. After she handed it to me, Tim and I headed toward the door. When we made it outside, Reggie appeared and pushed Tim, causing him to hit the door, making a thumping noise.

"I didn't want to believe it. So you're taking girls from our club and bringing them somewhere else?" he yelled, trying to bring things to a head.

Tim tried to walk toward his truck. When he stepped off of the sidewalk, Reggie pushed him to the ground.

"We're supposed to be partners on this thing. Instead of working with me, you're working against me. What's up, bro?"

"These girls just wanted to make some money. On the days our club is closed, they can make money—"

"Shut the fuck up, Tim! Just shut up. Our club's not closed, we're open every night. Just who do you think you're tryna carry, bama? This shit ain't right!" Reggie yelled, drawing his fist back, but he never hit Tim. Instead he pushed him once and caused him to stumble and fall. A crowd began to form.

"Just because you're my brother doesn't mean you know me," Tim said with blood trickling down his lip, as he rose to his feet. It sounded like he was issuing some kind of warning.

"Let's go," he told a group of girls. "Wait for me in the truck. I'll be there in a minute," he added.

As they walked away in silence, he pulled the bouncer aside and whispered something to him. Then he walked to his truck, wiping the blood from his lip. He got in and sped off. I was surprised that he backed down. In fact, I found it odd. People were still milling around, trying to figure out what had happened. While this was going on, I quietly left. I was growing tired of this constant reality show. It's not so funny when you are one of the actors. I figured out part of the puzzle: *loyalty*. Although I've heard of many girls dancing at more than one club, this couldn't be the case in the set up where I was. There was an air of possession. A big part of me didn't like that. I figured that where you go should be your business, so long as you didn't agree to show on a given night. Wrong.

I knew before long I'd find out the rest of the mystery behind Tim and the night's events. I'd figured out part of it, but definitely not everything. Just like Ayanna said, I was getting deeper and deeper in a world I knew nothing about. Still, this wasn't enough to scare me back to the daily prospect of wearing my apron and getting dishpan hands with nothing to balance out my life. In fact, all of this exposure to the adult entertainment industry was making me think twice about my lame sex life with Donavan. I decided I was going to put it on him, only because I'd been so sexually stimulated. Although I could barely stand my hubby as a person, I was about to show him who was boss. Whether I liked it or not, I needed to have sex!

10

SEX ON HIS DESK

After teasing men in strip clubs, and getting teased myself while showing off my goodies, my kitty kat had been dripping wet all night. I still had sex on the brain the next morning, despite our latest tiff. Realizing that Donavan has started up his Porsche, I knew that he was back in town. As if I hadn't learned the hard way, I ended up heading over to Donavan's office again . . . unannounced. The only difference was I didn't speed, and I had a trick up my sleeve, determined to get my rocks off for sure. I also decided not to let him know I got fired. Tending to our marriage had to come first.

When I arrived at my husband's office wearing a feminine looking summer sundress with bright flowers and a ribbon tied around my waist, he was engaged in a conference call. I boldly sat down across from him, glanced over at how fine he looked in his navy blue suit and coordinating tie, and picked up *The New York Times* that was turned to the stocks headline section. While waiting for Donavan to finish up, my mind wandered back to our relationship before we got married.

I thought of how my husband routinely sucked me until I exploded after he carefully shaved me, stroke by stroke with a razor, until my pussy was bare and my fat clit stared right at him. It was a joy for him to put a smile on my face in many ways, and in return, I didn't mind putting him first for treating me so good. We had something a lot of people didn't seem to have until he got that big promotion, and he proposed. After becoming social climbers, we got that big house, the candy apple red Porsche for him, Lexus for me, and Range Rover to transport our children, and we were able to put money in the joint bank account. By the time things changed financially, the only way I ever trembled from having the big O was if I grabbed my vibrator out of my panty drawer and fucked myself!

Donavan glanced down at his nearly three thousand dollar Tag Heuer link watch that was wrapped around his right arm. With every word spoken, I found myself fantasizing about past memories that consisted of Donavan burying his face in my pussy in my humble efficiency apartment as his saliva made a swishing sound. If I had my way, my head would soon bob up and down while sucking the hell out of Donavan's big, chocolate dick. My thoughts weren't just on kissing, licking, or sucking though. I missed the closeness of him being involved in my life. I treasured the companionship that became a fuzzy, distant memory. After nearly a month and a half of thinking it over while stripping, I decided that people do, and can, make mistakes. Maybe Aaynna was right. Maybe we just needed some spice in our marriage. We had been together since we were fifteen. He was my first love and I was his. Thus, I was willing to give my husband one free fuck up pass without going to jail in my little game. Determined to work things out, I was fighting to keep my foolish pride out of the way, so I sat in the same spot until I had the opportunity to strike up a conversation.

When Donavan hung up, I stopped staring at symbols I didn't understand, putting down the paper. I wasn't sure what to say to him since communicating with him was no longer natural and free. Still, I made up something to spark a conversation, taking the liberty of speaking first.

"From the looks of your desk, you need a good secretary in your life," I commented.

"I have one. By the way, we need milk," he said as I watched his pen move across a large, white writing pad.

"You don't even drink milk. The kids drink milk," I snapped.

"Well if you're here about the mortgage or any of the other bills, I paid them. Everything's taken care of."

"I'm not here about bills either. You always pay them on time. Since you don't come to me, I thought I'd come to you regarding a personal matter," I said, coaxing myself to calm down. I wanted to ball up my fist and lash out at my husband, but I didn't swing by his office to start a verbal war. I vowed to myself that I wouldn't slip into an argument with him, even if he was encouraging me to take the bait and do so.

"What is that supposed to mean? After getting in from my trip, I've been home. Just what are you doing here anyway?" he replied, never looking up.

"As you know, I have good clerical skills. After all, I am a legal secretary."

"I know that. Why aren't you at work?" he asked, finally looking up at me again.

"I'm on vacation, although it will be over before I know it," I lied.

"I didn't know that—it must be nice," he said in a condescending tone.

"That's because you didn't ask and we don't talk like adults anymore," I reminded him. "I'm not here to argue.

Let's keep this on a positive note. So anyway, could you use some extra office help or what?"

"Patty can handle it—that's what she gets paid to do—but thank you for offering."

"No, you don't understand," I said, wanting to taste his kisses.

I locked his office door and stood directly in front of his desk.

"The kids are still at camp, so this would be a really good time for you to get caught up on some paper work," I suggested.

"I don't know what in the hell you really want to tell me, but if it was important enough for you to come all the way down here, you may as well say it. You really are irritating me with this cat and mouse routine of yours," Donavan snapped, sounding mean and cold.

"Perhaps I can't say it," I said.

He sighed, misunderstanding my intentions.

"I don't have time for games. I've got a report to finish on a deadline. I really—"

"You don't understand. Perhaps I can show you better than tell you," I said, dropping my clothes. "You forgot your lunch, and your lunch is *me*!" I remarked, letting my dress drop to the floor. I stood in heels, showing off my black thong that left little to the imagination. The front of my undies spelled the word "Bitch" in sparkling silver letters. I thought they were a riot and picked them up at the store that sold stripper gear.

My husband's eyes glazed over as he stared at his sexy surprise visitor. I know he was floored, given that I was acting so uninhibited, which was out of character for me. While he remained frozen, I slowly sashayed toward him, swinging my hips just right, thinking about his eight inches of meat.

In a sultry tone, I whispered in his ear. "I'll do whatever

you want. It's been too long. Let's have sex on your desk, right now," I suggested, bending down.

Not allowing him time to answer, I let my lips brush the back of Donavan's neck as my kisses left a trail of passionate fire. The smell of his Bvlgari cologne drove me wild, filling my nose with a sensual blended scent. I walked around to face him. Next, I slowly unzipped his perfectly pressed slacks, and let my soft hand glide up to his chest.

"Suck on Daddy," my husband murmured. I was shocked that my effort to revive the sparks was working.

"Let's do it the way it should be done," I said.

After I unbuttoned his shirt and pulled it off of his body, I instructed him to get up on his desk. I sat on my knees and buried my face in his hairy groin, taking my husband's tool into my mouth as far as it could go. All of the sudden I began sucking on it hard, but not so that it would hurt him. I felt his throbbing dick swell into a solid rod as he moaned lowly, as if he were in sweet pain from being teased. Even the legs on his thighs were wet with saliva from the sloppy blow job I was giving him. I must admit, I sucked his dick like I wanted to drain his balls, as I stretched my jaws as wide as they would go. I finally looked up at him as he gripped my head while driving his tool in and out of my hungry mouth. His face was glistening with sweat, and when I knew that he was ready to enter me, I sprang to my feet, then pulled him up and told him where I wanted him to stand.

Next, I leaned over his desk with my legs spread apart, gripping the edge of his executive's desk. Donavan felt big and hot as he pushed himself deep inside of my tight pussy, filling my sweet, juicy walls. With deep strokes he pounded my kitty kat so hard, his balls were crashing into my backside. My pussy instantly began thanking me for giving it the proper physical attention it needed.

"Mmm. Oh honey. Mmm. It's been a long time," I said, half moaning.

Donavan kept driving himself so hard inside of me that my wetness began to wet my thighs and my knees began to tremble. It had been a long time since he moved my body to react like that, giving it what it craved. At that point, I changed positions, motioning for him to sit down in his roomy office chair. I slowly sat down on his tool and strad-dled him face to face, while letting my tongue dart in and out of his wet mouth. When our mouths separated I be-gan moving up and down on top of him, embracing him around his strong, wide shoulders, as my husband held my round hips with a tight grip.

"Damn, girl. Work Daddy. This pussy is sooo good. You've got the best pussy. You always have," Donavan said, mumbling. I couldn't believe he was saying that, given that the last time we spent that much time together, he was helping me make balloon animals for Brittany's birth-day party decorations.

"I'm going to cum, Donavan. I think I'm really going to cum. Do you want me to cum for you, baby?" I asked, half panting as quiet as I could in his ear.

"Yes, cum for Daddy, Vicious. Cum!" Donavan said with eyes shut.

"Yes, *who?*" I asked, sounding alarmed.

All motion ceased.

"I said, yes baby. What's wrong? Why'd you stop?" he asked, opening his eyes. I blinked, looking blankly at the man who was once the source of my strength. I felt weak, sick, and disgusted, all at the same time.

"Vicious, you said Vicious. Who's she? Did you fuck her, Donavan?" I asked, my voice pained with disappointment.

"No, honey. No," my husband insisted looking guilty.

"She's a stripper isn't she? That's a stripper name," I quickly remarked. Donavan furrowed his brow, stunned that I seemed to understand that. I knew I'd caught him off guard. His silence said it all.

"Me coming here, doing this to you was a big, big mistake," I said, shaking my head, wondering if I'd ever feel strong again.

Donavan reached for my right hand. I didn't want him to touch me, given that things hadn't turned out how it was supposed to. I felt alone more than ever. When he grabbed my hand, I snatched it away.

"It's no big deal. My guys and I go every now and then after work. I haven't fucked around on you—you have to believe that. All I do is watch the girls dance. They just dance. This is just a simple misunderstanding," Donavan said, struggling to convince me that his story was true.

"You called me another woman's name. That is a very big deal, and I'm certain that it's not a misunderstanding," I said, feeling insecure all over again. My self-esteem as a wife had completely disappeared, and I was also holding back from bringing up his bachelor party dirt. Still, I knew I had to be strong and keep that secret inside of me.

"Like I just said, it was just an accident. Don't make it out to be more than it is, *please*."

"And like I said, that name belongs to a stripper, doesn't it? I don't know why you find those clubs so fascinating when you have a wife and two children at home. You cheated on me. That's fucked up!" I exclaimed.

He moved close to apologize. Donavan knew I was really worked up when he heard me cuss, which I rarely did.

"Mystique, you're imagining things. I would never do something like that. You don't understand, it's work. I'm just so stressed out, I need the entertainment. It's just a fantasy. Yes, I may be a fan of that dancer, but it's you I come home to every night. Nothing else goes on in the clubs. I know how it sounds, but it's nothing like you'd think."

"Yeah, sure," I said, not bothering to reveal that I knew exactly what went down in, and out, of most strip clubs. "I understand job obligations, but CEOs, presidents of companies, and employees have lives! I work hard too, but I'm not out hanging in female strip clubs to drool over men in plastic pants. Get out of my face and just save the bull! I hate you, Donavan!" I yelled. "I can't threaten to ask you to sleep on the couch, because you do that shit every night anyway. Just go to hell!"

I quickly dressed and left him standing butt naked in his office, with his limp dick swinging like a miniature Tarzan's rope.

"Honey, come back," Donavan said.

"Bama, please! I'm not your honey, and I've heard enough. I hope it was worth it. You're an idiot!" I yelled.

Before I knew it, I'd thrown various items around his office, including an anniversary clock that I'd given to him.

I ran out of his office and straight past his nosey secretary, Patty. I think she finally got confirmation that we were having marital problems. Unable to pull myself together, the tears wouldn't stop. When I made it home I wanted to call Ayanna, then I remembered I couldn't. Plain and simple, I was an emotional wreck. Part of me wanted to call my husband and cuss him out until Jesus came back, but by the time I got home, the other part was too humiliated to talk to him. And to make matters worse my period started early, brought on by stress no doubt.

Instead of keeping my feelings bottled up inside of me, and frustrating myself by wasting tears, I decided that I was going to type his ass an email, telling him all sorts of things that were bottled up inside. But after I blew a fuse, I was struggling to decide what I wanted to say. Feeling anxious and frustrated and trying to gather my thoughts, I read some of my email. A cousin who was on the planning committee for our big family reunion the following year dropped me a line claiming that I didn't reply regarding if we would make it. I never received it though. After going back and forth in my mind about it, that's when I scrolled through my messages in the spam box, although I rarely bothered to go through the trouble. What a mistake. I did find that email about the reunion, in addition to another piece of information. When I clicked on an email with "hey there" in the subject line, that's when bad got a whole lot worse.

11

THAT MISTRESS BITCH

I got your email address from a very reliable source who told me you have been seeing Donavan for quite some time.

I would like to give you some friendly advice . . .

Accept him for who he is. He cares, perhaps loves you, but he will not settle down. If you are concerned about getting a veneral disease, use a condom. He respects that, and will use them as long as you demand it without fussing.

Stop asking for more than what he can, or is willing, to give. He's a good guy, but you will never be the only one and there are a lot!

I dated Donavan for a little while and was devastated when I found out the number of women he was involved with, and understandably so. He's smart, good looking, and a great lover. We're officially not dating anymore, although we fuck as often as possible.

He enjoys his world as it is. If you want to be in it and love him, accept him. Learn to know what you will and will not accept, but know that other women are ALWAYS going to be there.

While I'm busy sharing things with you, it would only be fair to admit that I love your decorating skills. The bedroom is especially nice, and your bed is very comfortable. Maybe I should get a canopy for my bed too. That shit is romantic as hell, and makes for great sex. It's unfortunate that Donavan pissed you off by calling out my name when you tried to get him to screw you in his office, but it is what it is. We're very close. He confides in me about all sorts of things. As soon as you left his office he called and told me the sad news. I told him how wrong he was for that, then I decided to shoot you this email right away! It's also unfortunate that he was in the shower at my place the day he took off work. I answered your text for him.

Well, at least I left you a present under your pillow. I do have a key to your house, I mean, my future house. I do believe Donavan will decide to be with me fulltime, VERY SOON. Don't worry, I keep our keys in a safe place. If you have any questions, you can hit me up. You may have found my cell number in Donavan's pocket. Oops! I forgot that I did change it. Silly me.

Life and love are gambles. You can have it all today and lose it all tomorrow, by all sorts of ways. Keep the faith. I hope you find peace.

After reading that real *classy* email, my head began to pound right away. I felt like someone had knocked me in the head with a hammer! I shook feverishly as I downloaded the attachment. All sorts of thoughts consumed me. Seeing Donavan? He's my husband! He proposed to me, I didn't propose to him. He asked me to move to his hometown, I didn't ask him to settle there. Nothing that happened between us pointed toward me twisting his arm to be with me, so what in the hell was this shit? Reliable source? How did some hoochie who can't even spell venereal disease get my personal email address? Either he told this mistress bitch I didn't even know to send this "friendly advice," or she went through his shit and decided to get through to me herself to let me know he had something on the side. I was scared and confused. I felt sick, assuming this woman could be the high-risk type, and she had obviously shared my husband in bed. How long, I just wasn't certain. All I could do was block everything out. I hunted down my bottle of Advil PM and popped three, not two, in my mouth. I was out for several hours. That way, at least I didn't have to cry.

When I got up from my nap, I found myself walking straight toward the computer room. I guess I was a glutton for punishment, but that email was still plucking with me. From working at the firm, I was aware that intelius.com could help me to cross-reference and perform an address, or phone search, using the sender's email address. If the name in the yahoo email address was indeed real, I would find it. For $7.95, I could get a one time report that included further information, such as the wench's criminal history, all addresses on file, liens, and much more. The other option was to reply with all sorts of choice words typed in bold, but I didn't want to make the typical move which was to let a person, who was out to start trouble, get the satisfaction of knowing how upset I was.

When the file revealed a picture of my naked husband asleep on his back in our bed, that's when I made that little investigative voice shut up. I officially realized that my marital problems had everything to do with a flaw in my husband's character—the exact same flaw many men have, but try and hide. The only thing better than the pussy some men are supposed to be committed to, is brand new pussy that will replace their old pussy. I couldn't believe he'd brought another woman into our home, our bed—a place that was supposed to be sacred—and even had the audacity to tell her when we had been intimate. I knew there had to be some truth to what the sender said, based on the delivery of her snide remarks.

Thus, I finally accepted a cheater won't change by force, and he sure wouldn't volunteer to man up. Even if I threw myself at my husband and opened my legs every night, he'd still creep and hunt to bang other women like the mistress bitch he obviously screwed in our bedroom. Only something ugly could come of me possibly learning her home phone number, or her physical address, so I decided to stop myself from falling into her trap, and opted not to break out my credit card to pay for that report.

I read the email three more times after I stared at what I believe was a camera phone photo, inspecting every word, period, and comma that burned my eyes and insulted my worth as a woman . . . and as a person. I felt as if I were living a nightmare, as the trust and love I had left for my husband dwindled into a serious case of hatred. It seemed as if each rung of hurt increased faster than I could blink. The only benefit was that this person who sent the email gave me a heads up and saved me the time of doing my own little investigation. My bedroom, my husband's naked ass, plus the bachelor party shit . . . I'd seen enough and decided that Donavan wasn't worth fighting for. To me, no man was worth fighting over, even if I did birth that man's babies.

I walked over to our dresser, threw our wedding portrait

that was encased in a silver frame across the room, feeling hatred build up within me as the tears came. I knew real love wasn't supposed to hurt that much, so I decided I'd buy some time because I did need to get a new gig and get my money right. I needed a good stash before leaving his trifling ass, then I'd see a lawyer about filing divorce papers, and also double check on what assets were in my name and so forth. I wanted to bleed him dry, take his kids, then take off. But first, I decided I'd stab Donavan in the back, the exact same way he stabbed me.

As I printed out the email and stored it in a secret place for safe keeping, I thought about something. By the time I got finished with Mr. Man, I felt that I wanted him to get everything back—every drop of hurt, plus interest. I became consumed with revenge, and the satisfaction of wanting him to think twice about ever pulling shit like he was pulling ever again.

12

TWO CAN PLAY MIND GAMES

By the time I finished reading that cruddy-ass email sent my way once more, I was more than happy to push my plump titties in men's faces and mouths when I worked at the club. It was sent on the heels of trying to reach out to him, so I did question the timing of my fucking and sucking quest. Putting two and two together I realized that my calls and visit probably threw off her plans that evening, since Donavan did come home, although late. My spirit told me that it was sent by some low-life desperate bitch, who Donavan was playing around with, and she was doing her piss on a fire hydrant dance, letting me know that there was another woman, and he had recently been with her. Whoever sent it hit the send button shortly after I tried to have great sex with Donavan. I suspected it was this Vicious woman. At first she did rattle my nerves, but then I started thinking a little smarter.

Although he obviously had a mistress—one or many who thought they had pussy power—I had the ring. He'd have to pay to make me leave and he wasn't trying to do that, at least not right then. At that point, I wasn't focused on the hurt and pain of what Donavan had done. I was fully in the frame of mind to seek revenge. I decided not to back down. Instead, I would listen out in the strip clubs, or on the private party circuit, for anyone named Vicious. If I ran into her ass, I planned to give her a real nice gift to remember me by. As far as Donavan, I now had the excitement of running in to him at a strip club. The excitement of getting caught made me more driven to keep hanging out near a pole.

I did need someone to lean on though, which brought me right back to Sapphire. Maybe a woman willing to listen to my woes didn't have to be such a horrible thing . . . so I thought. I began to overlook her bisexual tendencies and tried to focus on that fact that she was just a person who had been nice to me. Back then, someone was better than no one. Plus, I was bitter and in a serious man-hating mode when it came to taking the suckers seriously.

"I haven't heard from you in days. Don't go that long without letting me know you're okay," Sapphire told me.

"We're spending too much time together, Sapphire. I can't expect you to be there for me like this," I explained.

"I know, we're *friends*. How many times are you going to remind me of that? I don't like the way you sound, that's the bottom line. What's wrong? You sound upset about something."

Although I told her don't bother, Sapphire came over to comfort me before work. After I told her about some things that transpired with my husband that day, she brought me flowers and chocolates to cheer me up.

I gave her a friendly thank you kiss on the cheek. I really appreciated her concern, but a few things annoyed the hell out of me. For instance, Sapphire ordered me to fill my vase and put the flowers she gave me on my bedroom dresser. She said it would make me feel better every time I awakened and saw those pretty flowers. Second, before leaving, she held me around the waist and tried to kiss me when I went into the bathroom to wash my face. She watched my every move, then grabbed me out of the blue.

"He's proven he's being taken care of elsewhere. It's time for a plan B for us," she said, holding me around my waist.

"Stop it, Sapphire. I told you about talking like that. We're *just* friends. There is no plan B for us. Don't touch me like that. Get off of me and stop invading my personal space," I snapped.

"One day you'll want me all up in your personal space, but the invitation will be expired. My bad, I've got to be patient. Right now you're hurting."

After Sapphire left to dance her shift, I felt some sense of relief that she was gone. I was feeling extra moody because my period came on and I was retaining water slightly, which was just enough to make me feel fat and the opposite of sexy. I went to go lie down and take a nap to sleep off my depressed state, but my cell phone rang.

"Who is this?"

"You don't have my number programmed in your phone?" the voice said. "I called to see how you are."

"I'm ok, thank you," I replied. I finally realized it was Reggie from the club.

"I also wanted to be sure that you're coming tonight." I remained silent. "Tim won't be here anymore. I'm short on girls, well, not really. He took those busted bitches with him."

"Stop. That's not nice," I said.

"But it's true. I want to make sure my stars will be there. Will you?"

Reggie's flattery got him everywhere. I did agree to report to the club that evening. It continued to serve its purpose and that obviously wasn't making a lot of money. The spot was under-promoted, so I couldn't make *big* money, but the few dollars was more than acceptable to me.

"I just got back from a date, he smelled like cabbage," White Chocolate said.

"Cabbage?"

"Yeah, cabbage? Can't you hear? He stunk, girl! I think he was farting, too."

"Eeeew."

"He had a flat head and his fart smelled so bad, I thought he'd burst out in flames. Shit, I almost said fuck the money. I was about to call my ride and ask him to drop him off at an animal shelter. He was tore the hell up!"

I applied my lipstick in the dressing room, as a dancer reached down and grabbed a bottle of liquor. White Chocolate was already smoking like a steam train. The drama was thick and changed with every speaker.

"You want something to drink, Delicious?" White Chocolate asked.

"Naw. I'm trying to stop fucking around with the alcohol before I turn into a lush," Delicious answered as the other girl extended a nearly empty liquor bottle.

"What's the use now? You already are one!" White Chocolate answered.

"Look who's talking, you fart sniffing, wine-head!" Delicious said.

"For your information, I'm used to drinking champagne on my dates," White Chocolate bragged.

"Champagne and cabbage. Don't forget the brown showers you give for them sick freaks. What a good mix!" Delicious teased.

"He may not have smelled the best, but I've got money in my pocket for my time and energy, bitch. Maybe if you bothered cutting down that burning bush growing in your drawers, you'd earn enough money to get those big corns of yours professionally sawed down. You ever thought about that?" White Chocolate joked.

"Fuck you, trick! I have prettier feet than you. Who you think you are, trying to play the dozens like a sister—a member of the soul patrol? Why aren't you up in some white joint, where the girls move around in pasties and g-strings in Utah, or some place where rich bitches want to piss off daddy by stripping? You can't handle this! You outta ya league."

"Shut up, you ghetto skank. You know I am the best of the best. Are you afraid of some competition? You know I'm the most popular dancer in here."

"Please! The brothers know how the sistas get down. There's a special sumthin' sumthin' to the flavor of what we do. It can't be duplicated, but only imitated, mama. The only reason you get some brothas to dig up in your guts is 'cause you imitate me."

"That's what your mouth says, but don't get mad because I gave your man a lap dance last night. Maybe I should give him his money back, so he can lend his girl some laundry money. You do that shit every time," White Chocolate said, while smoking her cigarette. By this time she'd crossed her toothpick-like legs.

"Do what, Strawberry Shortcake?" Delicious teased.

"Don't act like you just didn't walk back and forth from the bathroom and use dish soap to wash your thongs. You never bring clean drawers—you probably carrying around a bushel of crabs in them filthy things. You're nasty!"

"Mind your business! Your man and your father don't call me Delicious for nothing! They got my crabs on their breath if I do got 'em!" she said, chuckling. Although it was toward the later part of July, Delicious had the nerve to turn on the radiator. I wondered what she was doing, but I soon found out when she laid her thongs on the radiator to dry.

"Now you know that don't make no sense. I ain't gonna fuck with your ignorant ass no more. I guess we better get dressed. It's time to make some pocket change," White Chocolate said, waving her tiny hand. She put out her cigarette.

"Pocket change, hell! I wanna make some money tonight," Delicious said, as she began looking through her bag. She had enough outfits to make me think I was at a semi-annual intimate apparel sale.

"It ain't even Thursday yet, so how you gonna make that much? You know the weekend is the time for that. Oh, I forget your trick's coming through," White Chocolate said.

"You play too much. I know you in a good mood 'cause you just got paid, but shut up! You got a big mouth to be so little. Here, you want this?" she asked, handing White Chocolate a shirt.

"Is it clean?"

"Shut up, bitch. You just fucked a man that smelled like farts and cabbage. Take it or leave it."

"I'll take it," she replied. White Chocolate leaned over to snatch it from between Delicious' long, painted acrylic nails.

Delicious and White Chocolate looked at the third dancer, who was quietly sitting near the dressing room door.

"Aren't you getting dressed, Silk? You ain't going out there to show them niggas what you workin' with or something? What's wrong with you?"

"I have to go to court. I'll be glad when it's over," Silk answered sadly. She looked Dominican to me and spoke with a slight accent.

"Oh," Delicious said after Silk poured her heart out.

Whether she realized it or not, I detected that Delicious was pleased that she'd have to compete against one less piece of eye candy. In her scheming mind, she had already probably begun counting the extra dollars before she collected them from the men. Silk got up and went into the entrance area to talk to the brothers. I ended up in that area too. I wanted to ask them to turn on some air, or at least a fan, because I was beginning to feel like a dry roasted peanut!

"I thought I was going to jail. When the police came, he played it off and grabbed the Bible. I hear they're trying to clean up that hotel," Silk explained.

"Why did you tell them anything? Don't you have a lawyer—let your lawyer talk for you," Reggie said. "You've got to be smarter and faster than law enforcement. Your mouth got you in more trouble than a $20-street walker. You should know how to talk by now. It never should've gone this far."

"I do have a lawyer. LE was asking for information . . . emails and stuff. What was I was I supposed to do?" she whined.

"You may have a lawyer, but you damned sure don't have a brain. If you had some smarts, you'd be dangerous."

Silk plopped down in a nearby chair, looking blue as she detailed her "date" gone wrong. Apparently she needed to vent and gave a fair amount of details about her computer date to Reggie. Putting two and two together I understood that she used one of several websites to advertise her services . . . and I'm not talking about dancing. I never did get to make my heat complaint since her dilemma had the partner consumed. I guess roasting a bit longer was worth it, since I left the room finally understanding that some of the girls were prostituting themselves via the information highway, and meeting men in the club.

Since no male customers had arrived yet, I wasn't busy doing much of anything besides torturing myself by watching a poorly written porn script. In the flick, some white woman told a black man that she had a hot, wet cherry that needed to be broken. She said she craved a big black dick because she always fantasized about having one. He told her that he traveled from state to state accommodating horny women just like her. I watched the man whip out an exceptionally long and thick dick, and then the woman began stretching her mouth to accommodate it, as she showed off her oral skills. I became so used to seeing porn play in the club, that I was not embarrassed that I was caught watching it when Tim came in sporting a slightly fat lip. Even though his lip was still slightly swollen, he didn't appear to be self-conscious about it. He sat down next to me and began talking.

"You're looking real good," he told me. "Real sexy."

"Thanks." I hugged him as I turned in his direction. "So you're back now?"

"No, I just stopped by."

"Are you okay here?"

"Besides this heat, I'm okay . . . I guess," I said, fanning myself. "Are you okay is the question? You really should keep putting ice on that," I commented, wondering if I should tell him about an incident I had with Reggie. When I was headed toward the dressing room to drink some bottled water that was in my bag, Reggie abruptly pulled me into one of the VIP rooms.

"I'm going to wait for you to come to me," Reggie said. "I'm not going to chase you!"

He grabbed a handful of one of my ass cheeks with one hand, and pulled my left breast out of my top with the other. Before I knew it he'd sucked my nipple until it grew hard. After that he flung me away and left. I leaned up against the wall, trying to catch my breath. While I was trying to decipher what had just happened between he and I, I could hear booty bumping and dick pumping through the thin, plywood divided wall. From the sound of things, a dancer's thighs were smacking against his legs, as she moved up and down, riding him like a horse. I couldn't hear words, just sex noises—bodies crashing and slapping. I felt safe with Tim—he had never laid a hand on me. Still, I decided to let what Reggie did slide.

"Oh this? I'm fine—just a little scrape. Are you making the money you want? How much do you need to make?" he inquired.

"I'm not, Tim. Let's just say . . . a lot. I need to make a lot more than I'm making now. I keep telling these men that all I do is dance. They just don't believe me," I shrugged my shoulders.

"A lot of contact at a cheap price is the norm, not the exception. I didn't know it would be like that in a lap dance spot. Friday and Saturday nights are the best though. I can usually make coming out a little bit worth my while before they stop wanting dances from me after they get too frustrated," I explained.

"You're a two-hundred-dollar girl. Do you hear that song? Listen to the words. When you're a bad bitch, you can get paid. Fly bitches like you can make good money. Whoever brings the most heat makes the most money in the strip game. Some of the prettiest girls make the least, because they don't know how to hustle until they sweat," he told me. "What I'm trying to say is, that there are two ways to look at this."

"What?"

"You can make much more. But . . ."

"But what?"

"Wallets go flat fast in the hood. To make that real

money on the dance tip, you need to get down with the get down in some other states. Atlanta, for example. The best strips clubs down there have ATMs in them. You got your celebrity crowd and all that shit—they'll pay you right to shake it like a salt shaker out there."

"I'm not going way out there to audition. And I'm surely not going by myself."

"A lot can be arranged in the ATL. I can have you set up in a place in midtown, get you hooked up in one of the best clubs, then you can come back with your money stacked. A lot of record folks and music artists go in there to see how the girls dance to their new shit. You never know if you could end up in somebody's video. But if you're not interested in going where the real business gets done, that's fine. I'm not ever going to push you to do anything you don't want to do. I just want to help you reach your goals. I don't want nothing from you. I don't want no sex either. My peeps take care of me. I'm just trying to help you out by using what you got, instead of giving it away for free," Tim said.

His cell phone rang and he answered it. From the tone of his voice I could tell it was a business call.

"Three to five of you looking for two thick-ass freaks to entertain at the last minute? I gotchu. I got some sisters for that—Fire and Desire. Naw, man. I can't send no face shots because they students. Of course they can make them booties clap. You want thick and nasty, so I'm sending thick and nasty. I can't say no more than that. Now I'd hate to have to hang up on you. You straight, they straight, we straight. I'll hit you back with the final details after I get out of a little meeting here. Peace." He hung up the phone.

"Those damn men know better than to get explicit over the phone. They a pain in my damn ass!" he mumbled. "So anyway, like I was saying, that narrows it down to option two. With option two, you don't have to hustle until you sweat. Yeah, you have to put in time, but not as much, and the money comes way faster. The competition is lower because the requirement to be good looking is higher. The only thing is that you'd have to do a *little* bit more than what you do now," Tim explained without missing a beat. He made a point to emphasize the word little.

"I'm not having sex. That's out!" I replied.

"I would never allow you to do anything you didn't want to do. I understand where you're coming from. You don't have to have sex to make a few hundred per client. Because of the way you look, they'd pay to be with you without sexual contact."

"Then what would I have to do?"

"Massage."

"What about it?"

"A few upscale clubs are about to be pushed out of downtown and forced to relocate. There's about to be more demand from the high rollers who like discreet service from high-end classy girls. You can make $1000 a day with the right clients—people like them can afford to pay. Some men might want to masturbate in front of you. Some may want to play with you a little bit. Some may want you to talk to them, or just watch TV while you rub them down. Others may want a hand job, while you give a topless massage, or something like that."

"I can't do massages and remain anonymous. Plus, that's not safe. How do I know those men wouldn't try to make me do more? I couldn't be the one to give a hand job, that's out of the question."

"There are ways to make sure they don't cross any lines. Most of them are lonely married men who don't want no trouble. They just want to relax and pretend that a dime-piece is their girlfriend for a little while. All you have to do is listen to them, do a little of what I told you, and be real sweet until their time's up. I would be there waiting for you. If anyone ever bothers you out here on these streets, tell them you fucks with me. The night we went to that other club, people were asking me about you. I told them I didn't know if you were down with extras or not. See, you got in their minds. By the time they figure out you don't, you've already gotten all the money they withdrew from the ATM."

"If you don't mind me asking . . . why were they asking you about me? I know we came together and everything, but—"

"I have something I should tell you," Tim explained.

"What is it?"

"I don't beat my girls, abuse them, or force them to do anything. I help women make money. I'm a pimp."

I tried not to look shocked or disappointed. The pieces all fit into the puzzle. His candid revelation explained how he knew so much, although his looks contradicted how I thought a pimp would appear. Jewelry didn't drip off of his neck, he didn't wear snakeskin shoes, and he wasn't dressed in a suit, or flashy outfit. So much for that stereotype too.

"I can handle all of your bookings. All you need to do is let me take a picture of you. I can have some appointments for you within a few days."

"No pictures. No way!" I said, still not over what he'd told me.

"Well let me take one from the neck down, just to show your body. Either that, or I can blur out your face," he told me.

When men began filling the space, our conversation was broken.

"Honey, you're on stage!" one of the brothers hollered. Although I was glad that I was temporarily off the hook with Tim, I walked toward Reggie to ask him about what I thought I heard him say.

"Me? Why not another girl who's been dancing longer?" I asked.

"What are you going to do if we book you for parties? You came from a club where they get on stage. Stop acting shy and get up there on stage!" he demanded.

"Not until someone gets some air circulating in here," I said. It seemed as if no one else thought to keep everyone cool, as Reggie turned on an old air conditioner high on the wall. It instantly began to cool down a bit. I guess he was trying to cut corners, cheap bastard!

All of the brothers stood around and watched as I shook it right to a pumping Trouble Funk tune. By the time I leaned forward, grabbed my ankles, and looked at many faces through my legs, I heard girls whispering that I was stiff and couldn't do my thing. Despite their remarks, by the time I got down, I felt like a bonafide sex goddess. Men threw enough dollars in four minutes for me to pay my $20.00 tip and have something left over to take home. I thought someone else was going to take a turn standing on top of the stage, moving seductively, but no one did. This was about keeping the girls in check and making the new girl feel special. Mind games go a long way in exotic dancing . . . a very long way.

When the next girl hit the club, she'd be the new next best thing . . . and so on and so on. These men are giving these girls some real head issues. No, they're giving themselves real head issues. Most of them have told me they've been stripping for four years or more. In some cases, since they were eighteen. From what I've gathered thus far, they also have no cars, no homes, and nothing real to show for their time in this environment. They are not self-sufficient within this vicious cycle. I'm only talking about some strippers, not all strippers, of course. These are the ones that think they know how to play the game, but really don't. They also include the ones who haven't thought of what they'd do after they got old, had no retirement, and hadn't cracked open a book since high school, that is, if they didn't drop out.

After I got down, a man grabbed me by the hand and asked me to go into the VIP room. I explained to him that all I did was what I did on the stage. The only difference could be that I'd gyrate for his viewing pleasure in the nude . . . if the money was right. He agreed, until I started winding and grinding in the booth. Midway between his fifteen minutes, he propositioned me for sex.

"I have a sister. I understand," he told me when I turned his offer down. He threw the money on the floor and left. These men simply couldn't understand that I didn't do extras, even the partners. When I came of out the VIP room straightening out my bills, Ray pulled me to the side.

"Let me holler at you a minute. Now this is just between us."

"Okay. What is it?" I asked.

"You still on your period?" Ray inquired.

"Yes," I replied. I began regretting that I let on that I had cramps the other day when he asked me. I kept complaining that it was hot in the club. Ray felt my head with the back of his hand after Reggie said I must be hot-blooded, and I told him that wasn't the reason I was feeling sick. After that, I whispered in Ray's ear what was ailing me. I guess he remembered.

"No you're not," Ray insisted.

"Whatever. What is it?"

"You want to make some money?"

"How?"

"I've got someone who wants you." He looked around

to make sure no one was walking by, or listening to what he was about to say. "Seventy-five for me, one hundred for you. No one will know."

"Tell him I'm not interested." I began to walk away. Ray pulled at my arm.

"Are you going to let all that go to waste," he asked, staring at my ass cheeks. "If you're going to shake your ass in next to nothing, then get butt-naked. You may as well make it worth your time," he added.

"This is for one man . . . and he's not here," I replied.

"Look, you might have to give him some head or something. If you don't like it, you'll never have to do it again. I won't ask you anymore."

"No," I repeated, feeling annoyed.

He was acting as if he had wax build-up in his ear. My answer hadn't changed. It was the same every time: No, no, no! He was wasting his hot breath, for sure.

"We could make some money."

"I'm a good girl. No."

After that, Reggie came walking by. "You need to be out there," he barked at me, pointing his finger toward the large room. "And you need to be up front," he said to Ray. "I'mma fire ya'll. I'm tired of this shit!"

I knew he wasn't truly in charge, so his words didn't count for much in my book.

"You ain't in charge. I'm tired of you always ordering me around. You better watch your step and tread lightly, dawg," Ray said as he walked away.

I began to notice the constant bickering and conflicts regarding managerial philosophies amongst the three men. If you said go right, the other said go left. On top of that, none of them were loyal to each other. This was yet another example of that, and the steady flow of side conversations was enough to make my head spin. We went our separate ways as soon as I quickly pushed the curtain back.

"He wants you!"

Silk sounded angry. I heard her mumble something under her breath in her native tongue, but I ignored her. It was obvious that she was jealous that I got more attention than she did.

"Thanks," I replied coolly.

"He wants change. I haven't made enough to make change!" she ranted.

As she puffed out her cheeks and headed toward the dressing room, I then understood that the man asked her to break a twenty to tip someone . . . but it wasn't her. In fact, it probably was for my benefit. I walked over in the man's direction. He was probably in his mid-fifties and had quite a gut on him. In fact, he looked pregnant with twins.

"Can you get my dick hard?" he asked bluntly.

"I think I'm good at what I do." I couldn't believe the man was so straight forward.

"I want someone to dance for my son . . . you."

"Is he shy?" I asked looking at him. His son wouldn't make eye contact with me. He looked like a tenderoni— cute and quiet. From my assessment, he hadn't been shaving, may or may not have had hair on his chest, and probably hadn't been turning down Yoo-hoo drinks too long!

"No, he's not shy," his father insisted. "It's his twenty-first birthday," he added. The man's son reminded me of a virgin, not in appearance, but demeanor. I wondered if twisted Donavan would make something like this a rite of passage for our son, Brian. I hoped not. The thought of it made my stomach turn. "Then again, I may want you for myself. I've got money to spend. Dance for me first, then you can dance for him."

After we struck a deal, and the man paid for the VIP room, I pushed the curtain back and swung my hips seductively as I sashayed inside. I obviously hadn't learned my lesson about taking a trip in one of those dark little booths. He asked me to bring a chair with me, so I dragged one along for the ride.

"Put that phat ass on me," the man said after he sat down.

I danced, removed my clothes, and then honored his explicit request.

"Now sit in that chair and open your legs. I want to see that pussy."

I faced him and opened my legs. The pervert had a flashlight in his pocket, shining it on my kitty cat like he was some sort of bootleg gynecologist!

"Never mind, you're good," he told me, turning it off.

"What?" I asked with concern.

"You should've cut the string," he said, referring to my dangling tampon cord.

"I can't. It would get stuck. I can't help Mother Nature, can I?" I reasoned.

I was a bit comforted in knowing that the appearance of my kitty kat didn't turn him off, it was just my string. *What am I thinking?* There I was getting caught up in this game on being judged on my looks and body parts. I had the power and control, and I was determined to put things back in perspective.

"Get dressed," he said, half ordering me.

As I did, I kept moving to the music to screw with his head. He changed his mind and threw down a twenty. I danced for him about two minutes before someone banged on the frame of the small room. When we came out, I saw a woman with cellulite all over her gigantic, stubby legs take the older man's son in a room. She had paw print tattoos all over her legs. The woman wasn't bad looking, just huge. As I sat in a chair on the other side of the VIP room wall, I thought I heard a steady slurping noise. To keep my composure, I got up and went to the front. I talked to Reggie about so many men wanting sex. In a way, I was playing musical chairs, all night!

"You aren't stupid, I've watched you. You're selling yourself short. I can't tell you what to do, but I can give you advice. Charge twenty dollars for a topless dance, and forty for nude. You have all the tools, but the mechanic is fucked up," Reggie told me.

I understood the concept of being eye candy, but I got tired of hearing him tell me I could pull that off because I felt otherwise. After his one-sided lecture was complete, I left and went back to the dressing room. I didn't realize he was behind me, but he was.

"Where's White Chocolate?"

"I'm not her keeper. I don't know," Delicious answered with attitude in her voice.

I walked out of the room, as if I was trying to help him find her. As I got closer to the VIP room, I saw two pair of feet—a woman's and a man's. One pair was facing the other, in a tight space. I quickly returned to the dressing room so I wouldn't have to tell what I'd noticed. When Reggie walked to the front of the club, White Chocolate suddenly appeared gripping a wad of money in her hand. The girls were bragging about how good the VIP room had been to them.

"She just let some man finger her pink pussy for $100," Delicious told me, pointing at her. I knew they were testing me to watch my reaction. I'd been in one of the rooms several times that night. They were trying to figure out what I'd done. I didn't comment. I just smiled slightly.

"That VIP room is all right . . . isn't it?" she pressed.

Once again, I didn't answer. I began packing my bag to go home and temporarily escape strip life. Thankfully, it was time to get dressed. I did manage to say one thing.

"I hope you didn't spill anything on my shoes. I saw

your feet in my shoes when I looked under the curtain in the VIP room," I said, slightly annoyed. I didn't want to lend any of the girls my heels, but I did in the name of peace. I'll never make the mistake of bringing two pairs of shoes again! What she did was her business, but did she have to do it in my sexy dancing shoes that I used my hard earned tip to pay?

"No, when I cum, I don't squirt." White Chocolate took my shoes off and handed them to me. "Your shoes hurt my damn feet! Where you get them thangs?" she asked, twisting up her face.

I felt like knocking her out. She just didn't understand how offended I was, nor did she thank me for allowing her crusty heels to sit in my shoes.

On my way out of the club, I passed Ray dumping bent up cigarette butts from ashtrays and stacking chairs. As I waved goodbye, I now understood how the girls made their *real* money in a place that didn't stay packed. I was thinking the point of men coming to the club was to entertain. At the most, I thought some would get excited, then go home and masturbate. Wrong! The girls were prostituting themselves in the back rooms, giving the brothers a cut unless they managed to sneak a man into the VIP without their knowledge. Dancing was just a means to get the men motivated to ask to take a trip to a back room—sort of like an oriental massage parlor, I guess. This revelation of seeing what really goes on, made me even more infuriated with Donavan, and I then believed his story a hell of a lot less.

I now understood that I was the only one who wasn't down with selling my kitty kat. I could easily comprehend how good girls who forgot to keep it a fantasy for men could go bad in this game. Thanks to Hollywood, rap videos, and stars who hit it big and admitted their stripper pasts, some young girls and women think strip life is so glamorous. If only they knew the part of it that extends far beyond booty shaking entertainment, they wouldn't want to live out that fantasy, or touch it with a ten-foot pole. On second thought, maybe it could be a fringe benefit for the needy like me.

Part of me still wanted to let Donavan know I wasn't sitting on my thumbs, distraught over his affair. If I had one thing to email my husband after Vicious caused his lies to fall apart, it would've been:

I've been stripping behind your back. Instead of looking at me all crazy when you realized that I knew Vicious was a stripper name, it should've made you think. But now that I know you have a mistress, it's all water under the bridge! I'm about to step up my game by having my cake and eating it too. I was too nice, so you treated me like a pushover. Let the cheating games begin . . . or in your case, continue. It's show time, Donavan. One monkey don't stop no show, even if I wear that monkey's wedding ring!
Honey

13

THE AFTER PARTY

One week later

"Where are my keys? Shit, I can't be late! The last thing I want to hear is Mr. Jiles's big mouth. I've gotta get out of here," I said, talking to myself. My heart was in my mouth the whole time I was lifting cushions, scanning end tables, and looking in various door locks. I found them at the very last minute in the most obvious place, my purse. On my way to the car, I straightened up a row of small white, plastic flowerpots that had been blown over during a windy summer rain. I turned on my headlights and windshield wipers and was off to return to work and my mundane responsibilities at the firm.

Ironically enough, after I stood up to my boss, he called me back a few days before the end of July. Something told me the work was piling up on my desk and no one else knew what to do. I knew he couldn't function without me when he apologized, and even approved of me taking the rest of my vacation days. The only reason I went back to D&R was because of my intended divorce. After I cleared my head, I realized that working in a law firm could be advantageous in the long run. I began playing chess with Mr. Jiles and he agreed a junior partner would supervise me for a while if I held off on my EEOC complaint. We called it a temporary truce.

I considered the fact that the kids would be returning home from camp in just under a month. I hadn't spoken to them too much. They were rarely quiet, and that made me nervous, so I called to check on them. When I did, they said they didn't want to leave—apparently kids can be as whimsical as men. After speaking with Brittany and Brian, I cooked myself dinner, read the paper, and listened to some old Jill Scott cuts. Donavan could've been eating steak, chopped mustard greens, and homemade macaroni and cheese whenever he got home, but no . . . he just had to act like a certified asshole!

Donavan was just taking up space in my book. He could eat greasy fast food burgers with his mistress for all I cared. When I went grocery shopping, I intentionally filled the mini-fridge with frozen food dinners, put a chain and pad lock on it, and posted a note letting him know that his food was elsewhere. He could figure out where to find it, or ask Vicious to cook his ass something real good! Two days after his slip-up, he left me Godiva chocolates on my pillow. Little did he know, Sapphire beat him to the punch when she high-tailed it over to our house with chocolates and flowers the day all hell broke loose. I knew Donavan's trinket didn't come from the heart though. He just didn't want me to divorce his paid ass and take half and his kids. There was no way his cheap ass ever would spend $75.00 on chocolates for me otherwise. He knew he was in hot water with me and that was that. How phony.

"Hey, Honey. How ya' doin', baby?" Sapphire said. I wished I never answered my cell phone.

"Just tired. This was my first week back at work. Papers

were piled a mile high on my desk. It seems like I'll never catch up unless I go in tomorrow," I complained.

"On a Saturday?" she questioned.

"Yeah, on a Saturday," I answered, then sighed at the thought of riding the elevator up to the eleventh floor of D&R.

"Will they pay you overtime?"

"Of course not," I said.

"Then why go?"

"Look, I have to go freshen up. I don't want to talk about my office job anymore," I explained.

I hung up the phone and walked to the bathroom to clean my face and take a shower. I opened my medicine cabinet and tilted my head back, as I put eye drops in my eyes. I'd developed chronic red and dry eyes because of smoke in the club and lack of proper rest. Despite it all, by the time I held my head upright, I was prepared to grab that shiny stripper pole. For all of the right reasons, I hoped that I'd proven myself to be a general, not a soldier. Staying home was not an option. I'd gotten too used to stripping under low, seductive lighting at night.

A few minutes before it was time for me to leave, Sapphire showed up at my front door.

"What are you doing here?" I asked as I looked through the glass of the storm door.

"Are you going to leave me standing here, or are you going to let your friend in?"

"Why aren't you at work?" I asked as I shut the door. "I really don't have time to socialize right now, Sapphire. In case you've forgotten, I have to go to my other gig now." I grabbed my bag and put on my coat.

"Stop acting like that. You know you're glad to see me."

"If you say so," I remarked rudely. "What are you doing here? You can't just show up like this. My kids will be back soon, and my husband could've been home."

"Lighten up. I'm going to work with you tonight. I told you I'd look out for you from start to finish in this thing. I meant it."

"Going with me, where?" I asked, playing dumb.

"Where do you think? I'm going to see my friend dance . . . show a little support."

"I don't want you going. Why would you want to see me in a compromising position, Sapphire?"

"Who said I have to look at you? I had a stressful week. I might want to get some attention from some dancers myself."

"Whatever," I commented, rolling my eyes.

I began walking toward the front door, turned the lock, and heard Sapphire close it behind her.

"Go home so I can concentrate on what I need to do," I said.

"I worked day shift today and I came straight from the club to make sure my friend was all right. You've been over here stressing. Earlier you were tripping over that trifling man of yours. Then, you're always talking about not wanting to wait in the dark by yourself. I came over here to show my face up in the club and make sure you're ok. Let me do that, okay? Damn you're bullheaded."

"And so are you . . . but worse," I replied to Sapphire. When she had her mind made up, there was no changing it.

Sapphire nearly clipped my heels following me into the club. The security guy charged her twenty dollars to get in. I never knew customers were paying so much to sit in some hard plastic chair in a hole in the wall! What men won't do for pussy. It's amazing. I proceeded to the dressing room to change my clothes. Sapphire sat in the main room in a chair, quietly sipping on a drink she'd gotten from somewhere.

Since the club wasn't popping right away, some girls were

busy calling men to come see them dance. One trick of the trade is building a customer base, and that takes time. Reggie even shot out emails from a laptop, and Tim and Ray fired up their cell phones to try and drum up business.

"Is anyone dressed?" asked Reggie. Smoke was swirling from the cigar he was holding in his right hand. "There's an African man out here who has money to spend," he added to motivate everyone to come out. When he looked around, his eyes met mine. Without uttering a word he pulled me by the arm and pushed me out of the dressing room into the main room.

Reggie walked into the area and I sat in a chair far across from a middle-aged man who was watching porn. Although he alternated between watching a woman give head, and staring at me, I was feeling timid and shy that night. I did my best not to make heavy eye contact—I just didn't feel like having much attention from anyone. A short while later more girls came out, accentuating their best features with carefully chosen outfits. For whatever reason, only one was brave enough to head straight toward the man's direction. After she danced for him, he waved me over and asked me to dance for him. As I did, he stuck dollars in my netted shorts. I questioned why he wanted the weakest one of all. I was the oldest, most inexperienced, and my outfit wasn't nearly as exciting as the others. I was wearing a military outfit with a black cover up. I eventually pulled my shorts down just over my cheeks. I bent over in his face. When I did, he inhaled my scent deeply over and over again, like he had some sort of smelling fetish. The next girl that danced for him grinded wildly and the most provocatively. The pair disappeared, and I did too shortly afterwards.

About an hour later, activity in the club picked up as men began to blow through. Many girls badgered the guys, asking them if they wanted a dance. I wasn't down with shoving my hip-gyrating services down their throats. I almost waited for a man to ask me, even though I was informed that I wouldn't make money that way. After a while, a man did ask me. I was beginning to get used to dancing for men who looked like they had a few felony charges under their belts, so I was relieved to move seductively up and down on a guy that looked clean cut. In fact, I felt like paying him for giving me the emotional break of not smelling weed on his clothes, or fighting not to get my heels caught on baggy pants legs. I danced for a few other men and the same man asked me to dance for his friend. He wore a huge cross around his neck and had on a hat. Something told me he had money to spend and he wanted to have a little clean fun. I decided that he'd be my guinea pig. I wanted to see how far I could go with a good guy . . . and so, that's what I did. I confronted my dark side . . . the side where I could test my acting ability for profit, especially since my period ended. After I got a second look at him, I realized we'd crossed paths elsewhere. It was the guy that turned me on my first time dancing at The Foxy Lady.

When T Pain's "I'm In Love With A Stripper" began to play, I straddled the stranger and softly embraced him around the neck. I inhaled deeply, enjoying the smell of Kenneth Cole Black that clung to his delicious looking skin. The music rattled so loud, it sent vibrations through the chair. I inhaled his cologne and pressed my breasts up against him, although he was wearing a thick down coat. As I moved up and down on his lap, I remembered to give him plenty of eye contact. When I got up and turned around, I smacked my own ass like I was a confident stripper with a dirty mind. To give him the first initial big thrill, I placed his right hand on my ass and directed him to smack my cheeks. I smiled as he made them jump over and over again. I could feel them redden as my ass began to sting. When he became slap happy, I smiled and winked to encourage our connection. My nipples were getting hard and my kitty kat was getting wet. I fantasized about touching him the first time, or him touching me, and then my desire turned into full-fledged opportunity. His ability to allow me to lead him was turning me on . . . for real. I could tell he wasn't a strip club regular, or macho stud out to grope a girl for a cheap thrill. It gave me pleasure to show him how to enjoy "the experience," the erotic way—by mimicking an authentic one.

I turned around once more, then slithered over another chair. I sat down facing him and opened my legs in the shape of a wide "V." It wasn't what I did, but how I did it. I focused my gaze on him. I held my sweet looking lips open so he could see everything it was made of. When he caught a look at my pinkness, he shook his head back and forth, staring at it like he could imagine his supple shaft stuck deep inside of it. He began letting dollars drop from his fingertips, as I moved my legs in various positions along with the beat of the music. When the next song began, I slid down in the chair and softly began to caress my clit like I was trying to get off. My own fingers acted as the toy that would be secretly used in private. I made my big lips open and close to the beat of the music while holding my legs apart. After that trick, I rubbed my purring kat gently. More dollars began to fall around me. I winked at the stranger again, then I began licking and sucking my own nipples so aggressively, anyone could've sworn that this was wild bachelor party footage captured on tape. That's something I rarely did, but it earned me another shower of dollars that lasted so long, he was fiending for change so he could tip me more. The DJ went to the front of the club and made change for him. After he did, I smiled warmly and winked at him again. I held my legs open and continued stroking my clit until my kitty cat grew slippery and wet. I got so excited that I began sucking one of my nipples at the same time. Within seconds, at least ten ones left his hands. I moved closer to him and locked my legs around his waist.

"You're teasing me," he said, smiling.

I winked again like he had my heart.

"Are you in love with this stripper?" I asked playfully, half smiling.

I knew my eyes were sparkling just right, giving him the fantasy the pimp spoke of. I was having fun with it—with him—and my sexual power as a woman. By that time, so many dollars covered the floor, the DJ periodically walked by and kicked them in a pile around my chair. I didn't want to break eye contact, so I never picked them up to put them in my garter belt. I was in a zone where I tuned out everyone but that man.

For my grand finale, I flicked my tongue as I closed my legs and opened them. When I reopened them, I gently stroked my clit and sucked my own juices. He was mesmerized and rewarded me by throwing more dollars on the floor. Smarter than the average "customer," the stranger recognized that he had no commitment and I had no obligation to act out any sex acts. Still, he was turned on and we continued our private show while the other girls did their sets on stage and the bright lights being turned back on as loud hip-hop music blasted. The only thing that broke our groove was me hearing someone on the mic announce that all girls would have to do sets. After the last person did her thing, I knew it was time for me to say goodbye. I hugged the generous customer and grabbed all of my dollars. In fact, he even helped me collect them before I rushed over to the stage to dance my set.

That night must've been my time to shine. Although I

was new on the scene, men were tipping me like I had done some mind-boggling tricks. At some point I turned in the stranger's direction, winked, and looked at him playfully. He was drawn to me like a magnet. I could tell me wanted to touch me, just one more time.

"Be strong," his friend advised him, as he watched me slowly wind my waist, making my stiffening nipples protrude.

Although he was warned, he walked up to the stage, smacked me on the ass hard, then tipped me three more ones. He also gave me his card with a number written on the back of it.

"Come here often?" I asked, then winked.

"Sexy, classy, nasty. No, I don't come here often, but hell yeah I remember you."

"Funny you should say that because I remember you too. Is that how you greet a lady, by smacking her on the ass like that, Daddy? " I replied, flirting. I was glad to see my admirer, although I tried to play it cool.

"Oh no you don't. I'm not letting you get away this time. My cell phone number is on the back. Call me so we can get together and have some real fun, Miss Lady."

"Real fun, huh? Let me be the judge of that, *if* I call. I have a man," I said.

"I'm not afraid of a little competition. Are you?" he said, running his fingers over his wedding ring. "Just don't let any other dancer find it this time. This is a standing invitation for you, and you only."

"Confident, honest, and open . . . I like that," I told him, winking.

"I know what I want, and I like what I see. Something about you is different. I like that. We need to get together at least once. I promise you won't regret it. Do yourself a big favor and make time to call your Daddy. We need to discuss some adult things in private," he said, pushing his business card into my right hand, then closing my fingers shut around it.

This simple act led to a few more men copying what he'd done. When my set ended, I had so much money and so many numbers torn from paper bags and scraps of paper, I couldn't believe my eyes. The stranger brought over his summer hat to use as a money bag, but took it upon himself to leave the other numbers on the floor. He and the DJ stuffed money in it as quickly as possible so the next dancer could get onstage. I'd been tipped another thirty dollars or so. After they gathered all of the money for me, one of them shoved the hat in my hand as I swiftly exited the area. My heart was pounding as I shot into the bathroom, and then into the dressing room. Girls stared me down as I sat in a chair and kept pulling ones out of the stranger's hat. I could feel the hate when the DJ asked me to give him all of my ones. I counted out ten ones at least ten times. We traded money. He put a rubber band around his and I secured mine in my garter. I felt three sensations at the same time: a sheer rush of pleasure, shock, and thankfulness. I knew that I'd done rather well for a novice.

"We need to do a girl-on-girl show and we've only been on stage once," White Chocolate complained.

I ignored them while freshening up, sprayed more body splash on myself, then I walked back out into the main area. When I returned, I saw White Chocolate and a dancer I didn't know putting on a serious dildo show. The men gathered around gawking as they slid the dildos in and out of their kitty kats, while fondling, kissing, and spanking each other. One customer walked up to one of the girls, and White Chocolate positioned herself on all fours then began groping and licking the man's jeans in the crotch area. The problem was that the men were being cheap. Tips were lean. Although the girls in the club had the dance moves down pat, and were willing to perform more exciting acts than I was, they'd missed something. They'd forgotten that strip life is about giving men a fantasy. And within it, too much is worse than too little. On stage is not the time to give or receive pleasure. That is the one sacred time that you can quietly harvest your crop without touching or being touched.

Little did I know, Sapphire saw everything that I'd done with my "special" customer. Although it was nearly three-thirty AM, the day's events were hardly over. A slither of the truth was about to rear its ugly head, riding on the back of something called sexual tension.

On the way home from the club I experienced a natural high. From what Ayanna told me about the research she'd done, I knew that the first month at any strip club is the most difficult period to profit and adjust. I felt slightly encouraged that I'd surpassed my typical meager earnings. By no means had I cleared a grand, but I took a step in a better direction. Sapphire and I discussed the club environment and her opinion of each brother. She told me to tell the partners that *she* was my pimp. She insisted that if I did that everyone would back off and stay the hell outta my pussy. All the partners did inquire to find out who Sapphire was, but I didn't think they thought it was because they feared her being my pimp. One even asked me if she was my sister. Why, I don't know.

Although I was tired and depleted, Sapphire and I were both curious about how much money I'd made. As soon as we got settled in my place, she said, "Give me the money so I can count it."

I turned on the light and dumped the stash on the floor in a messy pile.

"Here," I said, handing it to her.

"You hold it, I count," she explained, as we bent over the pile of money.

I complied as she straightened out each bill and counted it. When she finished, I had about $610. Sapphire placed the money on a small coffee table off to the side.

"It's something how pictures of these dead white men make the world go round," Sapphire said. "How much are you putting away for your future?" she asked.

"Sapphire, I don't have to do this for money. It's more for the thrill of it all and some other things."

"I want you to hear something," Sapphire told me, grabbing her cell phone out of her pocket. She dialed some numbers, then pressed the phone to my ear. "Listen to this," she told me.

"Your available balance is $40, 527.32," an automated voice said.

I handed the phone back to her.

"Did you hear it?" Sapphire asked.

"Yes," I answered.

"What did it say?"

"That your balance is forty grand, plus a few dollars and cents or so."

"I didn't let you hear that to brag about what I saved. I let you hear that to inspire you. Always put something away for you. Pay yourself first, even it's forty dollars. If you want me to, every week I'll come over and collect what you want me to put aside. I'll hold it in my bank account for you. I don't need it, you heard that for yourself. I also let you hear that for another reason."

"Which is?" I inquired.

"Let's build something together. I want to invest in you. I was serious about wanting to be your manager. If you let me market you, you can make some real money. I do it and so can you. I've made contacts beyond The Foxy Lady. You've got to get hooked into private VIP clientele. Do what you do in a controlled environment with men who have something to lose. I've got money saved from doing that, and I want you to know I'm serious. You don't have to make chump change at this, Honey. If you put the time in, you may as well reap the profits. With your looks, you can go far. No one has to know but us. Not your kids, not your husband, just us. In fact, if you don't want to use the money for yourself, you could use it for your kids' college funds or something."

I didn't answer Sapphire because I still didn't know how to read her. It was something about her that didn't sit right with me. She moved so close to me, our thighs touched.

"I noticed your legs are thicker and your ass has a little extra jiggle. Keep your weight up, it looks good on you. Keep eating, I love that you have something to hold on to."

I'd been making love to Soy Raspberry Yogurt, ice cream, high-calorie potato chips after three AM, and anything else I could get my hands on. Food had replaced sex. In fact, I'd gained three pounds in one week.

"You have beautiful eyes. They're beautiful . . . you're beautiful, Honey."

"No I'm not. I'm just a regular girl. I don't even know why anyone would tip me. I'm still fighting to rake leaves when my husband isn't around to do it, and making sure I put oil in the right place in my car. I just dance to escape my life at home. In fact, I don't know how much longer I can live like this."

"You've got to shake those demons. You have kids and you still look good! Plus, you have a good heart. Why are you settling for someone who isn't giving you the attention you need, anyway? I'm not hating on the brother, but that man never gave you the respect you deserve. If you save up the money I spoke of, you can move the hell on."

"My husband never saw me as true wifey material, just someone to cook, clean and push out his kids. Let's just chill. I don't want to talk about all of that," I said.

"Exactly. Always go by what you see. It's always about what a man does and never what he says. If it was really right, he would've made time for you and not been so selfish. When people change, you gotta change right along with them. He's got to be out of his damn mind to let this go. They tip you because of all this. Men see what I see."

"All of what?"

"You need to listen closely because I'm serious," she told me. "You're more than just a pretty face, and I'd love to have you in my life in every way. The most beautiful thing about you is your mind, Honey. You're like me; the only thing you really want is a chance to trust what you're feeling with someone worth their salt. And why did you give that motherfucker in the club your number anyway? Don't be doing that shit, it made me jealous."

This time, she pressed her juicy lips against mine. Her kisses became hard and passionate, beyond what they were the first time we'd played in each other's mouths.

"No, Sapphire. Don't. No," I said, begging her to stop, pushing her away.

"Shhh," she said softly. "Come on now. No matter what you're going through, it doesn't mean that you stop being a woman." She unbuttoned my shirt and began kissing my neck, then the corners of my mouth. "Aren't you tired of the same old thing?" she asked.

I didn't answer because I didn't want to admit that my panties were soaked.

"Variety is the spice of life," she said, squeezing my left breast with one hand, as her other hand crept toward my panties "Maybe this will help you decide to try someone new who can help you get your groove back. I want to be the one to help Honey get her groove back. You know what I'm sayin'?" Sapphire said while checking to see if I was wet.

Sapphire undressed too. She caressed my face, then positioned mine between her breasts. As I rested my head on top of her plush pillows, I found myself wondering what it would be like to touch her body from head to toe. Next, she pushed me from her body, then began sucking on my nipples. I gasped with pleasure as I considered pinching and sucking hers, just before she started sucking mine like a newborn baby to a bottle.

"There's no need to let all of this loving go to waste," she said, kissing the corners of my mouth again. "There's nothing wrong with giving your body the pleasure it needs."

This time, Sapphire stuck her tongue in my mouth and gave me a long, passionate French kiss. The long kiss was so soft, warm, and very wet. After our tongues rested, all I could do was stare at her, blinking my eyes.

"Get some candles, let's go into your bedroom. Your husband, men in the club, all of them turn us into objects. I don't even like men that way, and after peeping your game, I know I'm not alone. You are playing with those men's heads for some reason you haven't told me. Sapphire is a master at playing that game when I'm working my shift, but right now, this is real. That man that tipped you so good back there just wants you for sex, so I hope you plan on dropping his card straight in the trash can. Don't trust him. Like I told you before, every man that visits a strip club fantasizes about banging a stripper's back out. But I care about you, and all I want to do is bring out the best in you in every way," she said.

Over and over again, my mind wanted to tell my mouth to tell her to stay on the couch, but I couldn't shake the thought of making love to Sapphire. I really hadn't bothered to consider that the drinks she had with men in the club, the kisses she planted on their cheeks, and her pole twirling skills were strictly business moves. She deceived men to get what she wanted while getting back at them. Part of me liked that she was smart enough to toy with their emotions and profit from it. Her tight game turned me on more.

As my thoughts became jumbled, my kitty kat was doing the thinking, and I was in the mood to play a little dirty. First, Sapphire and I laid in bed together, just kissing each other while exploring our different bodies, as we took turns getting on top.

The next thing I knew, we were feeling each other up in my Jacuzzi. Sapphire was pressing my breasts together, and I was playing with her clit under the bubbles. The water made a swooshing noise when she opened her legs a bit wider, allowing me to move in on her. Next, I got on my knees, sliding in between Sapphire's legs, rubbing my nipples against hers as I kept playing with her love button. I guess she liked that, because she kissed me passionately, then clung to me in such an erotic way. She had me wondering what would happen next.

After about thirty minutes of foreplay, Sapphire found a clean towel in the linen closet, some massage oil in my bathroom, and lit two more candles that were sitting on my dresser. She dried me off and I returned the favor to her. She then told me to lay down on the bed. That's when she massaged my feet with Burt Bee's Coconut Foot Cream, and told me she'd pay for me to get another manicure and pedicure if I wanted one. After she did that, she returned to the room with a small hot towel that she lay across my neck, working on my tight shoulders. After it cooled, she dried me off with a large towel, then gave me a sensual, full-body massage making my back good and slippery with cinnamon essence oil. My kitty kat began to get wet from her touch. Next she caressed my ass, kneading my cheeks, rolling them between her hands, again and again. Next thing I knew she was playfully slapping my skin. As I began to breathe heavily, she kissed one cheek at a time, then began licking the small of my back down to the crack of my ass. As tingles shot through my body, Sapphire finally reached down and touched me in the gentlest way.

"You're so wet. You liked all that, didn't you?" she asked as she stuck her finger inside, pleasuring me a bit more.

"Your turn," I said, finally admitting that I wanted to feel her up in return.

I grabbed the oil and asked her to turn over on her back. After I lubed her up well, I began sliding around on top of her with my entire body.

"Damn, baby. That feels real good. I never had anyone do anything like this before," she murmured. I continued gliding over top of her, face to face, until the pleasure of it all became too intense when I brushed by her clit a few times. "Honey, don't you want something else now? I'm sure that I can please you. I might even turn you out," Sapphire cooed.

"Wait a minute, here. I'm not in the position to want anything else, so I hope you enjoyed your massage, Sapphire," I whispered in her ear as I lifted myself from on top of her. I pulled the covers up to cool down and catch a few winks. I didn't even care if Donavan walked in on us sleeping in bed. I was just feeling that bold.

The next thing I knew Sapphire pulled the covers off of me, slid down between my thighs, then licked them several times.

"Can I drink that up?" she asked next, gently resting her finger on my juicy clit. I didn't answer right away, so Sapphire parted my legs open, slid down to my kitty kat, and stopped. "How does it feel to have your clit licked? I love to eat good clean pussy like yours," she mumbled in a sexy voice.

"Ain't no shit a woman can do for me. The kiss and massage was nice, but—"

Sapphire cut me off, her tongue swirling around in the crevices of my wetness, giving me my first female vagina French kiss.

"Oh shit!" I said as my legs began to tremble.

She slid her tongue inside of my gushing pool, filling her mouth with my juices as I moaned. By the time I started screaming "fuck me, fuck me, yeah," I could tell she was a master pussy licker with a platinum tongue! I started licking my own nipples, realizing that Sapphire made me eat my own words. She was doing something for me beyond anything that Donavan had ever done.

"Mmm," I moaned as Sapphire sucked on my clit as the candles flickered.

"You like that, baby? I knew you would," Sapphire said, giggling a little. I giggled back.

She acted like she was trying to scoop me up, so I turned on my stomach. When I made it to my knees, she told me to move near the edge of the bed. When I did, she pumped one of her fingers in and out of my pussy. When my pussy began to make that talking sound, she stuck her tongue inside of my kitty kat from the back, while smacking my ass.

"Forget your man!" she told me. "He's no good for you," she remarked.

As she ate me from the back, I had noticed the candles went out, and we played around in total darkness.

"Oh shit. Shit. I'm cumming," I said, my body feeling like a mass of jelly.

Sapphire didn't pay me any attention. I enjoyed multiple orgasms as she instructed me to get in various positions. Pleasure consumed me. After hours upon hours of passionate play, Sapphire fell asleep with her tongue right on my stomach.

I know it seemed cold, but I just couldn't bring myself to go all the way with another woman. I'd be lying if I said I didn't enjoy all of that girl-on-girl action. All of that being served made me want to get with someone who owned a dick. Despite what Sapphire said about men wanting to use strippers to fulfill their sexual fantasies, the man who gave me the business card was at the top of my current to-call list. I didn't remember his name, but I finally decided to find the card I'd locked up in the glove compartment of my car to see if the one I was looking for was, or wasn't, available for a very early morning creep. Plus, it would've been rude not to return the stranger's hat . . . right?

14

MASS CONFUSION

"This is your morning wake up call. Get your butt out of that bed! I know you're probably still sleeping. I did a little over time last night at a private gig, so I ain't get done dancing until three-thirty this morning. Hopefully things went well for you. I plan on coming over there tonight so I can spend a little time with ya. Look on your step. I left a little something out there for my girlfriend. When you get this message, let me know how it went at your club last night, and holla at ya girl," Sapphire said cheerfully on the message the day after our private encounter. I had been sleeping.

I soon learned that staying up late at night, keeping stripper hours, was no party. I didn't see how the girls did it, then managed to deal with life during the day. When I stirred, I didn't call Sapphire back. Holding the cell phone in my right hand, I rubbed my eyes with my left, as my body craved coffee. Although I passed the kitchen for a jolt of caffeine, I managed to move enough to make it to the front steps. As I yawned and open the door, I found a bag. I picked it up and found a new Ann Taylor business

suit and two pairs of Seven jeans in it. I sighed and decided I'd return the items to Sapphire. I didn't like the
way she used the word girlfriend, and I also didn't want
her helping me with the club scene too much. I went to
the next message.

"Daddy needs to get with you, baby. You know who this
is." It was the guy with the business card. Rafiq. We'd
popped a bottle of Cristal, I spat on his tool and shined it
up real good to give him the best head action his dick ever
enjoyed. He did bang my back out real good, and I
brought in the beginning of August the right way by properly solving my "I ain't getting no booty" problem! Afterward, it was on and popping. Whenever we could, we
would slip away from home and do the damn thing.

I wasn't bothered by Rafiq hitting me up for another
round of getting down, but I did need a break from that
annoying Sapphire. Still, Ayanna was the only one I really
did want to talk to. Despite what we were going through, I
missed her presence in my chaotic world, and I wanted to
feel that comforting sisterly love.

"Let me start by saying that I don't want to lose you or
the great relationship I had with my sister over something
stupid. If I do, I could never replace you—no one can take
your place," I said. I can't remember a lot of the conversation, but much of it was spent pouring out my heart, exposing my insecurities, and crying. I cried so much that
my nose sounded stopped up. I wasn't playing . . . I really
cried out every fear, piece of heart, frustration and negative feeling I came to mind.

"Don't cry, sweetie. Don't—"

"I'm sorry. I just can't help it. I feel so alone and I miss
you so much, Ayanna. I didn't intend to call you and cry
like this. I really apologize. I did get my old job back, but
I've decided to get a divorce after I save up some money.
I'm just scared about so much, and I don't know what to

do. I couldn't believe you turned your back on me. You are so important to me and I *still* love you. We're sisters, forever," I rambled.

"Call me later. I'll come spend the night. Do you want me to?"

"I just heard it's supposed to be breezy with showers and thunder storms through the night. It's up to you, but I understand if you don't want to come out in bad weather. The kids are still away and I've been so lonely. Donavan, well he . . . when you and I weren't talking, he . . . I tried to . . ." I told her as I sniffed, struggling not to completely break down and cry uncontrollably.

"Never mind about him. I can already tell something's wrong again. We'll talk and I'll spend the night, ok sis?"

"Ok. Thanks, Yana," I said, pushing my hair behind my left ear.

At eleven-fifteen Ayanna called to let me know she was on her way over. I showered, left a message for Sapphire, and hid the shriveling flowers she gave me a while back in a junky closet.

"I'm having company tonight. I'll call you in the morning. Have a good night," I said as I heard the light rumbling of thunder roll in the background.

Ayanna made it over just before it started raining cats and dogs. Without speaking, we embraced. The way we hugged each other was mutually genuine. It was obvious that we both wanted to squash the argument that drove us apart. I told Ayanna what happened at Donovan's job, and she agreed that it was humiliating. I think she assumed I was still stripping, but had promised herself that we weren't going to get off track again by arguing over our differing view points.

After talking a while, and catching up on life, we enjoyed the beautiful solitude. I could hear Ayanna beginning to drift off to sleep. Suddenly, my home line began ringing off the hook. The person kept calling and calling like an emergency was in the works. Luckily, I'd turned my cell phone off.

"Should I get that or will you?" Ayanna asked.

"You can get it if you want. I know the kids are fine, so I'm not concerned about it," I answered. Neither one of us moved. We were so tired after talking. Just as we were beginning to get comfortable again, the ringing resumed. I guessed that the caller had tried my cell phone already.

"Who is that?" she asked while pressing the light on the clock to see the numbers.

"It must be my friend who works the night shift," I admitted. It had to be Sapphire, I could feel it in my bones. We heard someone alternating between banging at my door like they wanted it to cave in, and ringing the doorbell like getting someone to come to the door was a matter of life and death.

"Who is that?" Ayanna asked again.

"I told you, just a friend who checks on me."

"Who is this so-called friend? I want to know! You never have anyone coming over here like this. And it can't be Donavan, he has a key. Something's not right with this picture," Ayanna reasoned, jumping up barefooted, wearing nothing but a long T-shirt.

Sapphire banged on the door until I grew irritated. I knew she saw a car parked behind mine, so she knew I had company. She knew it had to be my husband or someone else. Now she was trying to make me look bad. I was livid that she tried to make me look like a liar. I didn't get up to answer the door and discouraged Ayanna from doing so. She wasn't going to at first until Sapphire began banging on the window while screaming my name as the rain poured. Then she resumed banging on the door, while yelling for someone to open up and let her in.

"Who in the world is banging on this door like they're

trying to break it down?" I heard her holler. "What in the hell are *you* doing here?" Ayanna shouted when she saw Sapphire.

"Can't speak?" Sapphire answered. "Boy, you do get around don't you? Since we broke up you just jump from one set of sheets to the next, although you couldn't commit to me. My new girlfriend lives here and you better not be fucking her!"

"Hold the fuck up. You need to stop telling sick lies. My sister lives here, so just leave and stop trying to start trouble."

"I'm not lying," Sapphire said shaking her head. "I'm here to see Honey," she insisted.

"What! You better not be sleeping with my sister! I swear I will kill you," Ayanna shouted.

"Well, I guess I fucked sisters then. No biggie. Why not keep all the lovin' in the family?" Sapphire said, shooting a devilish grin my sister's way.

"You better watch what you say to me! Don't you think you've done enough damage, bitch!" Ayanna taunted.

"No I don't, and you're the bitch!"

After that I heard nothing but the sounds of a wild cat-fight. I ran into the room and found two women rolling around on the floor, going for each other's throats like they were third-graders duking it out for the last ice cream sandwich. Arms, fists, and feet were flying fast in every damn direction.

"Hey, hey. Now wait a minute! I will not have that in here. Stop it, both of you," I said, prying them apart. I held Ayanna back, but she still lunged at Sapphire. I'd never seen her act like that before.

"Well I'll be damned. I guess the apple doesn't fall far from the tree!" Sapphire remarked as I pinned Ayanna's arms behind her.

"How do you know her, Mystique? Tell me now," Ayanna said.

"We, we . . ." I stuttered, as I led her to the couch, ordering her to take a seat.

"Yeah, tell her how I've been licking your pussy, looking out for you, having your back in the clubs. Just tell her you're bisexual. Why you gonna hide your freak now?" Sapphire asked me.

"I should bust your lip wide open," Ayanna exclaimed, springing to her feet. She balled up her fists like she wanted to start fighting again.

"Oh yeah. Same shit I did with you, I did with her," Sapphire taunted.

"I told you to stay out of the clubs, Mystique. All of this has really gotten out of hand," Ayanna told me while walking toward Sapphire.

"Don't you pretend like it's all her fault. And speaking of out of hand, tell her. If anyone has experience in being out of hand, I think that would be you. Go ahead, hit me. Cop a charge," Sapphire threatened.

"I have nothing to tell my sister," Ayanna snapped, backing down. "I have no problems taking this outside to finish your ass whipping. Why don't you just get out of here before I hurt you? Out of respect for my sister, I don't mind copping a charge if I light into your ass outside."

"You're not going to tell her that you and I used to live together? You're not going to tell her that we used to have a relationship? You're not going to tell her how you were *really* getting your money for school, hmmm?" Sapphire said, crossing her arms with a devilish grin. "This is your sister's house. If my woman wants me to leave, let her say it."

"Shut up you coke head. My sister didn't fuck you, you wish. Don't flatter yourself. Stop telling lies. Just get out!" Ayanna screamed.

"What do you want, baby? Do you want me to leave?" Sapphire asked, turning toward me.

"I won't stand for this raucous in the place where I raise my children. Ayanna, stay here and don't you move one inch. And you, come with me so we can settle this mess without you two ripping each other to pieces."

I pulled Sapphire to the side by her collar, pretending I'd listen to her in private, just to get her away from Ayanna and retrieve something that belonged to her. I shut my bedroom door, then I lit into Sapphire like nobody's business.

"Quite honestly, I shouldn't have been prancing around here half-naked when you came over, telling you about my personal problems, then letting you up in my bed like we were cuddle buddies. Even if I slipped up a little, this was never a competition. I told you from the beginning that I loved my husband, so don't act like that wasn't the case. You're wrong to come over here unannounced," I explained.

"Baby, don't leave me like this. We can work this out, I know we can. I'm begging you, please. I love you," Sapphire said with sad eyes. She moved close to me and tenderly wrapped her arms around my body. I pushed her away.

"How can I leave you if I was never with you? And you what?"

"I said *I love you*. There, I said it. I love you," Sapphire told me.

"Look, I appreciate you spending time with me, but this . . . all of this is just wrong. I have a husband, and you knew that from the gate," I said.

"It's your pussy, and he's not taking care of it. What is wrong with you? I know you've got to see that."

"Honestly, you're just too needy and clingy for my taste. You told me you'd never make problems for me and my husband if he and I tried to work it out. Now you cross the line and come in here acting like we didn't have that conversation, just because I did a little experimenting the other night. On top of that, I find out you and my sister had some kind of dealings with each other. I'm not into women, Sapphire. I like what I like, and what I like is dick. That's why I married a man," I said, grabbing clothes Sapphire gave me from the hangers, then stuffing them in a few empty shopping bags that I grabbed from my walk-in closet.

"Here! You obviously didn't give me these things from the heart, so I don't want them. I didn't take the tags off of them yet, so I'm sure you can return it all. Take this stuff out of here with you," I hollered, pushing the bags in her hands.

"Get out!" I yelled, pointing at the door. "I will report you to the police if you ever set foot on my property again! You are no longer welcome here, ever. I think you've done enough damage by bringing confusion into my home."

"Oh, so you're going to gang up on me without even knowing the whole story? I see how you are," Sapphire said, looking mad enough to start foaming at the mouth.

"This isn't over, Honey. You'll be sorry," she told me, opening the door.

"Please, little girl, give me a break! I'm not scared of you. I don't know what kind of baggage you have, but I'm already sorry for trying to befriend strip club trash like you. Just stay out of my life. That's all that matters."

I slammed the door after her and the whole room shook. Afterwards, I heard Sapphire cussing loudly, then the squealing of car tires. Once she was gone, I turned to Ayanna.

"Are you ok?" I asked.

She was crying and wouldn't talk to me.

"Sweetie, what's happened?" I asked.

"If I tell you everything, you've got to promise that it won't leave this room," Ayanna said, hanging her head down.

"I promise," I said, stroking her hair gently. "If it helps, I'll tell you everything, too."

Ayanna got up, went to get her purse, then pulled out the same journal she had before. She flipped through some pages, then sighed.

"Read days fourteen through seventeen. This time I'm giving you permission," she said, handing me the journal without making eye contact. She then walked into my bedroom and curled up in a fetal position on my bed.

I sat on the edge of the bed, and rubbed her back in circles like I did my daughter when she often climbed in bed with me after a nightmare or thunderstorm. Ayanna looked as scared as Brittany, leading me to wonder what secret she had been hiding. I gulped as I began reading the first diary entry. And what I was reading led me to decide that poor Ayanna didn't need to hear the truth about Sapphire . . . or the news of my real lover, Rafiq. Everything was suddenly falling part.

Just everything.

Day 14 in the life

Dear Diary,

I hope that everything that doesn't make sense today, will someday. So far, that hasn't happened. Today is Easter Sunday and I feel like shit on a stick. Thanks to the pain of rejection, I've been so depressed that I haven't answered the phone, taken a shower, or checked my email in days. I tried to shake off some of the blue funk by working up the courage to try to do a few productive things today. I used my last drops of gas to get to my P.O. Box, which is an hour away from my new location. I took the ride to clear my mind and see if anyone wrote me since I've been missing in action in the book business. Well, my damn keys didn't work. I came home and checked my receipt and realized I was four days late paying my box rental fee. Where will I get forty dollars for that? On my way home, I swung by a Chinese spot near a mall where I used to sign books. I ended up splurging on egg foo young and shrimp fried rice. On my way inside of my place, my neighbor spotted me.

"Did you make it to church?" she asked. She was a little old lady who made sure she drove herself to Catholic Church each, and every, day. She always moved so slowly and needed to grab onto things to steady her balance. I often wondered how she did it and admired her spunk. This neighbor also reminded me of the grandmother I never had.

"No Ma'am. I didn't make it this time," I answered in my most respectful voice.

"Well God is still with you," she replied sweetly. "The Lord loves us all, chile. Never forget, He loves us all. God is good all the time. Man will let you down, but God will never let you down. May He bless you always."

"Thank you, Ms. James. It was nice seeing you. Have a good rest of the day," I answered as I continued up the steps. As far as I was concerned, God turned his back on me which didn't motivate me to lift my arms to praise Him. I know this was a wrong way to think, but bitterness and frustration led me there. I felt abandoned by God, no matter how hard I tried to cease all negative thoughts about the Creator.

When I shut the door and locked it, I grabbed a paper plate and filled it up at least three times. I struggled to enjoy my food, as I faced the reality that my ex wouldn't at least check on me on Easter Sunday. X was out of the picture, as well as my so-called boyfriend. Strip life was all I felt I had although I could see what it did to my life in just a short time.

After stuffing my face, I tried to take the edge off of my loneliness by turning on my PC. I never should've checked my email, because reading a certain message added to my empty and glum feelings. Just as I suspected deep down in my gut, I didn't land the job that I interviewed for during the previous week. I gave it my best, and that was all I could do. I'm sure someone else would enjoy that $30 per hour. It's just not my time, I supposed. Why God, why?

Hi Ayanna,

I wanted to follow up with you on behalf of Mr. Hughes. He has come to make a decision and, unfortunately for us, we will not be able to bring you on as a ghost writer for Distinct Diamonds. Please know that Mr. Hughes was quite impressed with your skills, as we had more than 150 candidates apply for this position, and had the difficult process of selecting just 10 candidates for an interview.

We so appreciate your taking the time to apply for this position, and we regret that we could not choose all of our interviewees. If anything changes from our end, we will certainly let you know. In the meantime, please stay in touch. We will keep your information in our files for possible future projects.

Sincerely,
Mary Peters
Promotions Manager & Executive Assistant
Distinct Diamonds

After reading another neatly packaged rejection, I lost all traces of faith and optimism. I beat myself up and feared how I would pay my bills toward the end of the month. I walked back into the kitchen and sighed as I cracked open two fortune cookies. The fortune was pure bullshit. The second message stuck in my mind. It said something like: "You can have anything you want, if you want it desperately enough."

I laughed aloud and grabbed by cell phone to check my messages. I only had one.

"'Dis Cash. I got a whole bunch of new dudes in here for this Easter, locked-door party event. I need your help. I need you come up here and get some of this money. I got some heavy hitters in here. We not at The Foxy Lady. I spent some ends in this location, and I don't want these niggas roll out. I'm looking for a certain type tonight, and that's you. If you need some gas, I gotcha baby. I'm waiting on you to call, so I can tell you the address of where you need to be. Peace."

After hearing that message, something hit me. I suddenly felt wanted and needed. I called to find out where everyone was. I showered, put a sexy little stripper outfit on, turned on some music, then was on my way. After the beat dropped I moved more easily than I'd ever done. I explored my new moves that I'd worked out, then poured a glass of wine. After I seduced myself in front of a mirror for at least a half an hour, I got tired of looking at my own image. I suddenly felt the uncomfortable weight of loneliness drop on my shoulders, and was reminded that I had nothing, and no one. I guessed that I may as well grab my little bag, fuck-me pumps, and turn into a "get that money" chick tonight.

Day 15 in the life

Dear Diary,

I never anticipated the next twist. The music was bang-ing. Champagne bottles were popping. The mansion where the locked-door party was being held was hooked up with all sorts of party decorations and favors. Even I was im-pressed by finding out that Cash did have some good taste, although The Foxy Lady needed a make over, real bad.

Clientele appeared to mostly include men with money, big hustlers, doctors, lawyers, and other professionals—at least from what I could gather. It did have the feel of a locked-door adult fantasy party, by invitation only. I didn't see any of the regulars or locals who typically blew through to take their edge off of marital loneliness, or have a sip of liquor before negotiating a VIP visit. Then again, it was a special night. Maybe all of this was geared toward a certain crowd.

The aroma of weed was thick and overpowering like Los Angeles smog. I went to the bathroom to give my lungs a break, but I didn't have good luck getting that done. The door was half cocked and I assumed no one was in it, until I pushed it open a bit farther. When I did, I caught a glimpse of a couple of folks doing lines of coke in the bathroom. A big breasted blonde with implants was letting one man fuck her, as she sucked the other one at the same time. I quietly tipped away from the door and headed in the opposite direction. Shortly thereafter, drug boys that worked for Cash began showing up at the front door on occasion. I assumed "business" was booming be-yond expectation. The funny thing was that I thought I caught a glimpse of a well-known lobbyist and a few con-servative senators, all opposed to adult entertainment. Yet they were involved in some very interesting activities. I chalked it up to the side effects of inebriation and never thought of it again, while denying that I spotted women sitting on each of their knees.

The place was packed and buzzin'. Asses were shaking. Money was flowing. Being around other female hustlers aroused me. I began slapping women on the ass, just as they'd done it to me! The alcohol had me bent, for sure. I kept asking the bartender to pour me glass after glass. I sampled some of every kind of liquor from Belvedere vodka to Patrón, until my head felt light. I didn't want to vomit, so I stopped holding out my glass after a while.

I also noticed a lot of semi-model looking chicks in the house, adorned with glittering pasties that caught a kaleidoscope of colors every time they moved around in the light. Some of them were holding and licking X-rated lollipops. They were large, chocolate, and shaped like a penis.

The melting pot was boiling over. I saw some of everyone: tall, fat, skinny, small, thick, Puerto Rican, and Black, in addition to the new eye candy. I only spotted three girls from The Foxy Lady. I overheard them saying the less attractive, out of shape ones had been invited to leave the party after a big argument over tip out. There was also some sort of accusation made about one of the girls lying about change being given to her after a customer requested it. Word had it that her boyfriend came down to the club to pick her up after she called him ranting, raving, and making a scene. Cash had to pull out a pistol to make her back down, and him calm down. All I could say is that I'm glad I wasn't there to witness that ghetto drama!

I wore a see-through body suit and my five-inch heels with ankle straps. On this particular night, I treated every customer like I was genuinely happy to see him. I usually felt powerless, but from the moment I walked through the door, I felt powerful and full of energy like I was twenty again. I enjoyed the attention that I was getting, and made consistent eye contact. I didn't even have to try and keep a smile on my face . . . I had a *real* smile on my face. I'd been tossing drinks down my throat all night, and my inhibitions took flight. I showed men my breasts, shoving them in their mouths, and encouraged them to touch my kitty kat during dances. I even gave a few customers passionate kisses on the neck before walking away. Onstage, I was a pure exhibitionist, behaving like I was participating in a freak shoot in exotic Brazil! Obviously, I wasn't concerned about gathering more information for my research. I completely lost my focus—this particular night was all about self-gratification. My life was a mess, but men wanted me and made me feel like an exotic black butterfly. Men were mesmerized by the way I could make my vagina lips move on their own by working my inner muscles. They rewarded me well for burning up the stage. I was dulling the pain of unhappiness through sexual power, and I was also dulling the pain of being rejected by the man I loved, all at once. If I must say so myself, I was damn good at massaging my bruised ego.

When I put it up in the air and made my ass cheeks clap, an array of strange men balled up ones, fives, and even tens, and threw them my way, treating me like I was one of the hottest female dancers on the East Coast. A few came up to the stage, rolled money up like a cigarette, and stuck it in my kitty kat when I opened my legs. The classier men stuck them between my teeth as I flexed my ass, one cheek at a time. Even a female showed her appreciation with a tip after I grinded on her lap. She told me that everyone wanted to know when I was coming out to dance as I was walking to the dressing room. After I returned, I shocked her and her man by hopping on top of her lap. What can I say? I was in rare form that night.

Thinking back, I can't believe how much I acted like a nut.

While getting some air, a man walked up to me and led me to a table.

"Have you been here all night?" he asked.

"Yes," I replied.

"I didn't see you. I was leaving, but I'll stay now," he told me.

I sat on his lap to do my usual thing. "You don't have to do this," the man explained. Without warning, he told me," You're intelligent. This isn't you."

"How can you tell?" I asked as I moved around on his lap with a smile on my face.

"One intelligent person can recognize another."

"This isn't my life. There is more to me," I reasoned, wanting to tell him that I was in school, and was having some cash flow problems.

"Don't come back to a party like this anymore. You're not a whore. Reach inside of you and you'll get something better than all of this. There are other ways to make money. Look at me," he told me. I did. "What's the matter with you? You look like someone's wife. You're too beautiful for this. You know that, right?" he asked. He kissed in between my breasts, pushed a twenty-dollar bill in my hand and left the event.

His words rang like a massive choir of at least one million voices. What the stranger said hit me somewhere deep down inside. He made me feel so uneasy, I almost got dressed and went home on the spot. Instead of heeding his warning, I stepped it up a notch and proceeded to rebel, despite poignant words being placed in my ear. I blew off the warning and ignored my guardian angel's words of wisdom, reacting to it as if it were some one public service announcement. I sipped a few swallows of champagne and continued acting like a wild party girl. I was getting tipped so much, I had to give security my money to hold for me. My garter belt was way too full. Girls were shooting jealous stares toward me, but I didn't care about those green-eyed monsters. I wasn't there to be liked—I was there to get paid! Some dancers were lined up in rows, grinding on top of laps in between disappearing to the VIP rooms. I also overheard a wiry man I'd never seen before talking percentages with a stunning, thin French girl that had been over protective of him. It turned out that taking care of her entailed setting up paid dates. She was his in-house prostitute and girlfriend. We were all making money, one way or another.

When the crowd began to thin out, I noticed a man dressed in a tuxedo shirt staring at me with a fixed gaze. He looked as if he'd just come from some big event and I guessed that he'd ridden in many private elevators and limos. He never asked me to dance nor tipped me onstage. He just fixed his gaze on me all night long. I didn't know if he wanted me to save the last dance for him, or if I repulsed him so bad, he couldn't believe that they chose to allow me to work the event. I just didn't know what to think.

The party was ending, and the DJ announced it was the last dance. Then I heard the guest tell Cash, "I want her over there." After that, they mumbled something that I couldn't quite hear. Cash walked in my direction with a serious face. His eyeballs were red from drinking liquor like it was tap water.

"How did you do tonight, baby momma?" he joked as he smiled slightly.

"Everything's moving along. So far, so good. I'm not doing bad at all," I told Cash. "I haven't counted my money yet. Security is holding it for me."

"Look, remember what we talked about a little while back, as far as doing a little bit more to reach your goal?"

"Yeah," I answered. I though back on how I first met Cash, when I stumbled into The Foxy Lady after X tried to help me. I knew mixing business and pleasure wasn't smart, so I stayed away from him at first. All of the sudden, he stopped flirting in a trashy way. He changed his flavor by pretending he was a nice, humorous older cat, who just wanted to wine and dine me because I deserved it. After a lot of laughing, joking, and special times, he gave me money for my books, and bought me stripper outfits and expensive designer clothes. He never even tried to fuck me anymore. I grew to put stock in what he said.

"Everyone has a price. Tonight you can go home with the little bit of cash you made, or you can take home enough to get out of the game."

"What are you getting at? Are you insinuating something?" I asked.

"I told you I was going to help you get what you need. After events like this, I eat hot dogs or steak, depending on when, and how, I make things happen. Let's both eat steak tomorrow. That guy over there wants some *company* tonight."

"I don't know . . ."

"Don't half step in this game, Paradise. I been in the game a long time and know how the game is played. Every man in here tonight is paid, you know what I'm saying? I made sure that the ballers were in the building. When I say ballers, I mean all sorts of types. I just told that dude that you don't come cheap. He started out at $5,000, but I negotiated double by telling him you were a new girl who needed some convincing to get down and dirty on his clock. He wants a black girl, and he likes your look."

"He's offering $10,000 for one night? But why? Even if he's willing to pay all of that, I don't know if I could go through with it," I answered while noting that my financial goals now sounded realistic.

"Why? 'Cause you're the bad, bad bitch that everyone wants to be with. You act like a cloud will follow you, but it won't, baby momma. You can change your number. If anyone ever calls or asks you about what happened, say 'I don't know you.' Break all ties to the entertainment business, even with me, and move on with your life. By June, the sun could come out for you. It would be just like being with a boyfriend. He'd have on a condom. Now these dumb bitches that fuck with me are too dumb to make it count if they're going to do it, but the industry hasn't seen nothing like you in three years. You're sweet, innocent, and exotic. At the same time I know you're a business-woman. Here's an opportunity that may come only once in your life," Cash explained. "Look at him. That bama is the type that probably belongs to some golf or yacht club. He probably wouldn't even last a whole three minutes. You have nothing to lose, but everything to gain."

I turned towards the man, then back to Cash.

"If you want to make this money, let's go get it," he added.

After that, he got real personal and asked me about my rent, who was paying my bills, my job hunting progress, and of course, my business goal. I hung my head low while thinking of my father who'd been spotting me on the rent. I felt that nobody should wipe my ass. I was too old for that. Although he was pitching in here and there, I let a lot of things I needed slide. This was my chance to wipe my own ass in secret. Never had I imagined that crossing over into this lifestyle would begin to consume me the way that it had. I allowed curious emotions to cloud my judgment. What I was contemplating had nothing to do with research—layers of my morality were being peeled away. Everything right began to blur together into one big ball of temptation.

I thought about the movie deal that didn't pan out, my mother that up and died on me when I was only five, the money that all of the other girls were making because they were willing to have sex, my degree that hadn't made a difference when I sent out resumé after resumé with no great results, my student loan lender who was hounding me to death, my stomach that would be growling the next day, and the state of my pathetic, dried up career and love life. All of these thoughts began to swirl around in my head, leading me to consider that I'd done nothing up to that point, but let men touch my skin or graze either set of lips, or my nipples. I knew it was wrong to bend rules of my moral limits, but in a moment's time of feeling my worst, I said something that I thought I'd never say when I was propositioned: *yes.*

Initially I was troubled by why the stranger was willing to pay so much to sleep with me for just one night. Nevertheless, in a few short hours, I talked myself into imagining a positive outcome. Having all of the money I needed, and the ability to bow out of the game gracefully, played through my mind more times than I could count.

"Make sure he's got the money and set it up. Hurry up before I change my mind," I said. "If the liquor wears off, we'll both be eating hot dogs."

"Pay, fuck, and leave. It's that simple. Now think steak."

"Where are we going, Cash?"

"To a hotel downtown."

After he hooked up my date, he ushered out the few guests that remained, not even giving them a chance to drain the liquor from their last drinks. Then the real party began, and I learned the real deal about another part of the adult entertainment hustle.

Day 16 in the life

In the wee hours of the morning, Cash set up the discreet encounter with, what we thought, was a wimpy rich guy. He collected the money for my overnight tryst and agreed to pick me up from a pretty posh hotel in the morning. Since my "date" requested that I bring several pairs of nylons and heels so he could worship my legs in them, Cash stopped by a twenty-four hour Wal-Mart and bought a few pairs of nylons for me to stuff in my bag. I already had the heels covered of course. We figured he had some type of harmless foot fetish. Neither of us were necessarily alarmed that his request was indicative of him being some sort of perverted sexual deviant! The thing is, we were both wrong. There was no hint of normal intimacy in sight. That's how he caught me off guard in every way. I'd rather block out this experience for the rest of my life—it was that repulsive to me. Since I can't, I'll record what I can manage to admit and discuss. Quite frankly, Diary, writing it down is as bad as reliving it.

"So you're a few days old in this business?" the man said as he undressed.

"Yes I am," I answered shyly. "This is my first, umm, date," I said with embarrassment.

"I know. What a fine black girl you are. Slim natural curves. Sensual lips. Seductive face. I think I chose well. I hope you're very open-minded because it's playtime, Paradise."

"Thank you, and I'll do my best," I said, smiling a little, as I stood in black pantyhose and sexy shoes.

"Good. I'm glad to hear it. Did you bring another pair of panty hose?"

"Yes. I have them," I replied.

"Good. May I please see them?" he asked. I knew he was

watching me walk as I approached my bag and retrieved them.

My date quickly popped a pill in his mouth. I scrunched up my eyebrows and stared at him.

"Don't worry, it's just a little sexual enhancer. This stuff gives me the best erections of my life," he explained.

"Come here and stroke my dick," he said calmly.

I watched his facial expressions change as I slid my feet into my heels, and stroked his average-sized tool after he undressed. After that, he sat down on the bed, and motioned for me to walk toward him.

"You're going to love this. Now sit down on my lap," he said, whispering in my ear.

By this time, he was softly running his hands all over my body, then asked me to bend over on his lap. I was still quite lit.

"Daddy is always thinking of his little girl. Say 'I am a naughty slut' while I spank you," he said as he spanked me through the panty hose. I repeated his words as I prayed this man was just talking kinky during some type of role-play.

His demeanor changed within mere minutes.

"Now say 'spank me, I've been bad,' " he said. I repeated it again as he slapped my cheeks with a vengeance. "I guess you won't mind if I tied you up for a little while," he said. That's when he quickly bound my wrists. When I asked him what he was doing, and I told him it hurt, he told me to shut up, then moved on to something else.

"Get off my lap and get on your knees. Show me how sorry you are for saying I hurt you. Anything goes tonight. Now put your ass up and face down, *slut*!" he snarled.

When I submitted to him, my knees were nearly knocking together, and I ripped the pair of pantyhose I was wearing. When he put his finger through the hole, and wiggled it around in my pussy a bit on the rough side, I finally understood he was into some real freak nasty shit. Things were moving toward some sort of beginner bondage or domination sex play. I looked over at the door as I began to lose control of the situation.

"You're not even wet. Is this the best you can do? What you're doing is terrible. Do you even care if I leave happy? You're not working hard enough, cheap whore. Get your attitude right and cater to my fantasies, or you can go back to giving fifty-dollar blow jobs behind dumpsters, and I can get my fucking money back! Now turn around and stop wasting my time!"

Scared to death, and of Cash if the trick complained, I honored his request and turned around. The thought of getting my money kept me quiet, at least when it came to yelling for help. My inexperience had me confused, and I didn't know what to do.

"Look at those juicy lips. Mmmm. You have what it takes to make me happy. Lick my balls and act like you're my deep throat queen. Show me why you are the best girl for the job. Keep your sexy shoes on and show Daddy how much you love him," he added, sounding aroused.

With my hands still behind my back, I timidly licked his balls, wondering if I should say fuck the money and possible consequences with Cash, bite him, and run. Still, I sucked it all up and didn't stop.

"Now show Daddy. Sh–Show. Mmmm," he stuttered. "Pull those panty hose down," he told me as I stopped licking him and stared at his erect dick. "There's nothing like a sexy slut with pretty toes," he remarked.

Next, he began caressing my bare legs with his hands, then licked them, working his way down to my feet and toes. After he told me to turn around, without warning, he reached up and stuck his finger clear into my butt. I clenched my butt cheeks as my asshole began to burn. Stunned and completely shocked, I felt chills run through my body. After moaning a while, he pushed me, bending me over on the edge of the bed.

"Take it easy! What are you doing?" I said.

The trick didn't answer me. Instead, I heard him tear open a condom wrapper, then he started sticking me with his stiff penis. By this time, I began feeling numb, cold and violated. I was afraid to act like I wasn't in the mood to have sex with him, because this guy was just too weird for my tastes. Being petite, I didn't know if I could get away if I did hit him.

"What do you think you have, a platinum pussy? Cut the cutesy bullshit! What a mechanical job you're doing. You're not doing this for free, I'm *paying* you. You're a whore, so act the part! Hold your damn legs open, and that ass high in the air!" he shouted, pulling my hair, as my head fell back while he pumped me.

Sticking my backside up higher, I pretended that I wanted to give him pleasure as I closed my eyes and imagined my boyfriend inside of me. It was the only way I could try to get through this bizarre experience.

"That's better. Yeaaah," he cooed. "It's so wet and tight. Now you're acting like you're here to please me. Oooh yeah, that's better."

About a minute later, his dick grew limp and I prayed it was all over. He pulled the mushy tip out of me, then tried to beat his limp dick on my ass with ultra quick taps.

"Turn over, you dirty piece of trash. Hurry, turn over," he said, suddenly talking fast. I did. He must've snatched the condom off because the next thing I knew he was peeing all over my face, and some of the urine drained into my mouth, and ran all down my neck. As I listened to his sounds of relief, and felt the wetness of the warm pungent liquid, I cringed inside as he rubbed it in on my cheeks, neck, and breasts.

The man let me go early, untying me.

"Get your shit, and get out, you slut. You're finished now," he remarked.

I gathered my things as quickly as my pounding head would allow, ran down to the lobby and called Cash to pick me up. The stranger took me on a bizarre adventure that I'd prefer to forget. And no, turning a trick with a stranger wasn't like sleeping with a boyfriend, or a person you met at the club and had a one-night stand with. At the time, I thought I was getting a leg up on the competition by getting what I needed by any means necessary. In reality, I'd never forget how humiliating the experience was. I compromised my morality and opened up a can of worms I couldn't emotionally handle.

Day 17 in the life

The liquor began to wear off and reality began to set in, as I waited for Cash in the lobby of the hotel. Initially, I thought that my humanity made me vulnerable. I had made the same mistake as any one of those living in the motels that didn't have the facilities to fix school lunches for their little ones because they were taking care of their children in dirty hotel rooms. Upon considering all of these things, I thought of the girls that spent years dreaming of becoming a doctor, lawyer, teacher, letting it sail down the drain and go to waste. I'm talking about the college girls who got side tracked and ended up dropping out of school. I'm also talking about the ones who came in the game holding on to something and let go of who they were in the process of blowing money after every gig. Now I was on the edge of being added to the ranks of them. Me, Ayanna, Miss High and Mighty, Dean's List student, author, child of God, former debutant, and suburban chick. I too fell for it, although a woman like me was supposed to know better. *Right.* As so many thoughts swirled around in my head, I felt used and abused, until Cash shed light on the situation.

"Why are you crying, Paradise?" Cash asked when I got into his Yukon.

"That guy did some strange things. He tied me up, humiliated me, pissed in my face, and—"

"Stop right there, Paradise. Would you dance for a client with no history privately, without an escort?"

"No," I answered weakly.

"Then you should've already known rule number one. Never meet a new trick alone, when no one is nearby to look out for you if something goes down."

"Why didn't you tell me that?" I asked, looking at Cash.

"This is major. This ain't some cool little hustle, Paradise. Just like dancing, there's politics involved, and it's dangerous for a girl to be independent out here. Having sex for money is the next level, so you better know your shit. You had to learn the hard way. He didn't hurt you and you're fine. You have a little ride or die in you after all. You ain't no innocent victim. You got money to show for that," Cash said. "Well, it's not ten thousand. It's more like this. Count it," he continued, handing me some cash. With shaking hands, I reached out to take it. I counted the cash. Only three thousand dollars was there. I didn't comment as my thoughts continued to jump from one thing to another.

"I already took mine, Paradise. He said you were perfect. You did real good. Not bad for turning your first trick," Cash said. "Steak for me later, and now you have a decision to make."

"About what?"

"I can either take you back to your car, or you roll with me. If you really want to make some more money, this is only the beginning for us. Since you passed the test and didn't call me freaking out and shit, we can make some nice bread together, if you want to."

"I think I've done enough. Taking sex for money was a mistake, a big mistake."

"You knew what you were doing, and no one forced you to do it. Look shorty, once you take money for sex just one time, you're a pro—*a prostitute*. Since you decided to piss on the pot, you may as well profit and stay on it. Get with Daddy if you stay in this game. I'll watch your back, and next time you can get what you're supposed to. I know the right people like club promoters who are in the network of big names in the entertainment industry, plus I'm tight with some of them myself. You got a look they would like, and I can get you what you really need if you're willing to go to the next level. They don't call me Cash for nothing," he said. He lit up a cigarette and cracked the window to flick ashes out of it.

After Cash broke it down to me like that, I felt lower than shit hanging off of butt hairs. I saw his point, and I hated myself for having to face the truth. When his Nextel rang, he picked it up.

"I'm sick—I can't go on my date. I'm having withdrawal," a woman said. She sounded like she'd been crying for hours.

"Bitch, if you don't get it together quick and in a hurry, I'll put you out on the stroll!" Cash explained. "I gotta dip and go take care of something," he told me, turning in my direction as he exhaled smoke from his nose.

I heard his voice begin to escalate. Cash told the woman that a sick ho had no value to him and that since she decided to start shooting up and fuck with his money, she'd have to settle up what she owed, get out of the hotel room, and go back out on the stroll. It was hard to believe he'd just spoken to me in a smooth, silky voice. Still, when I realized it was someone I knew I told him I wanted to go along for the ride although I contemplated letting him pull off without me. I had my own problems. I felt dirty, disgusting, and used. I just wanted to make it home to take off my shoes and clothes, take a hot bath, and cry at the top of my lungs, but I didn't know what could happen to my friend, Sapphire. Among other things, I had no idea she was on drugs until she called Cash. So instead of bailing out and looking out for myself, I did what I thought was the right thing. I went with Cash that night. I wish I would've said I wouldn't go . . . because that was the beginning of my career as an escort.

When I finished reading the last entry, I lifted my head in shock. By that time, my sister had stopped crying, although she was still curled up in a fetal position. I felt her eyes watching my arms as I rested them in my lap. I felt numb all over and didn't know how else to feel. As I stared into space, Ayanna began to talk in a weak sounding voice.

"Oh my God, Yana! I can't believe that you—"

Ayanna cut me off.

"Let me finish where the diary leaves off," she said, her lip quivering. "It gets worse.

"Sapphire and I were roommates. I told you about things getting tight. Well, I couldn't make the rent one month. I just didn't make enough stripping. I was always worried about money and my grades were dropping. As a last ditch attempt to stay in school and get the money I needed, I-I, I started working for Cash after that incident. Sapphire and I both were."

Ayanna sighed.

"Sapphire swore she was clean for good, and she begged her way back into Cash's good graces. We were stacking lots of paper by stripping and doing extra freak nasty favors for upscale men: entertainers, athletes, politicians, big time hustlers, and high profile businessmen who said they were too busy to maintain real girlfriends. We traveled to Italy, Paris, Aruba, the Bahamas—many places together on the arm of men who were paying for us to keep our mouths shut about their fantasies and bizarre fetishes."

"You two did what!" I hollered. Ayanna just kept talking like she was in a daze.

"Dressing in designer gear became the norm, along with eating at the finest restaurants, and flying first class, buying nice little gifts and magazines to help the time pass. Saving money became a joke to us. Life had become about fucking, partying, and getting men off. I don't think I have to tell you that we've done threesomes together and got really personal. I think that's obvious.

"I even ran into X again, during my time spent in these circles. By that time, he hit it big and did make something real good out of himself, passing up his drug addicted parents with flying colors. He's a very well-known rapper today, in fact. Obviously his real name isn't X. I'm not trying to end up having Wendy Williams talk shit about me, or end up on some groupie chat room, in case my diary ever fell into the wrong hands. Hell no. To make a long story short, he cut me off socially after he realized that I was doing more than dancing, despite the fact that he introduced me to adult entertainment. When it came to a famous rapper on tour, Sapphire and I were only for the act and his staff. The freakier we were willing to get, the more we were paid, whether it was on a tour bus or in some penthouse suite. It just so happened, we were two of the girls picked out to be sent to X by Cash. But when we got to our destination, X saw it was me and went ballistic. He had the nerve to judge me and disown me for what I was doing. Negroes will flip the script ready to look down their noses and judge somebody, like they have never done any dirt.

"Despite all of that, everything was still pretty copasetic until Sapphire's drug problem came back to haunt her. She started popping ecstasy pills to relax her enough to do the other things, but it didn't stop there. Then she started snorting coke on the regular with those high rollers we were getting down with. Next, she hooked up with one of the hustlers who gave her a wifey experience. Everything went to hell in a hand basket in a very short time," Ayanna explained.

"Shortly thereafter, the hustle evolved into a hustle gone real wrong . . . and a *real* cruel one, too. Sapphire called Cash begging for help. This made time number two. I think she missed getting to live the glamorous life more than anything, and I think he only showed because all of the men who'd gotten to know us started asking for her. When those three agendas merged, I was made to make a tough decision. I had to choose sides that day."

I struggled to keep my mouth shut. Ayanna's story was more than I was prepared to hear. I found a bottle of Aleve and popped two in my mouth as I rubbed my temples real hard.

"When Cash and I laid eyes on Sapphire, she was in a very bad state, far worse than the first time. She was shaking. Her eyes were sunken in. Her skin looked kinda ashy, her hair looked like she hadn't combed it for days, and she had bright track marks on her arms. Cash was angry as hell since he'd let her back into his heart once before. Everything got crazy when Cash said he regarded me as his main girl, since I chose to hang tough. Sapphire had known him before me. As my initiation to prove my long term loyalty to him, he ordered me to take off my high heels and beat Sapphire with the heel of my shoe until she could take no more. Next, Cash grabbed a coat hanger from the closet, unbent it to from a straight line, and forced me to whip Sapphire with it, daring her to scream or even whimper. I watched welts form on her back as she looked into my eyes, non-verbally waiting for my comfort. Instead, after I beat her, I watched Cash kick her out of her own hotel room into the street. He cut her from his stable of women on the spot, then I took a shower to meet another high-priced trick with Cash."

"Days later, she called me, claiming all sorts of things about Cash she never had. Sapphire told me what Cash did to suck her into the game, and it turned out he'd roped her in too. She said he told her that she could make some extra bucks while he protected her. Supposedly, from the way he explained things, all she had to do was accompany high-class men to dinner. According to Sapphire, it turned out that Cash sent her out with a friend to make her believe what she saw was the real deal. It was a ploy to build her trust in him. It was just enough to impress her and make the game appear harmless and easy. Next, he convinced her to take it to the next level and sleep with the men she went to dinner with. Sapphire said Cash was a slimy dude, and that we should leave him the hell alone, and work our circuit independently. She wanted me to break ties with him and let her manage our 'careers.' Sapphire was always smart, with a magnetic personality, but she had a real weakness for drugs. Things got really out of hand when I told her I wouldn't jump ship with Cash."

Ayanna started sobbing.

"Then Sapphire blamed me for whipping her and all of that. I explained to her why I didn't stick up for her that day, and she said she understood my safety would've been in jeopardy. Still, she ended up holding it against me down the road. Little did I know a vendetta was in the making.

"As retaliation for me not leaving Cash and letting her suffer that day, she kept the money we split and saved later, after Cash took her back—the money we didn't blow on buying clothes and all of that. At the time, I didn't want my fitness of character to ever come up in my legal career, so I agreed to let her keep the money in an account in a safety deposit box. I'd already used the three grand for my book issue. I couldn't pay off the investor and my lawyer. Once again, there was no money left over for me to actually have more books printed. Plus, since I was being threatened, I spent all of the money I made with Cash that night making payments on my business venture, instead of putting any of it toward my tuition. After all I'd done to try and salvage my book venture, I still had no product, or a zero debt balance. By that time, I knew I was living wrong. I just felt stuck."

I handed Ayanna some tissue from a box on my nightstand, and also for myself. Before I knew it, I began crying too.

"Sapphire stayed screwed up real bad on drugs a while. Word on the street was that she had hit rock bottom, and also turned into a hardcore lesbian. They said she would only touch men if she ran out of money, but she preferred to finance her habit without having sex with them. I felt as though everything I did would've been for nothing if I didn't get my hands on that money she was holding before she blew it on drugs. You see, by this time the deadline had come for me to pay my tuition. I acted like I just wanted to see her and put our differences aside, but when I walked in the room and saw her naked and sweaty with a needle stuck in her arm, I knew she'd *really* lost it. I searched for the keys until I found them, but Sapphire wouldn't let me take her to get some of my money out of the thing. I couldn't pay my bill on time, and Dad wouldn't let me use his information to try and qualify for a financial aid loan. My name wasn't on file at the bank to the safety deposit box to gain entry. Sapphire said I turned my back on her and now she was turning her back on me.

"That wench needed another hit and ended up shooting up my tuition money. I left Cash for a while, but I came back to him too. I tried to get the money up other ways and couldn't raise much honestly, so I gave in. Months later, Sapphire showed up at The Foxy Lady, looking clean and acting calm, like nothing ever happened. She really is full of herself since Cash took the attitude that, so long as his big clients want to party with her on the drug tip, she can come back and forth until she destroys herself. History has a way of repeating itself. What I'm trying to tell you is that I'm a prostitute, Mystique, and have been for some time. I gave up on writing books. I gave up on publishing and I gave up on my education. You see, I've been lying about being in school. I really dropped out of school, and now your sister makes money by having sex with high profile men who can afford to screw her."

Ayanna began to cry again, as she released herself from the fetal position and buried her face in the bedspread. I felt so limp that I thought I was going to fall to the floor, but I didn't. My sister probably cried longer than the day she slid out of our mother's womb. Speechless and stunned, I tugged on her body until I managed to coax her to crawl into my lap. I held her in my arms, rocking her like a baby, finally wetting her with tears of my own. We cried for all of the hurt, our mutual hurt. Just when I thought it all meant something in a healing way, we heard Ayanna's cell phone ring. She wiped her eyes, her hands slowly moving down her puffy face, then released herself from my embrace. Ayanna picked up her phone that was sitting on my nightstand and answered it. Without her telling me, I knew it was the infamous Cash.

"Don't go, Yana. Stay here," I said softly. My head was all messed up beyond words, considering I'd shaken my ass at my sister's pimp's club!

When she didn't answer, I sighed heavily while gathering my thoughts. "Please, Yana. Don't do this anymore," I began to plead louder.

"You'll end up dead or catching some disease. Money's not worth playing the game you're in. Cash had knowledge of your weakness. Are you still messing with Cash or some other pimp?"

Ayanna remained quiet, so I figured out the answer to my own question.

"Ayanna, how could you have loyalty toward someone who sees you as nothing more than a means to an end? Between your legs, he sees nothing but a commodity. It has nothing to do with being a living, breathing person. It has everything to do with money, control, and abuse of pussy power. You didn't have any street smarts, which made you a perfect target to add to his brainwashed stable. Now that you've told me about this, leave him alone! He played you both. What's he's doing to you girls is insane!"

"Cash cares about me now. I don't even have to dance anymore. I don't like what I do, Mystique. I didn't have any financial help and I was just trying to get ahead when I started doing this. I never meant to get hooked on this lifestyle. I had no idea how few women who strip leave the game the same as they went in, until I learned that for myself. It's hard to dodge the shit. Not impossible, but damn hard. That's what I tried to tell you without coming out and saying it, when you wanted to start stripping, Mystique. Consequences can come to you easily in this game, and now I'm prepared to deal with more of them. I wanted to spare you from all of that. You just wouldn't read between the lines. Like you said, you can't tell a grown woman what to do, so long as she wants to do things her way. I'll stop when I'm ready, but right now I'm addicted to getting that fast money. I'm out, sis," she told me.

"But you have nothing to show for it and you've given up on everything that was important to you," I said, trying to pull her back into the room.

"And what do you have to show for the time and energy spent in your marriage?" Ayanna asked, stopping in her tracks. I couldn't think of anything new to say that would end the conversation on a positive note. "We both know the answer to that one, so let it go, sis. Don't judge my world." She sniffed. "You haven't displayed morals of gold either. Look at the mess you've made. I tried to tell you that I have it worse than you. Now you know that I wasn't talking shit."

I tugged Ayanna's arm again, and tried to restrain her in every possible way. I even put her in a headlock once and turned around and around in circles. We bumped into the dresser. All sorts of trinkets were pushed off. My favorite crystal lamp wobbled and fell. Glass flew everywhere. We kept wresting until we worked our way around the glass.

"You're not going out of this house," I exclaimed.

"Let me go!" she demanded, accidentally elbowing me in stomach after I hit her in the head with her cell phone. She finally slipped from my grip. I stood there staring at her.

Ayanna couldn't even look me in the eye, as I held my midsection, feeling winded. She let her head hang low, picking up her cell phone off of the floor. She rearranged her clothes, gathered her things, and closed the door. Of course I was bothered to find out that my sister was a high-priced groupie and escort to God only knew who, but who was I to judge her for what she'd done? I couldn't deny that it disturbed the hell out of me. With all my might, I tried to stop her and couldn't. The fight was useless.

I walked toward the utility room to get the broom and vacuum cleaner, while acknowledging that I'd developed bad habits of my own, just as she'd already pointed out. To deal with the pain of everything, I also turned to my new addiction of playing games with love . . . by using my body too.

15

PLAYING WITH FIRE

Around mid-August, my husband broke his silent treat-ment. He called to let me know he was coming to spend some quality time with his wife. You could've knocked me over with damn a feather. I didn't bother him about that email. As planned, I focused on myself and played the dumb wife game. The more scarce I became, and the more I treated my husband like an afterthought, the more he began to sniff behind me life a dog in heat. He even tried to talk dirty to me, suggesting having sex doggy-style in the shower, finishing up on the bed. Phone sex didn't even sound right rolling off of his cold lips—that had become Rafiq's job. It was nice not having to twist a man's arm to enjoy my company, compliment me, spend a little quality time with me here and there, or just straight up talk. As a result, I was no longer attracted to my hus-band. Rafiq had been filling his shoes rather lovely. I was being well taken care of, emotionally and physically. I didn't even give a shit about his mistress or mistresses. For once in our marriage, I was getting mine too. I was feeling like I had the whole world in the palm of my hand. I mean thong!

Since the ball was now in my court, I decided to have a little fun at his expense. I hightailed it into the bathroom, lotioned up with my best smelling scent, then slid on my stripper fuck-me shoes, with the sparkling heels. I also picked an outfit that I felt was sexy, but didn't scream, "I've been stripping." You could see through the netting, but it also allowed coverage with fringes on the wrap-around. I felt he would like it and wanted to look nice for him. When he arrived, I made sure the lights were turned off. I didn't want him to see my knees that were a little scarred from when I was first learned to jiggle my ass on all fours at The Foxy Lady. Nor did I want my face to tell on me. I looked out of the bathroom window and watched him turn the corner before his Porshe headed down my street. When he pulled up, I unlocked the door and left it open. He opened it.

"You left the door open?"

"No, I did it when you pulled up. I didn't want you to stand outside in the rain."

I stood there watching him as he undressed, then we went into the bedroom. I had rushed to put fresh sheets on the bed and hoped the bedspread didn't smell like Sapphire, although I could've lied and said an unfamiliar scent belonged to Ayanna, and she'd spent the night with me. Even so, I sprayed a little of my body splash between them for good measure. When he lay down to hold me, I remembered all of the nights that we'd spent together. Our lack of recent interaction couldn't stop me from gloating about feeling Rafiq's throbbing dick between my legs.

"May I?" I asked, stroking his tool like a purring kitty cat. I bit my lip in the corner, anxiously anticipating his reply.

"Yes," he answered. "If you make it hard, you can have it," he added. I felt tingles travel all over my skin.

Accepting the challenge, I closed my eyes, took his warm tool in my hands, then began licking, sucking, and slurping on him like a sweet popsicle. I let him push his tool all the way down to the back of my throat, and didn't miss a beat. As I listened to the rain beat against the widow pane, my tongue swirled around his swollen knob. I thought of all of the nights I wanted to taste him . . . Vicious was probably doing my job.

I seductively laid on my back, as Donavan made it to his knees. He surprised me and slipped his dick between both of my breasts. I began yanking and tugging on that fat stick like I wanted him to shoot a load on my chest. I watched the girls in the club give so many hands jobs that I knew exactly how to fuck his head up.

"Oh. Oh. Fuck!" he yelled. "Daaamn!"

After that, I took my rainy-day-hook up's chocolate tool into my mouth with one gargantuan swallow, cocking my head up a bit to look him square in the eye. Then I juggled his nuts in my mouth, sucking his balls just right until I heard him breathing deeply. When Donavan's dick got big and hard, I made it a point to catch myself and stop pleasing him.

"Mmmm. That's exactly what I'm talking about. Damn, baby. I like this freaky shit," he muttered. I knew I achieved superior results when he said, "I wanna cum, baby! Put your mouth back on Daddy. Keep going. Lick me again, baby. Suck me. Mmmm. I think it's time for us to make up, don't you?" Donavan rambled, trying to convince me to push his dick back into my warm mouth. "Damn. Since when did your oral skills get so good? You really—"

I cut him off, stopped what I was doing, then turned my head away. Donavan moved from on top of me, looking at me completely perplexed.

"Sorry, I'll have to get back with you later on this. The dishes are piled up in sink, dirty clothes are all over the floor in the laundry room, and the little ones are coming back in less than a week."

"No. Don't get up. Don't go!" he begged, sounding desperate.

"Oh, I'm not doing my housework yet. I'm taking a nap first," I calmly told him, pretending to sound drained. "As you pointed out a while back, everything's not about sex. Since you're just starting to come to bed again, how about just holding your wife? I miss that most, don't you?" I wasn't going to give my husband any ass. I still hadn't forgiven him for calling me the wrong bitch's name. At that point, I just played along. I'd become a good actress from stripping, little did dumb ass Donavan know.

"Of course I miss holding you," he answered. "I just thought that you also missed something else."

"Relax, honey. I'm going to finish what I was doing earlier. Don't worry," I lied, lifting up to plant a big kiss on his cheek. As I gloated inside, I laid back down, happy I'd turned the tables. Instead of Donavan rejecting me, I was rejecting him. I hoped that he'd feel bothered by my disappearance, the same way his used to bother me.

After my husband started snoring, I scribbled a note letting him know that I'd see him later, being sure to put in on the fridge under the magnet. I also left on the light, just as he'd done when he went to Seattle. I then snuck out of the house, started up my car, and turned on the radio as soon as I backed out of the driveway. Instead of listening to jazz, which I once used to calm my nerves and stay focused, I then knew nearly every new rap song that got airplay or strip club props. I blasted Da Wood's *Sex and Money 2* CD. The girls were fighting over it in the club after the DJ cranked it, but he hooked me up when they weren't even looking. I was sure that my son would think I was a cool mom for knowing who his favorite artists were by the time he returned from camp, in addition to those on the rise.

My personality was changing, too. I was quick to put people in their place, wanting to cuss more, and no longer moved away when someone lit up a cigarette or a blunt. I hit the club so much, that no matter where I intended to go, I automatically took the route of the club like my car was equipped with some sort of GPS device!

While deciding if I wanted to continue dancing at the main spot, I headed to another place . . . someone's apartment. I was encouraged to go when I was offered $100 just for showing up to entertain. I got "the call" while I was wandering around in 7-11 in search of a snack.

"**I**s the other girl going to do it? Who is it?" I asked Ray. "You know, Tasty? She knows you."

"I guess if I saw her face. Is it the girl who always dances in socks?"

"Not her," he said, laughing.

"Let me talk to the girl. I don't want to come over there and she not want to go through with it. I can't dance by myself," I explained. This was the only night the club was closed. I found out that so many people had side gigs to make more money.

"I'll take care of you, nothing's going to happen. Just come on. I'll give you $100. I got some guests from out of town just waiting to spend some bread before an NBA playoff game."

I gobbled a donut as I looked for the address of the "private party." Had I watched sports, I would've known that it wasn't even basketball season! It was all a big fat lie! I knew that $150 to show up to dance at a private party was the norm. Exotic dancers call this up-front guaranteed fee, a pay spot. Still, it didn't really matter, since it was more or less something to do. When I turned the corner I saw Ray standing outside. I parked the car under a street-light and crossed the street with my stripper gear. He spoke to me by giving me a pound, then I followed him into a basement apartment that was full of thick smoke, noise, music, liquor, and men.

"You doing all right? You look tired, Honey. Either that, or you fell off a roof-top and landed on your face," Ray laughed at his own one-liner.

"Cut the jokes, please. I'm tired and have a lot of personal issues on my plate."

"I'm just kidding. You're so serious. Come get this money in here. It'll make you feel better."

Almost everyone was puffing on something while chilling. Some men were wearing wife-beaters and jeans. Some were out on the balcony drinking out of paper bags. A few girls I'd seen in the club were drinking out of paper bags right along with another group of men they were talking to. They waved at me as I passed. At least one of them had a bad habit of smacking me on the behind every time I walked by in the dressing room. I put up with it, just like I did with the men. Never did I do more than smile and keep moving.

"You following me, beautiful?" one asked as I walked by. I pretended not to be phased by her smoking a joint.

"No. I'm sure not," I told her.

"But I want you to," she answered after passing the blunt to her girlfriend.

I gladly kept it moving, and walked to a back room after I was told I could get ready.

"You can change in here."

Ray shut the door. I noticed there were no curtains, so I got dressed as quickly as I could, feeling uncomfortable that anyone who could manage to see that high up may glance my way. Dirty pillows were thrown on the floor that was in desperate need of a good vacuuming. Trash was scattered around the room including beer bottles, pizza boxes, and dirty clothes. To top it all off, a mattress topped the floor that smelled like a baby had pissed on it hours before. A small, lumpy pillow with no pillow case was sitting on the upper left hand corner.

Despite all of that, I ignored the mess and quickly put on an outfit. When I reentered the room, all eyes were on me. I did my best to talk myself into giving about twenty men some of what they wanted, which was the best dance fantasy show I could deliver. Ray found some rap music and told me to get up on a wide coffee table after clearing it off. I had a feeling I wasn't the first girl to dance on top of it. As soon as I started to move like I was boss, men gathered around me like bees drawn to honey. I'd learned to flex one ass cheek at a time, slow and steady. But my neatest trick was the butterfly move, making both cheeks jiggle while alternating my muscle control skills. When I showed this skill while flashing a bedroom look toward my private audience, dollars began to fly out of their hands. Next, I moved up and down, then bent over and held my ass open, so they could see my cat from the back.

"I want this," someone said, grabbing a handful of my ass. "Yo, yo. What up? You wanna go back to my house? Are you wit' it, baby? How much for head? Fifty?" he asked, as I shook my stuff on top of the table.

"All this goodness would cost you way more than fifty. If you've got to ask how much, I'm not the one," I answered in a cocky tone, continuing to do my thing. He laughed at my brush-off as I shot him a quick wink and smile.

"She ain't fine for nothing. Come and tip, fellas. Honey, don't stop doin' what you're doin'! You're the best of the best!" Ray said like he was trying to get the men riled up.

I shook my ass on the table so long, my hair was drenched with sweat, but I still smiled real big as my skin began to shine from perspiration. By the time I wiped sweat from my eyes, someone went in a back room to get a fan to plug in to cool the place down. It didn't seem to help though—it was still scorching as I danced to some Ludacris cut.

"I like private dances. Get on down from there and give me one, so I can see exactly what's goin' on," another man said. He blew on my kitty kat, then slid a dollar over top of my lips, like he was swiping a credit card through a machine.

When I got down two girls named Tasty and Delight, who I now assumed were lipstick lesbians, began to mimic erotic sexual positions. They were the type of strippers that would show up drunk to work, probably stayed high on a regular basis, and spent about a half of what they made getting their nails and hair done, and buying expensive stripper clothes. The one called Tasty was rather petite. She straddled Delight and worked her hips, then they switched positions. When they did, Tasty began sucking and nibbling Delight's nipples like a man who'd been doing that to breasts all of his life. When they made it clear that they weren't shy about using two sets of lips and two tongues, the men went wild. Tasty stuck her head between Delight's legs and acted like she was trying to lick her dry, then they hit the infamous sixty-nine move. At that point, the pair was going hard like they had been lesbian lovers for the past ten years. I think they were really proud exhibitionists. Acting could only go so far.

"It's all chocolate up there," one of the men shouted. "You want them to turn you out? Get on up there. I'll tell them to do it if they wanna get tipped," he told me.

I smiled at him and thought of a quick reply.

"No thanks. It looks like they're doing a good job by themselves," I shot back.

"Come on. These girls need to pay their rent. The first

is coming. I'll take their asses back to the club if you don't tip right, fellas! This ain't no exhibition. Tasty and Delight's money in my left, Honey's in my right."

"Yeah, fuck these ones. We'll leave if ya'll don't do better than this," one said.

A few young looking guys tipped a little more. The other girl that was supposed to dance with me suddenly appeared dressed. When she saw Ray gripping a fist full of money in his hand, she was motivated to join in. She came into the room carrying a dildo. She blocked Tasty and Delight like she was waiting for them to move.

"Next up, Ice. Ice is in the house!"

Tasty and Delight moved toward two men that were sitting next to each other. Within one minute flat, Tasty was on her knees sucking on toes, and Delight was bent over licking a guy's butt crack. Both redeemed the spotlight as the men hooted for them to keep going. Dollars flew from their hands to the floor.

"Cut all *that* bullshit. Don't cheat yourself, treat yourself. Who wants their dick sucked and who wants to fuck?" a voice said loudly.

Ice licked the dildo up and down like she was licking a man's shaft, then she began sucking it a bit. Next, she lifted her right leg and stuffed a dildo inside of herself. After speaking such bold words, Tasty and Delight had no choice but to go their separate ways and begin lap dancing. Ice had all eyes on her, like it or not.

"What you know about that, Ice?" Ray asked. She shot a phony smile.

"Stop being cheap, fellas. Ice told you how she gets down, so if you want to find out what else she can do with that thang, show her how you ball!"

Ice moved the dildo in and out of her kitty kat like she wanted a man's dreams to come true. I watched her face, as she pumped the dildo in and out of her vagina. I could tell she wasn't getting off on the experience, but the guys didn't seem to care. She had too much control for it to appear erotic as far as I was concerned. A man drinking a bottle of beer asked her to take the dildo out of her kitty kat. After she did, he moved the head of a bottle in and out of her opening. I wondered if that stunt hurt her, but it was her pussy, not mine!

"Damn, I think Ice can take two dicks," he said to a friend who stood next to him.

The man with long, neat dreads whispered something in her ear. He tapped his partner on the shoulder and she disappeared in the back with both men. Obviously, her tongue and mouth were for rent . . . and probably more.

"That girl's off the chain," Ray said after she left. From what I gathered, I guess she didn't mind having high mileage. She was so high I don't see how she could manage to form a coherent sentence.

As I gave the man a lap dance, he kept trying to touch my kitty kat. I pushed his hand away, feeling annoyed.

"I'm not poison. I got someone home sexier than you," he told me, trying to use reverse psychology. "Why are you doing this, because you're pretty?" he asked, quickly switching up.

"No, I need the money," I lied. There was no way I was going to tell him about my dysfunctional home life that led me there. It seemed like someone was always trying to figure me out.

"My sister does this because she's pretty, too," he shared. I remained quiet.

"Well if you're going to do it, take their money. Grab their dicks while you're grinding, then jerk it off through their clothes," he whispered in my ear. "You still listening?" he added.

"Yeah," I whispered in his ear back.

"Slow is where it's at. Move slower," he explained as I sat perched on his lap.

"A little to the left," he added. I moved in that direction as instructed. "A little to the right," he added. I moved to the right. "That's it, shortie. You're almost done. I have money. How about giving me some pussy now?" he said. I could feel his erection bulging through his jeans.

"I don't do extras. All I do is dance," I said, feeling like a scratched up, broken record. I wanted to tell him that I wasn't getting paid to star in a high-paying lap dance video. Since Ayanna was in need of money, I understood how she ended up having sex to make more. Falling by the wayside after being tempted made so much sense, as unfortunate as the truth turned out to be. I suddenly became bored by my environment, tired of getting men off just because I could. My desire to put on my act was waning and began to trail off into apathy.

The thug got mad at me and shoved dollars in my hand. I gladly got off of his lap.

"Shit, I might as well call my girl," he mumbled grouchily. He whipped out his cell phone and began dialing some numbers as if I were supposed to be jealous. Not! The dollars weren't flying, so I decided it was time to leave. When I informed Ray that I was finished shaking my ass, he came into the room while I got dressed. He counted my money and told me we'd split it 50/50. My cut amounted to only fifty crummy dollars.

"If you want this other one hundred, let me lick it."

"You know I don't do extras, Ray."

"It's me, not those men up in the spot."

"So what if it is? It's just not appropriate. Not all dancers put out, and you already know my reputation," I told him while grabbing my bag.

"Give me some head then," he said, still trying to negotiate. Ray laid on the dirty mattress on the floor, but I ignored him. "Don't you want the other hundred?" he asked. When he lifted his shirt up, I thought I saw a money clip.

"Just give me the fifty. You can keep the hundred if I've got to go through all of that to get it. I took your word for what you said. I did what you asked me to do. If you want to switch up now, fuck it!" I told him annoyed.

"Take it," Ray said.

I could tell that I made him feel like the scoundrel he was.

"No, it's the principle of the thing. If you don't think I deserve it because I earned it in there, keep all of what I earned on your money clip," I said, putting on the rest of my clothes. "I'm going home to get some rest, I'm tired."

"I don't have no money clip," he explained.

"Don't play me, I saw it."

He lifted up his shirt revealing a gun.

"What are you doing with that thing?"

"I thought they'd tip more. They're all hustlers. Calm down. Ain't nobody gonna shoot you or nothing," he confessed. "I needed this piece to make sure everyone stayed in their place back there. I told you I wasn't gonna let anything happen to you. If I didn't like you, I could've scared you back at the club. I carry a piece all of the time."

"What did you say?" I asked. I felt stress build up in my head. I didn't want to appear to worried that I'd seen the gun, but I was. I tried to remain calm, cool, and collected without panicking and speeding off so fast the wheels of my car would leave the ground.

"Look, they all work for me. I'm one of the biggest dealers in DC. All the young'ins run product for me."

"I thought you had guests from out of town? Now they're hustlers?"

"A couple of my boys were from out of town. They just got in from a flight."

"There wasn't one dude in there who was thinking about an NBA playoff game. I see how you get down. That's cool. I don't appreciate you misleading me like this. People like you are poisoning our community, and misleading impressionable youth," I said, considering that Ray could've befriended someone like my son, and gotten him off track, just like those other young black men. "You knew that if you told me I'd think it was a totally different kind of crowd."

"I don't even want to do it to you now. Here, take this, this is my own money. It's $500. And I don't want anything from you. I'm going to look out for you like a little sister," he explained. "Look, I like being able to buy nice clothes, own property, and luxury cars. Don't hate the player, hate the game."

"I don't want your damn money. Keep that shit. You're pathetic!" I said, feeling guilty that even my meager stripping tips came from a room full of small time hustlers. After I said that, I heard Ice and a man arguing, then I heard what sounded like a fight break out in the living room. Ray jumped up with his gun drawn.

"Lock the door!" he yelled, bursting into the hallway.

I grabbed my bag, looking for a way out. By that time, Tasty and Delight were screaming, bullets were flying, and I was using my bag to shield my body as I crouched down, pushing my way out of the swelling crowd. As my eyes scanned the room, I noticed drug paraphernalia and alcohol out in the open. I had to drop to my knees and crawl through the sea of busy feet. I don't know how I did it, but I managed to make it to the front door and run down the stairwell. By the time I ran across the complex to my car, I heard police sirens howling in the background. It took all I had not to mash on the gas and burn rubber, but I knew it could draw undue suspicion to me. I held it together enough to drive a few miles, making it to the parking lot of an all-night supermarket so I could collect my thoughts.

I suddenly felt the need to see my man on the side, and leave the shady club characters alone for good! I'd taken all I could stand, although dealing with them did indeed serve its purpose. Ayanna was right about something. I wasn't streetwise, nor was I cut out to keep tipping around in the hood. As I whipped out my prepaid cell phone, I acknowledged that the most important thing was that I met my "marital insurance policy" Rafiq while out and about in the strip club. At that point, I had no reason to strip in public, or private, for a group of men ever again. Thankfully, I escaped without incident, while exploring my sexuality and escaping the pressure in my family, and professional, life. I considered myself lucky that I didn't get caught up in any serious mess and turned to a man with a professional career, instead of the many strange ones who did God knows what. As if I hadn't done enough to push my luck, I still hadn't learned my lesson. Little did I know, seeing Rafiq was still a risk that would eventually prove to jeopardize something other than my safety.

16

WHERE IS THE LOVE?

"I'm not wearing any panties," I said, licking my lips to get myself in the mood for phone sex.

"Damn, baby. Why you gotta tell me that shit?" Rafiq answered.

"Since you're still up, do you want to hear about what I'm doing?" I teased, feeling relaxed and comfortable enough to engage in phone sex.

"What is my girl doing?" Rafiq questioned.

"You didn't call me on my lunch break today after I sent you some naked pictures, so maybe I should stop here. Passing the time away at my desk wasn't easy. In fact, I struggled to get my work done."

"I didn't know you sent me pictures. I'm sorry I didn't call, sugar. I had a long, stressful day. In fact, this is the first time I've picked up the cell phone," Rafiq explained.

"I noticed. Thanks a lot. Now I'm too wound up to sleep, so I'm pinching and teasing my big nipples, while I'm thinking about you right now."

"What you're doing sounds, well, delicious. Please forgive your daddy and continue. I like what I'm hearing,"

Rafiq answered, breathing hard into his cell phone. It was Rafiq's idea to spring for two Virgin Mobile cell phones that allowed us to pay by the minute, without a contract. Activating the account required no real names or addresses. We often left each other sexy messages when we couldn't manage to see each other. I committed my pass code to memory, and I suspected Rafiq did too. These prepaid cell phones enabled us to cheat with no risk of having our calls traced by our mates. I had always wanted a man to understand me. I thought Donavan did, but I found that man in Rafiq.

"I miss you and I really need to see you. It sounds like you've been pushing yourself to the limit, so how about some hot, sexy playtime that can help you relax a little? Can you sneak out for a little fun, so we can finish this story in person, or what? " I finally asked.

"Are you proposing something like room service at the usual hotel?" my lover asked, perking up.

"Yeah, I'll be room service . . . coming to serve you, but only if your wife hasn't fed you yet. Last time we didn't get a room, I got cheated with a quickie cut short."

"You must admit it was fun almost getting caught by the park ranger though."

"Speak for yourself. It wasn't you struggling to get your clothes on, while your ass was up in the air."

Rafiq chuckled.

"You liked it, that moment was priceless. Now you're hooked on having sex in unusual places, when we are up to trying something spontaneous. Anyway baby, I can't wait for you to slide up and down my pole. I'm hungry for some sucking and poking. So tell me one thing first," Rafiq said.

"What?"

"Have you been saving that sweet, gushy pussy for me?"

"More than that. I'm saving it down to every little kiss.

You know I'm your down and dirty, freak nasty chick. I've got a whole lot of licks and kisses just waiting for you. My husband finally tried to get in my drawers, but I played him and held the pussy hostage. My kids come home soon, so we need to make this one count for all it's worth."

"It always does, and I want to hear the details about what you did to that stupid asshole later."

"He's so selfish, I don't even miss it like I used to. It's you that I can't get out of my mind," I said, boosting Rafiq's ego.

"That's because you've got me now, a man with exquisite, discerning taste. I've been constantly fantasizing about what you look like in that Victoria's Secret outfit I have in my trunk calling your name. And if you really need me, you know I'll be there. All you've got to do is call and say so."

"You're so good to me. Another present so soon?" I asked, beaming.

"You know I love dressing you, 'cause you deserve to look fly, and your husband isn't doing his job. You just wait until winter comes. Something tells me that someone is in for Jimmy Choos and leather skirts in every color this winter."

"All of that sounds great, baby, but right now my mind isn't on clothes. I'm imagining the way it feels when you touch me after I take them off. Are you going to cum on my back, my big tits, or my ass this time?"

"I'm bone hard from just thinking about pushing my dick inside of my Honey. You know I'm only getting it twice a year from my wife. So how about all three, one each time I cum? Now what are we waiting for? Let's roll. It'll be time to get to work before we know it, so pack your bag just in case there's no time to go home. We'll think of something to cover up where we were."

Both Rafiq and I became addicted to the naughty sexcapades that soon became a part of our daily routines. What began as doing impressions of our neglectful mates, turned into something hot and steamy. At first, the attention I received while stripping was addictive, but then finding Rafiq became the next best, exciting thing. We made it to our secret location. I got there first so I scattered rose petals on the bed, ordered some Cristal, then lit about fifteen candles enclosed in glass bowls I'd brought along.

"Yes. Are you looking for someone?" I asked, wearing a mardi gras mask to cover my face, a tantalizing stripper outfit, and a scent that Rafiq had given me the last time we hooked up. By that time I'd arranged the room, the lights were off, the candles were burning, and sexuality was oozing from my aura.

His mouth nearly dropped open. Rafiq's eyes looked glazed as he looked at me like I was some juicy steak. In no time flat we were tearing each other's clothes off after Rafiq hung a "Do Not Disturb" sign on the doorknob. The only thing that he didn't tear off of me was my four-inch heels that I slipped on in the parking lot of the hotel. Next, he smelled my neck to see if I was wearing his favorite perfume that he bought me. I was, of course!

"Damn. Look at you, girl. Can I get a lap dance?" my lover asked.

"With no music?"

"Let's make our own music. Come sit on Daddy Rafiq's lap," he suggested, patting his leg a few times.

Just looking at Rafiq always made me wanna grab a handful of pussy and touch myself. The candles illuminated the room just right. I could see quite a bit since I'd lugged in so many. I looked around the hotel room through my mask and led Rafiq to a plush chair on the opposite side of the room.

"I will, Daddy, but first there's something I want to show you," I told him as he sat down in the chair.

I positioned myself on the floor, then began slithering around seductively, ultimately laying on my back. I opened my legs wide and slowly pulled a long, shiny chain out of my kitty kat.

"Damn!" Rafiq said, watching the links appear before his eyes.

"*Now* you can have it your way," I said while standing. I sat in my lover's lap, then draped the beads around my lover's neck. I positioned myself on top of Rafiq, rubbing flesh on flesh, wondering how I was going to give Rafiq some naughty booty without inspiration from a songstress or rapper. I smiled as I placed both of my feet on the floor between his, while grinding slowly and seductively to the beat of our own music. After some time, I guided his hands toward my thighs, as I stroked my breasts while eyeing him, continuing to move around on top of him.

"Mmm," I moaned, feeling his stiffening dick caress the lips of my pussy.

"I know you've got to feel all of this," he commented as his warm, stiff tool began poking me in the leg.

"If I didn't know better, I'd think you set me up," I joked, between moans and heavy breathing. Both of our chests heaved as we continued to engage in this different kind of foreplay.

Fearing that my lover could slide his tool inside of me, I moved my legs around his sides. I then arched my back as I massaged my clit with my left hand, and stroked the back of my lover's back with my right.

I finished my nude lap dance, and openly watched Rafiq pleasure himself while I opened my legs on the bed and played with my pussy.

"Talk to me, baby. Tell me something good," I said, fingering myself.

"Honey, you're my kind of sexy. I want to stick my dick in that sweet pussy. I didn't know you knew tricks like that," Rafiq responded, stroking his beautiful dick. "Talk about kinky. I love a woman who is in touch with her sexuality like you are. The shit you do is off the hook. It gets me so turned on."

I finally took off my mask, letting it fall to the floor. I moved my left index finger in and out of my mouth rapidly as my lover spoke. The veins in his dick were getting thicker and more pronounce.

"C'mon baby," I said after I took my finger out of my mouth. I turned over, smacked my ass, then looked back at him. "If you think you can handle this, come get it. Fuck me, Rafiq," I added as he removed the chain that was dangling around his neck.

Before long, I felt like a porn director who was instructing new talent on the set. That Negro started twitching and quivering, and I had to tell him to slow down and hold back so he could be sure that my hungry pussy was well fed. After teasing him so long, he was so aroused that he kept saying he wanted to shoot cum all over my back, but I begged my lover to slow his roll and fuck me better than my husband ever had.

After that ego booster, Rafiq was primed to take his time. He opened a condom wrapper, and then started sticking me with steady thrusts from behind as I held on firmly to his toned butt. Rafiq didn't have a layer of fat on his body. His muscles were so defined I could see his lats, triceps, and muscles I didn't even know the names of. The man's abs were so tight he had this V-cut thing going on, reminding me of a chocolate Superman. In his case, age was sure enough just a number. As I considered all of what I was getting, I turned around to watch him do his thing as I smothered him with my big, round ass. Indescribable noises escaped from my mouth as my eyes rolled in the back of my head, and my knees pressed against fresh rose petals that set the mood right. I wondered if anyone in a nearby hotel room could hear my love sounds, but the neglected part of me didn't care as long as I was enjoying it.

We didn't talk nasty like we usually did. This time we just enjoyed our bodies and souls meeting again. Rafiq began smacking my ass harder and harder, proving his unwavering stamina. I began anticipating each love blow and grew wetter as I could feel the rhythm of his dominant stroking. I gripped the mattress by placing my arms between my legs—that's the beauty of being flexible! In fact, he had me yelling and screaming like I lost my mind, then I let loose and gushed like a broken water main was between my legs. I came so hard and long, I was surprised my toes didn't curl up!

Rafiq had impeccable manners, and he was tender and considerate. It appeared that he respected me, and I respected him. I looked to him to give me everything that I wasn't getting from Donavan, and because of that, he was on my mind constantly. During our first encounter, we clicked right away. He always pulled out the chair for me on our dinner dates, opened the door for me when we were headed to a mall, and always made sure that I was taken care of and wanted for nothing when we shared those stolen moments. Rafiq always told me how desirable and pretty that I was, and before long, we were no longer strangers. He made me smile on my worst days, and I enjoyed every moment of my time with him above and beyond the money he'd given me for stripping and keeping him entertained. With most of the other men I stripped for, there was an illusion of a connection since that was a part of my job. But in this case, the agenda was different, although we did meet in a strip club. Rafiq and I were two married people having a discreet affair, in the mood to play behind our mates' backs.

Rafiq kept me from falling apart when things got rough, and our relationship had moved beyond sex, although the sex was great. Although my initial joy was the attention I received, we went deeper on some other issues, such as HIV prevention. It all started when we were just about to get that pump action going, but Andrea was a guest on a popular R&B station in the DC area, pushing some concept she cooked up called PAS. The hostess explained that PAS stands for Personal Assessment for Sexual Activity, then she proceeded to address her listeners.

"I know my peeps in Chocolate City, and those listening on line, are probably mad at me right now for stopping the music tonight, but every now and then I feel like there's a reason to slow the love talk and gossip roll. Let's talk about something serious for a minute, ya'll. HIV. Now I know some of ya'll probably don't want to hear what's about to be said, but maybe at least one person out there won't hate on this woman and appreciate what she's trying to do. Don't send me no hate mail to give to her, 'cause I won't forward a damn thing! If you like the message, fine. If you don't, turn the dial, or keep your mouth shut, and take five minutes out of your night to listen, okay?"

The host belted out a phony sounding chuckle, then continued reading her script.

"PAS is a system developed by author Andrea Blackstone, in response to infidelity and dishonest dating practices, and the role that concerned singles can play in doing their part to attempt to prevent HIV transmission. She describes PAS as a tool that is meant to help sexually active singles learn more about their potential partners they seek to date, before they even sleep together. After speaking to numerous readers and observing the intricacies of the dating scene, Andrea sought to do something to challenge sexually active singles to guard their health, and also protect their potential partners. The challenge is a collection of important steps that involve questions and proactive measures.

"Welcome to the show, Andrea," Terry Towns said. "Could you tell everyone out there listening why and how you came up with PAS?"

"Thank you for having me here this evening on the Terry in the Town Show. I am excited about developing PAS," the author said. "After writing *Nympho*, I wanted to approach the issue of cheating, disease, and personal responsibility in a chic fashion. People are urged to get tested, but from my observations there is more that can be done to catch up with what's happening in modern times. People aren't going to stop having sex, but people can become more proactive by connecting prevention with PAS. With PAS, each partner must talk to each other about sexual issues, then pass the PAS test to engage in intimate activities. Earning a preliminary 'pass' to sleep with someone may not be a sexy premise, but it could save some lives. I want people to feel it's cool to empower themselves, as opposed to feeling embarrassed for being assertive."

"Let me play devil's advocate for a hot minute. What would you say to those that fear violating a person's privacy, those hatin' who think that you're trying to send a useless message 'cause people won't listen, or those who would argue PAS isn't a system that's guaranteed to work?"

"When a couple feels ready to invite sex into their relationship, PAS is supposed to serve as a preliminary plan of action, but of course it can't be a perfect process. The premise is, after developing a reasonable rapport with someone, both parties should open up about essential information linked to one's sexual history, desires, and typical habits. If a person is willing to sleep with another individual, discussion of certain issues should be mandatory, as opposed to regarding them as taboo. If a person is not willing to take reasonable steps to address the other party's health concerns, I hope that the person with a PAS assessment will quickly reconsider sleeping with a given prospect. Also, if a partner is reasonably suspected, or caught being unfaithful, the opposite party is highly encouraged to cease any, and all, physical activity with that person, taking time to sort out some pertinent health issues. Although some may feel that PAS may go against the grain, every step is reasonable and responsible. There should be no reason why any health conscious person should not want to do something savvy, such as celebrate the beauty of PAS."

After Terry interviewed Andrea, Rafiq and I looked at each other at the same time. It made us slow down and think about the health aspects of what we were getting ourselves into. We decided to take her challenge to screen each other before getting all freaky deaky, although PAS is meant for single folks more than married cheaters. Yeah, we messed up on some points, but we got the basics in, tailoring it to fit our needs at the time.

All of this made me open up about some specifics on the home front. I told Rafiq about the email I got from Donavan's mistress, among other things. He was supportive and even sympathetic. He held my hand through getting my health checked out, and I started my PAS file, after his results came back clean. His air of responsibility and compassion made me want some of what my eyeballs had been enjoying even more. The results were in—we were both, drug, disease, and drama free, and we decided to celebrate afterward. Rafiq was a player, but he was up front with his game. I knew what I was dealing with and so did he. I thought he was one of few men who understood that you could often get what you wanted *and* tell the truth. Candor we shared fostered honesty and trust, so I thought.

As a result, he got rather attached to me and ultimately paid me well to sex me exclusively. I understood his point about fucking men in the club, so I ruled out extras, except hand jobs and fingering in exchange for role play, blindfolds, handcuffs, hot candle wax, playing with toys, and even asshole licking. Rafiq and I didn't fear being kinky with each other when we were in the mood for something naughty, as opposed to spooning after something nice. Talking about willing to try anything at least once . . . that was Rafiq! I never even managed to slither into that sexy lingerie Rafiq wanted me to model for him, for obvious reasons.

Back then, I was thinking that one man's junk is another man, or woman's, treasure. Had I met Rafiq before I met Donavan, I could've easily pictured him being the father of my children. I just couldn't understand why his wife didn't want kids, among other things he told me about her. I found myself becoming a bit envious of her, since I knew I could never have him as my very own. Even so, I honored our nonverbal contract. The reason for two married people hooking up is to reinforce the understanding that neither party intends on disturbing what they have at home. That's just real. Divorce may be a fantasy, but not a reality. The nature of having something on the side demands that they should stay on the side. We both understood the rules to the game, and never gave each other drama about it. Rafiq and I were careful to focus on our adventurous encounters. Each time we parted, we looked forward to the next, and the next, and the next!

Some women are never satisfied, but I wasn't one of them. I once had thoughts of cuddling, kissing, and sharing a little pillow talk with someone that I could talk dirty with. After silently considering the way we made each other feel, I began to gloat. As luck would have it, I finally had a shot at having my cake and eating it too, and that made me feel like a real goddess. Neither one of us made it home that night, but I felt that sleeping in the arms of a man who knew how to make me feel like a real woman was truly worth it. And if anyone that knew me well observed a special new glow that women get when they're sprung, because they've got something good, I don't think I even would've cared.

During our next meeting, I made up my mind that I was going to surprise Rafiq with letting him know that it was no longer necessary to pay me when he saw me. I must admit that I was on my way to falling in love with a married man, even if I had to secretly share him with his wife who didn't even appreciate such a caring, sexy, and romantic black man. As I blew out every candle in the room, and the smoldering smoke rose from each wick as Rafiq waited for me to slide in between the sheets with him, I decided I didn't care if he belonged to someone else. Just like that email I received said, more than a fair share of men will never settle down . . . including the confused married ones. You can have it all today with a man, and lose it all tomorrow. No truer words were ever spoken, but eventually, the universe has its way of forcing those who disrespect it out of hiding.

17

DERANGED

Ms. Sapphire was tripping with a capital T. Had I known getting my kitty kat licked by her would've set her off like that, I would've kept my damn legs closed. While I was getting my hair done, her possessive ass blew up my cell phone at least five times. Her pages equated to eleven freaking calls. Does this spell stalker, crazy, or deranged? I let her know that I didn't want to talk to her and that I'd call the police if I had to take it to the next level. She claimed she was calling to check on me, but I didn't want anyone with Sapphire's mentality checking on me any longer. She was straight neurotic, showing every sign that I ought to stay away from her for the rest of my life.

"Don't call me anymore!" I yelled into the phone, as my hairdresser in Silver Spring was perming my hair. When Sapphire attempted to talk to me again, I hopped up from the chair and stormed into the bathroom. Given what already occurred, in addition to the new details that Ayanna provided, I was already irritable. It wasn't difficult for her to hit my button.

"I'll tell your husband everything about us!" she threatened.

"Stop acting like you've been played. You just played along with it, so don't get mad. I never lied to you. As I said before, I like MEN, and I have a husband. Before you tell my dirt, I'd tell him my damn self! He wouldn't care anyway. He's still doing his thing," I answered. "I have what I need now, and it's not you, Sapphire. No one in this world is going to tell me what I'm supposed to do, including you."

"Oh, so you think I'm some sort of girl toy?"

"I wouldn't say all that. You'll never have the top spot. Since you can't accept your position in the game, forget my number, and don't ever call me again. Game over!" I snapped in a mean, cold tone.

After I returned to the hairdresser's chair, everyone was looking at me sideways. To add insult to injury, the stress of everything that was unfolding prompted me to stare at myself in the mirror and cut a whole six inches! By the time she trimmed it up, it was barely grazing my collarbone. Six months from now, my long hair should be back if I could keep the scissors away from my head, but episodes like this weren't helping. I hoped I could learn to like my new haircut.

While my hairdresser was trying to fix this situation, the nut kept ringing my cell phone. The next time, my stylist answered it with my permission. She informed Sapphire that she was acting like a straight donkey. She didn't know what all of that phone ringing and yelling was about, but she was concerned about causing my hair to fall out if she couldn't concentrate on working with those chemicals. Who would blame her? No one wants to open themselves up for a lawsuit.

When Sapphire rang my phone again, I told her that I was at the hairdresser and that she should cool it. I couldn't believe that she called back and told a sixty-year-old, homemade biscuit baking, Southern Christian woman to suck her pussy! After being nasty to Ms. Betty for no reason, she sent a mountain of pages with "28424" as the return number. I was officially frightened of Sapphire after she left two messages for my listening pleasure. In the first, she rattled off something about thinking I'll become a successful dancer someday and that I should keep trying to make it to the top. She wished me well and hung up. In the second, she told me she'd *see* me at the top. She also let me know that she felt that I threw away a real friendship over silly things. The frosting on the cake was that she pretended as if I'd been begging to talk to her. After I listened to the message carefully, I understood that she'd turned the whole story around to make a new woman think that I was the one blowing up her phone like her number was about to change. All of this while she was getting some head!

"You can't fuck with shorty. Shorty came over, drops to her knees, and is giving me some vicious head. If you gotta go, you gotta go! When she comes through, I gotta go, baby. Don't fuck up a sister's groove. We're friends, okay, momma? I've accepted that. I'm dating new women. I've decided to concentrate on this dime piece right here. I'm not going to argue when she's over. She gets first priority in my life now. Always give. Always give . . . mmmm. Mmm, damn, Sadiqua! Always give a friend time to get back with you. I just called to make sure you're taking care of yourself, ok. I gotta go," Sapphire said in between moans.

When my knees started knocking in the chair, my hairdresser was so concerned for my safety she told me to pack a bag and crash at her place, which was about an hour away. That was nice of her, but I couldn't impose. Instead, I did take a piece of her advice and investigate how to pursue a restraining order. Thanks to Sapphire, the beautician did burn my head with that damn lye perm, but I convinced Ms. Betty that none of it was her fault and she had nothing to worry about.

I ran into Whole Foods, hopped on 495, and took my ass to bed after I turned off my cell phone. I only managed to get five hours of sleep though. I looked at the caller ID and Sapphire was ringing my home phone like her life depended on me picking it up. Every time I answered, she hung up. I got tired of playing her cat and mouse game and finally called 911. With my kids getting picked up in less than four days, I had to nip all of her shit in the bud.

"The commissioner's office can tell you how to get a restraining order to tell him to stop calling you," the 911 operator said. "Let me put you through to her," she added. Although I was frazzled, I managed to explain the situation to a woman in the commissioner's office.

"Did you hear her voice?" she asked.

"I did some of the time, but not every time. This morning she's been hanging up a lot."

"You can go after her for telephone misuse, but you have to have had heard her voice, that's why I'm asking. If you have any saved messages, that will help. Your other option is to get a peace order."

"Is that the same as a restraining order?" I asked, but she never answered my question.

"The peace order will be more effective if the police have an address where she can be served. They're not going to go looking for her if you press criminal charges. They'll try to punish her for the crime you're alleging."

"Thanks for you help. I appreciate it greatly," I told her.

"You're welcome," she answered politely.

The whole time the woman was speaking with me, Sapphire was busy beeping in, trying to get through. She continued playing her phone game for almost an hour. Finally, she spoke.

"You just shitted on me. Now you have an enemy for life!" Click.

I was shaking like a wind blown leaf. I couldn't believe my dealings with Sapphire had gone from sugar, to shit, so fast. I tried calling her to calm her down. I wanted to let her know I would be forced to turn over all of the saved messages to the police if she didn't stop harassing me. A grudge is a terrible thing when someone is unstable. Because I hadn't known Sapphire for years, I didn't know if she planned to kill me, take a hit out on me, or if she was just blowing off a whole lot of steam that she felt was justified. I called Sapphire one last time, but my efforts proved to be fruitless.

"Sweetheart, this isn't who you think it is. Sapphire is tied up for the moment," a woman said.

"Well someone just made a threat," I replied. After I said that short line, I hung up understanding that Sapphire hated my guts and was capable of anything. I called the drug dealing brother from the club. I figured I could put his street smarts to work for the sake of something good.

"Let me call you back on my other number. I need to put some more minutes on my cell phone," Ray explained.

"Why do you have a prepaid when you stay on the phone all of the time? That's a rip off." He got quiet. "Oh, I get it," I said putting two and two together. The police couldn't trace illegal activity through prepaid phones that weren't registered. When he called me back I told him the whole story.

"Anyway, don't go over to her townhouse in your car to get the address to get for the restraining order. It's too risky. If you want to go I can get a car for you to use from someone."

"That's okay. Thanks though," I answered. I was already on my way to her house. I hoped my memory held out. The other option was using her job address at The Foxy Lady, but I felt that could make Sapphire want to hurt me for real.

"You didn't take money from her or sex her? There's something you're not telling me."

"No, I swear!" I lied. I also wasn't about to tell him about the mess with Ayanna.

"We can deal with this my way or the police's way. I prefer you to use the legal way. I'm getting too old now for the street way."

"I don't want any trouble from you either," I told him. "That's not necessary. I don't want to add fuel to the fire," I added.

I hurried over to Sapphire's town house to write down the address. I was able to find it. Luckily, I made it before many people in the neighborhood got home from work. I didn't want anyone who knew her to possibly spot me. I returned home and hid it away with all of the information I had about Sapphire, including her home, cell phone number, and a picture she'd given me of herself. I inserted it in a sealed envelope. I neatly wrote the words "IF ANYTHING SHOULD HAPPEN TO ME PLEASE READ" on the outside of it, then affixed it to my note board in my office. My thoughts were all over the place. I turned on the TV, popped in an advanced aerobics tape, and worked out like I was on kryptonite. I needed somewhere to leave my frustration, and I knew I had to stay my ass out of strip clubs. I was good and frustrated. On my way back home, I checked my cell phone messages, praying it wasn't Sapphire again. It was. I supposed her girlfriend left so her tone was completely different. She sounded controlling, manly, rude, and slung around choice words, raw as hell.

"Damn, you know you act like I blew up your car or some shit. You sound like you out of your mind talking about you're going to call the cops on me for calling you, basically talking to you. All the shit I done for you! I been there for your motherfucking ass. But now, you acting all crazy. I knew your ass was crazy. You really is crazy! You need to get some medical attention. Take your ass to the strip club and dance for a dollar, bitch 'cause that's all you're fucking worth is a fucking dollar! When your husband was shitting on you, I was there. You're gonna stay with him so he can shit on you some more. Check your attitude and yourself. You's a weak-ass bitch. I need to call the cops on you for being a trick-ass ho! I did everything I could to show you I was real. I looked out for you. I showed you I was a friend to you, and treated you like a queen. I was trying to look out for a sista trying to do some things. This is the thanks I get, you stank-ass ho. You gettin' to be just like them chicken heads in the club, that sister of yours, and out here on the street. You playing a game you don't know shit about. *Fuck you!*"

18

ONE WIFE, TWO LOVERS

I thought I'd escaped the street politics of strip clubs and drama that seemed to go with it, but I started thinking about that twice. I was so alarmed by Sapphire's behavior that I fell into Donavan's arms, nestled within what I felt could finally be a bit of genuine tenderness. I'd always heard horror stories about crazy male customers becoming obsessed with strippers, but not strippers stalking and becoming obsessed with other strippers! Rafiq was a dream, but Sapphire turned out to be the lesbian "admirer" from hell, who was fucked up in the head.

I had no idea how many of the girls hooked up outside of the club for personal reasons. Part of me wanted to give peace a chance with my husband, and part of me just wanted to use him because I needed comfort. Either way, I wanted to wipe my slate clean of all dealings with Sapphire. I felt Donavan also wanted to chase me because he noticed I was no longer chasing him, so I made it a point to genuinely enjoy the "courting game" this time. Plus, I'd done away with my ponytail, and in his eyes, he'd assume I willingly got a fresh new haircut to update my look. The new me wasn't "soccer mom bland." Perhaps part of him did desire me again. I wasn't sure if it was the fact that I'd added some style or not. I suddenly felt the need to sport a stylish Prada bag, white-gold diamond earrings, and Versace shades that Rafiq bought me. Sweet.

With only one day left of being childless, I wanted to rest a little bit, since I stayed stressed the hell out, and had been out and about most of the summer. The only good thing that happened was getting off the hook with that reckless driving and speeding ticket fiasco in Virginia. I hauled my butt into traffic court one day before, and fortunately, the cop didn't show. No demerit points, no convictions or fines. No traffic school. God was looking out for me, no doubt, because Virginia doesn't play since they implemented all of those new speeding laws!

I slept until one o'clock that Saturday, and my cell phone was on vibrate so I wouldn't be disturbed. I checked my cell phone messages when I began to stir. I don't know if Donavan had a fight with his mistress or what, but oddly enough, he and I were acting like husband and wife that day. We spent the whole day watching TV, tickling each other, making love, and listening to jazz on 105.9. It was a romantic and nice experience. Unexpected, but definitely the kind that makes a girl feel like a million dollars. I even decided that I'd move past my male lover. Sapphire was pounding some sense in my head, and I was trying to reclaim my normal life, although I'd become addicted to sexual excitement.

To top it all off, for the first time in many years, Donavan offered to take me to a get together full of his closest friends and frat brothers. Actually, it was a 40th birthday party for one of his boys. Although I was his wife, my husband wasn't the biggest fan of bringing sand to the beach. He usually didn't invite me to accompany him to parties and get togethers. In fact, it was so rare that I'd forgotten

he was Greek, despite the fact that fifteen years ago our
wedding was full of his "brothers." I hadn't seen many of
them over the years, but I knew his membership was still
active. Since I had never been to college, I really had no
interest in male or female organizations of that nature.

I told Donavan that the party sounded like fun and
agreed to go with him. Before I thought about it, I'd soft-
ened up like the wife I'd been in the old days. As suggested, I freshened up and threw on a casual mini-skirt, a
tight top, and a sexy pair of stilettos that accentuated my
freshly done toes and sexy legs. I also highlighted my eyes
and lips, compliments of MAC cosmetics. I was the type
that normally sported sweats and had forgotten what a
tube of lipstick looked like after having our second child.
Although I decided to stop exotic dancing, it did do something for me besides getting back at my Don or making
me feel wanted. Just as I told Ayanna, it awakened my sensuality again and made me more daring. When I walked
out into the living room and asked him if I looked ok, I
could tell I did by the way he was staring at me. It had
been a very long time since he looked at me like that, and
it gave me that first date feeling again. I found myself feeling excited and happy, despite everything else that was oc-
curring in the other areas of my life. Everything was going
really well. We even had a real talk in the car as we headed
up Georgia Avenue, toward 16th Street. As we made it to
our destination, I realized that all of my lies were beginning to fall apart.

When we arrived at the gathering, the party was already
jumping, and we needed to catch up with the fun everyone else was having. Balloons, party streamers, and all
sorts of party décor was everywhere. Even so, I felt the typical discomfort that anyone experiences when meeting a
significant other's friends or colleagues for the first time.
Despite that, everyone was very friendly, and appeared to

be warm and inviting. I shook a lot of hands, smiled at a lot of unfamiliar faces, and watched Donavan beam as he escorted me on his arm. He and I ate a little of this, and a little of that. Everything from exotic cheeses to sliced fresh fruit, shrimp and cocktail sauce, veggie platters, and potluck dishes were displayed on two long tables covered with tablecloths in the living room. Shortly after we arrived, someone made an announcement that everyone should start gathering in the living room since some of the wives were getting things together to sing happy birthday and serve cake and ice cream in honor of the birthday boy.

Things were going well until I said, "Honey, this is a mean bowl of chili. Who made this? It's excellent. Boy would I like to have the recipe."

"That's Mad Dog's specialty. I'm sure he was the one that brought it. I showed up to many a spade games in college, just to get a bowl of this stuff," Donavan said, half laughing. "He never would tell anyone what he puts in it, so I wouldn't count on getting that recipe."

"Mad Dog? Why do they call him that?" I asked, wrinkling my forehead a little. "I don't recall you ever introducing me to this one. He must be some kind of nut," I added.

"It's a frat thing. That was his line name the big brothers gave him. He was my closest boy while we were pledging. After that, we became very good friends. He and his family just moved back to the area not too long ago when his job transferred him back to his home base. He's been away since we've been here. I guess I should have him over to the house some time soon," Donavan explained. "There you are. Hey partner, come here for a minute before we sing happy birthday to Dwight. It seems as though you've got another fan of your world-famous chili," Donavan joked, holding me around the waist while talking to someone. I was so into my husband, I wasn't paying attention to who was walking toward us.

While the man drew closer, Donavan resumed whispering naughty propositions in my ear. I was paying more attention to his rare offer of having my clit sucked until I came in his mouth! After that, he agreed to fuck me until another orgasm welled up inside of me. I responded to his flirting spree by offering to give him head in the car to warm him up. We alternated between acting silly and flirting with each other.

I had finally looked at the man, my lover, Rafiq. He came over and pulled my husband by the elbow, as if he didn't see me standing there. Realizing he was Mad Dog, my heart thumped so hard I could feel it pulsate in my throat. I plastered a fake cheesy smile on my face as the men distanced themselves from me, but I could still hear every word.

"Oh my gaaawd! Look at shorty right there. She's looking too good tonight! You slick dog! You brought Honey here to spice up the party tonight. On behalf of Dwight and every man in here, thanks for doing something special, dawg."

"You know her?" my husband asked, noticing that Rafiq was checking me out. I felt like running over to break up their conversation. I decided not to do it because that would make the whole thing look very suspicious. I figured that I should stay put and assumed Rafiq would brush it off properly. Instead, he didn't. As I heard bits and pieces of the conversation unfold, I began to feel frozen. For once that entire summer, I was feeling real chilly! I simply couldn't move or speak until it was all out, and it was becoming harder and harder to keep that smile plastered on my face. In fact, it had to leave.

"Do I? Is grass green? Of course I know that fine stallion! What time is she dancing? We got some stuck up bittys in here, but so what. If they don't like the show, they can leave and let the door hit them where the Lord split them."

"What do you mean dance? What are you talking about, share this one?"

"Okay, I'll let you in on a little secret, but this shit gotta stay between you and me. The first time I met with Honey, it was for dinner and drinks. I ran into her at a new spot where she was dancing. That night, I went to my usual spot, but the stage stayed empty too long. Only two girls were there because some baller was having his bachelor party in a secret location. He cleaned out the club. You know how all those hoes dream of living large with one of these athletes who only want to get in a new pair of drawers."

"What about it?"

"Anyway, I started coming in the club from time to time to watch her work them beautiful hips she's got. Her husband called her a wrong name while he was smashing that ass in his office. Old girl was really upset. I mean, how dumb could a man be to do something like not keeping his hoes straight? After we agreed there was some chemistry there, things got heated real fast. It started with phone sex. She said her husband was away on a business trip and she wanted to play."

"Oh really?" Donavan said, looking pissed as hell.

"Yeah, dawg! According to her, the husband is an excellent provider for the kids, but he has to be the most trifling person out there. Plus he had this strip club fetish that drove her to living her kinky double life and wanting a little fun outside of her marriage in the first place. I laughed my ass off after she told me how much she gets over on that idiot—I do the same thing to my wife. She said she spends far too much time hiding her dance bag, stripper shoes, and all of the other evidence. She went on to complain about being at home alone. That call and conversation led to me meeting up with her. We did a lot of kissing, hugging, and holding each other tight during some slow dances by candlelight with Barry White playing. After that, we took a sweet little skinny dip in my pool, and things ended with me smashing that ass all last Saturday when my wife was out of town. That broad can take it deep and long!" Rafiq commented, not noticing my husband's bottom lip was beginning to tremble. His face was getting red like my boss's, Mr. Jiles.

"My drawer full of Magnums are gone, and I'm not talking about from using them with the Mrs. As you can see, she's pregnant. I have a thing about screwing her when she's knocked up. Mentally, it makes me wonder if my dick is gonna smack the baby in the head or something, so I found me a little something new again. I'd say she was a welcome back to my hood gift from me to myself."

"So tell me more about this Honey," Donavan said.

"Now some things I ought to keep to myself. But the shit is so good, I've got to tell someone about it. Honey has the greatest stripper moves I've ever seen, and her head game is the best I've ever had! Pussy tastes so much better when it don't share your last name. Honey squatted on my face and smothered me good with that *sweet* kat and let me finish things off with some good anal sex. I can't tell you everything, but I will say that I tried out some positions on that ho I didn't think were humanly possible! That was the best $500 I ever spent for some private stripper shit. Are you hitting that tonight? If you're not, I might have to see if I can slip away for some more of that good, gushy shit. All I have is $50 on me. I've gotten so used to the sound of her high heels hitting my wooden floor on the regular, I hate that my wife's back in town. We've been kicking it at this hotel though."

"A hotel, huh?" Donavan asked, veins nearly popping out of his forehead.

"Yeah. We have this little spot we picked out. Talk about a hot affair! I'll need to run past the ATM too. So tell me what the deal is before I step to her about tonguing my ass tonight, unless you're down with running a train like I used to try to get you to do back in the old days. I'm sure that ho would be down, she's always down with everything and anything. I'm feenin' to pound that freak again, man. I just can't get enough of this one. So how do you know Honey anyway?"

Whap. My husband could contain his anger anymore. It was a bad situation. He threw a heavy-handed punch at his frat brother. Donavan caught Rafiq off guard, so he wobbled, then fell to the floor.

"It's about time you ask that question, you dumb motherfucker. That's my wife you're talking about!" he yelled. Everyone's at head swung in our direction. "My closest frat saw my wife's ass and has been fucking her! Oh hell no! You need a serious beat down." As soon as he stood up, whap, he punched him again.

"Take it easy, Donavan! Don't get crazy on a brother. I didn't know you were married to a stripper ho. You should've said something. God knows I didn't know. You know the world can be a small place," Rafiq insisted, looking alarmed.

"She's the mother of my two children, and she is *not* a stripper!" Donavan screamed.

Just after words heated up, a pregnant waddling woman blew through like a Texas twister spinning out of control. Take my word for it when I say that she made her presence known!

"I heard everything you said, Rafiq. Where's she at?" the woman carrying a beverage in her right hand yelled.

She picked me out based on where I was standing.

"I've got to take off my earrings and have a little talk about what my husband was doing with a slut like you. Stay away from my husband!" Rafiq's wife yelled, taking off her earrings.

"Who are you calling a stripper ho? Like my husband said, I'm no stripper," I shouted in defense of myself.

"She's talking to you . . . obviously," Rafiq said, holding his jaw.

"You stay out of this," his wife yelled. "You have the nerve to talk," she said, twirling her hair up in a bun.

"Now wait a minute. Before you start swinging and causing drama in someone's home, let me have an opportunity to defend myself. I'm a legal secretary at D&R. Clearly, your husband has me mixed up with someone else," I lied to the woman. She just stood there in silence with her jaw puffed out. I turned to her husband. "Maybe you meant what you said as a joke, but how could you insult me with my husband standing here? Show some respect to your wife and the other guests. This is supposed to be a happy occasion. Don't ruin Dwight's nice birthday party," I said, trying to give Rafiq a second chance to cover our asses, and claw our way out of the sinking quicksand. "You also owe my husband and me a speedy apology. I suggest you straighten this mess out right now! You know good and well that we've never met before tonight. Perhaps you are thinking of someone who favors me." I turned back toward his wife. Her swollen cheeks were deflating as she bought into my story. "And as for you, you can have your husband, I don't want him. Obviously, I have one of my own. Let's keep the peace here," I said to his wife.

"I never forget a face or a phat ass. I can *prove* I'm not just talking shit," Rafiq commented.

I couldn't believe he lost his cool in the valley, and actually planned on fessing up. His wife stopped in her tracks and made a U-turn. "Since the truth is all coming out in the open, what about that little brown flesh mole on the inside of the right side of your pussy lip? I can't live like this anymore. I cheated with her because I'm stuck in a dead end marriage with a woman I can't stand to come home to. It's been cheaper to keep Mya, but it's just not worth the aggravation anymore," Rafiq said. It became apparent that he worked hard at sabotaging his own relationship.

My husband looked at me in disbelief. A sour look covered Rafiq's wife's face, then she threw her drink at him. Mya smacked him repeatedly upside the head like she'd done it before. "If that's what you think, no problem. Negro, we have four kids together, you're going to pay me! I don't love your ass anyway. This is your second affair, and I'm tired of it. Once a dog, always a dog! Apparently, the dog I'm married to can't ever be trained," she said as cranberry juice dripped onto Rafiq's designer shirt. After that, she began grabbing anything in sight, throwing meatballs sautéed in sauce, dipping her hand in a pot of collard greens, and throwing an assortment of cheeses at her husband. All sorts of food was flying through the air, and guests were running for cover from the food shower.

"See what you've done! You have gone crazy, you idiot!" my husband growled, reminding me of a walking stick of dynamite. "You are supposed to be a reflection of me. Any one of my clients at the investment firm could've seen my wife shaking her ass! Then what? What about my accounts? What about my image? How could you have the audacity to do something trifling like that? So it is true! When we get home I'm packing my bags. I want a divorce and custody of my kids. I hope you're happy!" Donavan added, nearly shaking with uncontrollable anger.

The onlookers were confused as to where their eyes should focus while we continued our argument. Rafiq and his wife were still having a drama battle against Donavan and I. Both "shows" could've led to an Academy nomination for all of us.

"They're not your kids, they're *our* kids," I said to Donavan. "It doesn't feel so good to find out you've been disrespected, does it?"

He stared at me for about ten seconds, got real close to me, and towered over me like he was a bully trying to intimidate someone. For a fleeting second I wondered if he was going to raise his hand and hit me. He didn't though.

"They're my kids now. You're on your own, and now you can really do what you want without having to sneak and lie about it. If you want Rafiq, take him. But before you carry on, you might want to see how his wife feels about that first."

"Go ahead, Donavan, blame me like you always do! You're just so used to me being your little puppet on a string, but this time, I was the one who did something out of character by exotic dancing. I did my best to make the marriage work, but I couldn't make things happen by myself. I got tired of begging for attention and putting up with you acting funny. And okay, I admit it. I did fuck your boy. Since you seem like you need to hear all the details, his dick is bigger and he fucks better than you. Since everyone wants to air dirty linen, how about what *you* did? Getting cheated on doesn't feel so good, does it, player? You aren't any better. *Now* we're even," I said, ignoring Rafiq's wife.

"Please stop throwing food. I get the point!" Rafiq shouted at Mya.

"I'll have a list of things I want by Monday. If you're smart you'll buy every last one of them," she said. "And it *still* will be cheaper to keep me," she said, patting her stomach.

"Can't you connect the dots, Mya? I don't want to keep

you. I'm done. Finito. Ready to pay your ass for my peace of mind!" Rafiq explained, making motions like a referee with his arms. "When I divorce you, you'll be someone else's headache!"

"Did your ungrateful, sick ass need attention that badly? I haven't done anything but be with you for the last fifteen years, so I hope you're happy!" Donavan chimed in, yelling in my face.

"Oh really, is that right? Being married to you has been no walk in the park, and the way I see it, you have no grounds for divorce based on what I've done! Why bother to get married if you knew you still wanted to run the streets and cheat? I know about you sticking your tongue in some deadbeat stripper's coochie, and her sucking you off. I've been holding this in ever since I found out about your little boy's night out. The street goes two ways, my dear!" I said. Donavan froze.

"How did you find out about that?" he asked.

"I bet you do wonder how I know. Well, don't worry about it. Let's just get a divorce, but I want custody of *my* kids."

"They're my kids, and you'll never win. I'll fight this thing to the bitter end," Donavan yelled.

"If you've forgotten, I work at a law firm," I said, half smirking.

"Not after I'm through. We'll see about that, *Honey*. I think you've got some serious character issues to tend to. Mystique, you're nothing but a stripping slut who didn't know that some things are too sacred to be for sale! After all I've done to provide for our family, you showed me no respect." Donavan shook his head, slinging a fair share of disparaging comments.

"There's something that I want to say," Rafiq said, covered in an edible mess.

"Shut up!" Donavan yelled.

"Say it then. Tell your wife. If you don't, I will. It ain't right for you to flip the script on everyone but yourself."

"You just hold the fuck up. Keep your mouth shut, and stay out of this! This is family business."

"Whatever, player," Rafiq said. He inhaled deeply, then spoke. "I was holding the camcorder at the bachelor party. I left that night when my wife paged me because she went into labor with our first child."

"I said keep your mouth shut, *brother*," Donavan urged, trying to quiet his loudmouth friend.

"I told Donavan I was sorry I had to go. I'd make the wedding if I could but I couldn't promise depending on if my wife was having false labor pains or not. In case I didn't make it back, I told him I knew his wife must be someone really special, and that I looked forward to meeting her in the future."

"Rafiq, don't." Donavan ran over to him and did everything but drop to his knees to beg him to stop talking.

"It's ironic that I meet up with Honey, who turned out to be my boy's wife. Maybe it was fate that things were supposed to come out like this!"

"Why are you doing this?" Donavan asked Rafiq. He shoved him out of his way and walked forward.

"Fraternities used to be about community service, positive activities, bonding with men who behaved as men. But now, there's so much more to the brotherhood. Other things have taken a front seat in recent generations. Perhaps we have lost our purpose. Perhaps our focus has changed as times have changed with integration and so forth. Who said newer is better? As frat brothers, we've lived crazy lives and have done the basic juvenile dirt; pranks, poker parties, private games of strip poker. But some of us never grew up, really. Some of us are accomplished professional men who wear suits and ties, hiding secrets that we're keeping from our wives and families. But for the first time in my life, I'm going to do the right thing, despite the code amongst brothers, and a double standard many men take advantage of."

Donavan looked around the room as he broke out in a sweat.

"Shit. Don't believe a word he says," he commented.

"Now Donavan has always been a bit hypocritical, but he's also confided in me . . . just as I've often confided in him. We've always been close, just like real brothers. And real brothers tell each other real secrets. I've done my share of telling, and I've done my share of listening. We go way back as college roommates. That's a long time to tell secrets from mild to the most wild, in between studying, partying, and playing women. In fact, he always used to brag to me that he was the slickest motherfucker there is."

"I don't believe you're doing this. I trusted you!" Donavan shouted, pointing at his boy.

"Honey, I can answer the questions that led to everything you've done with me and your secret life. I'm doing this because I grew to really like you. What we did was wrong, sure, but deep down inside you have always loved this, this, this fool standing over here! You've done right to slip off his ring when you see fit. A woman always knows. Ask my wife. I mean . . . my soon-to-be former live-in gold digger."

"You're not supposed to do this. If you do tell, I'll be sure that you never work again in the DC area. And you're just getting settled here again," Donavan shouted, then balling up his right fist in a tight circle.

"I'm not one to be scared of threats. As well as you know me, Don, you know that I stand on my own two feet." Rafiq turned to me. "The reason why your husband has been absent, moody, and shifting the blame to you is because he has a fifteen-year-old son."

"What!" I shouted, holding the sides of my face.

"After the tape cut off, Donavan and that stripper kept going at it. According to what Donavan told me, the chick sat on top of your so-called husband, and rode him like she was the one marrying him the next morning. He got that dancer pregnant that night. They didn't use protection *and* it turns out that she was underage. That dancer's name is Vicious. Years ago, she threatened to file a complaint because Donavan stopped fulfilling the visitation agreement. She also threatened to file rape charges against a certain someone, since she was still seventeen, and she could use her age to help build a case with that lie she threatened to tell. So now the 'slickest motherfucker there is' pays her rent, light bill, car note, and child support. He still goes to see her dance to keep her satisfied with the arrangement. Word has it that if he ever rocked the boat too bad, she'd come to you to expose your husband. That's what the deal has been—he's been splitting his time between two families. He took his unhappiness about all of this out on you."

I remained silent as a waterfall of tears began pouring from my eyes.

When I finally could speak, I turned to my husband.

"Is this true?" I asked.

Donavan wore a face of guilt, looking stunned, dropping his fist.

"I can't believe this. How could you have the audacity to do this to me?" I said, snatching one of Donavan's lines from him. "You weren't even supposed to have a bachelor party, and you fucked that ho-ass bitch? You fucked her with no condom that night *and* kept seeing her too? How irresponsible and cold hearted can you get! How could you put my health at risk this way?" I said. "Apparently, you'll stick your dick in anything! Now I see why you wouldn't half way touch me right. It was guilt!" I screamed.

"Rafiq, that tape wasn't supposed to leave your possession. He booked one stripper that was supposed to put out, and two that didn't do extras. Ya'll didn't check her ID. It wasn't my fault. He and my boys set me up with a surprise party. They got me drunk. I really was headed to a local spot just to watch—"

"Don't blame him or them. Take some personal responsibility for this mess. It was your choice, so blame your fucking self!" I yelled, cutting my husband off.

Out of the blue, my fists suddenly balled up and I lunged toward Donavan. I was the one making my fists fly like a chicken head in a club battle. I pummeled him all over his body, jumped on his back, and even tried to claw his eyes out with my sharp, manicured nails. The birthday boy had to pull me off of Donavan as he shielded himself from my blows. After that, I ran in the kitchen to look for a good and sharp knife. I spotted a sterling silver one that Dwight's wife laid on the counter to cut the cake. As my fingers on my right hand wrapped around it firmly, I envisioned stabbing Donavan over and over again, cutting off his balls, and reducing them to a pile of bloody shreds.

19

OBSESSION CONFESSION

I felt as if my world collapsed all around me as at least eighty strangers watched me suffocate under the flying debris of it all. The public humiliation made me even angrier with Donavan, aside from the anguish caused by his willingness to give in to temptation fifteen years ago. I knew about the oral sex thing, but I had no idea about the rest of the story. I blamed Donavan for everything—he single-handedly caused our marital ship to sink as far as I was concerned. As these thoughts raced through my mind, I lunged toward my husband with a long knife. Thankfully, one of the male partygoers grabbed my wrist and foiled my attempt. In my fit of rage I had thoughts of attempting to kill Donavan, but I aimed at his penis instead. I missed his middle and stabbed him in the forearm. When the knife fell to the floor, I told Donavan that I'd take him for all he had if he pressed charges on me for assaulting him. I also threatened to find his baby's mother through my network of strippers and do some damage on that end. With those threats, one of his frat brothers wrapped his arm in towels and offered to drive him to the hospital.

"You've lost your mind. I'm moving out!" Donavan shouted as he held several towels around his arm, pulling them taut while walking of out the host's front door.

Embarrassed and shaken, tears continued to roll down my face. I somehow managed to address everyone whose eyes were staring down at me.

"What are you all looking at? You can all just go straight to hell!" I yelled in a shaky voice, looking back at them, snot nearly touching my top lip. Donavan and I were having a verbal tug of war and I couldn't fight the power struggle all alone. He had too many people on his side, although he was the one who stepped out of line first. Maybe it's a man thing, or an unspoken frat thing, I don't know. All I do know is that people were treating me like I was some cheap, low life, out of control skank, who reeked of trifling behavior.

Nevertheless, me and my wobbly knees made it to our car. After Donavan and one of his frat brothers pulled off, I tried my hardest to put the car key in the door and open it to drive home. I just couldn't do it right away. Just getting inside was an emotional struggle. After I heard people talking about me, I suddenly found the energy to get into the car. Struggling my hardest to forget the conversations we shared, all the sex we had, and the lies he told me about not having much sex with his wife and having no kids, I eased back in my seat and sat in the car for a minute or so before turning the key. Although I was humiliated as hell, struggling to regain my power as a woman and a person, I gathered my strength I pulled off feeling like the biggest idiot on earth. I couldn't believe that I'd allowed my husband to get me out of character on so many levels. I thought that getting even by deceiving and cheating on me would settle the score, but all it did was add to my pain. Realizing that made me consider the sum total of my actions. Would he decide to press charges on me? Would anyone in the room who witnessed what I did corroborate the events? Would my kids get taken away because of the entire mess? My heart began to pound as I wondered what Donavan was going to do next, and how I'd manage to hold it together enough to pick up my children at camp.

Due to my frame of mind I was a bit careless . . . just this one time. What I didn't realize was that I wasn't in my car alone. I wanted to believe that what was happening wasn't real. Unfortunately, it was.

"When you get out of this motherfucking car, you better not try no funny shit. Walk up to your door like you always do. I don't want no neighbors getting suspicious," Sapphire said as she gripped my throat with one hand, and a woman held a gun to my temple with the other. The woman with Sapphire was dressed in a white wife-beater, and had sagging pants and skinny braids that dangled about four inches. The strange woman looked like she didn't need an excuse to pick a fight. She had the countenance of a man in a gang. I followed her instructions to a perfect T. When we made it inside of my place, the pair forced me back into my office, then slammed the door. Sapphire grabbed my head with one hand and banged it against the wall as she spoke.

"I made you a good dancer. I made you hip to the game, and I protected you. I was there for you when no one else was, and now you wanna shit on me? I said, now you wanna shit on me just because I'm a lesbian and you're not?" Sapphire repeated as the woman aimed the gun at me.

"No! Not at all," I answered while crying.

"Yeah, right, you low down, lying skank! I fell in love with you the first time I laid eyes on you, and whether you like it or not, you belong to me. Now get the fuck over here right now!" Sapphire let go of my hair, spun me around, shook me as hard as she could, then pushed me to the floor. I felt dizzy enough to black out, but I didn't.

"I know you think you're better than me. You've got your eight-hundred-thousand-dollar house in the suburbs, you're married to some brother who's smelling himself a little bit, and you've got your kids, and some boring-ass office job. You can't just brush me off and return to your world like nothing ever happened. I'm going to make you take me seriously. If I can't have you, Honey, no one will. And I'll make sure you won't dance in any more clubs meeting men. I've been following you for weeks in another car. How dare you use me like this and cheat on me with some man you met, treating me like some convenient dick that gets hard when the wind blows. I know you thought I'd forget what you did to me. Well, I didn't. When the left your house the other day, I told you the subject wasn't over. Now you're gonna pay with your life," Sapphire yelled while straddling me and twisting my right arm.

I heard something pop in my arm, then Sapphire began punching me in my face with heavy fists. I begged her to stop brutalizing me, then she hopped up and grabbed the gun from the woman.

"What's the matter with you, Sapphire? This is all a misunderstanding. Please Sapphire, don't shoot me! I'll do whatever you want," I pleaded, as I attempted to slither away from her. Sapphire's rage was raw and cold. I regretted not following through with the restraining order, but regrets were a lot too late.

"Get your pitiful, sloppy ass over here! Where do you

think you're going? I thought we had a special connection. I thought you were my girlfriend. You led me on. You were playing me the whole time. You never mentioned you were stepping out with a man that wasn't your husband," Sapphire hollered while pulling me by one foot. "You shoulda acted right before, bitch. Now you wanna be out here dancing for dollars and turning tricks in private! Since you enjoy being treated like property, I'll give you what you want." Sapphire stopped dragging me, then began pounding and kicking me in the head, ribs, and stomach. It hurt to move, but I tried to curl up in a fetal position to cushion myself from her blows.

"I tried to look out for your monkey ass in every way. I bought you clothes. I bought you flowers when your husband had your mind all messed up. What thanks do I get from you? You're a two-faced phony slut, just like your sister. You don't never ever bite the hand that feeds you in this game, never! She whipped my ass back in the day, now I have a reason to whip yours. You both earned this payback," Sapphire yelled as I cried. "Cry Sapphire a gotdamn river, 'cause you's a real cruddy motherfucker! I let you into my life and you acted like you didn't want to be with homeboy anymore, then you turned around and acted like you didn't know me no more and slept with a stranger over me! "

"I didn't mean any harm, and I'm sure Ayanna didn't either," I said in between coughing up blood.

"You got some fucking nerve saying that! Yes you did, and she did too! I listened to you talk about your problems for hours on end. I did everything right. But no, you didn't want to act right. Instead, you stabbed me in the back after I was a real friend to your crazy ass, just like she did," Sapphire rambled. She didn't sound sweet and friendly like she usually did. Even when she was whiny and demanding, I never heard her sound so evil and curse so much.

When Sapphire saw that I couldn't move she grabbed my purse. I raised my head as blood trickled from my lip and face. She took her foot and knocked it back down like a nut being cracked by a nutcracker.

"Keep your head down."

I cried as I watched her laugh while running her fingers through money in my purse.

"Shut up, bitch!" she said as she kicked papers around in my messy office. Dancing such late hours left me too tired to even clean a lick, so papers were literally piling up everywhere.

Sapphire shoved the money in her pocket and picked up several photographs of my children and husband. "Aaaa-ha! It looks like I found something very interest-ing," she said as she picked them up. "I told you you've got an enemy for life. Now you're about to see how I can really get down. I don't believe in karma paying people back. I *am* karma. Before I go, my home girl is going to finish beating your ass, and it will be my pleasure to watch. Now that I know what your kids and husband look like—"

"Please, just leave them out of this!" I pleaded as she re-moved the photos from the frames, and shoved them in her pocket too.

"You don't listen very well. Shut up, bitch! I see you're all scared now. At first you were talking smack about not being scared of this little girl. What a change of opinion, huh?" Sapphire reminded.

That rough neck broad with Sapphire pressed the gun to my chest and revealed a blade that was hidden in her mouth. When I saw her flick it outward, and spit it into her hand without cutting her tongue, I knew I was in deep trouble.

"A razor can do more than give that perfect shave. Give

that cruddy bitch a reminder. Slice that bitch's pretty face. Make sure no man will ever look at her ass again, let alone her husband. Your marriage will be over for real! Cut her and leave her a reminder about not using people," Sapphire said to the woman as she stood over us.

A wicked smirk covered the woman's face as I wept and screamed, pleading for her not to do it. When the razor grazed my skin, I managed to strike her wrist and push it toward her face. I watched a gash form on the right side of her cheek, and felt her blood drip on me. My fight, or flight kicked in. I was about to either go for her eyes to blind her, so she'd drop the gun, or zero in on her wrists again.

When I noticed that woman was about to react to what I did, my plan changed. I threw up my hands to shield my face instead. She fired the gun and shot me in the hand, then aimed the gun at my head. Just as I heard a clicking sound of the trigger again, we heard a loud siren sounding off. After that, the pair took off running like two bats out of hell. I heard my back door slam. Feeling profoundly weak, I laid on my back, slipping in and out of consciousness. I was unsure what was truth and what was unreal, but I felt an incredible loving feeling that I could never describe. During this time, I saw a smiling angel with giant wings who instructed me to go toward a bright, warm light. The angel's light felt so loving, I wanted to stay, but I began traveling through a long tunnel. As I felt my body begin to move, the angel nodded and said, "Your work on Earth is not done. Hurry, go toward the light. It's not your time—Brittany and Brian needs you, Mystique. Go back. You must hurry. Go toward the light before it's too late, my child." Oddly enough, the face of that angel was that of my dead mother, affectionately known as Rosario.

20

THE HEALING JOURNEY

I'll never forget August twentieth as long as I live. In my state of physical and emotional pain, I suddenly regained consciousness after an array of medical staff worked on my severely battered body at Holy Cross. I remember riding in the ambulance, as they asked me if I understood what was happening to me. Shortly thereafter, I recalled mumbling Ayanna's cell phone number, and feeling dizzy as I was being wheeled into an emergency room. I closed my eyes as the piercing hospital lights hurt them. Dried blood caked my face and hands. I could feel the crust that it formed, and it made me felt unclean and dirty. In addition there was an IV that was forced into my sore arm.

I had two black eyes, a busted lip, broken arm, a severely swollen face, and bruised ribs. It took a fair share of stitches to close up the razor blade cuts, and surgery to repair my lip. It hurt to talk even move. As I lay in the hospital bed, I did my best to find the words to explain the reason behind why I'd been beaten black and blue to the police. At first I led them to believe I was seeing a man on the side in the city, who turned out to be obsessed. Then I decided to come clean, since I felt that Sapphire could hurt my family. When she took their pictures, it really gave me reason to put my foot down after the attack."

"Look at you. Look at my sister. Dear Jesus," Ayanna said. The way she kissed me on my head, I could tell he was heartbroken. "I called Donavan, told him where you were, and reminded him to pick up the kids at Camp Rising Sun. I knew they were supposed to come back. I didn't call Dad though. I wanted to ask you if I should in person first."

"Thanks, Yana. Please don't call Dad. You're right. It all blew up in my face. Go ahead and say you told me so," I rambled. "I know that you've always looked up to your older sister, and you always believed in me, but I let you down—I acted like a fool. Some example I turned out to be," I added, my speech slurred from my swollen lip.

"I know how you feel, but this is real life. People are imperfect in private. Even you, even me. How could I say anything about what you did, when I'm still living wrong?"

"Did you tell Donavan why I'm here?" I asked, speaking slowly.

"No, but he's going to find out. I mean, you did tell the police who did this. I know it took a lot for you to tell the truth, but you did the right thing. I hope they find her crazy ass, lock her up, and throw away the key," Ayanna said.

"Me too, Yana. Me too. She put the C in crazy, and really needs some psychological help."

"Sis."

"What, Yana?"

"I want out of prostitution. I want out of dancing. I can't live like this anymore. There's got to be a better way."

"Oh, Yana. I'm so glad to hear you say that."

"Yes, there were always presents under the Christmas tree. Yes, we had the benefit of attending the best schools, but Dad was always working in the church, looking after everyone when we needed him. He always did all the talking, and we always do all of the listening. I think part of what I did was about wanting a father in my life. I'm not talking about the deacon, I'm talking about my father. So much good for being a minister's daughter, huh."

"He did the best he could for us, Yana. I know he isn't too expressive and I've felt the same things you have. But Mom's death couldn't have been easy on him. He was left to raise two little girls by himself. You know, I think I burned myself out with my family, because I wanted everything to be perfect since we lost Mom so young. I wanted the white picket fence, the two-car garage, the husband with credentials . . . all for the wrong reasons. We were young and dumb—both of us. Maybe neither one of us was really ready to settle down."

"Think of Job, Mystique. You grew up living by the word—enough that you should always be able to keep your head up, and endure mostly anything that comes your way. God loves right and God is love. Anyone who has ever tried to get somewhere has experienced turmoil. There are no shortcuts and the world doesn't owe us anything, just because of what happened when we were growing up. Everything is not as it seems out here in these streets. The only constant variable is God. He's the one that will help us keep ourselves together, not a man's solutions. If we start thinking like someone who doesn't believe, you'll get cheated every time. Trust me when I tell you, I just remembered that when I walked in here, and saw you this way. It shook me up bad enough to realize I could've lost you, and you could lose me any day I meet up with a strange man in bed. I'm leaving the lifestyle—this time for good. Aside from the money, I just want to be loved. Now I realize I always had it in you . . . and even

Dad. Men offering me gifts, trips, cars, and money can't match the feeling of being cared about. I know they really don't care about me—we were just using each other for different things. I no longer want that kind of attention; it just feels too empty. Sisters forever?"

"Forever, Yana."

"Girl power, that's what's up. Now give me some love. Bam!" she said, giving me a high five like we often did. The only difference was that she touched my palm gently. Our watery eyes and snotty noses were running all over the place, so Ayanna found a box of tissue and wiped my eyes. She pulled out a few more and wiped hers too.

"I know it won't be easy for you to give up some of those things, Yana, just like I know that I can't heal my hurt over night. We're going to get through this mess together, and God will help us if we believe," I told her. "Come live with me and get a fresh start."

As my sister and I continued talking, the door to my hospital room opened slowly. The person didn't even knock.

"I was wrong," the woman standing at the foot of my bed said.

"Who are you?" Ayanna asked.

"I'm Vicious," she answered proudly. Chills shot through my body, and I felt a burning sensation shoot through my chest.

"Oh no she didn't! The cat that dragged her in, can drag her ass right back out! Get her out of here. After all the trouble she's caused and she has the nerve to come in your hospital room?" Ayanna said, turning to me. "Oh heeeell no!" She exclaimed, hopping up to usher Vicious out of the room.

"There's been enough fighting. Let her talk, Yana. It's ok. This hussy had the nerve to show her face, so let her finish," I said weakly. After all that had happened I figured that I may as well let my husband's baby's mother throw her two cents into the messy pile.

"I know you probably hate me. Donavan told me that you know everything now. I was young, careless, and in search of something I have yet to find—real love. You see, I grew up dirt poor in Arkansas. My alcoholic father used to beat my mother. Up until age sixteen I begged her to leave, but she wouldn't. So at age seventeen I ran away in search of a better life that didn't include harvesting crops under the hot sun. I guess I got sidetracked by stripping and doing many things I'm no longer proud of. All I can say is I now understand how families can get screwed up, and stay screwed up, for generations. That's what women do if we're not careful—pass on hurt to the next woman and to the next, disrespecting someone else's relationship just because it's not ours. Then our sons and daughters grow up confused and misguided, thinking that it's acceptable to treat other people this way. Yet, we expect them to have morals and respect for others. I'm here for the sake of three children—mine, and your two. I know I may look crazy coming here under these conditions, but I just felt moved to do so. I'm sorry for all the trouble I caused in your marriage, but I can't say I regret having my son. At first I was angry that Donavan didn't listen to his heartbeat to make sure the baby was ok at night. I wanted the man that I had a child with to do things like massage my feet and spend real quality time with me."

"Now you're supposed to feel sorry for her? This world doesn't owe her anything, no matter how much she feels she deserves it. You will not drag my sister through the mud any more than you already have. I really think you should be moving along. Go twirl around a pole. Go jump off a bridge. I don't care, just leave!" Ayanna rambled, while pressing my buzzer to call a nurse.

"Yana, let her say her piece," I scolded.

"I can understand how your sister feels. I wish I had someone who cared about me like she cares about you. Anyway, the trouble was, he went home to you and that made me feel so empty inside. I guess I wanted to force Donavan to man up and do right by his son, because I didn't have a father at home—I had a sperm donor that let me do what I wanted to do, dress like I wanted to dress, and was part of the reason I grew up much too fast."

All of the sudden, Vicious began living up to her name. Her tone of voice changed, as well as her body language.

"My job doesn't offer shit for my future, but that's ok with Donavan. He accepts me as I am. So now that you've kicked him out, I think it's fair for you to know what's coming next . . . *divorce papers.* I'm just here to inform you that your husband loves me, not you. In fact, he treats me like gold. He's going to divorce you and do right by me, once and for all."

"Says who?" I asked in a defensive tone.

"Whether you like it or not, I'm going to be your children's stepmother. I hope you can accept that for the sake of our kids. If not, don't say I didn't try to be civil. He doesn't want to hurt you by telling you the real deal, but your husband was screwing me as recent as last night. I'm the one that's been *corresponding* with you. If you haven't figured it out, I'm also his mistress. Donavan gave me your email address a while back, when I told him he had to prove he was ready for his divorce, but then he begged me not to ever write you, so I played it cool until now. Did you get that email or what, baby? I was tired of hearing about you when he was laid up in these arms." I did recall that email that sent me on a horrific mind trip. Now it all made sense.

"Let's be honest about this—look at you and look at me. I make $1500 a night, just for looking good. If you were a man, who would you pick? If it all came down to making one choice. I'm for real, but you're just a wanna be trying to come up to my level of having what Donavan needs. He's playing you to make things look good, so don't be stupid."

"Bitch, you're the stupid one for being pressed over a married man. I've seen more than my share of skanks like you 'cause I dance too," Ayanna said, pointing at Vicious like she still wanted to fight her.

Vicious moved close to my bed, ignoring Ayanna. She grabbed the shiny steel rails, smiling down at me like she was some friend of mine.

"Your *husband* said he loves me more than any woman he's ever been with, including you. I tried to tell you everything your stupid ass couldn't seem to figure out. Make it easy on yourself, go with the flow, and let him out of that jacked-up marriage."

Vicious began to laugh as my eyes started to water.

"You need to watch your mouth, you signifying monkey! My sister doesn't have to put up with hearing this! Forget calling security. You got five seconds to get out before my foot gets planted between your ass cheeks, then you'll have nothing to shake for dollars," Ayanna warned, gritting her teeth. She ran over to Vicious and tore her away from my bed, escorting her to the door.

"There's no need for all of that, *sweetie*," Vicious said, snatching her arm away. "I was just leaving. Oh, by the way . . . something almost slipped my mind. Do you like my engagement ring Donavan gave me on my birthday? Apparently, he's serious about upgrading, if you know what I mean. I just got my fifty grand for the down payment on a new town house, not that I'll need it since I'll be living in your shit soon enough. But I did get some ends, plus this," she said, flashing the shiny ring on her finger. " And what did you get on your birthday last time?

A big fat nothing, I bet. By the way, you look good girl, real nice. For real, for real, you been working out or something? Keep up the good work! Keep these as a souvenir. Like I said in that email, you can have it all today, and lose it all tomorrow," Vicious said to me in a condescending tone, tossing a pair of my husband's boxer shorts my way.

"I've had enough of you!" Ayanna said. That's when my sister lost it and hauled off and smacked Vicious something fierce.

She laughed, took one last long look at me, and switched while walking a few more steps like she was so special, the sun came up around her. "If that was supposed to hurt, it didn't work. Your husband smacks my ass way harder than that. I like it rough, so what you did was more like a tap on the shoulder, lil' momma. And wifey, just remember what I said. Donavan can't resist me. I own what's in those drawers," Vicious cautioned. "The ring I just showed you was proof. Now that you know the truth, I hope you find peace. Keep the faith."

After she dropped her last bomb, Vicious was gone.

21

VOWS

"If you've cheated with Vicious, you've probably cheated before and, probably would do me dirty again. I can't trust you after what you did to me," I scowled at my husband with hostility. That evening, I was able to talk a little bit clearer with less pain, although it still didn't tickle. Vicious really did a number on me. I was feeling very insecure as a woman, and a wife. My emotions were suffering from the after effects of her untimely visit. "You just remember what started this whole fiasco," I added.

"I could've lost you forever. You could've died. I'm so sorry, baby. This is all my fault for treating you the way I did," Donavan said as his eyes grew watery. "I don't want to fight anymore, and I'd never cheat on you again. I never should've done it. I had everything in one woman. I was so dumb," he admitted, while placing a dozen red roses on a small night stand next to me. I never thanked my husband for bringing them. In fact, I ignored the flowers all together.

"You should've told me everything when it first happened."

"How could I tell you? Tell me how I could've done that?" Donavan asked.

"Easy. As your wife, you should've been able to tell me anything."

"If I had, then what? You would've done nothing but gotten an annulment, and left me."

"Well look what *not* telling me has done. Our marriage was doomed before it even got off the ground. How did you ever expect this to fix itself? And who knows what kind of sexual history Vicious has had. I have one word for you: AIDS. After all we went through to convince our parents, who advised us not to get married at our ages, how could you be so stupid? How!" I snapped, feeling as if my husband was a traitor.

"I don't know. I was a twenty-two-year-old kid, who was dumb to drink so much that night. I just wasn't thinking straight. What I do know today, right here, right now, is that I love you. But you want me to leave, don't you?"

"Come closer," I said.

"Is this close enough?" my husband asked.

"No, closer. I'm tired, and I can't talk so loud."

When my husband was close enough to me, I stared at his face.

They say the eyes are the windows to the soul, and I wanted to study his eyes to search for real answers.

"I love you," Donavan said out of the blue.

"That's not the truth, not according to your *mistress.*"

"What?"

"Vicious was here. In fact, the evil whore did a good job picking me apart and just left," I explained. "She also explained whose idea it was to send me that damned email about you still running the streets to bed everyone, but me."

"Oh God. I. Mystique. I never meant for her to . . . I kept this from you because I really intended to spare you from the truth. I never gave her your email address," Donavan rambled. "She must've gotten it out of my telephone or something."

"Yeah, right! Apparently, she has a key you gave her too. She described our bedroom, and I know she's been in it."

"You're going to believe her over your own husband?"

"I'm tempted to, Donavan. She told me far more than you ever did. Where did you come from that night? You didn't come home straight from work. And were you slobbing her down in the stairwell? Are you setting me up with roses and an empathetic talk to make it look like you're sorry? How do I know that you and that whoring bitch aren't trying to pull one over on me again?" I said. "Just go ahead and be honest about wanting to divorce me and get with her. I saw the ring! Be a man and just get the truth over with! I bet you told her about Rafiq to make me look bad, too. How could you discuss our marital problems with the other woman?"

"No, baby. It's nothing like that," my husband insisted. "Ring, what ring?" he added.

"She came in here flashing an engagement ring. She was showing it off, saying that you proposed to her, and that you gave her a pile of money for a down payment on a town house. By the way, she dropped off a pair of your underwear. Nice gesture, huh?"

"She said and did what! She's lying. I never gave her any ring, or any money for a house," Donavan insisted, shaking his head. "Did you get a good look at the ring?" Donavan asked.

I shook my head as tears began to roll down my cheeks.

"Aww baby, don't cry. She's bluffing. It's all a big lie. Look, it was probably a cubic zirconia ring she got from somewhere. When she heard what happened, she didn't even want me to pick up the kids from camp. I was supposed to see her and my son. When Ayanna called me, I stood my ground for the first time in a long time. I remembered that I was your husband all along, and I also had parental responsibilities that I'd been neglecting with my other two children. She had no right, and no business, blackmailing me to behave as if I had feelings for her. Some people become ugly when they open their mouths, even if they are attractive. No doubt, this girl is that type. When most men look at her, they lust. That lust has earned her nothing but pain because she's ugly inside. Year after year she can only rely on her looks until the best years of her youth are gone," Donavan said, dabbing my eyes with tissue.

"Yeah, she reminded me she makes $1500 a night and men flock to her, including you. I can't compete with Vicious. She's obviously more interesting to you in every way."

"You're the one who's got it all, not her. She can't hold a candle to you, even on her best day. To be blunt, all she could ever offer me was a good lap dance and sex. She's not marriage material. I had to keep seeing her because I was scared of her crying rape, telling you about the past, and other things she drummed up."

"Well apparently, you wanted a freak, not a woman who carried herself like a lady. That tape I saw proved that you and your boys know firsthand how she really makes $1500 a night, and it's not from exotic dancing. You knew what she was all about."

"I admit, I did lose focus. But it's you that I love, and there's nothing Vicious can do to change that. That's what I say every time she looks my way. In fact, I'm sure that's the real reason she just wanted to come see the woman who has my heart, and always will. She's jealous of you, Mystique. She's just plain fishing for a way to justify not being able to move on. I'm ready to make an effort to rebuild a love stronger than it was before our crisis. I know our marriage won't fix itself, but I'm ready to put in real work. Your love is all I need, I swear. Faith-based marriage counseling, a trip to Paris so you can go to the top of the Eiffel Tower, a bigger new house, with more closet space you've been wanting in another zip code—whatever you want, it's yours. Name it and it's done."

"This isn't about material shit! It's about keeping your word. I thought you were a man of integrity. We're not rich, but we have enough stuff and we already live in a 4,000 square foot house! I don't care about the Lexus, the house, the stocks, investments, your prestigious job—none of it! If we lived in a two-bedroom house and drove two buckets, but had all the love in the world, I'd probably be far more happy than I am right now. Nice comforts are a blessing, but that's not everything. Not every marriage can be saved after something like this happens, and ours may not be one of them. It's about bonding and having what's real. All of that other stuff is extra. You reap what you sow, Donavan. You knew you were as good as married when you cheated with Vicious. I'm not blaming her, I'm blaming you. You did it once and you will easily do it again. You two had a child together behind my back. Fifteen years of suffering, Donavan. I think it would be best if you just went home and packed the rest of your things. I don't know who, or what, to believe. This is all so confusing."

"You made a mistake, a terrible mistake . . . and so did I."

"Apparently, your so-called mistake resulted in a child with an unstable woman though."

"I accept responsibility for every bit of that, and I hate what I put you through. But if you're willing to try to work this out, not just for Brittany and Brian, but for you and I too, then maybe we can think about—"

"Think about what?" I asked.

"Maybe we can think about rebuilding the trust we once had before that stupid bachelor party. I can have my wife back, and you can have your husband back. If we fell in love all over again, I think it would be a beautiful thing."

As bad as I must've looked, my husband pressed his lips against mine, on the right side, opposite the area where my lip was busted.

"Right now, baby. I'm willing to start right now," he said. "I'm willing to prove who, and what, I want. Let me care about you and show you what you really mean to me. Let me love you . . . *please.* Can we just try to work this out?"

"You have no idea how many sleepless nights I've had, and how many tears I've cried over our marriage. You've made my life a living hell, and I beat myself up, over and over again. I thought stripping and getting with Rafiq would provide me with some sense of vindication. Well, it didn't. Getting even was nothing more than a band-aid on our marital problems. Things have gotten so crazy. There's so much more to discuss before I can decide what I want to do. I can't make you love me, nor can I change a grown man," I said, struggling to grasp the root of a solution.

My husband reached out to embrace me, then he remembered that he couldn't since I was still so badly hurt. Instead, he carefully slid in bed next to me and said, "I naturally care about you—ashamed that you felt as if you had to make me love you back. I miss you and me." He began to cry, then my eyes began to tear up as well.

"I thought you'd forgotten me. I thought—"

"Heavens no. I was mad at myself, and mad at the world, at the bed I made that I had to lie in. It was wrong of me to lash out at you. I now see that the grass is not greener on the other side, and I'll feel so empty if you give up on this fool who took you for granted. As a black man,

I forgot how important it was to have a real queen through the good and bad times, having the kind of love our parents and grandparents had. The structure of the black family is crumbling. I don't want our home to turn out broken and become one more statistic. Black love used to mean something, and it still can if we retain our identities, one relationship at a time. I want to be a real man again— a man with a queen who loves me for who I am inside, not what I am on the outside. I got lost along the way of the journey, baby. I need you in my life, Mystique. My heart wants to know you again."

After Donavan revealed his true feelings, the floodgates of emotion opened. When it did, there was no stopping it, although I couldn't believe my ears.

"Knock, knock. There are some visitors out here to see you," Ayanna said.

"I'm spending some time with my wife, Ayanna. Can they wait?" Donavan answered.

"You picked them up from camp and I really think they'd like to see their mother."

"Mommy! Mommy!" Brittany exclaimed, running toward me.

"Dag, Ma! What happened to you?" Brian asked.

"Remember what I told you? Your mother needs her rest, Brian," Ayanna said.

"Mommy! I brought this for you," my daughter told me. It was almost as if she didn't notice my current state. That made me feel warm and fuzzy all over.

"The ceramic bowl you made at camp. It's beautiful, Brittany," I said as she held it up in front of me.

"Do you really like it? I hope it will make you feel better. Come home soon, Mom. Pleaaaase," she begged. "Who's going to get me ready for dance lessons? And who's going to have tea parties with me?"

"I love it. I'll be home soon," I replied, my eyes growing glossy.

"And this is from me," Brian said, beaming with pride.

"Your football jersey? Son, I can't."

"I figured it would help you get out of here, faster. I need you too, Mom. You're the one that's cheered me on at practice and forced me to do my homework, so I won't grow up as stupid as Brittany."

"Hey, boy! Don't you start with me," Brittany said, puffing her jaws with air. She threw her hand on her hip, while shaking her head back and forth.

"I'm just kidding, Brittany. Anyway, I took all of the things you did for us for granted. If it helps, I won't fight with Brittany anymore. Seeing you like this has made me appreciate the sacrifices. The sacrifices—"

"It's okay, Brian," I said. "I think I understand what you mean." I smiled because I'd been talking too much and I began to pay for it. The side of my mouth was hurting like the dickens, and I knew I'd have to buzz the nurse for pain medication.

"Say goodbye to your mother. She needs her rest now," Ayanna said.

"Aaaw, Auntie Yana. Do we have to go now? We just got here," Brittany complained.

"Leave your bowl for your mother and let's get going. It's bath time. You both smell like you brought the whole camp back with you!"

"But is she going to die?" Brittany said, tears welling up in her eyes. That's when guilt and reality set in. I was reminded that everything a parent does has the potential to affect one's children. In my case, my precious gems truly could've lost their mother sooner than they were supposed to, because of the risks I took.

"I'm going to be just fine," I said, reassuring Brittany.

"Come here, baby. Momma loves you and you're my baby, okay?"

"Yes, Mom," she said, tears still pouring from her little eyes.

"Now I need you to be real strong. Go home and help Auntie Yana by being a big girl," I continued.

"Bye, Ma. We miss you already," Brittany said, her face looking long.

"Yeah, me too. Who did this to you! That's what I want to know. I know people in Southeast who can look for the sucka and—"

"Brian, take your sister and sit in the waiting room. I'll be out in a minute," Ayanna said.

"Ayanna," Donavan said.

"What?" she answered.

"Thank you."

"For what?" Ayanna asked.

"Being there for Mystique when I wasn't."

"Just love her right, or let her go," Ayanna said, openly eyeing his bandaged flesh wound. "That's all I ask. If you really want to thank me, now you know how to do it," she commented, disappearing out of the door.

My husband spent the night holding my hand, pressing cold compresses on my head whenever he needed to stand over top of me to do it, and making sure that I had everything I needed. When I woke up in the middle of the night and realized that he was still wide awake, watching me like a hawk, that's when I wondered if my husband was telling the truth about how he felt about Vicious. Did we still have a small spark to work with, that was bigger than whatever he had with the other woman? Did he finally understand that I'd been the backbone of the family, even when it was a husband's place to hold things together? Why should I hang in there—why not just give up and go our separate ways?

I awakened to a dream about Vicious getting more sentiments off her chest, realizing that her visit was a feeble attempt to plant the seeds of doubt in my mind that Donavan wanted to work things out. That's when I realized that the grass wasn't necessarily greener on the other side, just because she was the mistress, and I was the wife. To want a married man so badly she'd confront me in a hospital bed, told me she had low self-esteem—even lower than mine. A woman in that frame of mind would do anything to get what she wanted. There was something about her I didn't trust, but I didn't want to assume that Donavan didn't have motives to manipulate me either. As soon as I was well enough, I decided to make it a point to test his story and hers. I refused to let Donavan run back to the safety of his wife with no work done on his part, even if I did have a slip up or two myself. There was no way around it. He'd have to be tortured by his mistake a bit more by enduring more questions about the history of his past with his "mistress." After asking him to enlighten me in some other areas, I'd know how to proceed. They say if you love someone and set them free, if they come back to you, they're yours. I did something that most women would never consider. I temporarily set Donavan free to be with the very woman that helped to destroy our marriage.

22

THE MISTRESS BLUES

Two months later

"Hi, Sunshine. Did you get my two messages asking you to please call me?" Donavan asked sweetly, using a nickname for me that hadn't rolled off of his lips in years.

"I got it. You said holler at you when I got a chance. I guess I really hadn't gotten around to it," I explained. I wasn't about to fall into my husband's sugary trap. I let him blow up the phone, since the tables were turned. The sweet talk act wasn't going to work.

"How are you, Brittany and Brian? I miss you guys."

"We're all fine. Now that you've checked on us, is there something specific that you need?" I asked, playing tough.

"Please do me a favor, Mystique. Let me come home. I'm begging for your forgiveness. I belong with my wife and kids."

"You know the deal. You have to spend six months living the single life, because I feel that you need some time to reflect on our time together, and what you really want.

As I've explained, if you don't do it, I'm divorcing you without further conversation," I said, then bit my lip. Saying that hurt me deeply, but I knew I had to be strong.

"Look, I've finally realized that stepping out of the relationship was a huge mistake. I don't want a mistress anymore. I want to be a fully committed, family man. I'm sorry!"

"If you really mean that, that's all well and good, but you have a bit more time to enjoy a bit of introspection. What's the rush? Take your time," I commented coolly.

"Lester put me out, and I don't have anywhere to go," Donavan finally admitted.

"So much for frat brothers," I said, chuckling a bit. Donavan had been renting a room in one of his brother's houses, but I guess he wore out his welcome.

"Well, there's always Vicious. I'm sure she'd be glad to put you up. From what I understand, you have been paying for her place," I reminded him. I knew that Donavan had already been forced to move in with Vicious, due to his weighty financial obligations on the home front—I did add all of the bills I'd been paying—plus whatever else his good old mistress was still holding over his head. I could hear Vicious nagging him in the background.

"I learned my lesson. Vicious is different. She's not like you. She won't fold towels, do the dishes, or wash my clothes like you do. You know I'm allergic to peanuts, and she almost killed me when she—"

"Donavan, you're rambling. Unless you have something new to say, I've got to do some things for the kids. No offense, but it's been a long day. I just want to tend to the children, catch a movie on cable, and get a good night's sleep."

"Please let me come home. Please! I'm trying. I've changed!" Donavan said, breaking down in tears.

"Unbeknownst to me, I shared you for fifteen years.

Now that everything's out in the open, a little while longer won't hurt. I'll holler at you later, baby. By the way, tell Vicious I said hello. She seems like she's getting upset with you about being on the phone with me. I wouldn't want you to be rude. Enjoy," I said, then hung up the phone.

Because of Donavan's actions, my power as a woman had been renewed. Through the pain he gave me, I began to value myself as I should once again. As odd as it was, he inspired a wonderful healing. Time spent away from my husband forced me to learn so much about myself as a woman, mother, and an individual, as I struggled to feel beautiful inside and out. I knew my confidence was improving when I realized that I already was all of those things and more. I never had anything to prove to anyone.

And not to gloat, but through the grapevine, I found out that he placed that call to me after losing his six-figure job behind that ghetto-ass stripper bringing trouble to his investment firm's door, after one of their heated arguments.

Having access to Vicious fulltime wasn't as nice as Donavan thought it would be, since I wasn't there as a buffer to take care of the mundane things at home. I let him suffer four more months, explaining to him that he had to make a choice between the streets and his family, as well as me and Vicious. Although he said he was sure about who he wanted, I made him deal with her until her crazy ass had him forgetting to shave. She ran the streets hunting him down, and he soon realized that a daily home-cooked meal was a blessing. When he hit rock bottom, he came home crawling to me, humble, funky, and dressed in wrinkled designer gear. His fingernails were unmanicured and his gray was showing because he hadn't been getting his touch-ups on a regular basis. I demanded that he clean up his ass in one hour flat and gather his faculties to interview for a new gig . . . or else.

23

GIVE ME THREE GOOD REASONS TO TAKE YOU BACK

February

My three requirements to even consider reconciling with my husband consisted of three simple things: 1) a restraining order taken out against his mistress, 2) taking an HIV test, and 3) a paternity test. Since Vicious refused to cooperate with Donavan and I regarding the paternity test, having a private paternity test was not an option. My husband had to petition the court for assistance, and I was more than glad to see him pay the fee for the test to get this thing resolved, once and for all. The test required a swab from inside the cheek from my husband, Vicious, and Donavan Junior. That event reopened Pandora's box, and then some.

The day Donavan landed a new gig through corporate recruiter hook-up, I did let him come home, but only under certain conditions. He was under a probationary period, during which I would do a lot of listening and watching to figure out if a divorce was what I really wanted.

I had Donavan by both of his balls, and he knew it, so he gave me props that it was my turn to run our show.

By the time he removed his suit, and changed into jeans and a white shirt, we both began hearing someone ringing our door bell continuously. Thinking it was some solicitor, we chose to ignore it, until the landline began to ring.

"How could you take a restraining order out on me? Why won't you talk to me? I miss you, baby," Vicious rambled, half crying.

"I hear you, but you're violating the rules of the restraining order," Donavan said on the phone, as I listened quietly on another extension.

"Don't you miss me too?" Vicious questioned, in between stuttering. Half giggling, she added, "I'm outside. I knocked and banged on the door, but you won't come out. I need you, baby. I've been drinking liquor all day, so I'm feeling kinda loose and thought I'd come see my boo. That was me throwing rocks at the window."

"What are you doing here, Vicious? Stop it and go home," he said, trying not to make a scene. We both looked outside and saw her standing in the middle of the yard, holding a bottle of liquor in one hand.

"I have a right to know if Donavan Jr. is biologically mine, Vicious. That's the only thing I have to say to you. If that turns out to be the case, you will hear from my lawyer about how I'm going to see, and take care of, my son. You are not welcomed here."

"What's that supposed to mean?"

"You already got me fired from my job, after you went down with your hair standing all over your head, making something up about me not paying child support."

"So! I don't give a shit about what happened to you. After all of these years, now you tryna say that Donavan Jr. isn't your child? Pleaaaase—you've got to be kidding me, you got-damn muthafucka. Talk to the hand and try again," Vicious said, sounding completely ghetto during her drunken bitch fest. I watched her from my bedroom window, as she stood wobbly-legged on the lawn, holding her cell phone to her ear.

"Just cooperate, would you? It would make it easier for all of us," Donavan said sounding frustrated. "Would you just cooperate like a normal, logical adult would?"

"All of us *who?*"

"That part's obvious, Vicious. I need to know for my own reassurance, as well as out of respect for my wife. The results will be in soon, so is all of this really necessary? If you don't leave and go home right now, I'm hanging up on you and calling the police."

Click. Donavan hung up the phone. When she continued standing in the yard, Donavan raised the window. Vicious ranted like a storm gaining strength. I could tell she was frustrated. Her voice had become high-pitched, and she began yelling loudly.

"I'm good enough to fuck, but I'm not good enough to come to your house? One minute you claim Donavan Jr., and the next you don't want to be around. Who you think you clowning? Oh, so now because your wife knows, you want to pretend like you didn't hit this pussy? Oh, you tryna perpetrate like you don't jump in the sack with me when you come to my spot? I'll tell you what, you're nothing but a no-good baby daddy! The nerve of you to even think about getting slick! He's yours and you know it! You haven't been over to see us in—"

"You've tried every trick in the book," I said, cutting her off. "You've threatened to harm yourself by swallowing a bottle of pills to get Donavan to come by. Then you start sending us both e-mails, trying to visit him at his office, calling our home at all hours of the night, and even mailing us a pair of his old underwear. Stop it, just stop all of your drama, Vicious! Since you didn't get a chance to hang up the phone when you heard my voice this time, there's something I need to get straight. There's a new sheriff in town, and that sheriff is me. Like it or not, he's made up his mind to come home, and I'll be right by my husband's side through this whole thing. It's time I've had him to myself. And just for the record, I'll be on you like white on rice!"

"You've got something to say to me? Come out here then, bitch!"

"No. Now *I'm* calling 911," I chimed in. Although I was still angry at Donavan, I wasn't about to let Vicious have the satisfaction of knowing that I still had mixed feelings about letting him come home and reenter my life.

Vicious walked toward her car, dropped the bottle of liquor, grabbed something, then stormed over to Donavan's prized candy-apple red Porsche, that he had moved out into driveway while straightening up the garage.

"Fuck both ya'll! Now you have a reason to call the police. I don't care, bitch! And he's late on my car payment!" Vicious screamed, as she used the bat to smash out all of the windows. When she began kicking the tires, she said, "This is just the beginning. Wait 'til I file rape charges today!"

"My Porsche! My Porsche!" Donavan screamed.

Brittany's activity bus pulled up in the midst of the argument. I heard Donavan scurrying to make it outside, trying to keep her from bumping into psychotic Vicious.

"Don't you dare touch my baby!" Donavan screamed, just as I was in the middle of placing a call to the police.

Brittany struggled to escape from Vicious, as tears wet her face. With a book bag on her back, mitten-topped hands, and a burgundy knit hat covering her head, she slipped and slid around, since a heavy layer of sleet was still fresh.

"Stop! Stop! Who are you? Let me go. Mommy! Daddy! Help me!" she yelled.

"Shut up, you little bitch. You act just like your momma. You're coming with me. Get in the car. Let's go!" Vicious said, twisting Brittany's arm in a drunken rage.

"Oh no I'm not!" Brittany yelled defiantly.

Next, Brittany bit Vicious on the arm through her coat, and broke free.

"Yes you are, you little devil!" Vicious said, trying to catch her, slipping on black ice.

They both ran in circles around the yard until Brittany began running toward the street. She wasn't looking at where she was going, because she was paying attention to Vicious clawing and chasing her instead. I could see the bus coming down the hill after turning around in the cul-de-sac and imagined Brittany darting out into the street. In sheer terror, I closed my eyes and covered my mouth with one jumpy hand, praying that my baby wouldn't get hit.

"Noooooooooo!" I heard Donavan scream. "Brittany, watch out, the bus is coming! Get out of the way! Get out of the street! Nooooooooo!"

I slid down the wall, assuming the worst, when I heard a high-pitched shrill scream, a horn, and squealing brakes. I began crying hysterically, too fearful to look out of the window, or run outside. I finally managed to gather the courage to stand and open my eyes.

Shaking terribly, I looked out of the window and saw Vicious flying through the air, then landing on her back. I breathed a sigh of relief, running outside to hold my baby and comfort her. I tore down the steps as sirens blared. Pushing through the crowd that formed, I grabbed Brittany, stroked her hair, and wiped her tears from her cheeks. Donavan ran over to Brittany and I, then we all hugged in a small circle. After that, everything seemed to happen so fast. I do remember standing over top of Vicious though.

"He loves me more, bi . . . bitch," she said, raising her head a little, speaking in a shallow voice. When her head fell, I was pushed toward the edge of a crowd. All I remember after that was talk of sending for a helicopter to fly Vicious to shock trauma, but before it touched down, she was pronounced dead at the scene of the accident.

Ironically, the day afterward, the paternity test arrived in the mail.

"The probability of paternity is 0%," the results read, just three days after all parties involved finally took the test. Thankfully, the lab offered rush results, at an extra charge. The confidential, notarized report confirmed that Ms. Vicious was just a trouble maker searching for a sugar daddy with deep pockets. It was obvious why she didn't want my husband to take a paternity test. She knew he would cut off all contact with her and no longer pay child support, or hook her income up. Just like I thought . . . her sexual history included running game on men with a little something, who got caught up in what they saw between her legs. Oh what a twisted, lying, scheming bitch! I wished I could say something better about the *dearly departed*, but I truly couldn't!

24

CLEANING OUT OUR CLOSETS

On Valentine's Day, Donavan sent the kids to his parents' house for the night, laid down a beautiful multicolored blanket with African proverbs written on it, and lit a row of tall red candles that flickered in the darkness as we sat on the living room floor. He prepared bologna and cheese sandwiches, chilled champagne, and dug out my favorite jazz record from a box in the garage. We talked privately, face-to-face. Under the glow of the candlelight, we reminisced about yesterday. We cried over our hurts, then laughed at each other's jokes.

Having a picnic basket dinner on floor with my husband while communicating was something that I never would've imagined doing in a million years. The living room picnic was something we used to do, when I made minimum wage and he held it down as a college freshman. We couldn't afford to go out to a restaurant, so this is how we used to get down, both struggling to live with gratitude in all possible areas of our lives. Years and years later, we returned to that place.

"I'll be back, Donavan," I said, getting up from the blanket.

"What are you doing? Where are you going? Did I mess up with the menu or something, Mystique? I knew I should've done the gourmet thing."

"There's something that I must do. Please hold your last thought," I explained.

While walking up the steps, heading toward the second floor, I reflected over many, many things that transpired between us. I once felt as though I had no control over my destiny, but now I see that's simply not true. When those who really loved me joined together and fused to strengthen my identity, I began to feel so much better. The day my kids busted into my hospital room, I realized that I wanted happiness with the man I shared vows with, but only if he proved his indiscretion was a one-time mistake. With that decision there would be issues of visitation, child support, and many other hurdles to jump while trying to be as understanding as I could toward my husband. That was our first step. Originally, my husband said he just panicked and gave in to Vicious, without thinking of her motives or her credibility, especially since Donavan Jr. seemed to favor him in more than a few ways. My first instinct was to make sure that Donavan Jr. was, in fact my husband's child by blood. I understood the part my husband told me about not taking the DNA test fifteen years ago, but doing so now was past overdue.

I had no idea how much Vicious was looking to Donavan to fill a void in her life, but she was. Somehow, he'd become her fantasy through building a makeshift family. Go figure. My husband and I both agreed that there was no need to send an innocent teen into foster care, if it didn't have to be that way. My husband wanted to be sure that I could handle it mentally, given the unusual circumstances. Don Jr. was already attached to my husband since he'd gotten to know him so well over the years. Obviously, his real father had never located him—or perhaps didn't care to look—and Donavan dropping out of his life because all of this wouldn't be the right thing to do, morally speaking.

For the sake of a teenager I didn't know, I decided to suck up the pain. Surprisingly, Don. Jr. making a transition from foster child to becoming a permanent member of our family was a real possibility. I am still healing and only time will tell if I can. There is no reason for setting up one more black male to fail due to the sins of his parents. Thus, I pray that I can forgive enough to make it that happen, as I heal over the history my husband had with his mother. Poor Brittany is still having nightmares after seeing that terrible accident, and I made an appointment for her to see a therapist because of it. Donavan and I considered sitting all of the kids down to explain the truth, but we're not quite ready to confess the ugliest details just yet, although they know a lot did go down in our marriage.

These days, my life is back to focusing on the ordinary things. I did put back on my apron and my two kids, plus the extra one, are still running me ragged. I also am grateful to still have an office job, although I was fired from D&R for missing too much time when I was attacked. Of course the old Mr. Jiles resurfaced, hit the ceiling, and called me up yelling that I'd been canned. I didn't fight it though. Instead, I accepted that the work place nightmare was finally over for good, and rode out the wave while I recuperated. After I regained a good bit of my strength, I sent out my resumé to other firms. I was blessed to find another position in a better working environment. In fact, I'm making more money at my new place of employment, than I was at D&R.

When I got to the storage closet, I reached in the largest suitcase, and pulled out a piece of paper. I sat down on the side of the bed realizing that Ayanna just up and disappeared one day. She did leave me a letter that was left in an envelope in my panty and bra drawer, a few months back. It said:

Mystique,

Now that I think Donavan is trying to be fair to you, I feel that I must look within and take steps to face things on my own, away from my sis. From what I've seen, the faith-based marriage counseling has allowed you both to make an effort to heal and plan how you can realistically take responsibility for your actions. I'm not saying I'm in the way, but I know you need some space to make some crucial marital decisions. If I stick around, you won't get off the fence with Donavan. It's time to work toward deciding if you want to be close to him again or not, with no added distractions. Turn to him, not to me. I never thought I'd tell you that, but I'm telling you this out of love.

If I don't say so myself, I have seen a change in my sis! You no longer complain about all you do for Brittany and Brian. You seem more than happy to shop for back-to-school bargains, run them here and there and everywhere, and mold them into who you're trying to show them they should be. I think you now realize how much joy those two knuckle-heads brought into your life, just like we probably gave Mom that same joy before she went on home. All good mothers make that sort of sacrifice, don't they?

Although you may have needed some "excitement" in your life, I think you now see that structure and balance is equally as important. That's what I was trying to tell you about believing in the hype of the exotic dancing world. A woman like you, who didn't need to stack her paper, didn't need to be in it. It just wasn't you! I know you are older than me, but all I wanted to do was protect you for once, just as you've tried to do for your crazy, screwed up baby sis-

ter. Thank God Sapphire was prosecuted and jailed for stalking, and assaulting, you though. She's just too far gone to see straight, but who cares about that sick broad. She's nobody, in the grand scheme of things! Life is too short to get caught up in holding grudges with people who really matter to us, and so forth. The journey of living is about self-discovery and taking proactive steps to find your passion, happiness, and inner peace. What I'm trying to say is that my sis has more than earned her turn at happiness and peace, so don't let it slip on by, ok? Just like you said, you spent the majority of your life looking out for Yana and everyone else.

You spent many nights trying to convince me that I did the right thing by leaving my pimp, and I know you're wondering if all of those chats over cups of chamomile tea really made a difference or not. There's just one more thing that needs my attention, in addition to my need to comb the classified ads and keep getting my resumé out there. No one's in a rush to hire me for a real job, so it's given me time to consider that maybe I'm going through this bout of unemployment for a reason. See, while everyone is getting a chance to come clean for good, I need to take care of something, as well. I don't want to pull your emotions in any more directions, so I won't elaborate right now. The bottom line is that now Yana has to find her own way, on her own, hoping to step up her game too.

Don't worry about me, just do you. Just love me unconditionally, because you know your sister feels the same way about you. Pray for me, and I'm praying for you and the family. That's all I need from you at this moment because I know that my big sister is with me in spirit. When things are taken care of in my world, you best believe that you'll be hearing from me. Please kiss Heckle and Jeckle for me. Oh yeah, the notes for our manuscript is in our hiding place. Who knows, maybe we can pick up on our project when I get

*back. Then again, it may be something for our eyes only—
our sexxxfessions! No real names, no blame, with a stamp of
fiction added to protect the not so innocent. You know that's
right! Seriously though, keep your chin up, gurl, and remember everything I've said in this letter. Sisters forever . . .*

Yana

I folded the letter that I'd been hiding in a small
square, while also considering what Donavan said a while
back about his desire to save our family. Next, I got up,
tucked it in a pouch of the large suitcase, then zipped it. I
lugged two other smaller suitcases out of the storage area,
then called my husband's name. Donavan appeared wearing confusion on his face.

"Don't just look at me, can I get some help here, baby?"
I said.

"What are you doing? You're leaving. But I thought—"

"There are two more bags behind me. Follow me,
please," I asked.

First, I stopped in Brittany's room and asked Donavan
to set the bag next to her closet. Next, we stopped at
Brian's room and did the same thing. Without asking, my
husband grabbed my bag, and followed me into our room.

"Look, I think I know where this is going. It's obvious
you had plans to leave before Valentine's Day. I asked you
to try and you did. You did your part. I can't blame you for
not wanting to spend a holiday celebrating love with me. I
suppose I deserve this trick being pulled on me today
after what I've done as a leader of our household," Donavan said, his voice sounding flat and disappointed.

I plopped down on the bed, pulled him on top of me,
and started kissing him all over his face. Unbuttoning his
shirt, I hungered to taste his neck with my tongue, but instead, I provided an explanation.

"What's the foundation of love? Name three big things

you named when we exchanged the vows we wrote all of those years ago," I said.

"They were trust, respect, and unity."

"Right," I said. I was literally beaming inside, surprised that Donavan did remember them! I didn't let on that I was impressed though. That's when I realized that he really was my first love, and I was also his. "So despite everything, I'm not quite ready to give up yet on the hope of unity. Together, I hope we can repair trust. But doing so will require a constant demonstration of respect."

"So we're not getting a divorce? You're not leaving?"

"Don't make me regret unpacking the emergency bags, Negro. Putting these things away where they belong will be an act of faith, so just make sure you stay on point in the upcoming year and beyond," I answered.

Donavan began to smile. I even noticed his eyes got glossy real fast. I know he was about to up and cry, but he held it in like most men do.

"The next phase of our journey will be a daily struggle, but if you continue working hard to make our commitment work, so will I. No more secrets, no more lies, and there's no other way we can have it again. A healthy marriage can't flourish like that. If you agree with all of what I just said, tomorrow morning I want to get out of bed, roll over, and find you sleeping next to me. I think that I'm ready for us to start sleeping in the same bed now, too. How do you feel about that?" I asked, my palms growing sweaty.

Donavan kissed my lips, then began sucking on my tongue, while pulling my body on top of his. I could smell his cologne and suddenly felt drunk from the scent of him. When he parted my legs slowly, and rolled me over, I swallowed hard because I was nervous. I was getting so moist, that my juices quickly made my panties wet. Donavan spontaneously peeled off my clothes and began licking my kitty kat, then talking dirty to me from the heart, wishing me a happy Valentine's Day. My mind began racing with thoughts of whether or not Donavan and I could really be soul mates again, or if the changes we were making in our relationship would stick for good. Fighting to enjoy my treat, I concluded the same thing as always—time will tell.

With all of the licking, touching, and physical and emotional spoiling I was getting, I knew that I just wanted to be happy with the man I exchanged vows with, and needed to try to remain positive about earning a second chance at love. There is something to be said about loving someone through mistakes made, and through the pain, when love is really unconditional and both parties are willing to put in work to mend broken ties. Whichever way this thing shakes out, the thought of having my husband back, mind, body, and soul, made chills run up my spine. By the time my husband slid his thick, black tool inside of me, and I began moaning and screaming, Donavan began calling out my name.

"Stop playing with me. You know your husband needs to make love to you. Give your Daddy that sweet, wet pussy. Mystique. Oh shit, Mystique—yes, girl. Oh yes! Give it to Daddy, Mystique," he yelled as I held my left leg high in the air. A broad smile covered my face, as he said my name time and time again—that led to physical relief that I didn't anticipate, or expect, after nibbling on a bologna and cheese sandwich!

"What you did to me felt so good, Daddy. Now I want you to give me some cum! Mmmm. Cum for me, Donavan! I need you to cum for me tonight," I yelled in a sultry tone, as my husband thrusted his dick inside of me, repeatedly hitting my clit. His rhythm became steady, and his stroke became deeper and longer.

"Here it comes," he said, looking into my eyes, unable to hold back.

"I feel it. I'm cumming, too. Oh shit. Oh shit, Donavan. Here it comes," I yelled, cupping my breasts to keep them still, biting my bottom lip.

Donavan dropped his head, sucking on my right nipple just before we both exploded in unison. I tightly locked my legs around his body, as we screamed and moaned. The headboard smacked against the wall the way it did when we first got engaged. Right in the middle of having a mind-blowing orgasm, I was thinking that there was nothing better than hot monogamy with someone you love, who loves you back. It took a whole lot of drama to remind my husband and I of that, and more may be coming our way. In fact, I got a call from my GYN today confirming my appointment for the morning. I'm keeping that to myself, as well as the fact that I'm *late*—very late. Plus, I've been feeling nauseous and weak. It could be a side effect of stress . . . or it could be another reason. Hopefully, I'm just overreacting, and there is no need to give what I'm about to say too much serious energy.

I know that you're probably thinking that I was way too easy on Donavan, right? Well, not exactly. My last sexxxfession that I have to tell is that Rafiq's wife may not be the only one with a bun in the oven. Could the baby be Donavan's or Rafiq's? If you've been a loyal "listener," you should be able to figure out what I'm getting at. My husband kept a secret under his hat for fifteen years, and I can't erase my past of looking for love and attention in all of the wrong places either, including the very last night Rafiq and I had hot wild, sex. As bad luck would have it, the condom broke on us, and when he withdrew from me, cum was everywhere. After what broke loose at the party that night, Rafiq did leave Mya. I don't think I can ever talk to him again though. The last thing I'd like to have looking at me every day, is a little one that would remind me of a side piece I almost fell hard for, but the probability is very high. Abortion is not an option in my eyes, so I pray to God that He's just trying to scare some sense into me.

Then there's the whole forgiveness issue. When it comes to that, it's all or nothing, so Donavan would have no room to single me out for my behavior. Plus, I never mentioned that my husband and Rafiq are the same complexion and have a few similar features. I just may have choices to make, including if I want to rock the boat at having a chance at real happiness in my marriage, if I am really eating for two. After what Donavan pulled, he'd be in no position to request a DNA test on the home front.

They say that a family that prays together, stays together. These days, my husband has remembered to be a praying man, helps do the chores around the house, and brings his tail home every night. For this reason, I think we've both been through enough, and there's no need to fan the flames of the fire, just when we're really trying to get along for good with God's help.

Women are often too quick to tell their dirt, but men are so much better at keeping secrets . . . well most of the time. The bottom line is that I'm not planning on going anywhere, and I did tie up some loose ends to make sure I have a back-up plan if Donavan even thinks about crossing me again. I started a secret savings account, and our house is now in my name. The house thing I negotiated when Donavan was making six figures, and he was scared shitless that alimony, and a huge child support check for two kids, could come back to bite him if I decided to divorce his ass. Before you judge me about my back-up plan, as well as everything within these pages, remember what the good book says, "Let he that is without sin cast the first stone!"

A WOMAN'S TRUE WORTH

A woman's true worth extends beyond what the world sees.

Real men always remember we birth and support them, in darkness and in dawn.

The lost ones do us harm by calling us video hoes, bitches, skanks, sluts, and words that cut us deep, nearly bringing us to our knees.

How much can our ears take before our self-esteem is slowly chipped away, and it finally shatters and breaks, under the weight of a self-fulfilling prophecy, for those of us who grow weak and take the bait?

Desensitized listeners hear it on TV, and emotionally battered women are left sore, behind closed doors where we are treated like we are the very words every person should hate, not adore. But when we begin mistreating each other, it then becomes our fault.

Young girls caught up in this fast moving world, gambling with fate, staining their lips with bright hues, wearing high-heeled shoes and fake bling, putting their bids in to play a game they have yet to understand, not legally old enough to stand on their own two feet.

They know not what they do, until the world shows them where a one-way street can lead you, in a place called trouble.

Glorification of the mistreatment of women fuses with commercialized seeds that grow into massive trees, which shade the essence of femininity, the definition of W-O-M-A-N, self-worth, and threaten to deplete the core of the black family. The fruit that tree bears invites division, intra racism, fatherless children, self-hatred, drug addiction, and countless other repercussions of game playing.

Woman, thou art duped, born into a society where getting ahead may involve contemplating offers to lay on our backs with power brokers who secretly part thighs, and whisper sweet, sugary lies, until lies fall apart during the last days of pleasure.

When it all comes full circle in life, the hurt is recycled, more often than not.

Some women don't care if they bring pain to the next woman's universe, so long as her purse, or her ego, swells . . . oh well. Oh well.

One person's hell is the next person's heaven, when women hand over our crowns, and get in where we fit in, reducing life and love to cold, heartless games.

The damage done is irrelevant, so long as the aggressor ends up on top. It's just business.

Collecting ends. Playing players. Seeking revenge. Grown boys disguised as men stray the wrong way. We seduce them, then we play a flipped game. This is our new dope.

But ladies, when we inhale this mentality to redeem our girl power . . . who wins, really?

Instinctually, we want and deserve more real love, and more self-respect, as we discover what it means to live life as it should be lived, with no regrets.

We're on this earth to fulfill our destiny. No man has a thing to do with any of that.

Forgive yourself for past indiscretions, remembering to savor life's lessons.

No life is left untouched by some, or all of these experiences, but there is something we can do.

Teach this world, and others in our lives, how to respect us the right way, whenever we get the chance to stand up, someday. Now that's a woman's true worth.

You may email Andrea your comments, or share a piece of your own world with her at dreamweaverpress@aol.com. If you have a sexxxfession, or a story of your own that you need to get off your chest, don't be shy. Tell her about it anonymously if you'd like—she'd still be glad to read whatever you have to say! Visit www.dreamweaverpress.net to read about her previous projects. For most recent updates, please visit myspace.com/andreawrites.

To learn more about the PAS challenge that was mentioned in *Sexxxfessions*, please read the message following this page.

DO YOU WANT TO TAKE THE PAS CHALLENGE?

Taking the PAS challenge involves six steps.

Step one:

Have the courage to be proactive. Get tested, even if you are not currently sexually active. Stop throwing your old HIV tests away. Keep a past and current record, or log, of being tested. Even if you test anonymously, the dates should be clear. Consider taking another test after your anonymous test shows that you are negative. If you want to add to your PAS file, you may also want to get tested for other common STDs. This step is foundational. It shows that you respect yourself enough to know your status, or that you've at least taken steps to track your sexual health. This sends a strong message to any partner that is interested in you. Also note that if your test reflects that there is a problem, immediately seek proper professional guidance, instead of proceeding with the challenge.

Step two:

Assess your sexual habits and desired quality traits of a sexual partner. Are you most comfortable in a monogamous relationship? Do you prefer casual sex? PAS is not about judging anyone by his or her past, or desires, but it is tied to disclosing important information. If you can't be honest with yourself, PAS is not for you. PAS is not for those who do not want to take the time to engage in a bit of self-analysis. PAS is also not appropriate for those who seek to sleep with many partners at once, change partners quickly, attract one night stands, or singles who are not be prepared to accept that bringing up this plan of action may cause some potential partners not to choose to interact with them. PAS requires a bit of effort and time spent beyond physical chemistry. If you seek to weed out those who do not think the way you do, on the most basic sexual levels, PAS is a starting point to invite responsible sexual interaction. Bringing up PAS should be less touchy, the more time you have taken to spend time with your prospective, before sex comes up at all.

Step three:

Record what questions you would like to ask a potential sexual partner. Develop your top six questions, tailored to your liking. Think over the main thoughts that you would truly like to know about someone you would consider having sex with. Write down your questions so that you won't forget what they are. Be prepared to answer whatever you ask. After a potential partner is aware that you require 1) discussion and 2) presenting HIV records, ask him or her if she has recent HIV records. If he or she replies that testing has occurred recently, kindly request to **see** his or her test result. Explain that you will show yours as well. If you are not comfortable taking this position, simply suggest that you get tested together.

If the potential partner reveals that he or she has not been tested lately, promptly request that he or she get tested. If both parties already possess rather recent test papers to present, you may either proceed to step four, or get tested together. As we all know, the accuracy of a test increases if a person addresses the last activity they engaged in approximately six months prior to getting that test and beyond. And technically, a single anonymous test can belong to someone else. You may note the statistical information to help determine if you think it matches, but that's no guarantee that it belongs to that particular individual! It's best to request seeing a test that was not taken anonymously. Keep this in mind, but don't appear to be paranoid either.

Step four:

Have a frank talk with your potential partner. Ask your six questions that are required to pass to the next phase. You should be willing to do the same.

For example:

1) What is our status? (What do we mean to each other, title wise?) Are you currently having sex with anyone else? The point is to clarify how this person views you, and what you both expect as a result of it. (Friends with benefits, girlfriend and boyfriend, etc.)

2) Do you expect monogamy from me, or do you engage in casual sex with your partners?

3) Are you currently in any other relationship—married, separated, committed to a boyfriend or girlfriend, or casually dating? Are you sexually active?

4) Have you ever had unprotected sex? If so, when was it?

5) Was your last partner tested, to your knowledge?

6) Would you agree that we should speak to each other about moving on sexually, before doing anything with anyone else, if things don't seem to be working out between us?

Optional:

A. Have you ever engaged in sexual activity with anyone of the same sex?

B. Are you a drug user, or have you ever been? This includes **any** type of illegal substance, even if you haven't been an IV drug user. If so, when?

C. Have you ever had any kind of STD? If so, what was it?

In turn, allow your partner to ask at least six questions of you. Encourage him or her to write them down, too.

Step five:

Assess if this person passed your PAS test. He or she also should decide if you passed his or her test, too. If you both passed, enjoy your interaction with protected sex. If you are unsure what options are available to you, do proper research to gather any and all relevant information that will lend itself to proper education. Be sure that the male partner knows how to properly put on, and wear condoms, and he has also selected the proper size.

*   *   *

The goal is to remain negative, assuming that you both have been cleared of having HIV, in keeping with the spirit of your PAS contracts. Adjust all steps to your liking, noting the long term obligation of what you agreed to. It is imperative that you observe your potential partner's responses, reactions, and willingness to be forthcoming. Follow your gut instinct, when it comes to assessing if that person is answering your questions honestly, but be sure not to attack him or her. Be cool to find out what you need to know. Remember, this person is at least agreeing to try and cooperate with you, and that is a step in the right direction.

Step 6:

From that point on, keep the lines of communication open, as you work on building intimate enjoyment. PAS cannot guarantee fidelity, but it can help a sexually active single foster accountability, and a plan of action if someone turns out to be unfaithful at any point in the relationship. The essential factor here is not to be afraid to revoke a partner's pass. If your partner ever violates the terms of PAS by being unfaithful (and it is provable or highly likely), promptly end any and all sexual activity with him or her. If you choose to try to work it out, the PAS process must be repeated, but remember to consult with your health practitioner to estimate the proper date when you both should be retested. Hopefully, all, if not most, persons who develop their own pass will seriously consider the possible ramifications of dealing with an unfaithful partner, as opposed to only assessing the emotional aspect of their partner's behavior. PAS is designed to send other singles a message that there are those who have decided that cheating and dishonesty are not only character issues, but also health concerns. Hopefully, after taking the PAS challenge, each participant will feel a sense of empowerment, as he or she attempts to find an appropriate party with whom a healthy sexual relationship can be shared.

Did your sexual partner earn a pass to be sexually interact with you? Did he or she pass your PAS? PAS . . . if you show me yours, I'll show you mine!

Disclaimer: PAS is not intended to be interpreted as dispensing any type of medical advice. If you need professional medical advice, consult your doctor, or a health care practitioner. Taking the PAS challenge does not guarantee that a person cannot contract HIV from another participant.

about the author

Andrea Blackstone was born in Long Island, New York, and moved to Annapolis, Maryland at the age of two. She majored in English and minored in Spanish at Morgan State University. While attending Morgan, she received many recommendations to consider a career in writing and was the recipient of The Zora Neale Hurston Scholarship Award.

After a two-year stint in law school, she later changed her career path. While recovering from an illness, she earned an M.A. from St. John's College in Annapolis, Maryland ahead of schedule and with honors. Afterward, Andrea became frustrated with her inability to find an entry-level job in journalism and considered returning to law school.

Jotting down notes on restaurant napkins and scraps of paper became a habit that she couldn't shake. In 2003, she grew tired of waiting for her first professional break and decided to create Dream Weaver Press. A short time later she self-published *Schemin': Confessions of a Gold Digger*, and the sequel, *Short Changed*. Andrea is also a finalist in *Chicken Soup for the African-American Woman's* Soul, and some of her original work will also be included in an upcoming urban fiction anthology. A lover of all genres and outrageous characters, Andrea aspires to write a wide array of stories. Her work will range from inspirational nonfiction to unconventional plots written under one of many pseudonyms.

SNEAK PREVIEW OF

My Little Secret

BY ANNA J.

Coming in September 2008

<u>**Ask Yourself**</u>

Ask yourself a question . . . have you ever had a session of love making, do you want me? Have you ever been to heaven?
—*Raheem DeVaughn*

February 9th, 2007

She feels like melted chocolate on my fingertips. The same color from the top of her head to the very tips of her feet. Her nipples are two shades darker than the rest of her, and they make her skin the perfect backdrop against her round breasts. Firm and sweet like two ripe peaches dipped in baker's chocolate. They are a little more than a handful and greatly appreciated. Touching her makes me feel like I've finally found peace on earth, and there is no feeling in the world greater than that.

Right now her eyes are closed and her bottom lip is tightly tucked between her teeth. From my view point between her wide-spread legs I can see the beginnings of yet another orgasm playing across her angelic face. These are the moments that make it all worthwhile. Her perfectly arched eyebrows go into a deep frown, and her eyelids flutter slightly. When her head falls back I know she's about to explode.

I move up on my knees so that we are pelvis to pelvis. Both of us are dripping wet from the humidity and the situation. Her legs are up on my shoulders, and her hands are cupping my breasts. I can't tell where her skin begins or where mine ends. As I look down at her, and watch her face go through way too many emotions I smile a little bit. She always did love the dick, and since we've been together she's never had to go without it. Especially since the one I have never goes down.

I'm pushing her tool into her soft folds inch by inch as if it were really a part of me, and her body is alive. I say "her tool" because it belongs to her, and I just enjoy using it on her. Her hip-length dreads seem to wrap us in a cocoon of coconut oil and sweat, body heat and moisture, soft moans and tear drops, pleasure and pain until we seemingly burst into an inferno of hot-like-fire ecstasy. Our chocolate skin is searing to the touch and we melt into each other becoming one. I can't tell where hers begins . . . I can't tell where mine ends.

She smiles . . . her eyes are still closed and she's still shaking from the intensity. I take this opportunity to taste her lips, and to lick the salty sweetness from the side of her neck. My hands begin to explore, and my tongue encircles her dark nipples. She arches her back when my full lips close around her nipple and I begin to suck softly as if she's feeding me life from within her soul.

Her hands find their way to my head and become tangled in my soft locks, identical to hers but not as long. I push into her deep, and grind softly against her clit in search of her "j-spot" because it belongs to me, Jada. She speaks my name so soft that I barely heard her. I know she wants me to take what she so willingly gave me, and I want to hear her beg for it.

I start to pull back slowly, and I can feel her body tightening up trying to keep me from moving. One of many soft moans is heard over the low hum of the clock radio that sits next to our bed. I hear slight snatches of Raheem DeVaughn singing about being in heaven, and I'm almost certain he wrote that song for me and my lady.

I open her lips up so that I can have full view of her sensitive pearl. Her body quakes with anticipation from the feel of my warm breath touching it, my mouth just mere inches away. I blow cool air on her stiff clit causing her to tense up briefly, her hands taking hold of my head trying to pull me closer. At this point my mouth is so close to her all I would have to do is twitch my lips to make contact, but I don't . . . I want her to beg for it.

My index finger is making small circles against my own clit, my honey sticky between my legs. The ultimate pleasure is giving pleasure, and I've experienced that on both accounts. My baby can't wait anymore, and her soft pants are turning into low moans. I stick my tongue out, and her clit gladly kisses me back.

Her body responds by releasing a syrupy sweet slickness that I lap up until it's all gone, fucking her with my tongue the way she likes it. I hold her legs up and out to intensify her orgasm because I know she can't handle it that way.

"Does your husband do you like this?" I ask between licks. Before she could answer I wrap my full lips around her clit and suck her into my mouth, swirling my tongue around her hardened bud, causing her body to shake.

Snatching a second toy from the side of the bed, I take one hand to part her lips, and I ease her favorite toy (The Rabbit) inside of her. Wishing that the strap-on I was wearing was a real dick so that I could feel her pulsate, I turn the toy on low at first wanting her to receive the ultimate pleasure. In the dark room the glow in the dark toy is lit brightly, the light disappearing inside of her when I push it all the way in.

The head of the curved toy turns in a slow circle while the pearl beads jump around on the inside, hitting up against her smooth walls during insertion. When I push the toy in she pushes her pelvis up to receive it, my mouth latched on to her clit like a vice. She moans louder, and I kick the toy up a notch to medium, much to her delight. Removing my mouth from her clit I rotate between flicking my wet tongue across it to heat it, and blowing my breath on it to cool it bringing her to yet another screaming orgasm, followed by strings of *"I love you"* and *"Please don't stop."*

Torturing her body slowly, I continue to stimulate her clit while pushing her toy in and out of her on a constant rhythm. When she lifts her legs to her chest I take the opportunity to let the ears on the rabbit toy that we are using do their job on her clit while my tongue find their way to her chocolate ass. I bite one cheek at a time replacing it with wet kisses, afterwards sliding my tongue in between to taste her there. Her body squirming underneath me lets me know I've hit the jackpot, and I fuck her with my tongue there also.

She's moaning, telling me in a loud whisper that she can't take it anymore. That's my cue to turn the toy up high. The buzzing from the toy matches that of the radio, and with her moans and my pants mixed in we sound like a well-rehearsed orchestra singing a symphony of passion. I allow her to buck against my face while I keep up with the rhythm of the toy, her juice oozing out the sides and forming a puddle under her ass. I'm loving it.

She moans and shakes until the feeling in the pit of her

stomach resides and she is able to breathe at a normal rate. My lips taste salty/sweet from kissing her body while she tries to get her head together, rubbing the sides of my body up and down in a lazy motion.

Valentine's Day is fast approaching and I have a wonderful evening planned for the two of us. She already promised me that her husband wouldn't be an issue because he'll be out of town that weekend, and besides all that they haven't celebrated Cupid's day since the year after they were married so I didn't even think twice about it. After seven years it should be over for them anyway.

"It's your turn now," she says to me in a husky lust filled voice, and I can't wait for her to take control.

The ultimate pleasure is giving pleasure . . . and man does it feel good both ways. She starts by rubbing her oil-slicked hands over the front of my body, taking extra time around my sensitive nipples before bringing her hands down across my flat stomach. I've since then removed the strap-on dildo, and am completely naked under her hands.

I can still feel her sweat on my skin, and I can still taste her on my lips. Closing my eyes I enjoy the sensual massage that I'm being treated to. After two years of us making love it's still good and gets better every time.

She likes to take her time covering every inch of my body, and I enjoy letting her. She skips past my love box, and starts at my feet, massaging my legs from the toes up. When she gets to my pleasure point her fingertips graze the smooth, hairless skin there, quickly teasing me before she heads back down and does the same thing with my other limb. My legs are spread apart and lying flat on the bed with her in between, relaxing my body with ease. A cool breeze from the cracked window blows across the room every so often, caressing my erect nipples, making them harder than before until her hands warm them back up again.

She knows when I can't take anymore and she rubs and caresses me until I am begging her to kiss my lips. I can see her smile through half-closed eyelids, and she does what I requested. Dipping her head down between my legs, she kisses my lips just as I asked, using her tongue to part them so that she can taste my clit. My body goes into mini-convulsions on contact, and I am fighting a battle to not cum that I never win.

"Valentine's Day belongs to us, right?" I ask her again between moans. I need her to be here. V-Day is for lovers, and her and her husband haven't been that in ages. I deserve it . . . I deserve her. I just don't want this to be a repeat of Christmas or New Years Eve.

"Yes, it's yours," she says between kisses on my thigh and sticking her tongue inside of me. Two of her fingers have found their way inside of my tight walls, and my pelvic area automatically bounces up and down on her hand as my orgasm approaches.

"Tell me you love me," I say to her as my breathing becomes raspy. Fire is spreading across my legs and working its way up to the pit of my stomach. I need her to tell me before I explode.

"I love you," she says and at the moment she places her tongue in my slit, I release my honey all over her tongue.

It feels like I am on the Tea Cup ride at the amusement park as my orgasm jerks my body uncontrollably and it feels like the room is spinning. She is sucking and slurping my clit while the weight of her body holds the bottom half of me captive. I'm practically screaming and begging her to stop, and just when I think I'm about to check out of here she lets my clit go.

I take a few more minutes to get my head together, allowing her to pull me into her and rub my back. Moments like this make it all worthwhile. We lay like that for a while longer listening to each other breathe, and much to my dismay she slides my head from where it was resting on her arm and gets up out of the bed.

I don't say a word. I just lie on the bed and watch her get dressed. I swear everything she does is so graceful, like there's a rhythm riding behind it. Pretty soon she is dressed and standing beside the bed looking down at me. She smiles and I smile back, not worried because she promised me our lover's day, and that's only a week away.

"So, Valentine's Day belongs to me, right?" I ask her again just to be certain.

"Yes, it belongs to you."

We kiss one last time, and I can still taste my honey on her lips. She already knows the routine, locking the bottom lock behind her. Just thinking about her makes me so horny, and I pick up her favorite toy to finish the job. Five more days, and it'll be on again.

COMING SOON FROM

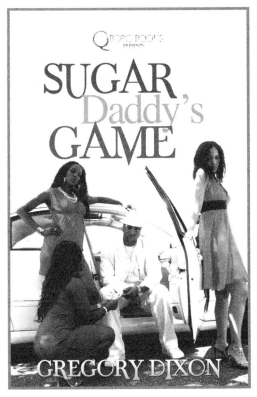

Jamell White is known as Sugar Daddy. Most of the people who know him assume that his nickname "Sugar" is a by-product of his cash-friendly habits with several beautiful, well known females. But they couldn't be more wrong.

MAY 2008

ISBN: 1-933967-41-2

NOW AVAILABLE FROM

Q-BORO BOOKS

NYMPHO
$14.95
ISBN 1933967102

How will signing up to live a promiscuous double-life destroy everything that's at stake in the lives of two close couples? Take a journey into Leslie's secret world and prepare for a twisted, erotic experience.

FREAK IN THE SHEETS
$14.95
ISBN 1933967196

Ready to break out of the humdrum of their lives, Raquelle and Layla decide to put their knowledge of sexuality and business together and open up a freak school, teaching men and women how to please their lovers beyond belief while enjoying themselves in the process.

However, Raquelle and Layla must learn some important lessons when it comes to being a lady in the street and a freak in the sheets.

LIAR, LIAR
$14.95
ISBN 1933967110

Stormy calls off her wedding to Camden when she learns he's cheating with a male church member. However, after being convinced that Camden has been delivered from his demons, she proceeds with the wedding.

Will Stormy and Camden survive scandal, lies and deceit?

HEAVEN SENT
$14.95
ISBN 1933967188

Eve is a recovering drug addict who has no intentions of staying clean until she meets Reverend Washington, a newly widowed man with three children. Secrets are uncovered that threaten Eve's new life with her new family and has everyone asking if Eve was *Heaven Sent.*

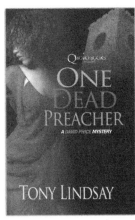

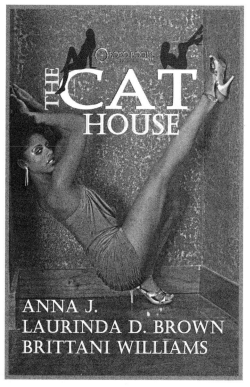

COMING SOON FROM

MARCH 2008
1-933967-39-0